Double

Daniel Faust, Book Seven

by Craig Schaefer

Publisher's Note: This is a work of fiction. Names, characters, places, and incidents are a product of the author's imagination. Locales and public names are sometimes used for atmospheric purposes. Any resemblance to actual people, living or dead, or to businesses, companies, events, institutions, or locales is completely coincidental.

Cover Design by James T. Egan of Bookfly Design LLC.
Author Photo ©2014 by Karen Forsythe Photography
Craig Schaefer / Double or Nothing
ISBN 978-1-944806-07-1

Contents

The Daniel Faust Series

1. The Long Way Down
    1.5. The White Gold Score
    2. Redemption Song
    3. The Living End
    4. A Plain-Dealing Villain
    5. The Killing Floor Blues
    6. The Castle Doctrine
    7. Double or Nothing

Also by Craig Schaefer

Harmony Black
    The Complete Revanche Cycle

Prologue

To some, he was the man with the Cheshire smile. To others, the Enemy. But the flickering photonegative shape—etched onto the film of the world, faceless save for his pearly, inhumanly wide grin—didn't care much for names. He flowed through the halls of Northlight Tower like a stop-motion animation come to life. At his side, primly dressed, heels clicking on Italian marble, Ms. Fleiss cradled a clipboard and ran through the day's agenda.

To her, he was the universe and everything in it.

"At two p.m., Ms. Green is having a follow-up discussion with Diehl Innovations to go over the new trade agreement," she said. "At four—local time—we've scheduled a meeting in Bristol with a representative from the Order of the Septic Blossom. Mr. Purple is handling that. Mr. Blue just reported in from Brazil; he's making considerable inroads with the local—"

"None of which speaks to the concern at hand. *Faust.* Where is he?"

Fleiss swallowed hard. "I've been working with a sketch artist. We're compiling dossiers on the people we believe to be his friends and allies, as potential pressure points to draw him out of hiding."

"So you have nothing."

"Nothing *yet*, my lord. The occult underground tends to be extremely insular, and considering Daniel Faust is both a sorcerer and a career criminal, on top of faking his death after the Eisenberg Prison incident—"

"If you can't tell me what I want to know," he said, "perhaps someone else can."

The double doors ahead swung open without being touched. His personal reception lounge—the walls done up in pale yellow fabric, chairs and a welcome desk carved to look like driftwood—waited just beyond. His visitor rose to greet him.

"My lord." Naavarasi bowed her head. A jade sarong, elegantly wrapped, draped her willowy frame. The color matched her fingernails. Her slender hand curled around a thin, unlabeled folder.

"Give me good news," he told her.

She held the folder out to him. "I've compiled a dossier on what we know about the Las Vegas underworld. Notable figures, their active statuses, and their alleged connections to this 'Faust' person."

"And Faust himself?"

Naavarasi shook her head. "I'm sorry. He's very good at covering his tracks."

His flickering hand snatched the folder from her grip. He shoved it at Fleiss.

"I want the two of you to coordinate your research. And I want *results*. Do you understand the situation here? Really, do you?"

"One hundred percent," Fleiss said. She glared at Naavarasi as she set the folder on top of her clipboard.

"All I need to know," Naavarasi said, "is your will, my lord. I live to serve you."

Fleiss's eyes narrowed to slits.

"A slice of my former power," the Enemy said, "my former glory, is locked behind the fifth act of my play. An act that can *only* be resolved by Faust's death. Every day he walks free, every day he draws breath, it's like a...like a mosquito, buzzing around my face, whining in my ear. A constant, maddening itch I can't slap away. *Find him.*"

"Perhaps, my lord," Fleiss said, "we should focus on the matter of Eastern Pines?"

He tilted his blurry head. "Are we ready?"

"In a matter of days. I've overseen the ritual preparations for nearly a year now, without fail, and attended to all the arrangements. Flawlessly."

"Well," he said, mollified, "that is...that is something to be pleased about. Well done, Fleiss."

She preened. "Thank you, my lord."

His Cheshire grin, obscenely wide, twisted into a grimace. "Now get back to work."

He gusted through the doors to his private office, the room beyond black as a moonless night. The doors slammed shut in his wake.

"That could have gone better," Naavarasi observed.

Fleiss got in her face and jabbed at the taller woman's chest with a manicured fingernail.

"You aren't fooling anyone," she snapped.

Naavarasi blinked, a picture of wounded innocence. "I'm not?"

"You're a *mercenary*. You aren't devoted to him like I am. You don't love him like I do."

"Sounds like I struck a nerve. Is it that hard to imagine that I might be drawn to our lord's cause? Maybe it's his charisma. Or his aftershave."

"I want to know what your game is," Fleiss said. "Do

you really expect me to believe you'd willingly work toward the destruction of your own world?"

Naavarasi's eyes went hard. She inched closer to Fleiss, looming over her.

"This is not *my* world. *My* world was a jungle paradise—and it, and my worshipers, and my kin, were taken from me by fire and sword. I care nothing for this Earth. And as long as our patron guarantees me a ticket *off* this miserable rock when he's done ravaging it, I'm happy to watch it burn."

Fleiss took a step backward, pushed by the heat of the other woman's glare. Naavarasi's voice dropped to a graveyard whisper.

"I am the last rakshasi," she said, "and my vengeance is this: I will be the last of all living things. I will see the death of the universe. And I will be the last to go. The one who turns out the lights and closes the final door."

Fleiss's upper lip twitched. She clutched the clipboard closer to her chest.

"From now on, you report to me, not to him. Don't upstage me like that again."

"Careful," Naavarasi said as she breezed past her, heading for the elevator. "Your insecurities are showing. It's a bad look for you."

* * *

A silver limousine waited for Naavarasi outside the corporate tower. It was early morning and a cool, grassy mist hung in the air. Droplets of dew clung to the limo's tinted windows. She slipped in back, closed the driver partition, and enjoyed the solitude.

Her phone chimed. A new message: "*Are you all right, Mistress? Just making sure.*"

Naavarasi's lips curled in a contented smile. It was nice

to be cared about. It was even better to be worshiped. Just like old times. Her thumbs rapped against the screen.

"*Fleiss suspects, but that's her nature,*" she replied. "*I've sold her a believable enough story. Grief, rage, vows of vengeance, very Shakespearean. Are you prepared for your next assignment?*"

"*I live to serve you, Mistress,*" came the response.

"I know you do," she murmured softly.

"*Approach Fleiss's organization,*" she typed, "*and offer your services as an assassin for hire. Kill anyone they tell you to. Go above and beyond, win their absolute confidence. I want you firmly embedded when the time is right.*"

"*And Daniel?*"

"*All in good time,*" she answered. "*When I command it, and not one moment sooner. Patience.*"

Naavarasi leaned back, snug in the bucket leather seat. She watched the world drift by outside the tinted window, a hammered-copper sun rising over another day. Endless potential.

"For now, though," she said to the sunrise, "our dear Daniel is about to render me a most valuable service. He just doesn't know it yet."

1.

Mayor Seabrook was a battleship in the form of a woman, pure steel under her lavender Chanel dress. For now, she kept the cannons hidden. Sitting across from her, in a low-backed lemon-colored chair by her office window, was Earl Harding. Harding had been the police commissioner of Las Vegas for over twenty years, and he'd worn his medal-studded uniform khakis just to remind us.

Between the two of them, they didn't have a single apology to offer. Just cold stares and bad attitudes. I suppose I couldn't blame them: it's not every day that a couple of representatives from your friendly local crime syndicate stop by for a chat. I sat on the far side of Seabrook's desk, casual, one leg folded over the other, feeling the reassuring weight of a nine-millimeter backup plan under my tailored jacket. Jennifer was right beside me. I was used to seeing her in tank tops and cargo pants, but lately she'd been rocking the corporate chic look. Primmed, pressed, and ready for the boardroom, though she still wore her tinted blue Lennon glasses, and a vaguely Celtic pendant dangled from one earlobe.

"I notice you didn't offer us coffee," I said.

Mayor Seabrook folded her hands on her desk. "Sorry. All out."

I pointedly looked to the credenza behind her. A shiny new French press sat beside two bags of imported coffee beans. She held her silence. So did I.

"You probably know why we're here," Jennifer said.

"That an admission of guilt?" Harding grunted.

"Everything stated in this meeting is off the record and hypothetical," she replied in her easy Kentucky drawl. "Like how *hypothetically*, when the Chicago Outfit came to town lookin' to bust heads, city hall took their side."

"We didn't—" Seabrook paused, catching herself. Mending the tiny crack in her armor. "No sides were taken. That said, it's the policy of this administration to act in the best interest of the citizenry and the Vegas economy. The gang war had to be quelled as quickly and quietly as possible."

"How'd that work out for you?" I set both feet on the powder-blue carpet, leaning forward in my chair. "Angelo Mancuso was ready and willing to mow down anybody who got in his way. We weren't the ones who firebombed that taphouse on East Charleston."

"No," Harding said. "You just shot up the Cobalt Lounge and left about twenty gangbangers dead."

"Oh. So I did your job for you? You're very welcome, Commissioner."

Harding pushed himself to his feet. "I don't need to listen to this—"

"*Sit*," Jennifer snapped.

He didn't move, frozen in midstep. He looked down at her, eyes slowly narrowing.

"What'd you say to me?"

Jennifer fixed him with her stare.

"Mrs. Mayor," she said, her voice like velvet wrapped around a switchblade, "tell your doggy to heel, before I have to yank his leash."

Seabrook chewed her bottom lip. Then she nodded, resigned. "Earl, sit down. Please."

He sat.

"You fucked up," I told Seabrook. "Fortunately for you, we're kind and forgiving people at heart."

"Generous to a fault," Jennifer added.

"There will be no reprisals, no payback. We're just going to pretend your lapse of judgment never happened. Of course, if you ever feel compelled to cheer for the rival team again..." I spread my open hands, letting the gesture speak for itself. "I'm hoping that our willingness to let bygones be bygones will pave the way to better relations in the future. We'd like to be friends."

"*Friends?*" Harding said. "You're nothing but goddamned mobsters."

Jennifer arched an eyebrow. "We're community organizers. See, an organized community is a safe and productive one. I understand you've been having a little problem on D Street the past couple of months."

He furrowed his brow, uncertain. "Well, it's a high-crime corridor—"

"I mean the serial rapist. Five victims, zero evidence. Dan, what time ya got?"

I eased back my jacket sleeve and checked my watch. It was a Gucci Swiss quartz with an onyx face and silver dials, slim and sleek. Caitlin had bought it for me as a present, to celebrate my first day of my new job.

My new job didn't have an official title. "Crime boss" wasn't something you put on business cards. I was still wrapping my head around the general concept.

"Just after nine a.m.," I said.

"Good, good." Jennifer turned to the commissioner. "Call the area command. I believe the culprit just turned himself in, asking to make a full confession. Matter of fact, he'll be begging for it."

He stared at her for a moment, like a kid watching the first moves of a magic trick. Then he got up and ambled out of the office, shutting the door behind him.

"So," I said to the mayor, "alone at last."

Her expression softened. Just a little.

"Earl's a hard-liner," she said. "That's why I like him. He gets things done. I'll tell you right now, he won't be making any deals with you people."

"If he won't," Jennifer said, "the people under him will. Some already have. We're not looking for deals, Mrs. Mayor, we're just here to share the facts of life. The New Commission is here, we're organized, and we're not going anywhere. We're not looking to hurt the tourist trade—we're *invested* in it—and we don't tolerate cowboys or shenanigans. You can choose to coexist with us, or you can choose not to."

The office door opened. Harding looked green around the edges as he shuffled back to his chair.

"Someone hammered roofing nails through his—" he stammered, trailing off as he stared at Jennifer.

She studied her short-cropped fingernails, perfectly casual.

"I don't like rapists," she said.

"*Some* things can be...tolerated," the mayor said. "Speaking entirely off the record, of course."

"Of course," Jennifer replied.

"And some things can't be. I just came back from the United Conference of Mayors in Boston. Let me be blunt,

Ms. Juniper. I know you're heavily invested in narcotics trafficking."

"Been falsely arrested once or twice," Jennifer said. "Don't even know what the inside of a courtroom looks like. Do carry on, though."

"Ink," Seabrook said. "We're not having it. Not in my city."

I shook my head, thinking back to an article I'd read in the *Sun* a few days earlier. "That's the new synthetic, right? I've heard it's spreading fast on the East Coast, but I figured that was media hype. You know, like when everyone was talking about bath salts for two months straight."

"It's not hype, Mr....?"

"Emerson," I said. Daniel Faust was legally dead, and I aimed to keep him that way. I was breaking in my new alter ego.

"And it's not just the East Coast," Harding said. "Maybe last month it was, but now that junk's all over the Midwest too. Somebody's flooding the market. Ink is part opiate, part hallucinogen. Addictive, cheap, and accessible."

Seabrook's fingers rattled on her keyboard. "In New York, they're calling it 'the new crack.' Except at least crack has a social stigma attached; ink is being sold as a party drug. Some addicts say that when they dose up, they can see the future. Some say they can see God. And for a few...here, I want to show you something."

"Mayor, you don't need to—" Harding said. She silenced him with a sharp glance.

She swiveled her monitor around to face us. A still from a security camera gave us a bird's-eye view of a room with padded white walls. A man in a paper gown stood frozen in the frame, his hands clutching his tangled hair.

"My former administrative assistant," Seabrook said. "He tried ink at a house party. Once. Had a bad reaction. This is him, two weeks later."

She clicked her mouse. The film lurched into motion and the man bounced off the padded wall, turning, pacing across the cell until he hit the opposite wall and started all over again. Tugging at his hair, mumbling an obsessive chant. I leaned closer to the desk.

"What's he saying?"

She turned the volume up. Under the hiss of static, I could make out some of the words.

"It smells like roses," he muttered. "Hedy, hold the book. Hedy, hold the...my name is, my name is—I don't know if that's your name don't know how this works, Hedy hold the *book*. It smells like roses in here, smells like roses. My name is—"

She paused the video.

"Total psychotic break. He still hasn't recovered. The doctors aren't hopeful." Seabrook laid her hands on her desk, palms flat. "This man was a friend of mine. This is *personal* to me, you understand? No ink in Vegas. Period."

"Don't seem like a thing I'd be inclined to promote m'self," Jennifer replied. "A healthy narcotics trade depends on repeat business. Ain't no money in sending your customers to a rubber room. Where's this flood of product coming from? If it started on the East Coast, that sounds like some Five Families business, them or the Brighton Beach crowd."

Harding snorted with his lips curled in an angry frown. "Nobody knows. All the usual suspects swear their hands are clean. My guys busted a small-time dealer with New

Mexico plates yesterday, and he said the whole operation is compartmentalized. Nobody knows any names more than one step up the distribution chain. Highly organized."

"A New Mexico dealer, coming here to push product?" I said. "Somebody's looking to get a foothold."

"And they're going to keep trying," the mayor said.

"What if they stopped?" I asked her.

Her eyes narrowed a little. "Meaning?"

I nodded toward Harding. "This might be the point in our discussion, Mrs. Mayor, where Commissioner Harding has more important business to attend to. Elsewhere."

"Mayor," he said, looking between us, "you can't possibly—"

"Earl." Seabrook put her fingers to her forehead and closed her eyes. "Please. For both our sakes. Don't hear anything you don't need to hear."

He grumbled as he shoved himself up from his chair. Then he kept grumbling, all the way out of her office. Seabrook stared at me in expectant silence.

"We could follow the pipeline," I said. "Theoretically, we could find the person trying to spread ink in Vegas, and have a little conversation."

"A conversation," she echoed.

"A come-to-Jesus meeting," Jennifer said. "In which they'll acknowledge their mistakes, repent, and sin no more."

"I'm not...asking you to...*do* anything," Seabrook said, choosing each word as if picturing herself repeating them in court.

"No, no." I gave her a reassuring smile. "This is something we'd do entirely on our own, nothing to do with you, no blowback to worry about. Your name would never come into it. It's just something we'd like to do as a gesture of friendship."

"And would this...gesture of friendship have any cost attached?"

"Never," I said. Then I held up a finger. "There is something, though, a completely unrelated matter I wanted to bring up. A friend of mine is trying to get a liquor license for his new bar. Now, if that process were to be streamlined, for the sake of speed, well, I think we'd all be very happy."

"New businesses are good for the economy," Jennifer said.

Seabrook nodded slowly. "I did run on a platform of economic development. So, while of course I'd expect that all laws and codes be obeyed to the letter, I could see myself putting in a phone call to the licensing board on your friend's behalf."

"We'll be in touch," I told her.

Out in the hall, Jennifer punched my arm.

"That's for volunteerin' us," she said with a smile. "C'mon, call for a sidebar before you sign us up for unpaid labor. You know better."

"If we can get that liquor license rushed through, *unpaid* my ass."

"Fair, fair, that's some long-term thinkin'." She paused, giving me the side-eye. "You okay, sugar? You've been a little weird since we watched that rubber-room video."

It stuck with me. Not the psychotic man bouncing off walls and tugging his hair out, but the words he was repeating. Four words. We stepped into the elevator, alone together, and I didn't speak until the steel doors glided shut.

"My last run-in with Ms. Fleiss," I said.

In my mind I was back in David Gosselin's private museum of magic. Watching, horrified, as Fleiss's skull distended and her elongated neck swayed. Her body bloating like a tumor-ridden hippo while her fingernails fell out and her hands sprouted claws of black iron.

"The man with the Cheshire smile's errand girl," Jennifer said. "Yeah, sounded like a bad party."

I remembered the rifle kicking against my grip, round after round rattling off as the twins and I gunned her down. The monstrosity staggering back in a fireworks storm of muzzle-flash, spitting blood but refusing to die.

"When she ran, she...carved a hole in the world, somehow. I've never seen magic like that before. It was a rent in space, with this hungry dark void behind it, sucking all the air from the room. And the one thing I remember about it, more than anything else—" I paused and shook my head. "It's got to be a coincidence, it *has* to be. It's just bugging me. Something the mayor's admin kept repeating."

"What's that, sugar?"

"Roses," I told her. "It smelled like roses."

2.

We had another appointment scheduled that morning. On our turf, this time.

Jennifer and I stepped into a cacophony of hammers and whirring band saws, a maze of nailed frames, stacks of drywall, and fat fuzzy rolls of pink insulation. Someday it would be a brand-new bar and lounge. For now, we walked through the wooden ribs with orange hard hats on, looking for a spot away from the noise. The warm, dry air was thick with the smell of fresh sawdust.

"Startin' to look like something." Jennifer surveyed the main floor. The rough wooden flooring bounced a little under our feet, spray-painted lines marking angles and roughing out a design plan.

"Sure is. Thanks for being a part of this, Jen."

"Ain't even a thing," she said. "Y'know, I could have kicked more money in."

The New Commission, rising in the wake of Nicky Agnelli's fall, had divvied up the city's territory and rackets. The Cinco Calles and the Bishops, the 14K and the Inagawa-kai, even the Blood Eagles all sitting down at the same table at the same time and forging an alliance. I'd finally stepped up and taken my seat at the table too, but that left a big question: what exactly did that mean?

I'd spent my entire career playing the henchman—first as Nicky's hired wand, then hanging out my shingle as a vengeance-for-hire specialist—or playing the lone wolf. I had a seat at the council table, sure, but what could I really bring to it?

Then late one night in the haze of a two-bourbon buzz, watching *Casablanca* with Caitlin, the answer came to me. We were standing in it.

"I know you could have," I told Jennifer, "but getting everybody to pay for a share was part of the plan. Once you and Gabriel bought in, Eddie Stone pretty much had to. Then Emma got *her* pocketbook out—"

"How many people own a slice of this place?"

"Caitlin makes a baker's dozen. But I still hold fifty-one percent. It's my baby." I gazed across the work site, taking it all in. Seeing where a bar would stand, the tables and chairs, imagining the mood lighting. "The Tiger's Garden will always be home, but if you're not a magician, you can't even find the door. Club Winter is...Winter. If you don't have friends in low places, forget about it."

"And we can't exactly rent out Margaritaville again," Jennifer mused.

"You got it. And so..." I swept out my arm. "The American. Owned, on paper, by our good and fictional friend Rick Blaine. Neutral ground for the occult *and* criminal underworlds. Safe harbor with top-shelf drinks. And seeing as the heaviest hitters in Vegas, from racket bosses to hell's emissaries, all own a stake in the operation, it'll be the safest place on earth."

Jennifer snickered. "Daniel Faust, legitimate businessman. Never thought I'd see the day."

"Not *that* legitimate. For starters, that fortified vault I'm having installed? That's for escrow. If anyone needs to make a deal or hand off hot goods, the American will happily facilitate a safe transaction. For a cut off the top, of course. Also, there's the backroom poker tables and the sports book. The casinos report winnings to the IRS. We won't."

"Daniel." Jennifer put her hands to her chest in mock dismay. "I am shocked, *shocked* to find that gambling is going on in here. Or will be."

The foreman trundled up, pulling me aside for a moment. Another clipboard, another form in triplicate, another material purchase to sign off on. I didn't know anything about building a business from scratch, but I was getting a quick education. As he walked off, I caught Jennifer staring at me, a little smile on her lips.

"What?" I asked.

"I ain't seen you this energized in months. Not since the start of that whole Lauren Carmichael mess. Just been one damn thing after another. You took some hits—"

"We both took some hits."

"Yeah," she said, "but here we are. I hope you're letting yourself soak up some pride. A little, anyhow."

"I've never trusted feeling too proud or too happy. Always feels like I'm setting myself up for a fall." I folded my arms. "Anyway, this whole idea could crash and burn. Let's see how it plays."

"It ain't the succeedin', sugar. It's the *tryin'*. You're off the sidelines, you got your sleeves rolled up, and you're going for it. That's all any of us wanted to see."

"Time will tell." I gave her a sidelong glance. "And there's still the...other thing."

Jennifer pursed her lips. "Cheshire."

"The Enemy is out there. He isn't going away, and from what Carolyn Saunders told me, he doesn't just want me dead, he *needs* me dead. His old power is locked away in some kind of reliquary, and offing me is one of the keys to popping it open."

"Point of order," Jennifer said, "he's just gotta off 'the Thief.' If you can put that title on somebody else's head, the way he put it on yours—"

"Then the Enemy gets stronger. This thing destroys planets for fun, Jen. And if Fleiss wasn't lying, he's done it a *lot*."

"Didn't Carolyn Saunders say this cycle always ends with him facing off against the Paladin?" Jennifer tapped her chin, thinking. "Seems to me, we oughta get proactive. Find this Paladin feller and arm him up. Do everything we can to hand him a winning edge."

"Cheat our asses off," I said.

"*That's* a given."

We had a visitor. He stood at the edge of the work site with his black hat in his liver-spotted hands. Big, broad shoulders with a coat too heavy for October in Vegas, but the expression on his face was like that of a kid standing outside the principal's office, dragging his heels before he went in to get a paddling.

I greeted him with a smile. "Mr. Petrocelli, I presume."

He came over, his polished Italian loafers unsteady on the rough flooring, and shook my hand. His smile was even less genuine than mine.

"Looks like this is going to be quite a place," he said, his gruff voice seared by decades of cigar smoke. The odor of a fresh stogie clung to his coat, stronger than the sawdust. "Nightclub?"

"More of a lounge," I said. "Piano music, live singers."

Now the smile was more genuine. "Ah, classy. Good to hear there's still a little of that old Vegas charm left. These days it's all—what do they call it, electronic dance music? That *untz-untz-untz* garbage the kids like. Anyway, I wanted to come out and speak to you in person, considering...well, considering."

"We appreciate that," Jennifer said.

He talked right past her, his eyes fixed on me. "I want you to understand that what the Mancusos did—that was not sanctioned or authorized by our people. If they'd even spoken to us about it—which they did not—the Petrocelli and Accardo families would have stood in strong opposition. The very *idea* that he'd go to the mattresses against you people without provocation, and sully our good name...it's unprecedented. That's not how we do business."

The Chicago Outfit was closing ranks and running scared. An overnight siege that left the don and twenty-odd wise guys dead tended to have that effect. Maybe he was telling the truth about not being on board with Angelo Mancuso's doomed crusade; maybe he wasn't. We'd already made a near-unanimous decision at the Commission table to pretend we believed him.

"We understand completely," Jennifer said. "These things happen. You can't be held responsible for the Mancuso family's poor decisions."

He didn't even look at her, still focusing on me as if he hadn't heard her speak. Now he was starting to piss me off.

"We're hoping to mend relations," Petrocelli said. "A clean slate on both sides. *Tabula rasa.*"

I knew what he was doing, and I wasn't having it. He knew perfectly well that Jennifer was the top dog in Vegas, but for an old-school midwestern mob guy, kowtowing to a woman was out of the question. He thought he could make peace the easy way and protect his masculine pride. No dice. I gave him a polite little chuckle and gestured to Jennifer.

"Hey, good to know, sir," I said, "but I'm not sure why you keep talking to me. I'm not even on the board. I'm just hired to watch Ms. Juniper's back. She's in charge here."

Now he looked at her. The smile died on his lips like a wilting flower.

"Ms....Juniper," he said. "Of course."

She offered her hand. He took it with all the enthusiasm of someone mucking out a horse stall with his bare fingers.

"Chairperson of the New Commission," she said. "I'm surprised nobody told you."

Surprised. Right. I struggled to keep a straight face as Petrocelli stammered his lying apology.

"It's just been a very, that is, tumultuous time—"

"And the war is over," Jennifer told him. "We agree. I've spoken to the members of the board, and no one wants to push this matter any further. The offense came from Don Mancuso, and he and his people paid the price. Honor is satisfied."

Petrocelli's face softened a little. Maybe it was relief that his house wasn't going to turn into a shooting gallery like Mancuso's did. Maybe he'd found something in Jennifer's manner, the way she carried herself and shot straight, that he could come to respect once he'd given her a chance.

"I'm glad to hear that." He crossed his fingers, holding them up. "Y'know, back in the day, Chicago and Vegas were thick as thieves. We built this city."

"I've got a lot of respect for that," Jennifer told him,

working her diplomacy. "I'm too young to have seen those days firsthand, but I believe they should never be forgotten. Once the Outfit reorganizes, I'd like to extend the hand of friendship."

He nodded, slow, a faint twinkle of gratitude in his eyes.

"Yeah. Yeah, we'd appreciate that. I'll take your message back home. Thank you, Ms. Juniper."

She raised a hand in parting. "Mr. Petrocelli."

As he walked away, I caught Jennifer's eye and mouthed a single word: "*Ink.*"

"Oh, Mr. Petrocelli?" she said. "Just one last thing."

He turned back, looking her way.

"We've been hearing rumors on the grapevine about what's happening back east," she said. "What do you know about ink?"

He grimaced. "What a headache. One night, it's nowhere and nobody's heard of it. One night after that, it's *everywhere*. You'd think whoever's making this junk would come to us. Offer respect, let us dip our beaks. Not one word."

"So you don't know who's behind it either?" I asked.

"Nah. My guys nabbed a street dealer last week. Asked him nice where he was getting the stuff. He didn't wanna be nice, so then they asked him with a blowtorch. We gave him some time alone in a dark room to think about his answer. Maybe he'd wanna start cooperating before my guys got more creative, know what I mean?"

"What'd he tell you?" Jennifer said.

"Nothing." Petrocelli shook his head, disgusted. "He bit off his own tongue. Then he swallowed it and choked himself to death. Damnedest thing you ever saw."

"He was that afraid of what you were gonna do to him?"

"No," Petrocelli said. "He was that afraid of his supplier. We told him it wasn't a secret worth dying over. All he had to do was give us a name. We'd let him walk, even put a little cash in his pocket. My boys started working on him, he's *still* too scared to talk. I said, kid, you're bein' crazy now. Acting like this supplier is the devil himself."

His gaze went distant, thinking back. He gave a humorless little laugh.

"He said it *was* the devil."

3.

Petrocelli left. Jennifer punched me in the arm.

"Ow." I rubbed my sleeve with exaggerated indignation. "Now what was *that* one for?"

"You didn't have to do that," she said.

"Do what?"

She pulled down her tinted glasses, staring at me over the rims. "You think I didn't catch that? Pretendin' to be my errand boy, to force him to talk to me."

"You're our chair. He disrespects you, he disrespects all of us." I shrugged. "Besides, maybe I wanted to see him squirm a little."

"Mission accomplished. You think he's on the level?"

I glanced to the cluttered floor where he'd been standing a moment ago. A pair of workmen ambled past, hoisting a stack of wooden beams between them.

"I think so. We didn't just give the Outfit a black eye; we proved we won't be shy about dishing out even more punishment if we feel so inclined. They won't be a problem for a while, at least not until they figure out who's running the show now that Mancuso and his kid are six feet under. Right now I'm more intrigued by this ink business."

"And thinkin' about our liquor license."

I waved a hand, taking in the room. "Even if we finished construction tomorrow, no point opening until we get that license. And we can't exactly go the conventional route, seeing as we can't allow a full inspection of the grounds, half our bar inventory is stolen property, and the legal owner only exists on paper. Getting fast-tracked by the mayor would fix everything."

"Hmm. We gotta find this ink supplier. On the bright side, he probably ain't the devil." She tilted her head. "Could be *a* devil, though. Commissioner Harding said they just caught a dealer; if he's still in town, maybe he could help us solve the mystery. Want me to talk to these construction guys, see about borrowing a blowtorch?"

A high-pitched whine split the air as a circular saw carved a beam down to size. My eardrums stung. I shouted above the noise.

"Figured I'd try finesse first." I waved a hand toward the wooden ribs of the room and held up my phone. "Gonna step outside, make a couple of calls."

Ever since my "death" in prison and my subsequent miraculous resurrection, I'd had one constant thorn in my side. Detective Gary Kemper. He was still raw about how I'd blackmailed him once, back during the Lauren Carmichael business, and he jumped at the chance to return the favor. He knew that Daniel Faust was still among the living, and now my continued cooperation was the only thing keeping him from a phone call to the FBI.

So far, he had wanted the same thing I did: stopping the gang war between Vegas and Chicago. Now that the war was over, the thought of what he might do with his leverage was enough to keep me up at night. I could end the problem with one bullet, except for a couple of problems. First, Kemper wasn't stupid. No chance he hadn't worked out some kind of contingency plan, a way to screw me from beyond the grave.

Second, I wasn't big on killing cops. That used to be a solid rule of mine, until I'd gunned down a pair of corrupt detectives on the Outfit's payroll. Now it was more of a guideline. I wasn't looking to bury any *good* cops, anyway, and Kemper was a good cop. He was more or less honest, on the job for the right reasons. That made him my enemy, but I figured his continued presence in the world was a net good. Sometimes the choice that lets you face yourself in the mirror every morning is the only choice worth making, even if it causes more headaches down the road.

He picked up on the second ring. "Kemper."

"It's me. I need some information."

I waited for his incredulous pause to end.

"Seems you forgot how this works, Faust. I call you. You do what I tell you to. Then you go away until I feel like telling you to do something else. It's kind of a one-way street, this thing we've got here."

"Spoken like a man who's lousy in bed, Detective. When you're fucking someone, you should at least give 'em a reach-around. Besides, I'm doing my civic duty and helping to stem a dangerous new drug epidemic."

"Do tell."

"I have it on good authority that Metro busted an ink dealer," I said. "Not one of our people, and not one of the usual suspects. An out-of-towner, driving a car with New Mexico plates. I need to know if he's still in lockup."

"Which sector did he get picked up in?"

"No idea," I said.

He grunted into the phone. "So what, I'm supposed to call all of 'em? Who told you about the bust?"

"Commissioner Harding."

"Don't even joke about that," he said.

"No joke. I was having a morning sit-down with him and Mayor Seabrook. They don't like me very much, you'll be pleased to hear. They like this ink stuff even less. I've got avenues of information that the boys in beige don't, and I'm looking to help out."

"We've got this handled," Kemper said. "Ink's not getting a foothold in Vegas."

"You've got a buddy in the Chicago PD, Detective. Call him up, ask how *their* plans went. C'mon, you've got nothing to lose. All I need is a little information. You do your thing, I'll do mine, and we'll see who's got something to brag about when the dust settles."

"I'll call you back."

Twenty minutes later, he had the inside scoop. The pusher was a career loser named Charlie Malone, a drifter with a history of racking up two strikes in states with three-strike laws. A "habitual offender," Kemper called him, but his real habit was feeding the hungry mouth in his arm. His usual business was ripping off drug dealers; apparently he'd gone from beating 'em to joining 'em. He'd bonded out two hours ago.

"He's from out of state and a flight risk," I said. "Who was dumb enough to post bond for this guy?"

According to the card they left behind, Coughlin and Son Bail Bonds, Inc. was dumb enough. I got their address and called for a cab.

* * *

The wobbly ceiling fan inside Coughlin and Son's shoebox of an office spun as slow as a revolving door. Barely kicking up a breeze, just pushing the sluggish cigarette-flavored air around. The garish sofa by the door looked like it had been bought from an elderly grandmother's estate sale; the ten-year-old issues of *People* magazine littering the coffee table probably came from the same place. Farther in, a bullet-headed man with a missing front tooth—Coughlin or Son, I wasn't sure—looked up from his mammoth of a monitor and gave me a wave.

"Afternoon," he said. "Help ya out?"

The door swung shut at my back.

"I hope so," I told him. "I'm here about one of your clients. Charlie Malone, busted on possession?"

A glint of recognition. "Yeah, my kid bonded him out. Pretty standard, they got him on a Class E, that's five grand for bail."

"You know he's from out of state, right? And doesn't have any reason to stick around. Why'd you take the risk?"

His eyes narrowed. "And we're having this discussion why exactly?"

Time wasn't on my side. I thought about playing it hard, locking his front door and leaning on him, but there's a time and a place for that kind of maneuver. Bail bondsmen deal with tough guys for a living; intimidation would just make him dig his heels in. I gave him a smile instead.

"I'm a PI," I told him. "Keep it on the down-low, but certain people in high places are worried about ink dealers from New Mexico suddenly darkening our city's doorstep."

Coughlin showed me his open hands. "Hey, I got nothing to do with that. We issue bonds to anybody and everybody, no matter the crime. Innocent until proven guilty, am I right?"

"No judgment here. Just seems like a waste of five grand."

"Nah," he said, "the money's guaranteed. We would have turned him down flat—like you said, he's probably gonna jump bail, and I don't feel like driving to New Mexico—but the guy's lawyer is good for it."

"Lawyer?" I tilted my head. "Since when does Legal Aid vouch for a client's bail money? Most of those guys can barely be bothered to show up for court."

"Uh-uh. This ain't pro bono. Guy's got a *real* lawyer." He tugged open a desk drawer, rummaging around until he came up with a rumpled business card.

I took it from his outstretched hand and twirled it in my fingertips. Gold on cream, elegant and precise. *Weishaupt and Associates*, it read. *Mr. Smith, Esquire.*

I owned a card like his, but mine had bloodstains. The warden of Eisenberg Correctional had given it to me thirty seconds before I shot him dead. It was a golden ticket, he told me: all I had to do was show some mercy, let him walk, and call the number on the card, and I could have anything I wanted as a reward. He caught me on a bad day; I was all out of mercy.

Since then, my buddy Pixie had been digging into Weishaupt's business. Her shovel mostly hit bedrock. The firm was a sham, as far as she could tell. Their website was a rat's nest of dead links and spyware, their street address was a vacant lot, and their "lawyers" were stock-photo actors. Their computer system had bulletproof security that stopped her cold—and considering Pixie broke into government mainframes for fun, that said a lot.

I already knew Weishaupt was up to some nasty business. Apparently they were expanding their repertoire. I pocketed the card.

"I need to have a word with Mr. Malone. I assume he

had to give you an address? Wherever he's supposedly staying while he waits for his hearing?"

"Sure." Coughlin looked me up and down. "Thing is, I don't need some pissed-off junkie with an assault record storming in here, demanding to know why I gave out his personal information."

"If he asks, I got it from the court."

"If you're really working for people in high places," he said, "I should tell you to go and do that."

I gave him a tired sigh and a just-us-working-stiffs smile. "C'mon, pal, I'm trying to earn a living, just like you. Sure, I could do that, but it's a drive across town and at least an hour sitting in some pencil jockey's waiting room. Help me out?"

He stared at me, he stared at his computer screen, then he hauled his keyboard across the desk.

"Just keep my name outta your mouth," he told me. "He's staying at a transient motel on Paradise Road, stone's throw from the airport. Do me one favor?"

"Name it."

"I saw that look in your eye just now. Seen guys like you before."

"Do tell," I said.

"All I'm saying is, when you're 'having a word' with this guy? If you gotta hurt him bad enough that he's gonna miss his court date, a courtesy call would be appreciated."

4.

Malone was holing up at the Paradise All-Suites, a fancy name for a roach motel that was a hellhole in the fifties and hadn't been fixed up—or cleaned—since. The daylight faded as my taxi pulled into the lot, the silhouette of a jumbo jet soaring like a steel vulture in front of a rippling orange sunset. In the distance, rising up over the tenements and condos, the Strip opened one sleepy neon eye.

A television squatted in the corner of the lobby, blaring some old sitcom. Canned laughter washed over my back as I stepped up to the check-in desk. The clerk had bloodshot eyes and shaky fingers. He barely glanced my way as he droned, "Forty bucks a night or ten by the hour, no pets."

"Looking for one of your tenants. Charlie Malone."

Now he looked at me. "Who's asking?"

I set a couple of ten-dollar bills on the counter. "Alexander Hamilton."

He stuffed the bills in his shirt pocket.

"Tell Mr. President he's on the second floor. Room twenty-three."

I turned to go, then paused. I looked back at him.

"You...do know Hamilton was never president, right?"

The clerk shrugged. "You know history, but I got your money. Which one of us is *really* smart here?"

I couldn't argue that.

"Got another ten-spot," he said. "I'll tell you something you oughta know."

I fished in my pocket and tugged out another bill. I set it on the counter—then yanked it back when he reached for it.

"Info first," I told him. "I'll pay what it's worth."

"Saw Malone visiting the room of a long-term tenant this morning. Aforementioned tenant is a successful small business owner."

"Drugs?"

"Guns," he said. "Saw Malone leave with a pocket thirty-two, But that's none of my business."

I gave him the ten.

I jogged up bare concrete steps to the second-floor hallway. Up ahead, the door to twenty-three jiggled and swung open. An emaciated guy in a yellow tank top and prison tats, three days of stubble on his cheeks, wandered out into the hall. He looked my way. Our eyes locked. He knew.

Malone darted back into his room and slammed the door behind him. I heard the metallic click of a deadbolt as I broke into a run. I hit the door shoulder-first, and the cheap wood shattered like a broken promise. The room beyond was a grungy kitchenette strewn with crumpled beer cans and dead roaches. Malone was on the far side, halfway out the window; he looked back with big wet puppy-dog eyes, like he was emotionally hurt that I was chasing him. Then the .32 in his hand spat fire, and I threw myself to the soiled carpet, rolling behind the sofa as shots whined over my head.

I came up on one knee with a brace of playing cards in my left hand. I flung them like throwing knives and they lanced across the room trailing heat-mirage ripples in their wake. Two went wide, digging halfway into the rotting plaster, and a third sliced his tank top and scored a red line across his hip. He yelped and tumbled out the window. The fire escape rattled as it caught him like a baby in a rusty cradle.

"Don't run," I shouted. "It's only gonna get worse if you—"

He ran. The fire escape groaned as he thundered down the metal steps. I leaned out the window then ducked back, another bullet cracking past my face and blasting the wooden sill into splinters. I took a deep breath, counted to two, and jumped out after him.

Lights were clicking on all over the complex, eyes peering out from behind dusty drapery. I didn't need this kind of attention. The cards stayed snug in my breast pocket; doing magic in public was the definition of a bad idea, and drawing my pistol was only marginally wiser. Malone was either smart enough to stop shooting or he was just too scared to think about anything but getting away from me. He dropped down to the pavement, stumbled, and raced for the street with his arms flailing.

I was right behind him, my heart a jackhammer, shoes pounding the sidewalk. Slowly slipping farther behind as the distance between us grew and my lungs burned with every breath. Maybe I was getting old, maybe the fear or the drugs or both were giving him an edge, but I was losing this race. Traffic on the side street was sparse, but it was still there, and the occasional wash of headlight beams at my back was the only thing keeping me from pulling my piece and going for a leg shot.

A car cruised past, a snow-white Audi Quattro. Smooth and easy—until it suddenly swerved right, jumped the curb, and slammed on the brakes. Malone ran headlong into the car's hood, flying off his feet and rolling, coming down on the other side in a tangle of limbs. I ran around the car and slapped the gun out of his hand. Then I gave him a backhand hard enough to loosen the few teeth he had left.

"Told you," I panted, "not to make me run. *Asshole.*"

The driver's-side door opened and a goddess stepped out. Well, the closest thing I'd ever seen to one, anyway. Tall, her pinstripe blazer and slacks perfectly tailored to her frame, her scarlet hair falling over one shoulder in an elaborately braided twist. She wore an impish smile.

"Sorry to interrupt your evening exercise," Caitlin said, "but you were late for our dinner date."

Malone clutched his arm, the skin purple under his twitching fingers, and gritted his teeth. He was a mess of cuts and scrapes. "My arm," he whined. "Think you broke my fuckin' arm—"

I rested my hands on my knees, crouching, still trying to catch my breath. "Oh, we haven't started breaking things yet. Cait, help me get him into the back seat?"

Caitlin snickered and hoisted him up under one arm, like he was lighter than a sack of groceries. She unceremoniously tossed him into the back, then leaned over his pale, sweaty face.

"If you even think about bleeding on my car seats," she murmured to him, "then after my lover is done with you, *I* get a turn."

She got behind the wheel. I sat beside her and buckled

in. We pulled away from the curb, off the side street, and into the flow of nighttime traffic.

"How was LA?" I asked.

"Delightful. Tanesha sends her regards, by the way. She treated me to an early listen of the new album, now that it's finished. It's going to be *amazing*."

It was a sore spot, but I still had to ask. "How about her, ah...ghost problem?"

"She doesn't know she has one, and ideally never will." Caitlin sighed. "I caught a glimpse of Monty's shade in one of her hallway mirrors. Still clinging. Doomed romanticism is lovely in poetry and song, but a bit sad in real life."

"Some people just don't know how to let go."

"Hey," Malone groaned from the back seat. "Where are you taking me?"

I ignored him. "Nicky's out of the hospital and back in hiding. The twins are taking care of him while he rests up, which sounds like a special kind of hell."

"I heard they tried to make chicken soup once." Caitlin's nose wrinkled. "Twenty chickens died and a small farm was wiped from the map. I'm told a grenade launcher was involved. What about Paolo?"

Another sore spot. A much fresher wound. I didn't answer right away. I looked out the window and watched the Vegas skyline slowly come to life.

"They discharged him this morning."

Caitlin's glance flicked my way. "Did you go and see him?"

"Not yet. I mean, I visited him in the hospital, twice, but he was all doped up on morphine."

"You should go see him," she said.

"I know."

Hunted by the courts of hell, Damien Ecko decided to go out with a bang, focusing his rampage of revenge on my friends and family. He got his hands on my buddy Paolo and mutilated him. Nothing personal between them, he did it just to spite me. When he was finished, Paolo—a world-class forger and a hell of an artist—only had two fingers left.

Ecko chewed off the others, one at a time, while Paolo screamed for mercy.

"What happened wasn't your fault," Caitlin said. "Paolo knows it wasn't your fault."

I shifted in my seat, leaning my weight against the armrest as oncoming headlights washed across the windshield.

"I talked to the Commission," I said. "Everybody's in agreement: he took that hit for us, collectively. So we're gonna...I mean, we can't make him whole. Nobody can make him whole. But he'll have money. He won't want for anything."

Anything but his hands. Anything but the craft he could never practice again.

"You should go see him," Caitlin said again.

"Hey," Malone piped up from the back. "*Hey.*"

I turned in my seat, swallowing down a white-hot flash of anger.

"The fuck is your problem?"

"My arm. I need a *hospital.*"

"Yeah, we'll get right on that." I faced front again.

"Brought you a present," Caitlin said.

"For me? You didn't have to do that."

"I don't *have* to do anything I don't want to do," she said. "Look in the glove compartment."

Her gift lay coiled on top of the Audi owner's manual

and a pristine registration card. Black leather straps curled like octopus arms around a long, thin tube. I took it out, brow furrowing as I turned it in my hands, buckles catching the moonlight.

"Is this..." I started to ask as I tried to figure it out. I nodded my head at the junkie in the back seat. "Is this something I don't want to be showing off in mixed company?"

Caitlin arched an eyebrow at me. Her pomegranate-stained lips offered an amused smile.

"This particular toy isn't for the bedroom, pet."

"I'm never quite sure."

"*That* gift is in the trunk, and I'll show it to you later tonight," she said. "This is a spring sheath. The straps buckle around your forearm and hold the opening of the sheath against the bottom of your sleeve. Bentley referred me to a shop in LA where they make custom gear for stage magicians."

"For..." I grinned, fingers running along the black leather tube. "My wand. You got me a concealed sheath for my wand."

"Well, seeing as you finally stopped wearing that damn top hat in public, I thought you deserved a reward."

"I *like* that hat."

"I know," Caitlin sighed. "I really wish you didn't."

I held the sheath against my forearm and flexed my wrist, getting a feel for the action. "This is fantastic, Cait. I love this."

I looked her way. I didn't say these words often, but now they spilled out on their own, natural as breathing.

"I love you."

Her smile softened. Almost wistful.

"Love you too," she said in a faint voice.

Malone let out a guttural wheeze and twisted on the back seat, the tan leather creaking under his weight. "Guys, c'mon, I really need a hospital."

The moment shattered. Caitlin glared into the rearview mirror.

"I will *give* you something to whine about." She turned the wheel, headlights strobing off construction pallets and sawhorses as the Audi's tires rumbled on loose gravel. "Good. We're here. Can I torture him now?"

I took out my phone and dialed Jennifer's number. "Hopefully that won't be necessary."

She got out, slamming her door, and opened the back. She grabbed Malone by the scruff of his neck.

"Torture is like a good bottle of wine," she said. "It's never *necessary*, but it's a fine way to liven up a party and is best savored in the company of friends."

5.

By night the build site was quiet and dark, the cold of the desert night seeping through bare wood and drywall. The wind ruffled the edges of plastic sheeting, the unfinished windows tarped and taped. I turned on a construction light, a single high-powered bulb dangling in an orange plastic cage, and it cast long and shifting shadows across the unfinished floorboards. That sawdust taste still hung thick in the air. The woody aroma mingled with the faint scent of blood.

We had Malone on the floor, a leash of rope tethering his good arm and his neck to a portable generator. Jennifer showed up fifteen minutes later. She'd dressed down for the night, trading her corporate look for a windbreaker over a concert T-shirt and a ripped-up pair of blue jeans. Her steel-toed boots clunked on the raw flooring as she came over and clasped hands with Caitlin.

"Welcome home, Cait. How'd la-la land treat you?"

"I *did* feel eminently refreshed." She pointed a baleful finger at Malone. "Then he bled. On my car."

Jennifer winced. "Ooh. That's a hangin' offense."

"Indeed. I just haven't decided which body part to hang him by."

"I don't even *know* you people," he moaned, his face a twist of pained confusion.

I stood over him and put my hands on my hips.

"Hi," I said. "We own Las Vegas. You probably should have found that out before you tried to set up shop here."

"Let's talk about ink," Jennifer told him.

Malone shook his head like it was full of marbles and he thought he could force them out one ear.

"Can't," he said. "Can't talk about that."

"Look," I said, "temporarily putting aside the issue of my girlfriend's car, we don't *want* to get rough with you. But you are gonna talk. And you are gonna tell us what we want to know. This little conversation is only going to get as nasty as you insist we make it, understand? This could end with us driving you to the emergency room and putting a nice wad of cash in your pocket, smiles and good feelings all around, or it could end with us picking an assortment of construction tools and finding out what they can do to a human body. It's your call."

His headshake was a spasm now, a borderline seizure as he thrashed against the rope around his throat.

"Can't," he stammered, "can't talk 'bout that. Can't. Can't."

Jennifer stepped up to stand beside me, frowning. "Sugar, something is *wrong* with this critter. I thought he just had junkie brain, y'know, coming down and getting hungry for a fix, but..."

"But," I echoed. I held up my hands. "It's okay. Hey, buddy. Forget it. We don't want to ask you about ink. We wanna ask about your favorite football team."

The spasms stopped. He blinked, cow-eyed and dull.

"The...the Broncos?"

"Yeah," I said. "Just think about the Broncos for a minute. We'll be right back."

I waved Caitlin and Jennifer aside, dropping my voice to a murmur. I kept my eyes on him as I spoke. All three eyes. My psychic senses roused, sleepy, stretching out tendrils of concentrated thought that writhed in my second sight like violet sea anemones. A shadow lived inside Malone's body, wriggling, buried deep with legs like fishhooks.

"Somebody put a whammy on this guy."

"A geas?" Jennifer asked. "Some kinda curse to keep his mouth shut?"

"That'd do the trick," I said. "Explains the dealer those hoods from Chicago caught, too. He didn't talk when they tortured him because he literally *couldn't*. And committing suicide by biting his own tongue off? A geas could make somebody do that."

"A scary-strong one," Jennifer whispered, glancing over at Malone.

"Can you remove it?" Caitlin asked.

"Tricky," I said. "A geas is a binding curse. A taboo enforced by spellcraft. It's designed to protect itself. Trying to pry it out might kill him."

Jennifer spread her hands. "We got an alternative?"

"Point. Okay, I'm gonna run out and grab my ritual kit. Babysit this guy until I get back." I gave Caitlin an apologetic glance. "Sorry. This was not the five-star evening I planned on treating you to."

"I think I know a thing or two about the demands of a busy career," she said, her voice dry. "And this has the potential to be entertaining. You gather your supplies, and I'll order some food for the three of us. Indian, Chinese, or pizza?"

I said, "Indian" at the same time Jennifer said, "Chinese." Caitlin beamed at us, looking content.

"Pizza it is, then. Good choice."

* * *

Caitlin chose the toppings, of course, picking up our pie from a gourmet shop over in Summerlin. Neapolitan style, rich and chewy, with San Marzano tomatoes, peppers sliced paper thin, garlic, spinach, and fresh mozzarella. The big, steaming box shared space with a tray of breaded calamari and a black plastic bowl of Caesar salad. A plywood sheet, balanced between a pair of sawhorses, served as a makeshift table.

"I picked up a nice earthy Sangiovese to go with it," Caitlin said, turning the wine bottle in her hands and giving the label a critical eye. "The store only had plastic glasses, but needs must. We'll make do."

"You do realize I spent my formative years drinkin' outta mason jars, right?" Jennifer said. "Plastic is fine. It's like we're having a picnic."

Malone wasn't having a picnic. I had him laid out on the floor, his wrists tied to the generator, the rope around his ankles lashed to an eighty-pound bag of concrete mix. I circled him, moving in a crouch as I drew a ring of white chalk upon the rough plywood floorboards. Then another smaller circle inside the first. A scattering of open Tupperware containers sat to one side, the tools of the trade at my fingertips.

"What're you—" he stammered, his voice weak. "What're you doin'?"

"Maybe saving your life, so shut up and let me concentrate."

Between the rings, my stick of chalk scratched swirling glyphs from memory. Hebrew letters, words of protection and expulsion. The names of forgotten entities some books claimed were angels, some claimed were demons. I didn't care what they were. I only cared if the spell worked. In my mind's eye Malone slowly took on a pale scarlet sheen. A neon glow over his body rippled like a bank of morning fog. And buried in the fog, I saw the dark and squirming shadow that had taken up residence behind his rib cage, its tarantula-leg pincers hooked into his heart.

"I conjure you, o instrument," I whispered with a quick glance at my watch, "in the hour of Mars, in the day of Mercury. By Dalmaley, by Lameck—"

"I think I'm gonna throw up," Malone wheezed.

I grabbed his chin, feeling clammy sweat and stubble under my fingertips. Turning his head toward me, I dipped my free fingers into a pot of white salve. I drew a seal on his forehead, glistening swirls against his pale skin, then let him go.

"By thrones, powers, and principalities, you are driven forth. You are exiled." I reached for another plastic tub, scooping up a handful of sea salt. I sprinkled it over Malone's body, crystals landing in his tangled and greasy hair, catching in his dirty bootlaces. The fog was roiling now, the shadow over his heart twitching like a centipede. The ritual was turning the geas parasite's formerly cozy home into a very unpleasant place.

Now to give it an alternative. I waved to grab Jennifer's attention and pointed at an empty work bucket in the far corner of the room. She ran over, snatched it up, and jogged to my side as I picked up the little treat I'd bought on my way over. A cardboard container, like a Chinese take-out box, lined in plastic. A coppery stench filled the air as I unhooked the flaps.

When it comes to ritual magic, there's a time and a

place for blood sacrifice. In a pinch, a stop at a late-night butcher's shop is almost as good. I poured the cow blood into the bucket, thick burgundy rivulets splashing the sides and rolling down. The bucket stood right at the chalk circle's outer edge, close to Malone's face. He groaned again and writhed against the ropes.

"That's right," I murmured, watching the shadow begin to crawl up his rib cage. "Got someplace warm and comfy for you. It's closing time; you don't have to go home, but you can't stay in there."

I'd done this ritual twice in my life. The subject survived once, so I was batting fifty-fifty odds. All the same, I knew the moves and how things would go from here. The curse would gust from his mouth and nose in a wisp of almost-invisible smoke, like the last gasp of a blown-out candle, and fly into the bucket of blood. We'd take the bucket out back, dig a shallow hole in the sand, splash the blood into the hole, and bury it. Easy. Done.

His chest swelled. The soiled cotton of his tank top rose up as his skin flexed and stretched. Malone's wrists twisted in the ropes, skinned raw. He let out a strangled cry.

"That ain't supposed to—" Jennifer started to say.

"I know." I grabbed another handful of salt and splashed him with it, grainy crystals scattering across the circle of chalk.

Malone bucked against the ropes, seizing. His jaw wrenched wide in a scream that devolved into wet, ragged choking. His throat bulged. Something was inside him, clawing its way out, and it wasn't a wisp of smoke. I grabbed the bucket and inched it closer, tilting it toward his head. The coppery smell of blood mingled with a new odor rising up from Malone's open mouth, something like the stench of an open sewer on a hot summer day.

Four-inch antennae wriggled in the depths of Malone's throat. I saw the first gleam of a brown chitinous shell as his bloodshot eyes rolled back in his head. My stomach clenched, revolting, as the creature slithered up into his mouth and pushed his cheeks back.

It was a cockroach. A cockroach over half a foot long.

I jumped back as the monstrous insect crawled from Malone's mouth, spilling over his blood-flecked lips and skittering down his chin. It raced down his neck and across the floor, running circles around the bucket. Jennifer's chromed .357 roared like a cannon as she opened fire, slugs pounding fist-sized chunks in the plywood. Splinters flew and the roach ran in a blind panic. A pair of playing cards leaped from my breast pocket and into my outstretched fingertips. I fired them one at a time, razor-sharp cards carving into the floor like throwing knives, each one landing a fraction of an inch behind the fleeing insect.

A stiletto heel slammed down. The roach twitched under Caitlin's foot, speared through the middle and dying in a slowly spreading pool of yellow goo. She glanced over at us, head tilted in curiosity, and took a bite from her slice of pizza.

"I presume," she said, chewing thoughtfully, "that's not how this spell usually goes?"

6.

I took the bucket out back, dumped the blood, and washed it out with a hose while Jennifer took a sponge to the circle of chalk. The plastic tub of salad was sacrificed for the cause of occult science: we needed something to keep the dead roach in.

"Honestly," Jennifer said, shuddering as she snapped the lid into place, "don't know why you're savin' this thing."

"Because I want to know what it *is*."

"Giant bug," she said.

"Giant bug that shouldn't exist. And this isn't how geases work. At all." I looked over at Caitlin, who was starting her third slice of pizza. "What do you think? Demonic?"

She shrugged and reached for her plastic wineglass.

"We *do* grow them big back home. But no. This doesn't have the right feel. It's more..."

I stared at the thing, nestled among a few stray leaves of lettuce under a clear plastic dome. Half expecting it to start moving again.

"Artificial," I said. The only word that fit the strangely

sterile energy wafting off the roach's impaled corpse. Caitlin nodded.

Jennifer put her hands on her hips and sighed, surveying the damage. Bullet holes and gouges littered the floorboards.

"Gonna have fun explaining this to the construction crew tomorrow," she said.

Malone let out a hoarse, racking cough as he came to. He opened his eyes, squinting.

"Feel better?" I asked him.

"Feels like I just got my tonsils taken out," he rasped. "What happened?"

"Probably for the best that you don't remember." I crouched and untied the ropes at his ankles. "I wish *I* didn't remember. So. You were about to tell us who you work for."

"I can't—" He paused, then blinked. "I...I *can*. It's like I had this...block in my head."

"It wasn't in your head, but close enough. Where'd you get the ink? Who told you to start pushing it in Vegas?"

"I got jammed up with these guys," Malone said. "See, I was dealing horse. I got a little problem, just a little sweet tooth, you know?"

"You were selling to feed your habit," I said.

He nodded, weak. I finished untying him. He put his back to the generator, still sitting on the floor, cradling his fractured arm.

"Problem was, I was selling on a corner I didn't have a right to be selling on."

"And now here you are on *our* turf," Jennifer said. "Wow, talk about not learnin' from your mistakes."

"This guy, an OG with the Fourth Street Counts, he said I had a choice. I could pay back all the money I 'owed' him from stealing his business, plus interest, or I could work for him. Told me to go to this address, he'd hook me up with his supplier. Pretty simple decision. I could toe the line or *lose* my toes, you know?"

"Then what happened?" I asked.

His gaze went distant, confused.

"I...I don't know. That's God's honest truth, man. It was a blur."

"Must be where they put the roach in him," Jennifer murmured.

Malone gaped at her. "What?"

"Never mind." I waved a hand. "Continue."

"Next thing I know, it's two weeks later and I'm driving across the Nevada state line with cash that ain't mine, in a wallet I don't remember buying, and two crates of ink in my trunk. There's these...gaps. I know I was supposed to sling the ink in Vegas, but I don't know who told me that. I got the product, but I don't remember where."

"How about your lawyers?" I said. "Weishaupt and Associates. How'd you know to call them when you got busted?"

"Found the card in my wallet." He shrugged, helpless. "Stab in the dark, you know? Had a phone call coming, and I figured they had to be better than a public defender. I gave 'em my name and they knew exactly who I was. They said to stay put, keep my mouth shut, and they'd take care of everything."

I held up one finger. "Sidebar."

Off to the side, Jennifer, Caitlin, and I huddled close.

"Turning drug mules into mind-enslaved drones," I said. "That's a new one."

Jennifer frowned. "A street gang like the Counts doesn't have that kind of juice. New Mexico, though, you're looking at a lot of *narcotraficante* action down there. Think this is coming in from south of the border? What do we know about these lawyers?"

I took the card for Weishaupt and Associates from my pocket. Turning it over, running my thumb over the gold embossment.

"These guys were behind the gladiator fights at Eisenberg Prison, too. Figured they were taking a cut from the gambling action. Looks like we've got a new player on the scene, and they don't have much respect for territory lines."

"We need solid intel," Jennifer said. "Feel like takin' a trip to New Mexico on behalf of the New Commission?"

"Do I *want* to? No. But that's the job I signed up for, isn't it?"

She put her hand on my arm, nodding with mock solemnity.

"Sorry, sugar, you're on the payroll now. Some days you get the cash and the cars and the good champagne...and some days you gotta go to Albuquerque."

"I'm still waiting for the cash and the cars," I said.

Caitlin glanced over at Malone. "What about this one? You know, there's an old superstition that burying a corpse in the foundation of a building brings luck to all who cross its threshold."

"I...have never heard that," I told her.

"Maybe it's a new superstition."

Jennifer contemplated the man, curling her lip. "I think we ought to leave him in play for now. If he goes missing, the folks holding his leash might get froggy and jump outta sight before Danny gets a good look at 'em. Wait a week, and I'll send a couple guys to keep eyes on him in the meantime. If you're still feelin' raw about the blood on your back seat, I'll bring him to you myself."

We walked back over to Malone, and I laid down the law.

"The lawyers told you to stay cool and stay put, and that's exactly what you're gonna do. Go back to your shitty hotel room, wait for their call, do whatever they tell you to, and forget we ever had this conversation." I looked at Caitlin. "Let's get this guy to the ER so they can patch his arm up."

"Don't worry," Malone said, "I won't say anything about any of this. I'm not looking for trouble, swear."

I helped him to his feet. "It's not us you need to worry about. It's the people you work for. Know those blackouts and brain glitches you've been having? If you don't want to go through that all over again, you'd better pretend to be as dumb as you look."

* * *

I rode with Caitlin. We took Malone to Desert Springs Hospital over on Flamingo Road, dropped him off in the parking lot, and peeled away as he staggered to the emergency room doors. He was his own problem now.

My problem was six hundred miles away. I had an address, the place where Malone got the whammy laid on him, and not much else to go on.

"Albuquerque," I muttered.

Caitlin tapped her phone when we paused at a stoplight, pairing it with the car speakers, and set it in the cup holder between us. A Howard Jones album started to play, peppy strings and synthesizers washing in.

"Might do you good to get out of town for a few days," she said. "Travel is healthy for the heart. I'll check in on the construction for you until you get back."

"Thanks. But it doesn't matter *when* construction's done if we don't have a liquor license. So I'll go out there, poke a stick around and turn over a few rocks, and see what squirms out. All I need is some kind of win I can bring to Mayor Seabrook. If I can find the ink pipeline, maybe a production facility, and leak it to the local cops so they get a big bust...yeah, that should do the trick."

"Worry about it tomorrow, pet. Tonight is for us." She drummed her manicured nails on the steering wheel. "I want to dance. Let's go to Winter."

I slouched in my seat. "A nightclub packed with hip, beautiful twentysomethings. I am too old for that crowd."

"Nonsense. You're as young as you feel." She winked. "Trust me. Then again, I could think of some other ways to get a good workout..."

My phone buzzed in my pocket. "Hold that thought."

I fished the phone out and glanced at the screen. The call was coming from the Blue Karma Restaurant in Denver. "Oh, hell."

Caitlin flicked her gaze at my phone and wrinkled her nose. "Indeed."

She turned down the music. I answered the phone.

"Faust."

"Daniel." Caitlin's voice oozed through the phone, smoldering. "I was just lying here in bed, thinking about you. What are you wearing?"

I leaned my head back and rolled my eyes.

"Cait's sitting right next to me, Naavarasi. Also, this thing called 'caller ID' was invented around thirty years ago. Knock it off."

She chuckled, a smoky sound, as her Indian accent returned and she spoke in her natural voice. "I can't fool you. Still, what *are* you wearing?"

"A chastity belt," Caitlin muttered darkly. I gave her the side-eye.

"I'm wearing my patience," I told Naavarasi. "No, wait, I mean *you're* wearing *on* my patience. What do you want?"

"Straight to business, then. You owe me two boons. One for my aid while you were in prison, and one for my elimination of that shape-shifting wretch who dared to pretend at being one of my kind. I'm calling one of those favors due."

I knew this was coming. Sooner or later, those two swords dangling over my head were going to drop. Might as well get it over with.

"Fine," I said, "come on out to Vegas. We'll sit down and talk it over."

"No. You'll come to me in Denver. As soon as possible—tomorrow would be best."

"I can't just—" I shook my head. "Why can't you come here?"

"Because I don't want to. And because of protocol. By the codes of the Cold Peace, when it comes to the exchange of owed boons between members of two courts, said exchange must always take place on ground belonging to the owed party. The case law is extremely clear on this matter. If I came to you, it would be demeaning to my station as a baron of hell."

I furrowed my brow. Naavarasi wasn't a demon—the rakshasi matriarch had been drafted into her court at sword-point centuries ago, when Prince Malphas sieged the pocket dimension she called home. She was the last of her kind because Malphas, the prince she owed allegiance and loyalty to, had murdered all the rest.

Suffice to say, "Baron" Naavarasi wasn't a fan of demons or infernal politics. Hearing her quote the dictates of the Cold Peace like a veteran trial lawyer had my suspicions tingling. More than they usually did when dealing with her.

"You're forgetting something," I told her. "I'm not a demon. Not a member of *any* court. Those rules don't apply to me."

"But you are Caitlin's consort. Thereby, she must bear the shame of a social indignity committed by you, so sayeth the Learned Commentaries of the Scholar Snikar'doweis."

I put my hand over the phone and looked at Caitlin. "Is there such a thing as the 'Learned Commentaries of Snickerdoodles'?"

"Snik—" Caitlin paused. Then she sighed. "Yes. You have to go to Denver."

"Or else what?"

"Or else she complains to Prince Malphas, who complains to my prince, who calls me on the carpet and demands to know why I didn't make you go to Denver. And then I have to make you go to Denver. So let's cut out that unpleasant middle step, hmm?"

I put the phone back to my ear. "I'll be there."

"I will prepare a welcoming feast."

"That's okay," I told her. "I'll grab food on the way. Don't put yourself to any trouble."

I hung up. "My schedule just got busier."

"I'm having a thought," Caitlin said. "Road trip."

"Road trip?"

She gave me a nod and flicked her turn signal.

"I'm coming with you, of course. So let's take a few days and turn it into a little vacation."

"You don't have to do that—"

"Daniel," she said, her voice firm. "Have you ever had

an interaction with Naavarasi where she *didn't* try to manipulate, maneuver, or otherwise put you on the losing end of a bad deal?"

"You're still pissed off that she kissed me that one time, aren't you?"

We paused at a red light. She fluffed her bangs in the rearview mirror, quick and precise, then glanced my way.

"I was joking about the chastity belt. Was. Don't tempt me, or this drive will be a lot more fun for me than it will be for you."

The light shifted. We pulled through the intersection, the Audi turning slow like a white steel shark.

"Anyway," Caitlin said, "I want to know what Naavarasi's 'favor' is, and be able to veto it on the spot if necessary. If I'm not there, she'll pull all sorts of court and protocol games, banking on you not knowing any better."

"Yeah, doesn't that strike you as a little bit weird?" I asked. "Naavarasi *hates* infernal politics. She hates her own prince, hates her title. We made an ally out of her in the first place—well, as much as she's anybody's ally—by playing on that. Now she wants to act like nobility all of a sudden? Something smells off about this."

"She's clearly plotting something. It won't take long to find out what. We're fortunate that the woman has a compulsive need to show off and make sure everyone knows how clever she is. If she could keep her designs to herself, she'd actually be dangerous. So, road trip? You and me and the open highway? I think we've earned a little relaxation."

I liked the idea. I'd spent some time lately wrestling with my own momentum. Pushing myself nonstop for months, pinballing from one catastrophe to another, no sleep between lighting fires and putting them out. Taking a little breather, just for us, sounded like a plan.

"Deal," I said. "And I know just the car to do it in. I asked Pixie to track down the Hemi Cuda. They impounded it when I got busted, but it's been long enough that the heat's gotta be simmering down. If it's going up for police auction, I should be able to send a proxy in there and win it back."

Caitlin smiled contentedly. "I *do* enjoy driving that car."

"I know you do. Okay, so first thing tomorrow morning, I'll go see Pixie and see what she's got for us."

7.

"What the hell?" I shouted. "*Harmony Black stole my car?*"

I caught looks from the far side of the room, but I was too pissed off to care. It was breakfast time at Saint Jude's, and the vintage dance-hall-turned-soup-kitchen was filling up with the castaways and forgotten tribes of Las Vegas. Dusty light filtered down from the high windows, the aroma of burnt hash browns and powdered eggs thick in the air.

Pixie glared at me over the rims of her chunky black Buddy Holly glasses. The tips of her short-cropped scarlet hair were dyed ice white. "Number one, use your inside voice. Number two, don't shoot the messenger."

"You don't steal a man's ride, Pix. You don't do it. You especially don't do it when said ride is a painstakingly rebuilt 1970 Barracuda with a four-hundred-and-twenty-six-cubic-inch Hemi engine that can pull a fourteen-second quarter mile."

"I did like that car," Caitlin said, standing beside me.

"She didn't *steal* it," Pixie said. "It was being held in the police impound lot over on A Street. According to the quartermaster's inventory, it was 'temporarily requisitioned by Special Agent Black of the Critical Incident Response Group, pursuant to an ongoing investigation.'"

I spread my hands. "What investigation? As far as she and anybody else in the FBI know, I'm *dead.* No. She stole my car. She stole a dead man's car, and that's even *more* morally unacceptable. That's grave robbing."

"Really?" Pixie stared at me. "You're gonna talk about morals. You."

"As an FBI agent, she should be held to higher standards than me, that's all I'm saying. Where's the car now?"

"Your guess is as good as mine," she said. "I'll keep an ear out, and if she puts it back in impound, I'll let you know."

I looked to Caitlin. "You realize this means war."

"Ah, yes," she said, her voice bone-dry. "The thousand injuries of Harmony Black you have borne as best you could, but when she ventured upon insult..."

"Are you humoring me? I feel that you're humoring me right now."

She stood behind me and rested her hands on my shoulders, leaning in. I felt the warm tickle of her breath against the back of my neck.

"I am absolutely humoring you," she whispered. "Come on, we'll take my car instead."

With two destinations to choose from, we decided on Albuquerque. First, because we wanted to strike while the iron was hot—and before Malone's bosses had any chance to figure out we'd flipped him and learned their home address. Secondly, because it'd keep Naavarasi waiting.

"You do have to go," Caitlin said, "but there's nothing

in the terms of the Cold Peace that says you can't be fashionably late."

We set off on Highway 93, just me, her, and the open road. An hour later we crossed the state border into Arizona, cruising smooth and easy on the open highway. I rolled my window down and basked in the arid sun. Away from the neon, away from the noise, gliding past looming mountains dotted with scrub and ponderosa pines.

"You were right," I said to Caitlin. "I think we both needed this. Just a little time to get away from it all."

Her phone rang.

She pushed a button on the steering wheel. The call routed to the Audi's speakers, killing a bouncy pop song in mid-crescendo. Emma's voice flooded the car.

"Caitlin. There's a problem with the money train."

Caitlin arched an eyebrow. "Last I checked, the money is your department."

"Until it becomes a matter of security, then it's your department. Our friend from Reno is skimming. Two of the last shipments of laundered cash arrived *short*."

"Wonderful," Caitlin said. "Put a bag over his head, throw him in a closet, and let him stew until I get back. I assume he's protesting his innocence—"

My phone buzzed against my hip. I tugged it out, checked the caller ID, and took the call.

"Dan," Gabriel said, his melodic voice sounding apologetic. The boss of the Cinco Calles was built like a brick wall but spoke like a lead soprano. "Sorry to bug you, *ese*. Jenny told me you were on a road trip, but this ain't gonna wait."

"Of course he says he's innocent," Emma complained over the car speakers. "Humans always say that until you find the right way to *hurt* them—"

I cradled my phone close, cupping my hand over my mouth. "No problem, Gabriel. What's up?"

"Got an issue with the territory map. See, one line kinda squiggles on a street east of Fremont. Bishops say the patch oughta be theirs. Winslow says it's Blood Eagles turf. The rest of the Commission's already weighed in, and it's a tie. You got the deciding vote. Sorry, man, somebody's gonna be pissed at you no matter what."

"No torture until I get back," Caitlin said to Emma.

"Of course not," Emma said. "I assumed we'd share the fun part together. But we have to move these shipments, and Reno isn't reliable anymore. That's your problem to solve."

I thought fast. "Gabe? Hold on a sec."

I put my hand over the phone, leaned in, and whispered in Caitlin's ear. She nodded, whispering back.

"Okay," I told Gabriel, "here's what *I* say. That patch near Fremont goes to the Bishops. Have Winslow call Emma Loomis at Southern Tropics Import-Export. She's got some sensitive cargo that needs a regular escort, and she's gonna give him the job."

"Emma," Caitlin said, "you'll pay Winslow and his Blood Eagles what you were paying that Reno lot, plus ten percent. They're reliable. Agreed?"

"Will they *bathe* before I have to meet with them?" she asked.

"I'll take that as a yes."

"Will he go for that?" Gabriel asked me. "I mean, sounds like more work. How's the money?"

"Maybe not as good," I said, "but more importantly, ask Winslow what sounds like more fun. They can sit on a couple of pool halls, collecting extortion money, or his boys can do what they do best: jump on their Harleys, ride the open road, and stomp anyone who looks at them cross-eyed."

Gabriel laughed. "Yeah, that sounds more their speed."

"Also," Caitlin added, "if Emma adds any more routes or requires additional convoys to be secured, she'll grant Winslow and his friends exclusive rights."

"I will?" Emma asked.

"It's a security matter," Caitlin said. "As you just pointed out, that's *my* decision to make. The Bishops receive territory and stable income, the Blood Eagles receive a more entertaining task with the potential of more money in the future, and you receive top-notch security from a reliable and accountable provider."

"Deal," Emma said.

"I'll give 'em the good news," Gabriel told me.

They both hung up. I set my phone down, resting it against my leg. We rode in silence for a minute or two, just watching the sandy mountains drift by.

"Something occurred to me," I said. "I think we're a power couple now."

Caitlin thought that over. She pursed her lips and nodded.

"An apt description," she replied.

Her phone rang. She sighed and took the call.

* * *

We cruised into Albuquerque with the setting sun at our back, rippling down in a grimy tequila-colored sky. The place had a strange vibe, like a small town that had somehow become a big city without realizing it. Adobe and remnants of the pioneer days shared space with the high-rises on Central Avenue. Tourist traps and hotels stood a block away from streets lined with hand-built houses from the twenties. I checked the address Malone had given us. Now we were rolling south, where everything was vintage except for the steel bars on the windows and the graffiti tags on the clay-brick walls.

Dirty plastic shopping bags blew along a desolate side street. One caught on the prickles of a tall cactus and fluttered in the hot wind like a flag of surrender. Our destination was up ahead, along a tangle of industrial parks and warehouses. It was a long and low-slung factory with glazed windows, its tired beige eaves buckling under the weight of time. Sanchez Brothers Baby Formula, read a sign smeared with delivery-truck exhaust and road grit, Established 1932.

"I think the Sanchez Brothers have been out of business for a few decades," I said as Caitlin pulled over to the curb.

"And yet," she murmured, "the lights are on. Plan of attack?"

"Let's get inside and check the lay of the land. Always a chance Malone lied to us. I figure we'll see what we can see, snap a few covert pictures so we've got something to show the mayor back home, and call in an anonymous tip to the local PD. Let *them* do the heavy lifting."

"Not as much fun as a massacre," Caitlin said.

"No, but they still get shut down, Mayor Seabrook doesn't have to deny her involvement after the fact, and we keep our hands clean. We still don't know who's behind this ink business. We just *finished* fighting a gang war; I don't want to drag the New Commission into another one without intel."

I opened the passenger door and stepped out. It felt good to stretch my legs. I smoothed the lapels of my suit jacket and took inventory. My deck of cards nestled in my breast pocket, ready to dance. They softly crackled with magical energy, like a constant kiss of static electricity rippling against my chest. On my other side, my favorite backup plan: a Colt 1911 semi-automatic nestled in a calfskin shoulder holster. When it came to handguns I was a "whatever works" kind of guy—I'd packed everything from a suppressed .22 to a monstrous Taurus Judge in the past—but I'd been putting in some range time with the Colt lately and it felt like a solid all-purpose tool.

The final piece of my arsenal was literally up my sleeve: my new wand sat snug in the spring-release sheath Caitlin had bought for me. I'd brought it mostly out of curiosity, seeing as I didn't know how the damn thing worked. The ebony wand originally belonged to Howard Canton, a stage magician and closet occultist from the 1940s. The ends were capped in white bone. Human bone. One tip came from the skull of an ancient Egyptian illusionist, the other from debunker and skeptic par excellence Harry Houdini. Lies and truth, the power to weave illusions and the power to rip them away.

I'd only used the wand twice, battling Damien Ecko then taking the fight to his mob allies in Chicago; both times it had sprung to life in my hand and I'd harnessed its magic on pure instinct. Destroying Ecko's human guise, conjuring smoke and mercury mirrors. I just had no idea *how*, and since then the wand had sat dormant. To tell the truth, I wasn't even sure I was the one weaving the spell. Canton's relic seemed to have a mind of its own and opinions it didn't feel like sharing.

All I knew for sure was that the Enemy, the man with the Cheshire smile, was obsessed with finding anything and everything connected to Canton and his career. That made things simple. He wanted it, which meant I wanted it more.

Caitlin and I skirted the crumbling brick wall to find a parking lot around back, ringed by a rusted fence. Coils of barbed wire rotted in the dark like a promise of tetanus. Two men stood guard by the driveway gate, and I knew we were in the right spot. One wore a windbreaker with bulges in all the wrong places, and the other didn't bother with the camouflage: a MAC-10 dangled from a shoulder strap, freshly oiled steel half an inch from his open hand.

"You want the one on the left, or the one on the right?" I breathed.

Caitlin crouched like a cat beside me. For a moment her eyes shifted to swirls of molten copper. She smiled, flashing rows of shark teeth.

"Now *this*," she purred, "is my idea of a couple's vacation."

8.

The ace of spades leaped from my breast pocket and into my hand, streaming sparks of golden light as I burst around the corner. I charged the guards head-on, shoes pounding the pavement. The one in the windbreaker turned and his mouth fell open. I flicked my fingers. The card sliced through the gloom like a laser-guided knife. It slashed his throat before he could shout, painting the pavement with spatters of hot blood. The card spun, still going, then lodged crumpled and spent in the rungs of the chain-link fence.

He dropped to his knees in slow motion, mouth still gaping and nothing but a wet gurgle coming out. His buddy grabbed the MAC-10; the machine pistol swung up as Caitlin ran ahead of me, bounding like a lioness. She threw herself on him before he could pull the trigger. One hand clamped over his wrist. One hand on his throat. Both hands dug in, her nails black iron claws, and *twisted.* Bone and cartilage snapped. His final breath, as his broken body fell at her feet, was a graveyard rattle.

She smiled, pleased with herself, and sniffed at her bloody hands as I jogged up. Her claws melted back into their human shape, a perfect French manicure dripping burgundy red.

"Let's get these guys out of sight," I said and grabbed my victim's wrists. I heaved him toward a grime-caked dumpster on the edge of the lot, dragging him on the asphalt. Caitlin just scooped the second corpse up under her arm, toting him like a bag of trash. We tossed both bodies inside. Nothing left but slug trails of blood, shimmering black in the gathering dark.

I kept my ears perked. No commotion, nothing but the sound of traffic on a distant freeway and the rustle of the bone-dry wind. I led the way to a side door, corrugated steel, no sign and no window, and fished out my oilskin lockpick sheath.

"Time me," I said, crouching down.

She tapped the stopwatch on her phone. I tugged out a tension rake and a pick that curved like a white-water river, pocketing the rest. The tumblers slipped and jiggled under my picks as I probed at the lock's innards, working blind, racing the clock. The final tumbler slipped, caught, and rolled over, rewarding me with a satisfying, hollow *click*.

"Two minutes and thirty-four seconds," Caitlin said. "I think you bested your average."

"I'm feeling lucky tonight. Let's see if that holds up."

The door led to a narrow cinder-block hall, with black rubbery tile that sparkled like a bowling-alley floor. No guards in sight. I took the lead.

"What happened to 'ladies first'?" she whispered in mock dismay.

"Still not sure what we're up against, and I'm the only one carrying a piece," I whispered back. "You know, you could have grabbed a gun off one of the guards outside."

"*You* know I don't care for them," she replied. "In the course of my executive career, I've found that my preferred style of conflict resolution is more personal. Hands-on."

The hallway opened onto a wide factory floor, lit by stark white overheads dangling from the vaulted roof and circled by a second-floor balcony and steel catwalks that crisscrossed overhead. The place hadn't changed much since the thirties, but the assembly line—standing silent, its conveyor belt rusted and dead—wasn't pumping out baby formula anymore. Two rows of grim-faced men, stripped down to their boxers and wearing surgical masks, labored on a narcotic production line. They mixed chemicals in plastic dishes and flasks, spun vials in centrifuges, an elaborate dance that didn't look like any production process I'd ever seen. Plastic jugs sloshed on a rolling cart as a laborer brought in another load of raw materials. On the far end, two workers carefully measured the final product—black, spiky grains like bristly ocean pearls—into clear plastic baggies.

The factory stank, the kind of odor that clung to the very bricks and sank into the fibers of my suit. An unholy cross between pool chlorine and the musty smell of a wet dog. The smell didn't bother me as much as my magical senses did, though: fire-alarm bells rang out in the back of my mind, and my third eye squinted at the chemical cart. Whatever was in those plastic jugs wasn't just toxic, it was magically active. From the frown on Caitlin's face, she sensed it too.

We kept moving. Skirting the outer edge of the factory floor, keeping to the long shadows, ears perked. A lone sentry walked the floor with a rifle cradled in a careless grip, and we pressed our backs to a brick pillar until he moved along. Others patrolled the catwalks, or made slow circles along the second-floor balcony. I counted five guards in all, but those were just the ones I could see. We glued ourselves to whatever cover we could find.

I had my eyes on a door up ahead. Closed, with dusty blinds drawn over a long glass window alongside it. It would have been a foreman's office, back in the day, and hopefully it still was. I wanted to get my hands on whoever was running this operation. Using spellcraft to put mental blinders on their street dealers was one thing; if they were actually infusing occult ingredients *into* the drugs, I needed to know why.

As we inched closer, I heard a muffled voice from behind the door, nasal and strident.

"I'm telling you," he said, "it's a bad idea. We shouldn't set foot in Vegas. Hit the towns *around* it, and let ink spread virally. Why? Because there are some crazy motherfuckers in Vegas. Trust me, I know. Firsthand experience here."

I narrowed my eyes and drew my Colt, holding it close to my chest.

"I know that voice," I murmured.

"Yes," he went on. "My previous employer. You know, the one who turned into a plant monster, changed her name to Eve, and wanted to destroy half the planet to save the other half? You know who stopped her? *Worse people than her.*"

I tried the handle. It gave, slowly. Unlocked.

"Swear to God," he said, "if I never have to see Daniel Faust again—"

I swept into the office, Caitlin right behind me.

Dr. Francis Nedry, draped in a white lab coat, his eyes

shrouded behind form-fitting mirrored glasses, froze with a phone receiver in his pale hand. His lips twitched.

I pantomimed holding a phone and whispered, "You'll call them back." Caitlin shut the office door.

"I gotta call you back," he said and hung up the phone. Then he slumped into a cheap office chair behind a cluttered desk. He had a battered filing cabinet, a stepstool in the corner, and not much else. A streaky mirror on one wall captured the tiny room and reflected it back at us.

Not much of a fiefdom, compared to the last time we'd crossed swords. He'd been on Lauren Carmichael's payroll back in the day, a scientist-sorcerer helping to fuel her rise to godhood. With Lauren he had funding, his own laboratory, and a steady supply of test subjects culled from Vegas's homeless population. Looked like he'd fallen on harder times since then.

Nedry's gaze shifted to a beige box beside the desk phone, with a little red button on top.

"Panic button?" I shook my head. "I wouldn't do that."

He looked down the barrel of my .45 instead. "You gonna shoot me?"

"Probably. Haven't yet, though. Tell me what I want to know and you might stay lucky. Ink is nationwide and I doubt you're running the show from some rust-bucket factory in Albuquerque, so let's start with this: who's the top dog?"

"They'll kill me," he said.

I glanced sidelong at Caitlin. She cracked her knuckles.

"*Really*," she told him.

"Worse than you can, sweetheart. See, after that mess with Lauren, me and Dr. Clark went job hunting. We got...recruited. For Clark's skill with, you know, various recreational pharmaceuticals and toxins, and for our shared background in trans-dimensional experimentation."

"Oh," I said, "like Viridithol? Like how you took snippets of cancerous plant life from the Garden of Eden and fed it to women who thought it was a new fertility drug?"

He held up an irritated finger. I saw my reflection loom in one lens of his mirrored glasses, Caitlin in the other.

"*Test subjects*," he said. "Those women signed full releases and engaged in a proper clinical trial. But yes, mistakes were made. And learned from."

I pointed at the closed door. "Ink? Don't tell me you're putting Viridithol in this shit."

"You kidding me? After what happened to Lauren? Oh, *hell* no. Mistakes made, lessons learned. Iterate and optimize. That's called science, Mr. Faust."

"So who's calling the shots?" I asked. "Five Families? Bratva? Cali Cartel? This isn't a penny-ante operation—whoever's behind it has a hell of a bankroll and nationwide reach."

Nedry chuckled, but there wasn't any humor in it.

"Nationwide? You *wish* they were just nationwide. Nah." He leaned back in his chair. "Hell, you should probably just shoot me. You won't believe me anyway."

"Try me," I said.

Nedry turned his mirrored shades my way. He tilted his head and sized me up.

"The Network."

"Bullshit."

He shrugged. "Told you."

Caitlin looked my way, her brow lightly furrowed. "Network?"

"It's an urban legend," I said. "Criminal underworld spook stories, a cartel so secretive that nobody even knows their real name, or if they *have* a real name. They're just 'the Network.' See, it used to be a popular scam back east. Guys would claim to be working for the Network and recruit local talent who thought they were being scouted for the big leagues. It basically boiled down to 'rob this place while I supervise—in other words, do nothing—and give me most of the take.' Then the recruiter would skip town and leave the locals holding the bag."

"*Used* to be a popular scam," Nedry said. "Know why it stopped?"

"Because everyone figured out the Network isn't real, and the last few guys who tried it got their skulls split."

"It stopped because the Network doesn't like having its name taken in vain." Nedry shifted in his chair. His arrogance coming back to the fore, even at gunpoint. "And you haven't seen the proof because you're not invited to the party. The Network is compartmentalized. It runs tight, silent, and with its tentacles in a thousand different pies. Anyone at street level, anyone who might flap their gums to the wrong people gets a little insurance plan installed in their intestinal tract."

"The geas-roaches," Caitlin said.

"You've seen those?" Nedry asked. "Huh, explains how you found *this* place. Kudos for that. They're supposed to kill their hosts if they somehow get pried out. Dead men tell no tales."

"I could maybe buy the feds not knowing about all this," I said, "but why wouldn't we, or the Outfit, or the Brighton Beach crowd? It'd be in their best interest to do business with us. They're leaving money on the table."

Nedry turned his ugly smirk my way.

"It's not about money, Faust. The Network has a philosophy."

"Which is?"

"Above my pay grade," Nedry said. "I just know it exists. This isn't a criminal syndicate. It's a holy order."

"For an organization obsessed with secrecy," Caitlin observed, "you're being rather loose-lipped."

Nedry shrugged. "I was bored. Nobody to talk to around here. Besides, why not? You're not getting out of here alive."

I'd been watching his body language. His slow shift to the left, chair slightly turning. The way his head inclined toward the mirror on the wall. I couldn't see his eyes behind those shades, but I knew exactly what he was looking at. And what he was planning to do.

"Focus on the gun," I told him. "We've faced off before, remember? I know your tricks, Nedry. Don't even think about jumping into that mirror. You've got about four feet of space to cross, and my trigger finger is faster than you are."

"Oh, I've got a new trick or two," he said. "See, Lauren Carmichael might have given me money and a fancy lab, but she wanted all the power—the *real* power—for herself. My new employers? They believe in rewarding loyalty. Observe and learn."

He lunged for the panic button on the desk.

I shot him between the eyes. The Colt boomed in the tight office, my eardrums ringing as Nedry's head snapped back. He slumped in his chair, dead.

I heard him snicker. My gaze shot to the mirror where his reflection, unharmed and smiling, gave us a wave.

"I don't control reflections anymore, Mr. Faust. I *am* the reflection now. Iterate and optimize."

His hand slapped down on the reflection of the panic button. A grinding klaxon sounded, echoing through the musty factory, letting Nedry's guards know they had intruders. And telling them exactly where we were—in a tight little killing box, over two hundred yards from the front door, and with every gun in the building standing in our way.

9.

I shot the mirror.

I knew it was pointless even as I pulled the trigger, but I did it anyway, watching jagged shards scatter upon the office floor. Nedry grinned out from each and every one of them, reflected a dozen times as he flipped me the bird. Then he darted out of sight, his image vanishing.

I bolted for the door, flung it open—then jumped back as a full-auto blast of rifle fire raked through the doorway. It tore the desk to scrap and shredded papers into a cloud of confetti. Caitlin's hand clamped on my shoulder, firm.

"I go first," she said. "You provide covering fire. We stick to the pillars and go out the way we came in. Yes?"

I clenched my jaw, bracing for the fight.

She lunged out in a blur of motion, and I was right on her heels. Muzzle flare from the catwalk above. I snapped off shots on the run. The rifle tumbled from the shooter's hands as his shoulder spouted blood. He stumbled back, losing his footing, going over the rail and screaming as he plummeted to the concrete fifteen feet below. We jumped behind a pillar and another gunman rounded the corner right in front of us, weapon to his shoulder. Caitlin knocked the barrel upward just as he pulled the trigger.

The slugs chewed into the rafters, point-blank muzzle flash leaving streaks of white across my vision. Then she ripped the rifle from his hands and spun it around, putting two shots in his chest and the third through his skull.

I tried to break cover, falling back as another burst of gunfire rattled across a row of dented steel lockers to my left. Two shooters were perched behind the old conveyor belt, hunkered down and locked onto our cover, pinning us like bugs. I heard a voice shout over the deafening klaxon, "Bring up the grenades! Flush 'em out!"

Caitlin leaned against the pillar, gritting her teeth. My stomach twisted into a knot. She was bleeding, dark ichor oozing from ragged holes in her blouse.

"I'm all right," she breathed. "Bullets, I can endure."

I wasn't sure about grenades. My chances weren't too good either, but in that moment I wasn't thinking about myself. Just her. Wanting to protect her, feeling like I'd failed. Helpless, trapped, out of ideas and waiting for the hammer to drop.

The wand throbbed against my forearm.

It was a tugging sensation, pulling at my veins and making my blood pulse in strange rhythms. I flexed my wrist to trigger the quick-release sheath. Canton's wand dropped into my fingers. I caught it and whipped the bone tip upward in a flourish.

I wasn't in the factory anymore.

The world washed out in static, turning black and white and flickering, as if I'd stepped into an old-time newsreel or a silent movie. A jaunty but off-key melody played on an invisible piano. Bodiless, I gazed upon a theater stage where a man in a top hat and tails—Howard Canton, I recognized him from his poster—stepped into a trunk and crouched down. A smiling showgirl shut the lid and Canton spoke, his tinny words reverberating inside my skull.

"Translocation is an essential tool of the magician's craft. Yes, sir, this staple technique makes the ideal climax for an escape—a guaranteed crowd-pleaser every time."

The newsreel camera took a dizzying spin and dragged my mind along with it, following a spotlight as it landed upon a balcony high above the stage. Canton emerged, arms high, brandishing his wand. The roar of the crowd broke into crackling static before the image vanished.

"Daniel?" Caitlin said.

I snapped back to reality, gunfire pinging off steel and stone all around us. I looked to the bank of lockers against the wall, most of them raked by bullets, a couple of them safe behind our cover.

"Cait! Can you pull that padlock off?"

She tilted her head at me. "Why?"

"Just do it!"

She grabbed the padlock holding the locker shut and twisted it. The old, dented hasp groaned in her fist. Then it broke, showering flakes of rust as she ripped it free. The locker door yawned open. Nothing but cobwebs inside.

"Trust me," I said. Then I kissed her on the cheek.

The wand pulsed in my hand. I threw myself inside the locker, grabbed the door, and slammed it shut. Entombing myself in darkness.

The world lurched sideways and my stomach lurched along with it. I heard the faint jangling of wind chimes and smelled the scent of fresh, blooming roses.

Then the darkness cast me out. I staggered into sudden light and noise and found myself up on the catwalk, standing behind two of the shooters. One had a grenade in his hand, raising it high to throw—and far below, I saw Caitlin's shadow, pinned behind the brick pillar.

I put two bullets in the back of the grenadier's head. His buddy turned, shocked. My third shot went straight through his open mouth and punched out the back of his neck. The grenade, a slim metal cylinder, clattered to the catwalk.

The live grenade, with its pin pulled.

I ran like hell was on my heels, racing across the catwalk, high above the heart of the factory floor. And hell came, a roaring explosion that washed hot across my back as it slammed me to the scaffolding. My ears rang and the stench of smoldering steel shoved acrid fingers down my throat. The catwalk yawned, its moorings twisted and smoking, and leaned to one side. Tortured struts snapped like twigs, and the ground dropped out from under me.

The far end of the catwalk fell to the factory floor, turning the rough metal into a slide ending in cold concrete, fifteen feet down. I hit my back, skidding, my stomach lurching into my throat. I landed hard on my shoulder and rolled, crashing against the edge of the dead conveyor belt.

I looked up, dazed, and stared into the barrel of a gun.

One of the chemists, in his boxers and surgical mask, gripped an oversized Magnum in both trembling hands. He stood on the belt, legs spread like an Old West gunslinger, and thumbed back the hammer as he aimed down at me. I fumbled for my gun, somewhere off to my left, fingers closing over the grip, but I knew I'd never bring it up in time.

A blur hit him from behind, knocking him from the belt to the concrete. The Magnum roared and the slug cratered the floor inches from my head. I flinched, turning my face from the shower of chipped stone and dust. A broken chunk of floor shot past and carved a stinging razor slice along my cheek. Caitlin crouched over the chemist like a lioness who'd just run down a juicy gazelle. Then her teeth sank into his throat, and his last breath turned into a ragged, blood-choked gurgle.

Up on the balcony, on the far end of the factory hall, steel doors burst open. Reinforcements. And we were out in the open. I snapped my fingers and a handful of playing cards leaped from my breast pocket, landing in my outstretched hand. I shoved myself to my feet and stumbled over to Caitlin, my back and legs burning and sticky-wet. My ride down the falling catwalk and the hard stop at the end had left my jacket torn, my slacks looking like someone had taken a cheese grater to the backs of my calves. No time to worry about it now. I threw the cards behind me and they hung in the air, twirling, a pasteboard shield to cover our escape. Riflemen on the balcony opened fire and the cards dropped in a dead flurry, each one catching a bullet for me.

Caitlin jumped from the throat-ripped corpse and snatched up the dead man's revolver. She ran alongside me, looking back over her shoulder and firing wildly until the hammer slammed down on an empty chamber, then tossed the gun aside. The covering fire bought us a few seconds as we crossed open ground. Then we were charging up the access hall and bursting out into the parking lot, still hearing the alarm klaxon muffled behind the antique brickwork.

We couldn't stop now. My heart hammered my chest, every breath a burning splinter in my side. We ran up the block, to the waiting Audi, and Caitlin tossed me the keys. I jumped behind the wheel. The engine roared to life and I whipped the car around, screeching away from the curb and hooking a hard U-turn on the empty street. I stepped on the gas, aiming for bright lights and traffic, no destination in mind beyond getting the hell out of there.

Caitlin's seat yawned back as far as it could go. She lay beside me, eyes shut, her face and chest wet with fresh blood. The blood on her mouth wasn't hers. The blood plastering her torn blouse, molasses-thick and nearly black, was.

"Cait?" I said, hearing the tightness in my throat. "What can I do?"

"You can drive," she said, exhausted. "What are those bullets called, the ones that...expand inside of you?"

"Hollow-points?"

"Mm. Those." She shifted on the seat, wincing. "That's what they shot me with. Don't fret. I hear you fretting."

My hands squeezed the steering wheel. "My girlfriend is sitting next to me with three *bullets* in her, so yeah, I'm *fretting*."

"Takes more than that to stop me." Her tongue trailed over her upper lip, tasting the dead chemist's blood. "It just hurts. Excruciatingly. Not the enjoyable kind of pain, either. I'll be fine in a few hours. Just need to rest and rebuild my body. How did you do that, the...teleportation thing?"

Good question. The wand sat snug in its wrist sheath, dormant now. Keeping its mysteries to itself.

"I think...I think Howard Canton just showed me how," I said. "It's weird. Back when I faced off with Ecko and grabbed the wand for the first time, I felt a hand passing it to me. I think part of Canton's spirit is still around. Clinging to his wand, his hat, maybe other pieces of his gear."

"Thank him for me," she murmured. Then she fell asleep, or what passed for it with Caitlin, closing in on herself and conserving energy as her body stitched itself back together.

* * *

Sunrise found us on the outskirts of Santa Fe. The gas needle was flirting with the edge of a cliff, so I pulled into a Shell station, staggered out of the car, and swiped my card at the pump.

"The Network," Jennifer said, her sleepy drawl echoing in my ear. "That old urban legend? For realsies?"

I cradled my phone against my shoulder and popped the Audi's gas cap. "Well, either it's a new twist on the old recruitment scam or it's the real deal. Nedry believed it, that much I'm sure of. And he's gotten a serious power upgrade since the last time we crossed swords, so whoever he's working for, they deliver the goods."

"We gotta dig deeper into these lawyers. I got some guys trailing our buddy Malone around—when he has his next meeting with Weishaupt and Associates, we're gonna have ears in the room."

"Tell them to be *careful*," I winced as I squeezed the pump trigger, a pulled muscle twinging along my shoulder. "We could be at the edge of an iceberg here. No idea how big it is under the surface."

"I'll show 'em the dead giant cockroach. They'll be plenty careful."

I was being stared at. On the opposite side of the pump, a guy with a minivan—stick figure family in the back window and a school-hockey bumper sticker—kept looking from me to the Audi and back again.

I caught my reflection in his tinted window. My hair was a mess, one shoulder of my jacket ripped at the seams, my pants dirty and torn. I followed his gaze to the car. Caitlin lay slumped and unconscious in the passenger seat, her mouth crusted with dried blood.

"Costume party," I told him. I raised one hand, hooking it into a claw. "Rarr. I'm a zombie. Rarr."

He found something else to look at. I went back to my phone call.

"Keep me posted," I told Jennifer. "We've got another six hours on the road before we hit Denver."

"Havin' a good trip otherwise?"

"Oh, sure," I said. "A nice romantic vacation, you know, aside from nearly getting killed by a mad scientist and a gang of drug dealers in the middle of goddamn Albuquerque. You know where I don't want to die, Jen? Albuquerque."

Hockey dad was staring at me again. I locked eyes with him and slowly opened my jacket, showing him my shoulder holster. He stepped backward until he disappeared behind his side of the pump.

"And now we have to visit Naavarasi," I said. "She eats people. So that'll be fun."

"She still insisting Chicago's shape-changer wasn't one of her kin?"

"She's the last of her kind. She's adamant about it."

The thought had been nagging at the back of my mind, though, ever since our showdown with the Chicago Outfit. They had a shifter of their own, Kirmira. We fought fire with fire and hired Naavarasi to lure him into a killing room.

"Jen," I said, "out of curiosity, how's your place fixed for surveillance?"

"Like every good purveyor of medicinal substances, I cultivate a healthy sense of paranoia along with my crops. Damn near every inch of the compound is wired for video and sound. Why?"

"Right before Naavarasi took him out, Kirmira said something. I don't know what language it was, but he definitely said something to her."

"And then she snapped his neck. Musta been the wrong question. You want me to pull the audio?"

"Yeah, if you've got the time. I'll take it over to the university when I get back, maybe see if they've got a language-studies department or something."

"Done and done," she said.

The pump clicked. I shut the gas cap and got back in the car. Caitlin murmured as I fired up the ignition, her blood-flecked fingertips sleepily brushing against my hand. I drove north, heading for Denver.

10.

Colorado was a field of green and faded gold, mountains and rolling forests dressed in the colors of autumn. A late October chill hung in the air, crisp as a ripe apple, and I smelled the musty tang of a leaf fire in the distance. Caitlin stirred a couple of hours into the drive. She groaned softly, shifting in her seat and rubbing at her eyes with one balled-up fist.

"Hey, sleepyhead," I said. "How are you?"

Her hand closed over mine. She gave me a contented smile.

"My guardian," she sighed, "standing watch over me while I heal."

Her other hand rummaged inside her torn blouse, digging through matted gore. Her fingers plucked out the remnants of a mushroomed slug, the metal blown-out and jagged. She gave it a dubious look and flicked it to the mat at her feet.

"Almost good as new," she said.

"You hungry?"

"I am." She glanced down at her chest. "That said, I'm not exactly fit for being seen in public at the moment, and you're only marginally better-off."

"Relax," I said. "I've got this covered."

I found a motel just off the highway, and she waited in the car while I ran into the front office and checked in. Inside room eight, floral curtains opened onto a clean queen-size bed and a span of faded beige carpet.

"Here we go," I said. "Privacy, a shower, and all the hot water you can use. You can get cleaned up while I run out and buy us some new clothes. Don't know about you, but everything else I packed is vacation-casual, and I assume we need to look sharp for this meeting."

"I'll write my sizes down."

I tapped the side of my head. "Already know 'em."

"You memorized," she said with a tilt of her head, "my clothing sizes."

"You memorized mine. Only seemed fair."

She reached out and took hold of my shirt, bunching up the fabric in her hand, and pulled me close. Her blood-encrusted lips brushed lightly against mine.

"You," she murmured. "I'm keeping you."

* * *

I came back with an armload of bags, squeezing my way through the motel room door. Caitlin stepped from the bathroom wrapped in a white towel, her skin scrubbed pink, trickles of steam leaking out from the doorway.

"Found a diner down the road that does carry-out," I said, setting half my bags on the bed and spreading out the rest on a long dresser beside the TV set. "Got scrambled eggs, hash browns, sausage links, they threw a couple of Danishes in. I told them to give us a little of everything."

"'Everything' is exactly what I'm hungry for." She dipped her hand into a Macy's bag, tugging out a ribbed cashmere sweater in the color of a gathering storm. Her eyebrows lifted. "Catherine Malandrino? Considering you had to shop retail, nicely chosen on short notice."

"I know it's not your usual haute couture, but I did my best."

I was already wearing my purchases. No time for a tailor, so I kept it simple: pleated slacks and a mint-green button-down shirt. Business casual.

We dug into the food. I didn't realize how hungry I was until I started eating, but my growling stomach made sure I got the message. I walked to the bathroom with the last strip of bacon dangling from my mouth, unbuttoning my shirt on the way. My own wounds were mostly under the surface, splotchy bruises already rising across my back and my scraped-up legs, but a hot shower sounded like a little patch of paradise right about then. I luxuriated under the spray and let the heat and the steam sap my tension away. My steel-tense muscles finally started to unclench.

The curtain rattled. Caitlin stepped into the shower with me. Her warm, naked body pressed against my back.

"Thought you might want company," she murmured in my ear.

I turned to face her. The cascade of water flowed down over my scalp, coursing against my bruised shoulders, as our lips met and my hands caressed her hips.

"Besides," she said, "I used up a considerable amount of energy healing myself, and I have to replenish my strength. I'm hungry for more than hash browns."

I put on a face and pulled away, but not too far. "Ooh, so it's not about me at all. I'm just a food source for you."

"A delicious and nutritious one," she said, nodding earnestly. "You're better than chocolate."

"I feel so...filthy," I said, kissing her again. "And used."

Her hand slid up my back. Her fingers twined in my wet hair, pulling tight.

"Good," she purred, playful. "Wouldn't want you to misunderstand the situation."

I traced the curve of her hips with my fingers, the curve of her neck with my lips.

"You know we're going to be late for the meeting," I said.

"Fashionably." She gave me an impish smile. "Besides, Naavarasi has an exceptionally keen sense of smell."

We turned, slowly, guided by her hands. She pushed me back against the shower wall, the tiles cool against my back. Her fingers tugged at my hair and urged me to lift my chin. To bare my throat to her. I felt the pearly touch of her teeth.

"I'm just marking my territory," she whispered.

* * *

Caitlin drove the rest of the way, smiling like a cat in an aviary. I rode at her side, pleasantly aching, watching wisps of cloud drift over the white-capped mountains. We rolled into Denver a little after three in the afternoon.

Baron Naavarasi's domain didn't look like much from the outside. The Blue Karma was a strip-mall Indian restaurant squeezed between a nail salon and a liquor store. It didn't look like much on the inside, either. Just a hole-in-the-wall with cheap, wobbly chairs and faded ivory tablecloths dotted with blue flowers. The scent of hot curry hung in the humid air. Caitlin gave the waitress a polite smile.

"We're here to see the proprietor. She's expecting us."

The girl silently pointed to a beaded curtain in the back of the room.

My stomach muscles tightened as we walked through

the restaurant. I'd been back there before. Once. Caitlin didn't say anything, but I knew she sensed what I was feeling. Her hand closed over mine. She gave it a reassuring squeeze as we stepped through the beads and into another world.

A stone corridor lay beyond the curtain, lit by guttering torchlight. It stretched out into darkness, too far to be possible without cutting into the alley behind the strip mall. Yet here it was. We walked side by side into the shadows.

Another beaded curtain waited at the end of the corridor. And beyond it, another restaurant.

It was the same size and shape as the Blue Karma, the same layout, but that's where the similarities ended. The flowered tablecloths in the Blue Karma weren't crusted with dried gore. No black roaches, their antennae wriggling, squirmed across blood-soaked carpet. No shades sat in rusted chairs, flickering in and out of sight as their forms writhed in silent anguish.

The coppery stench of blood lodged in my throat, choking my breath. And under that smell, under the odor of rancid meat, lingered something faint and almost indescribably sweet. I looked across Naavarasi's tiny kingdom, across filthy plates and skittering vermin, and my mouth still watered.

Our hostess sat at a banquet table, the long tablecloth bleeding crimson like a sheet over a murder victim. I watched as a long, thin serpent, red and yellow bands rippling, slithered around covered silver trays. It wound itself around Naavarasi's slender wrist and coiled there like a living bracelet. She rose to greet us. Her jade-painted nails glimmered as she beckoned us forth.

"Welcome to my home," she said. "Please, join me."

We took our seats on the other side of the table.

"Could I offer you some tea? Coconut water? *Aam panna?*" Naavarasi locked eyes with me as she lifted the silver dome from a serving tray between us. "Perhaps you're hungry from your journey."

The platter was a steaming dish of *rogan josh*, chunks of lamb in vivid red curry. The steam wafted my way, slithering into my nostrils and coiling around my brain. It bore the aroma of chilies, warm spices, supple meat cooked to exacting perfection.

"You enjoyed my cuisine," Naavarasi told me, "the last time you visited. I thought you might enjoy seconds."

She was trying to rattle me. And it was working. I'd eaten at her table, all right: it had been a prerequisite to doing business with her. And considering how much had been hanging in the balance at the time, I had to take the risk.

I couldn't say if the dish I'd tasted that day was lamb or...her preferred variety of meat. Either she had made me a cannibal that day, or she hadn't. She wouldn't tell me, and I didn't know. I only knew that it was the most delicious thing I'd tasted in my entire life.

"No thank you," I said, holding her gaze.

"Are you sure?" She inched the plate closer to me. "Just a nibble?"

Caitlin narrowed her eyes. She leaned in, digging into the plate with her fingers and scooping out a chunk of meat. She popped it into her mouth and chewed thoughtfully.

"It's lamb," she told me.

Naavarasi's lips pursed in irritation. "My invitation was for your consort."

"And yet," Caitlin said, "here I am. You should have

known I'd be here, Baron. You chose to make this a formal matter between the courts. If my prince's name is invoked as part of Daniel's debt to you, then I *will* be present to oversee the discussion."

"Indeed." Naavarasi rolled her eyes. "'A hound is a prince's weapon. His sword and his shield, his whip and his crook.' I understand perfectly."

Caitlin gave her a tiny smile. "Verse thirty-nine, chapter eight of the Dictates of the Cold Peace. You've been studying the law."

"So I have." She turned my way. "You owe me two boons, Daniel Faust. This will repay the first."

She lifted another serving-tray dome. Underneath lay a glossy photograph.

I picked it up and studied it. The picture showed an obsidian knife with a flared, black blade, the surface pitted with craters. It made me think of a leaf, fallen from a diseased and dying tree. The handle, carved from yellow-green stone, rippled like the coils of a serpent. The pommel had been shaped to mimic the roaring mouth of a lion. A strip of black punch tape stuck to the bottom corner of the photo read, "Museum File 3397-8C."

"I know this picture. I know this knife." I looked to Caitlin. "This is the blade Ms. Fleiss hired me to steal from Damien Ecko, back in Chicago, right before I landed in prison. Well, technically Cameron Drake hired me, but he was Fleiss's puppet."

"It is my understanding," Naavarasi said. "that you were the only survivor of that ill-fated heist. But you did survive, and succeed. That's why I chose you for this task."

Ill-fated was one way of putting it. Our wheelman turned traitor. One of my partners got his brains blown across Ecko's wall. Another ended up a zombie in a torture cell. As for the traitor, well, he took the fall for a different crime, one I committed. And Nadine, one of Naavarasi's court-sisters, took him.

Not a lot of good memories in Chicago. I rapped the edge of the photo against the scarlet-stained tablecloth.

"What's this about, Naavarasi?"

She steepled her fingers and smiled.

"A heist," she said. "You stole the knife once. Now I want you to steal it again. For me."

11.

Believe it or not, there are some people and places I won't rob. Orphanages. Public schools. Nuns. Well, most nuns. Now that I wasn't a lone wolf anymore, representing Vegas's New Commission, my choice of targets was even more selective by necessity. A couple of years ago, for instance, I might have ripped off an Outfit front without thinking twice as long as I could cover my tracks; now, seeing as we were trying to make nice with Chicago, their businesses were off-limits. Politics.

This was an entirely new level of complicated. Cameron Drake, lottery-winner-slash-hostage, was a puppet for Ms. Fleiss. And Ms. Fleiss was working for the Enemy. When I delivered that knife to Drake, I was basically delivering it to *him*. I didn't mind indirectly jabbing at the Enemy where I could, like when I stole Howard Canton's old top hat before Fleiss could get at it. But actually coming at him, on his home turf?

I set the photograph down.

"Not interested," I said. "Pick a different job."

"The knife is currently being stored at a private estate west of Austin. It's a ranch called Eastern Pines. I believe that's where you met with the former client, Cameron Drake—"

"Hello?" I shook my head at her. "Are you listening? I'm not doing this."

"Daniel, when I aided you in your time of crisis, languishing in prison, I was explicit, was I not?" She ticked off her points on the tips of her jade fingernails. "One, I required a boon, to be named later. You agreed. Two, I told you it would be a theft. You agreed. I specifically said that it would be an object well within your ability to acquire, and that it did not belong to any member of the Court of Jade Tears. You agreed."

Her face rippled, distorting and turning pale, her hair shortening as if it was being sucked into her scalp. Her black gown flared out, growing sleeves, brightening in color.

I sat across the table from myself, dressed in a prison jumpsuit. Naavarasi nodded, firm, and spoke in my voice. "'You've got a deal.' Does this jog your memory?"

"Point made," I said.

The rakshasi transformed again, her flesh running like melted candlewax until she was back in her favored shape.

"I believe that you're a man of your word, Daniel. And just as importantly, you know the perils of being known as a deal-breaker in your line of work. Uphold your end of the bargain, or I will *not* be silent about it. Everyone—and I mean everyone, from the courts of hell to the criminal underworld—will know that you reneged on a simple agreement and can't be trusted. If I understand correctly, you're trying to forge a coalition in Las Vegas. Making deals, negotiating arrangements. How much success do you think you'll have once your reputation has been destroyed, hmm?"

I pushed my chair back.

"Give us a second."

Naavarasi reached with her left hand to the plate of *rogan josh*, digging her fingers into the scarlet curry. "Take as many as you like. I am generous to a fault."

Caitlin and I stepped back from the table, conferring in low voices.

"I don't like this," I whispered. "She set this up all the way back when I was in prison? And that photograph. I remember that strip of punch tape stuck to the corner. It's not a copy of the photo, Cait, it's the *original*, the same photo Cameron Drake showed me when he hired me for the heist. How the hell did Naavarasi get her hands on it?"

Caitlin's eyes darkened. "Normally she'd be falling all over herself to tell us how. She's being...uncharacteristically reserved. What about this dagger? What's it capable of?"

"As far as I could tell when I had it? Nothing. Unless it's got some deeply, *deeply* buried magic—which I'm not ruling out—it's just a knife. I mean, it's a well-preserved antique from the Aztec Empire, thing's at least five hundred years old, so it's gotta be worth a small fortune to the right collector, but—"

"The odds of this being about money?" Caitlin asked.

"Zero." I glanced at the table. "I want to know what she knows."

We returned to our seats. Naavarasi favored me with a hungry smile.

"I've decided to sweeten the pot," she said, "though I'm certainly not obligated. You currently owe me two boons, the second for helping you to destroy that...pathetic specimen that pretended to be one of my kin. Acquire the knife for me, and I'll wipe the slate clean. Your entire debt to me, satisfied."

"Attractive offer," I said. "Why do you want the knife?"

"I thought a good thief never asked. It's unprofessional."

That was all I'd get out of her on that subject. I shifted gears. "What do you know about Cameron Drake?"

"Former roofing contractor who won the Powerball. He grew up watching *Dallas* on television and wanted to be J. R. Ewing. So he bought Eastern Pines for a little over ten million dollars, sight unseen, and moved to Texas. My sources indicate that these days he's mostly a recluse and a professional alcoholic. Overnight success was not healthy for him."

My gaze drifted to the photograph. And the little strip of black punch tape.

"So you've never met him?" I asked.

"My sources have."

"And have your sources told you anything about a woman named Fleiss?"

"She's his personal assistant," Naavarasi said, "though these days she's rarely at the ranch. She conducts her business elsewhere."

"Where?" I asked.

Her nostrils flared as she tilted her head.

"Drake's secretary is a person of interest to you, Daniel? Why? And would that information be...valuable to you?"

So Naavarasi didn't know the truth about Fleiss—that she was Drake's captor, not his assistant—which meant by extension she didn't know about the Enemy. Good. There were too many players in motion, and there was too much at stake, to let the rakshasi queen get any closer to the action. On the other hand, if Fleiss wasn't living at the ranch, knowing where she *did* hang her hat could be a hell of an advantage.

"Maybe we can talk about that," I said. "After the job."

"After the job," she echoed. "That's a yes, then?"

"That's a yes. But just because I'm doing the job for free doesn't mean I'm *losing* money. You'll cover my expenses. Travel. Equipment. A reasonable per diem for me and my crew."

I held up the photograph.

"I'm keeping this."

Naavarasi reached for another serving-tray lid and lifted it up. A red and yellow serpent coiled around a banded stack of crisp hundred-dollar bills. She wriggled her fingers and the snake slithered off across the table. Then she scooped up the cash and offered it to me.

"Bring me my knife," she said. "Don't keep me waiting."

* * *

Afternoon sunlight shimmered through the evergreens as we drove west on I-70, heading home. The light, the cool autumn wind, the scent of pine needles—it all seemed a little unreal. Plagued by the memories of Naavarasi's magic, part of me was afraid we'd never left the Blue Karma—that it was all some grand illusion that would rip away at any moment and I'd be back in that lightless hell. Bound to a chair, with a fresh plate of meat in front of me and blood on my lips.

"She has that effect," Caitlin said. She kept an easy grip on the steering wheel.

"I didn't say anything."

"You didn't have to." She glanced sidelong at me. "*Her* knife, she said. I wonder if that was a slip."

I thought back to the first time around. "Damien Ecko was a facilitator for the Chicago underworld. He'd hold valuable objects—art, relics, gold—as collateral. Sort of an escrow service for drug dealers. He was holding on to the dagger for somebody, but I never did find out who. You think it might have been Naavarasi's?"

"Or someone who took it from her. If she was tracking the dagger's movements, it could have led her to Drake. Which would explain why she knows about him, but not about his true mistress."

"If," I said. Lots of ifs. Too many. "We know the Enemy wanted that knife. He's been sending his thief—*the* capital-T Thief, until he whammied me with the title—all over the world to snatch artifacts. An Aztec bowl from Dubai, Howard Canton memorabilia...he's got a plan in motion."

"A plan that taking the knife back from him would hopefully disrupt," Caitlin said. "Regardless of *what* Naavarasi wants with it, this could work in our favor."

"Not keen about facing Fleiss again, but if she's not at the ranch—and I gotta figure the Enemy isn't there either—then this is almost a straightforward job. Hell, I've been wanting to hit that place ever since I found out Drake's being held hostage. Have to imagine he'd be pretty grateful if we got him out of there."

And he'd undoubtedly be willing to show that gratitude in the form of hard American currency, not to mention the intel on Fleiss he might be able to provide. We needed every scrap we could get.

"Sounds like you're talking yourself into this," Caitlin said.

"I'm good at that. Do you object?"

She thought about it for a moment, then shook her head.

"No. It might unveil more information about the Enemy. And while it's certainly personal—given that he's determined to kill you, and I take a dim view of that—I have a professional mandate as well."

"Your dad?" I asked.

"Prince Sitri is concerned, to put it mildly. The other princes are barely acknowledging the situation, but if this creature is capable of destroying parallel Earths, has already *done* so, and ours is next on the menu..."

"Y'know, I had a thought about that," I said. "Okay, so if other worlds exist, are there other hells, too?"

"My prince would like to know the answer to that question." Caitlin's lips curled in a determined smile. "Either he has countless rivals, scattered across the multiverse, or countless opportunities. So, what's our next step?"

"She gave me money for a crew." I took out my phone. "So we get a crew."

I tapped the speed dial and listened to the ring.

"Scrivener's Nook," said the reedy voice on the other end of the line. "Purveyors of rare books and quality literature."

"Bentley, hey. Got a line on a job. Sort of a command performance, but there's a chance for a big score. You and Corman doing anything this week?"

"We have opera tickets on Tuesday. Beyond that, our schedules are wide open."

I heard Corman's gruff voice shout in the background, "Our schedules are open on Tuesday, too!"

"Hush, you." Bentley sighed.

"We're on the road," I said, "driving back from Denver. Long way to go yet. Maybe we could meet up tomorrow night? The Tiger's Garden."

"That would be ideal. And...Denver, Daniel?"

"Yeah. Naavarasi's bill just came due."

"Well, regardless of my personal feelings about that...creature," Bentley said, "you have to repay your debt. It's the right thing to do."

"I know. And as usual, doing the right thing is a pain in the ass. I'll see you tomorrow night."

I made a few more calls. We drove without stopping—reenergized and healed, Caitlin could get through the night with nothing but ten minutes of meditation, and she liked to drive. It was midmorning when we crossed the Nevada state line, bound for home.

"While you're rallying the troops," Caitlin told me, "I'm going to confer with my people. If this 'Network' organization is real—and their *bullets* were certainly real enough—I want my field agents out there and chasing leads."

I glanced at my new watch. I had some time to kill before heading to the Tiger's Garden. Caitlin caught the look on my face.

"You know what you have to do now," she said. "No excuses."

"I know," I replied. "No excuses."

12.

On a street lined with foreclosures and boarded windows, the Love Connection had held on through thick and thin. Not for the virtue of the porn business, that was a front, and a half-hearted one at that. The real regulars were in it for the backroom action: Paolo was the best paper-man in the West, elevating the forger's craft to an art worthy of Picasso.

That was then. Now an Out of Business sign hung prominently on the door, the old window display swept out. I saw a shadow shuffling around inside. I stood out on the stoop, where I had waited for Paolo's ambulance, and wrestled with my regret. Eventually I settled on the hard truth: if I walked away, I'd be an even worse friend than I already was.

I knocked on the glass door.

Paolo opened up. He looked tired. Bags under his eyes and a couple days' stubble growing over tiny nicks and cuts on his olive cheeks. I didn't look at his hands.

"Hey," he said.

"Hey."

"I was wondering if you were gonna come around. I got outta the hospital a few days ago."

"Yeah," I said. "I heard. I was on the road, had some business out of state. I just got back."

"You wanna come in?"

"Yeah," I said. "Thanks."

He stepped aside. Held the door for me, with a plastic two-pronged pincer. It looked like the claw arm from one of those old stuffed-toy carnival games. Just like those old claws, it was less sturdy than it looked. The door slipped from his grip and hit my shoulder. I brushed past it, into the darkened, empty store, the wire-frame DVD racks stripped bare.

I nodded at the pincers. "They took the whole hand off?"

He raised the claw, turning it slow. The fingers of his other hand—the two he had left, just his index finger and his thumb—trailed along the cheap rubber-coated plastic.

"Infection. Guess the bastard had something in his, you know, his spit. When he..."

Paolo fell silent.

"Paolo, I'm...I don't even know how to do this. Sorry isn't a big enough word."

He met my gaze. "Did you come here to say sorry, or did you come here for absolution? This about me, or is it about you?"

"Both," I said. No point lying.

He raised his mutilated hand and made the sign of the cross.

"Sin no more," he told me, a humorless smile on his lips. His hand fell limp at his side. "I'm not mad at you, Dan. I was. When it was happening, he just kept telling me, you know, telling me he was only doing it to get at you. That you were the reason he was here—"

"He wasn't lying."

"I know. But I had a lot of time to think in the hospital. It was either think about stuff or watch shitty TV, you know? So I thought about stuff. Fact is, when you get into this life, this world, you run certain risks. It's the price of doing business."

"You weren't a combatant," I said. "You, Doc Savoy—you should have been untouchable. There are rules."

"C'mon, Dan. I'm a professional forger. I'm a criminal. I supply products and services to other criminals. You can talk about the rules all day long, but the second somebody who doesn't feel like following 'em comes along..." He held up his pincers. "What I'm saying is, it could have been him, or it could have been some other guy with a hate-on for some other regular client of mine. I'm not saying it's my fault. Not saying it's yours, either. It just *happened*, and what happened could have been a hell of a lot worse. I'm still breathing. So, the guy. Is he...?"

"Not breathing," I said.

"Thanks for that."

I gestured at the claw. "That's the best thing the hospital could give you?"

Paolo laughed. "*Give* me? Man, I don't have health insurance. I was lucky they gave me a couple of aspirin on my way out. I bought this piece of crap myself. Got it on eBay."

"Well, look up whatever the top-of-the-line model is, because that's what you're getting. The Commission had a talk: you took a hit for us, getting dragged into our war, and we owe you. We can't fix what happened, but you're gonna be taken care of."

"Yeah, Jennifer told me. I appreciate that."

"Well, seeing as."

I paced the floor, taking in the vacant storefront, the empty light fixtures overhead. An entire life, moved out, over.

"Seeing as?" Paolo said.

"I mean, he took all this."

Paolo blinked at me. "Wait. Wait a second. Did you think I was really out of business?"

"You aren't? Your hands..."

He cracked a smile, a genuine one.

"Come on back," he said. "I wanna show you something."

I followed him into the stockroom. A single dangling bulb cast stark light across the empty shelves. His old rig, the real center of his business, was still set up: two folding tables laden with a twenty-seven-inch iMac, a digital tablet made for artists, at least three different printers, and stacks of paper in every conceivable weight and color. The bloodstains had set into the concrete floor, their long black smears the only reminder of what had happened here. Paolo stepped over them, pulled back a rolling chair and sat down.

"Art was always my bag," he said, reaching for the tablet. The pincers caught on the edge and slipped. Then slipped again. I wavered on my feet, wanting to help, not wanting to insult him by helping. Eventually he latched on, dragging the bulky plastic rectangle front and center.

"I remember," I told him. "You almost went upstate for trying to sell off a bogus Renoir."

Paolo shrugged. "Hey, how was I supposed to know the guy already owned the original? After that, I realized the real money was in fake paper. The safe money, anyway. Steady work and happy customers. But art...that's how I taught myself. Sitting in a gallery with a pencil and a pad, learning how to draw what I saw. Style, texture, layering. I put in the work, and it made me who I am."

He leaned over and turned on the iMac. I stared at the picture on the screen, vivid azures and shades of yellow bursting to life. A black, jagged tower rose up in the foreground, a village stretching out below. And above, half-finished, currents of blue and white swirled in a sky studded with lemon lights.

"Is that *Starry Night?*" I asked.

Paolo picked up a plastic stylus with his pincers. He held it over the tablet and made slow brushstrokes. Clumsy at first, almost fumbling, then more confident. The sky painted itself, coming to life before my eyes.

"From memory," Paolo said. "So the details are off, but it's close enough for practice. When van Gogh painted the original, he was in an asylum in southern France after cutting his ear off. This was what he saw when he looked out his cell window."

"You're teaching yourself. Starting over."

"Not starting over. I still got the basics, the fundamentals. The stuff that takes years to lock down, I got that. I just gotta learn a different way of doing things. A different way of doing almost everything."

He turned toward me, swiveling in his chair.

"It ain't easy. It's so beyond *not easy* I don't even know where to start. I mean, just living like this...it's rough, and life ain't ever gonna be easy again. But I figure, look at Vincent. Man was mutilated, depressed, he had voices in his head, he was locked up, and he kept painting. If he did it, I can do it."

I started to open my mouth. He held up his two-fingered hand, silencing me.

"And please," he said. "If you're about to say

something about me being brave, don't. I've been a cripple less than a month and I'm already well past sick of that shit. You get hurt and everybody and their brother wants to tell you how *brave* you are for living on. Like, what, as opposed to dropping dead? Because those are my only two options. Same two choices everybody else gets."

"Can I tell you you're pretty cool?" I asked.

He cocked a smile. "Yeah, I'll settle for cool. Honestly, though, it's just who I am. It's what I love. I love my art. So I'm not gonna let these fucked-up mitts stop me from doing what I want to do. I figure anything worth having is worth fighting for, right? The more you want it, the more you gotta fight. That's what makes us human."

I held out my hand. He held out his. We clasped them together, as best we could.

"So rejoice," Paolo said. "When you inevitably fuck up and burn that new identity I spent so much time working on, just like last time, I'll still be open for business."

"Your confidence is duly noted," I told him.

* * *

Darkness fell over the city. The city responded by firing up its own sun. The Strip blazed to life and I inched through molasses-thick traffic while the world became a whirl of flashing neon. My destination was farther afield: Fremont Street, and the Tiger's Garden.

I parked a couple of blocks from Fremont, in a bad patch of neighborhood where the tourist crowd—if they were smart—didn't stray. It was also Bishops turf, so I wasn't worried about leaving my rental car at the curbside. If anyone was dumb enough to steal it, I'd have it returned with an apology, a wash, and a wax job by tomorrow afternoon.

I had to admit, I was feeling all right. The idea of

pulling a heist for free still didn't sit right with me, but if we sprang Cameron Drake along with his lottery millions, we might make out like bandits. And the last thing the Enemy expected from me right now, I had to imagine, was a direct attack. We could hit the ranch, snatch Drake and the dagger right out from under his nose, and win an advantage. It wouldn't be easy, but it wasn't impossible.

Things were actually starting to go my way.

"*Faust!*" shouted a voice from the alley, across a desolate and dusty street. I stopped in my tracks.

David Gosselin looked like he'd just stepped off a Broadway stage. He wore painted-on black satin pants and a lacy white poet's shirt, his immaculate dark hair slicked to one side. He pointed at me.

"You have something that belongs to me."

"Dressed like that," I said, "I'm guessing it's your self-esteem."

"Canton's top hat. That hat cost me a million dollars. One. Million. Dollars."

"Which you make in what, a day or two? Go back on TV and make the White House disappear again. I could watch that trick all day long."

"You violated the sanctity of my museum," he seethed. "You locked me in a *milk jug*—"

"The twins did that. You know, the ones you were trying to have sex with? Hey, you took 'em home, not me."

"I will have my revenge!"

He raised one hand before him and a wind, desert-hot and gritty, rose with the curl of his fingers. It swept along the empty street, kicking up a flurry of plastic bags and crumpled newspapers.

"Are we doing this?" I asked. "I mean, right now? Are

we really doing this? I'm kind of in the middle of something."

David's other hand swooped high. Clouds of white fog billowed down the alley, capturing his silhouette while he struck a pose. Then great, shadowy rotors began to spin at his back, the fog spreading across the street like an ocean of foam.

"Prepare yourself." His hair shone and his poet's shirt ruffled in the wind. "Prepare yourself to experience...*the magic of David Gosselin!*"

"Okay," I sighed. "So we're doing this."

13.

I couldn't shoot David Gosselin. Technically, I could—I mean, I had the Colt, it was loaded, and he was standing right across the street—but I would have felt bad about it. The man was a national treasure. Besides, he was actually in the right, seeing as I did steal his million-dollar hat. I would argue that he didn't do a good enough job protecting it, but I understood why he might not share my point of view.

My cards crackled in my breast pocket. I could wing him, go for his leg—and then he'd be out of action while he healed up, have to cancel a week's worth of shows, and probably come at me twice as hard next time. No, this was definitely one of those "only way to win is not to play" situations. I flexed my wrist. Canton's wand dropped into my hand. David wasn't the only one who could summon fog. I'd done it twice before, battling Ecko and the Outfit, and a little cover was exactly what I needed to slip away without a fight.

I waved the wand, and...nothing happened. It sat dormant in my grip, as powerless and silent as any other stick of wood. David wasn't waiting for me to make a move. He spun his arms, raised them high, and a swarm of white blurs burst from the fogbank. They fluttered under his arms and streaked straight for me.

Doves.

"What the fu—" was all I had time to say before the first one hit me. Wings flapped in my face, a tiny beak slamming against my forehead like a stapler drilling into my skin, and I flung up one hand to ward it off before it could go for my eyes. A second dove buffeted my shoulders, flapping frantically, and pecked at my neck. Doves trilled in my ears, swarming around me like I was a birdseed buffet on two legs.

I did the only dignified thing a man could do in this situation. I ran for it.

Beaks hammered at the back of my skull. I waved them off, bending low as I sprinted along the sidewalk, catching a cut across the back of my hand.

"Ow. Stop it." I hooked a sharp left, taking a shortcut along an alley as the white fog rippled around my feet. "*Dove bastards.*"

The lights of Fremont Street loomed up ahead. The fog dwindled, dropping low then vanishing, as the last dove made a half-hearted attempt to peck my ear off before winging away. David knew the rules as well as anyone: no magic—no *real* magic—in public view. And Fremont was about as public as you could get.

Fremont was a carnival by night, a street packed with sound stages and open bars, thousands of tourists toting plastic margarita cups and moving to the rhythm of an '80s hair-metal cover band. LEDs flared and fired streamers of light across an overhead canopy. Tonight's light show had a patriotic flavor, a cascading dance of lasers in red, white, and blue. I got lost in the crowd. Then I lost my waking mind, pushing aside my pounding heartbeat and the irritating sting on my forehead, slipping into a meditative trance.

I walked, but with no destination. My eyes were open, but beyond the glow of the light show and the churning, confusing crowds, I saw nothing. I wanted to go to the Tiger's Garden. Thanks to the enchantment laid on the place—or a curse, we weren't quite sure—the only way to find the entrance was not to look for it.

A brass bell jangled. Suddenly I was pushing through a door, past a grubby welcome mat and onto faded and cigarette-burned carpet. No crowds, no blaring music, just seventies-era wood paneling and a short bar strung with tiki lanterns. The stench of body odor and cheap beer vanished, replaced by the warm, welcoming aroma of *naan* and hummus.

Around the corner, in the dining room, my family shared drinks around the table. Jennifer raised her bottle of Amstel as I stumbled across the threshold. Mama Margaux was on her left, sipping some mammoth tropical concoction that matched the orange of her dress. Judging from the empty glasses, Bentley was on his third martini. Corman, the stocky, broad-shouldered Oscar to Bentley's Felix, nursed a straight bourbon.

"Hey, Dan," Jennifer said. She pointed at her forehead. "You got a—a thingy."

"Yeah." I pulled back a chair. "Ran into David Gosselin on my way over here."

Corman furrowed his brow. "What'd he do, hit you?"

"He threw doves at me." I shook my head, still processing it. "He threw *doves*. Who *does* that?"

Margaux stirred her frosted goblet with a straw. "I thought doves were supposed to be nice birds."

"They are, normally," I said. "I think he recruits his

from bird reform school. No. Gangs. Bird gangs. One had a switchblade."

"I hope you didn't hurt him too badly," Bentley said. "I know how you feel about the man, but he is a national treasure."

"See, that was my line of thinking—" I paused as Amar swooped in, bearing a brass-rimmed tray. Amar was the Garden's sole employee, its waiter, bartender, presumably the chef, and possibly the owner. He was notoriously tight-lipped when it came to anything but the tiny restaurant's menu. He'd come bearing gifts: the Jack and Coke I was just about to order, and a white napkin. I took the drink, tossed back a swallow, and pressed the napkin to my forehead.

The door jangled. David steamed into the room like a freight train on a collision course. Amar got between us, fast.

"This isn't over," David snapped, trying to sidestep around him.

Amar didn't let him. His voice was soft velvet with a steel core.

"There is no violence in the Tiger's Garden, sir."

Jennifer leaned back in her chair. "I'd listen to him, sugar. Bad rule to break."

"For God's sake," Bentley sighed into his martini, "it's a hat. Let it *go*, David."

"I expect better from you in particular," David said, turning his ire on Bentley. "You and Corman have *pedigrees*. The fact that you'd defend this cheap little hustler—"

"Hold up." A warning hung on the edge of Corman's gruff voice. "You're talking about our kid, Dave. Watch it."

Amar stepped closer to David, locking eyes with him.

"Sir. It would be best if you stepped outside for some fresh air. You may return when you can conduct yourself as a gentleman, at which time we will happily serve you."

David took a step back. Then he looked my way.

"I'll be waiting outside, Faust."

He stormed for the door. As the bell jangled I called out, "The exit *moves*, dipshit."

"Sir," Amar told me as I sank into my chair, "far be it from the staff to speak to our favored clientele about their personal lives, or make any course of recommendation..."

"But?" I asked.

"But you should give his hat back." Amar held his tray and stepped back behind the bar.

Margaux pointed at him with the tip of her straw. "He's right, you know."

"It's rapidly becoming a matter of principle," I said. "Besides, I'm starting to get a clue about why the Enemy is fixated on snapping up all of Howard Canton's old stuff. I think Canton is still around somehow. Me and Caitlin ran into a little trouble out in Albuquerque, and his ghost stepped in to give me an impromptu magic lesson."

Bentley frowned, mentally walking the timeline. "They couldn't have known each other. If we understand correctly, the Enemy was trapped in that prison dimension until Dr. Payton's unfortunate and ill-advised experiments set him free twenty-odd years ago. Canton was long dead before that."

"Got me," I said. "But on that note, Naavarasi's calling her marker due."

I gave them the abridged version of our sit-down with the rakshasi queen. They listened, sipping their drinks, and Bentley had me backtrack a couple of times to go over the finer details.

"I could believe the knife used to belong to her," he mused, "or that she had some theoretical connection to Damien Ecko, explaining why it was in his safe. The notion that she followed the trail to Cameron Drake's doorstep is plausible, beyond the detail about the photograph. But."

"But that's a ten-clown-car-pileup of coincidences," Jennifer said. "I don't like it. Too many connections being drawn between people who ain't got any business knowing each other."

"And it's Naavarasi we're talking about." Margaux finished her drink. She held the empty glass out to her side. In a heartbeat, Amar snatched it away and set a second frosted goblet—this one neon blue—in front of her.

"She does fancy herself the spider at the core of a tangled web," Bentley said. "She has also, sad to say, boxed you into a corner quite effectively."

"If I pull this off, though, we're square," I said. "This is the first and *last* favor she's ever gonna get out of me. So that's the score: grab the knife for her, grab Drake for us, and learn anything we can about Fleiss and the Enemy. You want in?"

Margaux eyed me over her glass. "You really think Drake's gonna share his lottery winnings if we snatch him away from that place?"

"I wasn't planning on giving him a say in the matter."

"Knowledge," Bentley said, "could be the greatest treasure of all."

Jennifer kicked back, her chair leaning at a dangerous angle.

"You always say that." She shrugged. "But you ain't wrong. If Fleiss and Cheshire are fixin' to cook up some kinda doomsday plot, we *are* gonna scrap with 'em sooner or later. I wanna know exactly what we're up against and how to take these critters down for good. Drake might know something. Is Caitlin in?"

"Oh yeah," I said. "She's in. We might be able to get Pixie too, if her dance card is open."

"And this 'Ms. Fleiss,'" Margaux said, "Naavarasi claims she's not at the ranch right now? So we won't have to fight her?"

"Claims," I said. "That said, Naavarasi lies...well, even more than *we* do. Even with Fleiss out of the picture, it's not a soft target. There's armed guards patrolling the compound twenty-four seven, a full security grid with cameras and alarm systems, and we don't have eyes inside the main house. I've only been in there once, and I didn't see anything like a safe or a vault. This job's going to take a lot of improvisation. I figure we make Drake the priority. Once we get our hands on him, hopefully he can tell us where the dagger's being kept and open any code-locked doors for us."

"We better make it fast," Jennifer said. "I'm admittedly bein' superstitious, but have you been keeping an eye on the clock?"

I glanced at my watch. "What about it? It's barely nine. The night's still young."

"The *date*, sugar. It's the twenty-ninth. Halloween is two days away."

14.

We got an early start. And an early flight, riding from McCarran to Austin-Bergstrom International. Our base camp was a penthouse suite at the Omni, a warm and tan expanse with leather upholstery and a top-floor view of the downtown skyline. We rearranged the furniture, pushing together tables and clearing floor space, then set out the Do Not Disturb card.

A heist is like a battle: sometimes victory is all in the planning and success is decided before you take one step onto the battlefield. And sometimes the plan goes straight out the window and you live or die based on how well you can think on your feet. I decided to err on the side of optimism.

Pixie was too busy to come, until we told her the job might give us a shot at the Enemy. For that, she freed her schedule up. She spread a blueprint-sized roll of photo paper out on the table. A satellite overview, showing the grounds of Eastern Pines in grainy black and white. We gathered around, cradling paper cups of strong black coffee from the lobby cafe, and studied the map.

"This is the best resolution I could pull," Pixie said. "Current blueprints are a no-go. When Drake bought the place, it was falling apart; he paid for a massive renovation of the main house. The contractors never filed updated paperwork, and it looks like the state just kinda 'forgot' to do any kind of inspections or regulation."

"What about the people who did the actual construction work?" I asked. "*Somebody's* been inside that house."

"Funny story. One week after the renovations were done, the contractor's next job site went up in a fireball. Gas-main eruption."

Jennifer stood on the other side of the table. She had dressed for the Texas weather, ditching her corporate look for cargo pants and a tank top that showed off her tattoo sleeve. The centerpiece, depicting Elvis as the Gautama Buddha, flexed as she tossed back a swig of black coffee.

"Lemme guess," she said. "Everybody who built Drake's new house bit the big one."

Caitlin leaned in and trailed a scarlet fingernail along the blurry access road. "All we need to find, assuming we make our move after nightfall, is the room where he rests his head. I think I can convince him to be our tour guide. Getting to the main house, that's the conundrum."

"I can tell you what I know from the last time I was there," I said. "This fence circles the entire property. Razor wire, and it could be electrified."

"What about the front gate?" Corman asked.

"*Looked* decorative, like hickory wood, but it might just be fake veneer over a metal core. I wouldn't try ramming it unless we absolutely have to, anyway. Opens by keypad access or remote control from the guardhouse. Speaking of." I tapped two long rectangles on the map. "Bunkhouses. Instead of cowboys, Drake has private security. They move in two-man patrols, regular radio contact, equipped with sidearms and rifles. They work a tight grid formation. They're good. They've also got the outer grounds blanketed with security cameras, but without eyes on their control room, no telling how many guards are watching the feeds or how much attention they're paying."

"Speaking of cowboys..." Margaux gestured at a penned-off patch of land east of the main estate. "Is that a corral?"

"Yeah. When you drop ten million bucks on a ranch in Texas, I'm pretty sure horses are mandatory."

"Where's the ranch legally located, when it comes to municipal stuff?" Jennifer asked. "What kinda police response time are we lookin' at, and which town's gonna be sending 'em?"

"None and none," I said, "considering Drake is being held hostage and there's zero chance the guards supposedly working for him aren't aware of that fact. I guarantee they're under orders *not* to call the cops. They'll either shoot first and ask questions later, or hold any intruders until Fleiss comes to deal with them."

"So don't get caught," she said.

"Bingo."

"There's a bright side," Pixie said. "That means they're not using a commercial security provider. This isn't one of those alarm systems that automatically calls an outside service center when it gets tripped, then sends the cops to check things out. If we can take control of the cameras, the whole ranch goes deaf and blind."

"Their self-imposed isolation is our opportunity," Caitlin murmured.

"Reckon we could hit the place with two teams," Jennifer said. "Alpha goes in and monkey-wrenches their generator plus any backups. Kill the power, kill the lights, shut it all down. Bravo hits the main house and grabs Drake and the knife. Maybe we set a few fires on the way out, give 'em something to keep the guards busy while we make our exit."

"We need to know where that first team is going, though." I looked to Pixie. "No way you can tell from the satellite view, huh?"

She shook her head. Her eyebrows knitted as she weighed her options. "Once dark comes, I *could* get a drone in there. Keep it high and quiet, scope out as much as I can through a remote camera. Of course, if the guards spot it, they'll know they've got trouble coming."

"I want to know how far their security perimeter extends beyond the fence. And if the fence is electrified or alarmed. Basically, if anything's gonna stop us from cutting our own entrance." I turned to Bentley and Corman. "You two in the mood to do a little acting?"

"Always," Bentley replied. Corman gave an agreeable grunt and drank his coffee.

I stepped back from the table, taking in the gathered faces.

"Okay. We're looking at a two-day job. Today we shop for supplies and probe their security. Tonight, Pixie gets eyes-on inside the fence. Tomorrow we firm up the plan of attack, and tomorrow night we go in."

"On Halloween night," Jennifer said.

"On Halloween night," I said. "What are you worried about? We're the scariest people in town."

* * *

Six hours later I was west of Austin, down on my belly in pale grass, surrounded by oaks and scrub. A humid wind ruffled the back of my shirt, the fabric clinging to a patch of sweat between my shoulder blades. I peered through binoculars set to maximum zoom.

I'd found a hill just elevated enough to let me peek past the chain-link fence ringing Drake's ranch. Gray silhouettes of security guards patrolled the grounds in a slow and mechanical rhythm, two by two, on foot or kicking up dust on golf carts. There were the outbuildings, the bunkhouses, some kind of utility shed, the horse pasture...and the rising, grand mansion at the head of the compound, ivory white with Grecian pillars and a salmon shingled rooftop. I was too far away to get a look inside the windows, but I didn't dare move any closer than this.

My phone, nestled in the grass to my left, buzzed softly. I took the call and put it on speaker.

"Yeah."

"So far, so good," Bentley said. "First we were 'broken down' just off the highway, where the access road begins, for nearly an hour. Then we moved up to about three hundred yards from the front gate and 'broke down' again. Nobody came out to investigate, and as far as we can tell, the guards haven't even noticed. Cormie even got out and brazenly took pictures of the ranch, which you'd think would draw a bit of attention."

"Great. Gonna go for the gold?"

"Wish us good fortune. I'll leave the phone on."

I watched through the binoculars as their rented car, a blue Ford Focus already caked in Texas road dust, rumbled along the outer fence line. They stopped about midway along the compound, pulling over, and Corman ambled out of the car.

"He's walking to the fence now," Bentley said. "Can you see us?"

"I'm watching you."

I wished I were watching through a sniper's scope, so I could provide some real backup. This wasn't the dangerous part of the job—not compared to what we had planned for tomorrow night—but they were closer to the action than I wanted them to be.

Dust blossomed in the distance, a heat mirage rippling in the wake of a speeding golf cart. "You've got incoming."

Bentley got out of the car as Corman stepped back from the fence. He left the door open and gave a wave to the new arrivals. The cart stopped short. Two uniforms hopped out, rifles slung over their shoulders.

"You're trespassing," I heard one say, his muffled voice carried over Bentley's phone.

"*So* sorry about that," Bentley said. "We're trying to make our way to Austin and we seem to have gotten lost."

"You," the other guard said, nodding at Corman. "What were you doing over by the fence?"

Corman grabbed his belt, giving his pants a hike. "Had to drain the snake. Been in the car for four damn hours. That a crime?"

"Yeah, *actually*—" the second guard started to say. The first one waved him off and pointed up the road.

"Forget it. Look, this is private property. You can't be here. Turn your car around, head up the road that way. Twenty minutes, you'll hit the highway. Go east on two-ninety and follow the signs, that'll take you to Austin."

Bentley and Corman got back in the car. The guards stayed right on their tail, the golf cart chugging along behind them until both vehicles slipped around a hill and out of my binoculars' sight.

"Tell me you didn't really pee on the electric fence," I said into the phone.

"Nope," Corman said. "Made that mistake once, in my

twenties. Once was enough. Anyway, it's not electrified. You can tell by looking at the posts: on a regular fence, the wire's just stapled or tied off. Electric fences have insulators. Also, no alarm feeds, at least none I could see. They're *watching* outside the fence line, but if you can slip past 'em, nothing's stopping you from cutting your way through."

If. There were a lot of *ifs* in play here.

"Fair enough," I said. "Once the golf patrol stops following you, swing around and pick me up. The others should be done with their shopping trips by now."

15.

Austin welcomed us back with a skyline in evening bloom, city lights shimmering against a gentle orange sunset. We came back to the suite with armloads of paper bags from an Italian place up the block, ravioli and lasagna and meatballs in greasy crimped tins sealed by paper lids.

"Didn't know what everybody wanted," I said as I stepped through the door, "so we basically just ordered the entire menu."

Caitlin was draped on the leather sofa, one leg up and her knee bent, remote control dangling in her hand as she watched the news.

"I could have told you what everyone wanted," she said.

Sitting next to her, Jennifer craned her neck and stared at the bags. "Cannoli?"

"Of *course* I got cannoli," I said.

We hadn't been the only ones shopping. While Bentley, Corman, and I were out at the ranch, Pixie had turned the table into an electronics graveyard, scattering odd parts and tools and what looked like the half-dissected guts of a quadricopter drone. A tiny rotor whined as she tapped a probe against the exposed circuit board.

"Vegetarian options?" she asked.

I cleared a little space at the edge of a counter and set the bags down. "Eggplant, tomato, and mozzarella salad, and you're welcome."

"You remembered."

"I remember things. Occasionally." I looked to Mama Margaux. "How'd we do on the essentials?"

She pointed to a pile of plastic bags, tossed onto one of the leather armchairs. "Halloween masks and leather gloves, each bought from a different store in a different part of town. Think you might be a little paranoid, Danny."

"Nah, you wouldn't believe how many crews get tripped up on the basics. Knew this guy who pulled a five-man bank heist a few years back: perfect, got away clean, didn't leave a trace of evidence behind. Two days later, the FBI was kicking their door in."

"How's that?" she asked.

I took the tins out one by one, setting out a feast. The room filled with the aroma of fresh pasta and rich, meaty sauce.

"Their planner bought five identical ski masks from a sporting-goods store two blocks from the bank. In the middle of a July heat wave. And he paid with a credit card. Amazingly, the cops do tend to notice these things."

Jennifer pushed herself up from the couch. She scooped up a duffel bag, black and branded with a white Nike swoosh, and toted it over to me.

"Meanwhile, seeing as we couldn't bring our artillery on the plane, I went up to North Lamar and made a new friend. Gabriel did time with one of the locals, a few years back, and he fixed us up with a sweet deal."

She held the bag open like a kid showing off her Halloween candy haul. Except Jennifer's flavors came in full metal jackets, hollow-points, and wadcutters. I reached in and pulled out a nine-millimeter automatic with faded walnut grips and a trace of rust on the sights. A second gun, a snub-nosed .38 revolver, had a loose, jangly feel in my hand.

"Wow, these are...unique pieces."

"Of crap," Jennifer said. "Don't gotta sugarcoat it. But considering we only need 'em for one night and we're not taking them home with us, I wasn't looking for museum quality. We can either bury the lot out in the scrub once we're done, or the guy says he'll buy the whole bag back for ten percent of what I paid. Sort of like when Coke came in bottles, and you could turn 'em in for recycling and get a little change back."

"A socially conscious gunrunner. You test-fired these, right?"

"Did I—" Jennifer gaped at me. Then she turned to Caitlin. "You hear this guy? Did I *test-fire* 'em? Talkin' like I never ripped anybody off before."

I put the revolver back in the bag and held up my open hands. "Okay, okay! Sorry I asked."

"Besides," she said, "I figure they'll mostly be for show and crowd control. If we actually have to pull the trigger, something went *real* wrong."

"I brought my whip," Caitlin said offhandedly.

"You brought it with you? On the airplane?" I asked. "Like, you actually put a bullwhip in your checked luggage?"

"No, silly. It was in my carry-on bag."

I held up a finger. "*Now* I understand the looks we were getting in the security line."

With no room left at the pushed-together tables, everyone just ate where they could find space, spreading out on the chairs and sofa. I demolished a meaty hunk of lasagna, down to the last scrap of gooey mozzarella on my greasy paper plate, and patted my stomach.

"Needed that. Pix, how's the drone looking?"

She held it up to show me. It was an off-the-shelf model, a hobbyist's toy, but she'd spent hours tinkering with it. Reassembled, the formerly white shell glistened with a fresh coat of matte black paint, and its bright, decorative LEDs had been scooped out.

"Ready to rock. A buddy of mine is working on his own drone project and he kicked me his design specs. I can only do so much on short notice, though. I was able to wring a *little* range and battery-time boost out of the stock parts, but I still have to get close to the action."

Corman tossed me the keys to the Focus. I caught them in my open palm.

"Back to the ranch, then. Don't wait up, everybody, we're probably gonna be late."

* * *

We ended up lying flat in a patch of scrub not far from where I'd been perched earlier that day. By night the Texas heat turned to shivering autumn cold, a late wind ruffling the sparse grass. Pixie opened her laptop, our side-by-side faces lit in the screen's pale glow.

"Okay," she said, "this should be good for about twenty-five minutes of flight time, and that has to include getting there and back again. What's priority?"

"Security room, generators, comm trunks," I said. "Anything we'll have a shot at disabling. After that, if you can peep in the windows in the main house and try to find Drake's bedroom, that's gravy on top."

She tapped a few keys. A window popped open, the drone's camera going live, and the feed reflected our own faces back at us.

"Done and done. So, I gotta ask."

"Yeah?"

The drone's rotors whirred, whisper-soft, and it lurched off the ground as Pixie steered it.

"Jennifer," she said.

I sighed. "Look, I know you're big on the whole straight-edge lifestyle thing and you don't like drugs—"

"No, that's not it. Every time we work together she's kinda like...around? A little closer than she needs to be? I mean, I thought she was hitting on me, but I know the two of you used to date."

I winced as the drone winged off toward the compound fence, gaining altitude.

"Briefly. Very, very briefly. Jen's kinda bi but mostly prefers women. I think I was the last guy she got with." I put on a stoic face. "I like to think that I was so good, I was the last man she ever needed. No one could possibly compete after that."

"Yeah. I don't think that's it." She gave me the side-eye. "So, wait, does she think that *I'm*—"

I shrugged. "Nobody knows what you're into. I mean, nobody's ever seen you dating *anybody*."

Spotty electric lights burned in the distance, beyond the fence. They looked like blurry smears on the drone's eye-view, pixelating as the quadricopter moved in close. Pixie cursed under her breath and rattled off a few quick commands. The camera window bloomed wider as the focus tightened.

"This camera's a piece of—hold on, that's better. Anyway, I don't date. At all."

I held my breath and watched the feed as a guard patrol rounded a corner. The drone zipped upward, hovering over their heads. They passed underneath it without a second glance.

"The patrols have penlights clipped to their uniform pockets, *and* Maglites. Good to know." I glanced at her. "So you jump straight to the sex stuff? Don't even have to buy you dinner first?"

She gave me a look that could curdle milk.

"I don't do the sex stuff either. I'm just not wired that way. I like a good snuggle, that's about it." She pointed to the screen. "Here. This outbuilding is the only one with a guard posted outside. The windows are tinted, but see that glow coming from inside?"

"Like security monitors," I said. "Think the main generator's in there, too?"

"Can't tell. But over here," Pixie said, the drone winging off to the left, "we've either got a *very* expensive outhouse with a padlocked door, or that's some kind of utility shed. Could be electric, water, comms—"

"Or the lucky trifecta. Let's check out the main house."

"So," Pixie said, "I hate to ask..."

She didn't have to.

"I'll talk to her and let her down easy," I said. "Don't worry about it."

Jennifer wouldn't be thrilled—she'd been lusting after Pixie since they first met—but she wouldn't be brokenhearted either. At her most optimistic, she knew it was still a coin flip at best.

The copter took a detour, going long around the edge of the compound, keeping away from the foot patrols. A few horses lingered out in the corral, lonely shadows in the dark.

"Thanks," she said. "You know, I don't say this a lot. I don't think I've ever said it. But ever since I got dragged into this world. You know, demons, monsters, craziness..."

"As I recall, *I* dragged you into it."

"As I recall, I insisted. You tried to warn me. I should have trusted you." She focused on the screen, concentrating as she steered the drone. "Anyway, I know I get on your case a lot, but you've really gone out of your way to make me feel like...well, part of the family. And that means a lot to me. Thanks."

"Don't mention it. Nobody's looking out for us in this world. We gotta look out for each other. There—that window's lit up. Can you get closer?" I tapped a faint glowing rectangle on the screen, just out of focus. "Anyway, I'm just sore because I had money in the betting pool."

"The betting pool?"

"Yeah, see, I put fifty bucks on you being robosexual. I figured you were building contraptions in your garage, like with pistons, and weird attachments. That's what I told everybody, anyway."

"Daniel Faust," she said with a sigh, "you are an enormous asshole."

"I know, Pix." I patted her on the shoulder. "I know."

A silhouette sat in the second-floor window. The drone dipped closer, bouncing on a sudden gust of midnight wind, and the camera went blurry. Pixie tapped a few keys, muttering under her breath, and the screen snapped into focus.

It was Cameron Drake. He sat in a wheelchair and stared out the window, looking twenty years older than the last time I'd seen him. He wore a tattered bathrobe, stubble caking his cheeks, and his eyes were haunted and distant.

"Whoa," Pixie said, "is that Drake? Looks like he went full Howard Hughes."

I squinted at the screen. "When we met, the guy was working overtime to murder his liver, but...that's not just booze. There's something *wrong* with him."

The bedroom door opened. Pixie zipped the drone upward, rocketing away. A tiny battery-status bar in the corner of the screen started flashing red.

"Gotta reel it back in," she said. "So, uh, he looked kinda catatonic. Do you think he's even gonna be able to talk? I mean, a big part of this plan is hinging on Drake's cooperation."

Good question. And another uglier one loomed in the back of my mind. When I'd squared off with Ms. Fleiss at Gosselin's magic museum, she'd plunged me into a nightmare world—forcing me to vividly experience my friends' deaths, over and over again, while only a second or two passed in the real world.

Drake had been in her clutches for months. What had she been *doing* to him? And could it be fixed?

16.

We got back to Austin in the dead of the night, crashed for a few hours, then woke everybody up to work out the final plan. The whole crew clustered around the satellite map while we refueled with black coffee and doughnuts. I popped a chocolate munchkin into my mouth, grateful for the sugar boost.

"Gonna need a fallback," Jennifer said. "If Drake's really catatonic, I mean, searching the house without his help is still an option."

"It's just going to take longer. And the longer it takes, the harder it's gonna be to get away clean. What we need is a really good diversion, something we can set off to buy some time and cover our exit." I tapped the edge of the map, thinking. "What we *need* is a little chaos."

"Sounds like we need a bomb," Corman said.

Jennifer shook her head. "If we were back home, easy, I could line up a few sticks of boom-boom before suppertime. My only contact out here is Gabriel's buddy and, well...you saw the quality of his merchandise. I'm not lookin' to blow my hands off."

"Drake owns horses," Caitlin said, cradling her chin in

her fingertips. "Probably not trained for war, wouldn't you think?"

"It's the twenty-first century. When's the last time anyone outside of a Renaissance fair trained horses for—" Pixie paused, remembering who she was talking to. "Oh. Right. Yeah, no, probably not. They looked pretty docile when we flew the drone over, though, and most of them were in the stable for the night. A few gunshots won't start a stampede."

"So we encourage them," Margaux said. "*I* encourage them."

I looked her way. "What've you got in mind?"

"Sometimes my spirits like to dance inside people's skins. And sometimes they can be convinced to...go down-market. Especially if you ask the right ones, with the right offerings, and there's a little mischief to be made." She pointed to the map's far edge. "I can set up here, behind the hillside—in the open, but out of sight from the ranch—and make my plea to the *loa*."

Jennifer looked dubious. "Don't you use drums and rattles when you do your thing? Sound carries pretty far out there."

"If this works, by the time anybody thinks to check it out, they'll be neck-deep in spirit-mad horses. All the same, I'll need somebody watching my back just in case. Preferably somebody with a gun. My hands are gonna be occupied."

Bentley gave her a formal bow. "Cormie and I would be delighted to be your dates for the evening."

"We still need a little help gettin' in the front door," Jennifer told me. "Or through the fence, as the case may be. I figure you and Cait are storming the house, finding

Drake and the knife. That leaves support, and we're a pair of hands short."

"I'll be running overwatch with the drone," Pixie said. "I can steer you around the foot patrols, no problem, at least so long as the battery holds out."

Jennifer shook her head. "Obliged, but that ain't the issue. Now I can do some damage in that utility shed on my own, but taking control of the security room, that's not a one-woman job. Don't know how many guards are in there, where they're positioned...one wrong move and I'm dead. The plan's dead too. But mostly me."

"So I'll go," Corman said. "Bentley can cover Margaux on his own."

"That won't work either," I said. "I need one of you acting as our wheelman. Best-case scenario, we slip in and out and nobody's the wiser. It's a lot more likely that this job is going to get loud and nasty, and we're all gonna have to get out of there *fast*. Which means we need somebody positioned with the escape vehicle, buckled in and the engine running. Every second counts."

"If one of *them's* gonna be driving," Margaux muttered, "it should definitely be Corman."

"Because I'm a better shot?" Bentley asked.

"Sure," she said. "Because you're a better shot."

I fixed my eyes on the satellite map. Tracing lines in my mind, calculating distances. I rapped my knuckles on the table.

"Okay," I said, "change of plans. Caitlin, you're with Jennifer. I'm going after Drake and the knife solo."

Caitlin arched an eyebrow. "Excuse me?"

"Drake knows me. And I know that knife. I mean, I already stole it once. I can move in, nice and quick and quiet, and get out the same way. Meanwhile, Jennifer's end of this job is a lot more likely to get violent. I want you backing her up."

"When it comes to violence," Jennifer told her, "you *are* kind of an artiste."

"And what if Naavarasi is wrong?" Caitlin asked. "What if Fleiss is there?"

"Then I get the hell out before she spots me, we scrub this whole thing, and Naavarasi can go pound sand. By which I mean I'll find some way to make it up to her. Maybe chocolate, and a nice floral arrangement."

* * *

Sourcing a getaway car was easy. We rented it. A black Ford Explorer with seating for seven and a V8 engine, perfect for getting around in the scrub. We pulled off to the side of the highway, just shy of the access road to Eastern Pines. I unscrewed the license plates, tossed them in the cargo nook, and took a razor blade to the Budget bumper sticker. If the guards happened to spot the car on our way out, they'd have no way to trace it back to us.

Finding a couple of live chickens for Mama Margaux's ritual had been a little harder. They were in the cargo nook too, squawking up a storm, and ten minutes into the drive the SUV filled with a stench that had us clutching our noses and rolling down the windows.

"That is *rank*," Bentley said, fanning his hand in front of his face. "I have nothing against the occasional blood sacrifice, when needs must, but couldn't we have bought *packaged* chicken for this? From the grocery store, for instance?"

"And where exactly do you think packaged chicken comes from?" Margaux asked him.

"I like to imagine it just spontaneously appears there. I prefer not to engage with my food any further than that."

Margaux folded her arms, stoic. "Can't kill the chicken, don't eat the chicken."

Behind the wheel, Corman made a sour face as we rumbled along the access road.

"Definitely not getting the cleaning deposit back," he said.

"Reminds me of growin' up back home," Jennifer said. "Good times, good times. So Mama, how long is it gonna take to do this thing?"

Margaux shrugged. "It's not a science. Twenty minutes if the *loa* are feeling generous. An hour if they're feeling less generous."

"And if they're not feelin' generous at all?"

"Well," Margaux said, "at least we'll have a home-cooked chicken dinner tonight."

Pixie stuck her head out the window and gulped down fresh air. I was testing my memory, rehearsing in my head, mentally following the trail the drone had laid for us the night before. Then I passed out my new purchase, courtesy of Naavarasi's per-diem money: a handful of new Bluetooth earpieces, slim and storm-gray.

"We'll make our staging area over by the dunes, same place Pix and I staked out last night. Once me, Caitlin, and Jennifer go in, start the clock. In exactly one hour, if we're not out by then, get the ritual underway. We'll also be in phone contact and Pixie's drone will be doing flybys until the battery dies. If you see anything hinky, if the job goes sideways—"

"Start the ritual," Margaux said. "You'll be covered, Danny, don't worry about it. We'll get it done."

She handed me a pair of black leather driving gloves, thin and supple, and a rubber mask. I turned the mask and squinted at it.

"Is that...Ronald Reagan?"

Margaux held up another pair of masks. "I also got Richard Nixon and Jimmy Carter."

Jennifer and Caitlin shared a glance. Caitlin tilted her head, noncommittal.

"Dibs on Carter," Jennifer said.

A mile out from the ranch, Corman killed the headlights and cruised in slow. The starlight guided our way across the scrub. Far from the city, the night was a canopy of twinkling lights, an ocean vast and deep.

The Explorer rumbled to a stop. The engine fell silent. We synchronized our earpieces.

I felt that familiar tension in my gut, the cold certainty that I was walking into a world of trouble that could end in a prison cell or a shallow grave. I preferred to dull it with alcohol when I could, just one drink before a job to settle my nerves, but I didn't really mind the feeling. It was an old professional companion of mine. The night I *didn't* feel that tension was the night I'd get sloppy and screw up.

It would only take one bad night to end it all.

I pulled on my gloves. They were tight, like a second skin, and thin enough that they wouldn't slow me down. We piled out of the SUV and Jennifer set her duffel bag down on the ground.

"It's go time." She unzipped the bag and opened it wide. "Arm up and mask up."

I opted for the snub-nosed .38 with the rattly grip and loose cylinder. It looked like the least reliable choice in the dodgy arsenal, which was why I chose it. I had my cards to rely on—plus Canton's wand, if it felt like cooperating—and if I did my job right, I wouldn't have to pull the trigger. If any gunfighting came into play tonight, it was most likely going to fall on Jennifer's and Caitlin's shoulders, so I wanted them to have the better tools for the job.

Pixie set up her laptop on the Explorer's hood, running preflight checks on the drone, while Margaux herded the chickens. Bentley and Corman helped her with the rest of her magical gear—bags of flour, pouches and sachets, a small hand drum with a wicker frame—and unfurled a roll of plain black carpet over the sparse grass.

"While you go after Drake and the knife," Jennifer told me, "me and Cait are gonna shut down that security room. Once we strong-arm it and make sure nobody's gonna be calling for reinforcements, priority two is finding the generators. Plural. You know this place has at least one backup."

I nodded as I tugged on my Reagan mask. "Find them, but leave the generators online until I say otherwise. If we can keep this quiet from start to finish, all the better."

"And if we can't?" Caitlin asked.

"Then you blow the generators, Mama does her thing, and the guards have to deal with a total blackout and a horse stampede at the same time. We'll be back in Vegas and counting our money before they know what hit 'em."

"Counting our money," Jennifer said. "Sure, if we were gettin' *paid* for this job."

"Drake is our paycheck. Hopefully."

Caitlin frowned. "Too many hopes and not enough certainties for my liking tonight."

"You and me both," I said. "But that's the job. So...let's do this."

17.

The three of us went wide around the compound, avoiding the front gates and the lights from the guard shacks, keeping clear of the access road. We stayed low as we skirted the fence line. Pixie's drone whirred overhead. It wouldn't have enough battery charge to stick around for the whole job, but it would last long enough to help guide us in.

"You're clear," Pixie's voice said in my ear. "Foot patrol just went by, about forty feet ahead of you, and I don't see another in sight."

I took a pair of tin snips to the fence and snapped the chain links one at a time. A couple of feet to my left, Jennifer did the same. We cut an arch and met in the middle. The fence rattled as we shoved the sawed-off section in, making a hole big enough to wriggle through. Jagged links tugged at my windbreaker and scratched my back as I squirmed past. Caitlin and Jennifer were next. With a silent nod, we parted ways: I broke left, they broke right, and the drone zipped ahead of them.

I was on my own now.

I jogged in a crouch, balancing speed and silence, keeping to the loose dirt along the fence and away from the paved walkways. I heard the whine of a golf cart's engine and pressed my back to the bunkhouse wall until it passed. A Maglite's beam strobed by, a guard keeping a casual watch, then moved along. I moved along too, in the opposite direction.

The Ionic pillars of the main estate rose up ahead, hard-angled eaves looming in the dark like ravens' beaks. A light burned in the second-floor bedroom window, just like last night. That was where I'd find my first target. As for the second...I'd just have to improvise. I steered clear of the front door and made my way around to the side of the house. A service entrance wasn't far away, and the window set into the door looked in on a dark, silent kitchen. I got low and fished out my lockpicks.

Jennifer's voice whispered over the Bluetooth link. "Security room is ours. We got access to the alarm feed, cameras, the whole kit 'n' caboodle. Four guards. One made a move. The other three decided to live."

"Noise?"

"Cait took him down quiet. We're foxes in the henhouse at the moment."

"How long until shift change?" I asked.

"She's askin' our hostages about that right now. They decided to act tough, so she's explaining the need for open and honest communication." I heard something in the background, an anguished whimper. "She's getting her point across."

I worked the lock, picks delicately scraping, threading a needle in the dark.

"How about those camera feeds," I said. "Got any eyes inside the main house?"

"Sorry, sugar, you're going in blind. Either there's no cameras in there..."

She left the rest unspoken. Either there weren't any cameras, or Drake's house had its own independent security. The service door swung open. I drew my .38.

I cradled the revolver close as I swept through the kitchen, then the gloomy, long gallery of the dining room, past a twelve-foot mahogany table and a double-wide china cabinet. When Drake won the lottery he must have dreamed about lavish parties, entertaining his friends in grand style. Instead, he wound up in a gilded prison. I still didn't know why they'd targeted him, or what the purpose behind this charade was beyond siphoning his cash, but one way or another I was taking him off the board tonight.

If he wasn't completely brain-fried, he was coming with me. If he was, a mercy killing was the best I could offer him. Either way, I wasn't leaving him in Fleiss's hands. Not for one more night.

Ears perked, I pushed a swinging door open just a couple of inches and eyed the foyer. A crystal chandelier hung in the gloom, chimes rattling in a chilly draft. No guards in sight. I padded up a long, curving staircase, footfalls soft on the blue velvet runner, and paused at the landing to get my bearings. Up a short hallway, a strip of light glowed under a closed door.

I turned the handle, slow. It gave. The door opened with a long wooden groan.

Drake was where we'd seen him last night: in his wheelchair and bathrobe, hair matted and stringy, staring at the window while a lamp burned at his side. The light turned the glass into a black mirror. I saw his reflection—and mine, holding a gun and shrouded under my dead-faced Reagan mask, right behind him. His eyes went wide and his mouth opened, like he was about to shout for help.

I yanked the mask off. "Hey—hey, Cameron, wait. It's me! I'm here to save you."

He blinked, tugging a stubborn wheel and rolling the chair around to face me.

"M-Mr. Faust?" he whispered.

"Yeah." I tossed the mask onto his bedspread. I took him in—and my stomach clenched when I looked down at his bare feet. They were brutalized, covered in splotchy bruises and burst blood vessels, his heels black and three of his toes broken. "Jesus, what'd they *do* to you?"

His jaw trembled as he swallowed. "Ms. Fleiss gets...impatient. It's my fault. I made her do it. It's all my fault."

"Hey, none of that. We're getting you out of here, okay?"

That's what I said out loud. The debate in my head hadn't been settled yet. Now I understood why they didn't bother stationing guards in the house: Drake couldn't walk on his own, and he wasn't getting down that staircase in a wheelchair. I could wrestle his chair down the steps and wheel him out of here—and then we'd be a slow-moving target all the way to the escape car.

A mercy killing was still on the table. Take him out, deny his resources to the Enemy. Quick, easy, and clean.

He squeezed my hand. His eyes glistened wet, pathetically grateful as he looked up at me.

"Thank you," he whispered. "I'd given up hope."

Damn it. I hated doing the right thing. I sighed and tapped my earpiece.

"I found Drake," I said. "He can't walk on his own, looks like Ms. Fleiss went all Annie Wilkes on his feet with a hammer. We're definitely going to need that distraction."

"You want me to blow the generators now?" Jennifer asked.

"Nah, hold up, still have to get what we came for." I looked to Drake. "That Aztec dagger, the one I stole for you—do you still have it? Is it here?"

"It's...it's in the basement." He cringed. "It's a bad place."

"Well, we really need it. Is Fleiss here? She's not down there, is she?"

"I don't...think so. The days run together. They've been bringing food to my room. I don't really leave anymore."

"What about—" I racked my brain, trying to remember his name. "Pachenko. That big slab of muscle she had with her last time I came here?"

Drake shook his head. "Nobody comes around after dark. Just me. And the voices. Sometimes the walls whisper at night."

I sighed and jammed the .38 into the back of my belt, under my windbreaker. Needed to free my hands up. I walked behind his chair and took hold of the handles, wheeling him toward the door.

"Pal," I muttered, "you're gonna need a hospital and some serious therapy when we get out of here. Maybe not in that order."

I eased his chair backward down the foyer steps one at a time, wincing at every *thump* of his wheels against the runner. It sounded like a drumbeat calling out the guards, but nobody came to check it out. By the time we reached the bottom, one shoulder was aching and my back felt like I'd been digging a ditch.

He pointed toward a side corridor off the foyer,

opposite the way I'd come in. An elevator stood at the end, with a single sliding door and a brass button.

"You have an elevator," I breathed. "I just hauled your dead-weight ass down that entire flight of stairs, and you have an elevator."

"It doesn't go to the second floor. It only goes down."

"Peachy." I pushed the button. It lit up with a cool amber glow. "What kind of security you got down there? Is the knife in a safe? Some kind of vault?"

"It's sitting on a pillow."

The door glided open. A spacious cage, wood-walled and somber, waited on the other side. I wheeled him in. Sure enough, there were only two buttons on the panel inside. I hit the bottom one.

"*Lots* of therapy," I said.

I braced for trouble. Ms. Fleiss—and the Enemy, by extension—had gone to a lot of trouble to get that dagger. If it was really just sitting on a pillow, no vault, no locks, I fully expected that pillow to be stuffed with nitroglycerin.

Or more likely, they trusted sorcery over electronics. There were more ways to lay a whammy on your loot than I could count. Curses, hex-wards, conjured and bound guardians. Any or all of them could be waiting for me, and I'd have to move fast to identify and defuse whatever defenses Fleiss had concocted.

The elevator sank like a stone. And kept sinking. I didn't know how far down this basement was, but if I had to guess, we were a good fifty feet under the house. It finally jarred to a stop and the door opened onto a long and unfinished corridor. A smooth stone floor, unadorned drywall, nothing but a string of bare and dangling bulbs overhead to light the way.

One by one, the bulbs flickered to life on their own.

All the way to the door at the far end of the hallway. Slate black, with a polished brass handle.

"I don't want to go in there," Drake whispered.

"I can't leave you here," I told him. "Some guard comes along and finds you, we're both screwed. Don't worry, I'll keep you safe."

The corridor was just long enough to feel like a march to the electric chair. I studied the door at the end. No lock, no keypad, just a handle waiting to be turned. I took hold of it, the brass cold under my palm, tingling with static electricity. The door opened onto darkness.

And a stench. It wafted out on a gust of humid air, almost shoving me back a step. Cloying, and rotten, and coppery-sweet. Blood. Not from a cut or a wound, not even from a single body. Bodies. Hundreds of them. It was a slaughterhouse smell.

I held my breath and pushed Drake's chair over the threshold.

18.

As we stepped through the black door, fires roared to life. The flames billowed, bellowing like twin lions from great brass braziers, and lit the chamber in flickering shades of scarlet and gold. The room was a vault, stone floor and unfinished walls like the corridor outside, at least fifty feet high and twice as deep. A vault built to hold a four-sided pyramid of weathered stone.

The pyramid, a burning brazier at the two closest corners, bore a staircase along each of its faces. The steps rose to a flat summit about seven feet up, where a stone altar stood beside a trio of low, round pillars. Carved serpents ringed the pillars, and engraved faces—jaguars, herons, animals I couldn't begin to guess at—leered out at us from the basalt steps.

I tapped my earpiece. My voice came out softer than I wanted it to.

"Caitlin? Jennifer?" I listened to the faint hiss of static. "Anybody?"

Four mirrors of polished obsidian, each tall as a man and twice as wide, stood on wooden frames around the pyramid summit. Their black reflections captured the altar and the pillars—one bearing a jade bowl, one a clay flute, and the third an emerald silk pillow. I couldn't see from the foot of the pyramid, but I was willing to bet I'd find the dagger nestled on top of it.

I took a hesitant step toward the stairs, the blood stench overwhelming now. As I got closer to the pyramid, I could see why. The stone, naturally dark, had a sticky, flaky patina to it. The kind of dead-beetle sheen you get from spilling gallons of blood and leaving it to dry in the hot, stale air. I didn't see any bodies, but people had died in this room. People had been murdered in this room.

I opened my third eye, stretching out my psychic senses, and wished I hadn't. My first trip to Eastern Pines, I'd sensed something malevolent beneath the house. Now I saw it. Human shadows, the remnants of souls, lay strewn across the steps. Psychic echoes of victims tortured, broken and bled to feed the thirsty stone.

"It's a battery," I breathed.

I'd seen this before. Lauren Carmichael had turned her casino penthouse into a psychic resonator, designed to harvest life-energy from human sacrifices. We had stopped her just before the grand opening.

This one, though, was fully fueled. The pyramid thrummed with dormant power, ripe to the point of bursting. A powder keg just waiting for a match.

"Do you see?" asked the voice at my back.

I whirled. Ms. Fleiss stood in the doorway, one hand resting on Drake's shoulder. Drake trembled, his face fish-belly pale and glistening with fear-sweat.

"Do you see the glory?" Fleiss raised a languid hand and pointed to the pyramid. "Unbelievers sought to steal my lord's magic and imprison him. But he could not be chained. And he would not be denied. Even in his weakened state, he sought other means of restoring his power."

I thought about my cards. Thought about my gun. The last time I tangled with Fleiss it had taken a firing squad to drive her off, and that only *hurt* her. The wand sat in my wrist sheath, dormant. No help there.

"The Aztec relics your boy Marcel's been stealing," I said. "The bowl, the mirrors..."

"Every world is a pearl, Mr. Faust, floating in the shadow in-between. Sometimes they bump against one another. Sometimes pilgrims cross over. And they bring things with them. Ideas. Beliefs. Relics."

She didn't give any warning. One moment she was standing perfectly still. The next she was lunging at me like an Olympic fencer, crossing the space between us in a blur and throwing a knuckle punch. Her fist cracked against my sternum and my heart jolted with an electric shock. I fell back, landing hard against the bottom steps of the pyramid, the rough basalt shooting lances of pain up my tailbone. She swung up a stiletto heel and brought it down in an ax kick that whistled to a sudden stop against my throat. She leaned in. The pressure, just shy of breaking the skin, was a warning.

"*Don't* move," she told me. "*Do* witness. Witness the glory."

I felt the pyramid shift. Blood-caked stone vibrated against my back, the buried power rising in voiceless recognition. Plumes of black smoke billowed from the obsidian mirrors, as if they were pits of oil and someone had tossed a match into their bottomless depths.

"We once graced an Earth where the Aztec Empire had never fallen," Fleiss said, wearing a fervent smile. "They greeted my lord as a god, as was good and right, and many miracles were performed before we laid that world to ruin. Pilgrims from that world crossed over to this one, over a thousand years ago, and carried trinkets that had been blessed with my lord's touch. Kissed by his power."

The pyramid sang now, a tuneless keening somewhere between a hymn and a scream. My heart jackhammered, sweat plastering my shirt to my chest as the brazier fires rose and the vaulted chamber became an inferno of smoke. The air stank of cloying incense and burning corpses.

"Do you see, Mr. Faust?" Fleiss hissed with a fanatic's devotion, her gaze locked upon the roiling smoke and the obsidian glass. "Do you see what he is, now?"

I saw.

A figure stood on the pyramid, wreathed in black smoke. He had the form of a man but no depth, no color, just an empty void that crackled around the edges as he stepped forth. It was like some divine animator had sketched a charcoal figure in the air, erasing and redrawing him with every passing second, his edges never staying quite the same.

He had no face. Only a pearly, inhumanly wide smile.

"They mistook me for Tezcatlipoca," he said. "The Smoking Mirror. But you know who I really am, don't you, Daniel?"

"The Enemy," I whispered.

He spread his arms wide, as if in greeting.

"I'll answer to that name, and many others if it pleases. How does the old saw go? You can call me anything you like, just don't call me late for dinner. In my weakened, *hungry* state, I needed to amass some bits and pieces of my old magic. Just enough to get the ball rolling and begin opening my reliquary. A process that you, my friend, have made rather difficult."

"So that explains the Aztec stuff," I said. "It used to be yours. Then you built this...*thing*. Harvesting life-energy."

The pyramid moaned against my back. I felt ghostly hands pressing against the inside of the stone, trapped in anguish.

"One plan gives birth to another," he replied. "With every step, my lost power returning."

"What's the connection to Howard Canton, then?"

As I spoke the name, Fleiss's heel shoved harder against my throat.

"Ah, good old Canton," the Enemy said. "You have his top hat. Where is it, please?"

"Go to hell."

Fleiss leaned in and pressed her foot down. My breath became a wheezing trickle, blood welling under the spike of her heel. I had one advantage: he didn't know I'd found Canton's wand inside the hat. It wasn't much of an edge, but I'd take whatever I could get.

"*Don't* kill him," he said to Fleiss. She gritted her teeth and the pressure let up, just a fraction of an inch. He shook his head and clicked an invisible tongue. "Not yet, anyway. Not here. It's not your fault, Daniel. You're an ant, drawn into the machinations of a god. How could you possibly understand?"

"You're not a god," I said. "You're nothing but a cosmic glitch, a bug in the system. Somebody told a story, back at the dawn of time, and the story came to life. You're the villain."

"I'm the victor," he said.

"You're *trapped*. Just like all the other characters. Doomed to dance the same dance, make the same mistakes, over and over again. For eternity." I grimaced as

Fleiss's heel dug into my throat. "You think I'm scared of you? I *pity* you."

The creature's smile faded.

"And yet," he said, "my imprisonment in that barren hell-dimension was an opportunity in disguise. You see, those righteous and good-intentioned sages who cast me into the Pessundation—thinking they'd seal me away for eternity—made a slight miscalculation. They wounded the cycle. The reincarnations fell out of sync, characters popping up on random worlds, the fabric of the universe frantically struggling to keep the story intact. And that taught me something very valuable."

He walked to the pillars. His flickering hands picked up the Aztec dagger, cradling it, and he carried it over to the altar.

"If the cycle can be wounded," he said, "the cycle can be killed. It is my compulsion, my nature, and my fate to devour worlds one by one. That's how the story was told. Don't blame me, blame my author. This time, though? This time I'm playing for *all* the marbles."

"And it's the Paladin's compulsion, nature, and fate to kick your ass. I hear that's part of the story, too."

The Enemy chuckled. He rested the dagger on the altar, placing it carefully, as if observing some sacred geometry.

"And you are not the Paladin," he said. "You can't defeat me, Daniel. The fabric of reality itself will fight to stop you. Thanks to the power of the cursed story that spawned me, I'm fated to die at my nemesis's hands and none other's. And when I find the Paladin *this* time..."

My sweat ran cold as I put it together.

"The Pessundation," I whispered. "You're going to do to him what the people who locked you away did to you."

The Enemy clapped his hands. His Cheshire grin grew wide enough to split his shadowy face in half.

"The only force in the entire universe that can slay me, gifted with eternal life and eternal imprisonment. That's how this cycle of the story ends, Daniel: *it doesn't*. It will go on and on, because *I* will go on and on, and this 'cosmic glitch' will be the ruin of the universe. I'm not a bug. I'm a virus with no cure."

He glided to the edge of the pyramid steps.

"As for you, I'm afraid you're destined for a rather painful and ignominious death. Seeing as I have a schedule to keep, you get to keep breathing for another hour or two. Lucky you."

"Shall I put him in his cell?" Fleiss asked.

He shrugged. "Eh. Let him stay. Let him watch. Let an ant gaze upon miracles, and hope to comprehend."

The Enemy loomed over me. Even without eyes, I felt the heat of his steady gaze.

"Before you die, Daniel, you *will* acknowledge that I am a god."

19.

"I have many plans and many projects," the Enemy told me. "Many fingers in many pies. This is but one of them. Are you familiar with the myths of the *Rex Nemorensis*? The sacred king?"

"It's a fertility rite," I breathed. Blood trickled down my neck, tickling my shoulder, as Fleiss's heel dug in. "You crown a 'king,' then sacrifice him at the year's end. Supposed to ensure a bountiful harvest."

"Indeed. A king who wants for nothing in the year before he goes to his death, blessed with bounty and fortune." His eyeless gaze shifted to the broken, whimpering man in the wheelchair. "Like a lottery winner. Isn't the natural cruelty of the universe funny, Cameron? If you hadn't stopped at the 7-Eleven on your way home that day, if you hadn't chosen the random numbers you did—one in almost three hundred million odds! If you hadn't, someone else would be in your position right now. And you'd be living your pointless, mundane life, never touched by the winds of magic."

Drake, dripping sweat, moved his cracked lips in a silent plea.

"Tonight, we end the reign of the sacred king." Fleiss

pointed to the pyramid. “It’s the thirty-first. Samhain. The end of the harvest season.”

“I realize we’re monkeying with the theme a bit,” the Enemy said, waving a flickering hand. “Aztec ritual, Celtic holiday, Greco-Roman myth cycle...but we like our magic nice and chaotic around here. We’ll go with whatever works. I think you can relate to that.”

“So you stored up all this energy,” I said, “and you’re going to release it all at once. Why? What are you going to *do* with it?”

He glided to the altar. His sketched-in fingers caressed the obsidian blade.

“This item you so generously stole for me,” he said, “is a Cutting Knife.”

“All knives are cutting knives.”

“Not like this,” he said. “They’re very rare. Very special. And they hold secrets upon secrets. Tonight, this one’s mysteries will be exposed. And I will add a new weapon to my arsenal.”

He began to chant. A slow, sibilant call in some language I’d never heard. His words were feathery, tangled like twine, then musty and leaden. Vowels and consonants brushed one another in ways they were never meant to, the sounds slipping inside one another and coming out twisted. The stone pyramid shuddered and groaned.

“*Witness*,” Fleiss hissed. She twisted her foot, grinding her heel into my throat.

I witnessed.

Energy rose from the pyramid like wisps of vapor, squirming silver in the air. Worms of raw power, sucked into the four obsidian mirrors. And the mirrors, full to bursting with the souls of the damned, responded. Streamers of smoke coursed from their faces, four black chains that fell upon the knife with a sound like cold water on a red-hot skillet.

Pinioned by the smoke, the knife lifted into the air. It hovered above the altar, shivering, then began to change.

The blade opened. It unfolded down the middle, growing longer but not thinner as its size doubled from nowhere. Again, then again. The obsidian and jade buckled and twisted, opening like the petals of a lethal flower, every change in its configuration making it grow.

"Rise," Fleiss said to Drake. I turned my head, as much as I could manage, watching in mute horror as his broken feet touched upon the hot stone floor and he pushed himself up from the wheelchair. His face contorted in pain as he stumbled toward the pyramid. No control over his body, a puppet under her control, but fully aware—and feeling every agonizing step. I heard tiny bones snap as he mounted the stairs. His breath came out in labored wheezes.

The Enemy glided to the pillars and lifted the clay flute. He played a trilling, discordant tune, a song devoid of rhythm or sanity but every note placed with absolute precision. Carefully, exactingly mad. And Drake danced. He shuffled, hopping on his blackened feet as he climbed the pyramid, his body jerking in spasms while tears streamed down his sweat-soaked face.

The knife wasn't a knife anymore. It was a formless mass the size of a jaguar now, leaves of obsidian and jade continuing to unfold, to grow, to lengthen upon the altar as it reeled against the chains of black smoke.

Drake twirled on the steps with his arms flung out to his sides. As the flute trilled, hitting a high note, he leaped in the air. His left ankle snapped as he crashed down on the step. His foot wrenched to one side, a shard of bloody bone jutting out from the bruised and ravaged skin. He shrieked through gritted teeth and continued his ascent.

The knife, whatever it was now, bucked and rippled. Colors of obsidian and jade muted, the razor-edged stone becoming soft, colors running together. It flung out tendrils that blossomed like fractal explosions.

Drake reached the top of the pyramid and stood before the Enemy. He spun one last time, a pirouette that wrenched his mangled foot until it was turned completely backward. He stood frozen and trembling as the flute played its final note. His jaw wrenched open in a voiceless scream, and his eyes were rolled so far back in his skull I could only see bloodshot white.

The knife had finished its transformation. It thumped against the altar, suddenly still.

It was a woman.

She had olive skin and amber eyes, her body draped in a snowy-white gown that made me think of an ancient Greek tunic. The chains of black smoke held her fast, leashing her ankles and wrists and binding her to the altar stone. She bared her teeth at the Enemy, letting out a yawp of raw outrage.

The Enemy casually untied Drake's bathrobe. It pooled around his feet, soaking in the blood from his mangled ankle as Drake stood trembling and naked. The flickering shape scooped up the Aztec bowl and a thin knife with a curved, scything blade.

The first cut drew along Drake's outstretched arm, carving a red line from his shoulder to the inside of his elbow. The Enemy caught his blood as it welled up and began to drool down, pattering into the bowl. Still chanting, his formless words squirming inside my ears, he floated to the altar.

He flipped over the bowl. As the blood splashed across her body, staining her tunic scarlet, the woman threw back her head and howled. It was a scream of unendurable anguish, of someone having their life and their mind torn away, one inch at a time.

"What is he *doing* to her?" I gasped as he returned to Drake, slicing open his other arm and harvesting more blood.

Fleiss gazed up with a look of pure awe. Beatific.

"Teaching her," she said. "Taming her. You have to break a wild horse before you can ride it."

I came to the quiet conclusion that I was probably going to die.

I was outclassed. Outgunned. Cornered by two creatures that might as well have been gods, for all I could do against them.

But if I was going to die, I'd go out on my own terms. Spitting in their faces and, if I could manage it, leaving them with some scars to remember me by. I tallied my resources. Fleiss hadn't bothered patting me down, didn't take my cards or the .38 revolver jammed down the back of my belt. No need to: she'd *caught* my cards the last time we fought, plucking them out of the air and melting them with a glance, and a storm of bullets had barely managed to wound her. Then there was Canton's wand, strapped to my forearm and useless as a twig.

Come on, Howard, I thought. *Any other tricks you want to show me, now would be a damn good time for it.*

Another bowl of blood rained down. My stomach clenched, twisted with nausea as the bound woman's shrieks rang out over the Enemy's incessant chanting. I had six bullets in the .38. As the Enemy drew his blade along Drake's quivering, pale chest, I knew exactly how I was going to spend them.

Fleiss was distracted, focused on the spectacle. She didn't notice me slipping my hand under my back, wriggling the gun loose and curling my fingers around its wobbly grip. She didn't even look as I took careful aim and steeled myself, preparing for the last fight of my life.

The hammer cracked down and the first bullet punched into her chin, snapping her jawbone and spattering hot black ichor across my face. She stumbled back with a furious howl of pain. I jumped to my feet and ran up the pyramid steps, one eye squinted and aiming down the iron sights. My next shot slammed into one of the obsidian mirrors. The stone shattered like cheap glass, billowing down in a cascade of razor-edged shards. Then another, and another, the chains of smoke whiplashing through the air as the vault filled with the sound of breaking glass. The last mirror burst in a glittering torrent. As Fleiss recovered, shaking off her shock, her jaw already reknitting itself and spitting out the crumpled slug, I had just enough time to take my final shot.

The bullet plowed into the Aztec bowl in the Enemy's hands, covering him in chunks of broken bloodstained jade.

I stood halfway up the pyramid, between Fleiss and the Enemy. I tossed my empty gun aside. It clattered against the stone as the ritual energy sparked, whimpered, and died.

The vault fell silent.

"You..." the Enemy said. "You *ruined* it. You ruined *everything*."

"I'm Daniel Faust." I shrugged. "It's kind of what I do. Somebody probably should have warned you."

I heard Fleiss rush me from behind, her feet thundering on the steps. She stopped, frozen, as the Enemy held up his open palm.

"*Don't* kill him." He shook his head, slow. "No. I won't be goaded into slaying you like this. To unlock my full power, your death has to take place under very specific circumstances. And how fortunate for me that said circumstances fully allow for endless, excruciating, and *unimaginable* pain."

The woman on the altar—still panting, her face ashen and gown soaked in sacrificial blood—forced herself to her feet. She looked my way, her amber eyes glowing like candles dancing behind a pair of stained-glass windows.

"Catch me," she said.

Then she ran at me, flinging herself into the air, doing a swan dive off the top of the pyramid steps.

Her spine snapped in half, her body buckling backward, jackknifing. Her arms broke at the elbows, then her knees, the woman's body folding in on itself with blinding speed. As she twisted in the air, shrinking with the sound of a hundred crackling bones, her olive skin turned to hardened stone.

The Cutting Knife, transformed back to its original shape, landed in my outstretched palm. My fingers curled around the jade hilt.

"My lord..." Fleiss said, her voice suddenly uncertain.

"You don't even know how to use that thing," the Enemy told me. "And it doesn't have time to teach you. Its magic is sealed, denied to you."

"Magic?" I turned the dagger in my hand. Firelight glinted off the pitted and glossy blade. "Maybe so, but I gotta tell you, right now, I just want to find out if you can bleed."

The Cheshire smile grew wide. He snapped out his empty left hand, fingers open.

"If you like," he said. "Fleiss! *To me!*"

Ms. Fleiss broke into a run, thundering up the pyramid steps, and leaped. Her grin, as wide and mad as his, caved in as her skull collapsed. Her body buckled, shrinking, flesh turning to tempered steel.

A dagger landed in the Enemy's hand, thumping against his flickering palm. A trench knife, like something a World War II commando might have carried, with a stained wooden grip.

"I can't kill you here," he said, "lest the reliquary stay sealed forever. But nothing says I can't cut you. Carve you. Reduce you to a screaming, mindless lump of *meat*."

My fear and my adrenaline were two warring armies raging in my veins. One force telling me to freeze, to cower, to run and hide, the other telling me to fight for every heartbeat I had left. Adrenaline won. If I was going down, I was going to make him work for it.

A knife fight with a wannabe god? There were worse ways to die. I dropped into a fighting stance, knees bent and limber, my body turned to one side to give him a smaller target. I squared my feet on the pyramid steps. Then I reached out with my empty hand, curled my fingers, and beckoned to him.

"C'mon, then." My lunatic smile, driven by desperation, was almost wider than his. "Show me what you've got."

20.

The Enemy strode toward me, and suddenly halted.

Cameron Drake got between us. He was a shell of a man, broken, ragged, and bleeding, his weight on one blackened foot while the other hung mutilated from a shattered ankle. But he still blocked the flickering shadow's path.

"Defiance," the Enemy murmured, sounding almost perplexed. "We broke you. Bled you. But you still think to stand in my way. Why?"

Drake didn't have the strength to speak. Only to stand. I found some words to speak for him.

"They say you've been to a lot of other worlds," I called up from the pyramid steps. "Can't imagine the things you've seen. Which is why it's so funny."

The Enemy tilted his head, looking past Drake to me. "Funny?"

"Yeah," I said. "All those years, all those worlds...but if you really don't know why he's standing in your way, you don't know *shit* about the human race."

The Enemy considered that. He looked back to Drake. Then to the dagger in his blurry hand.

"Maybe," he mused, "as a species, you're simply too

collectively stupid to know fear. A reckless and violent breed of mammal which should have rightfully gone extinct by now. Let me rectify that."

His open palm slapped against Drake's forehead, fingers clamping tight. The Enemy's form pulsed and shimmered, rippling with sparks like scratches on a film negative.

"You were twelve years old."

"I was twelve years old," Drake echoed, his voice a strained rasp.

"You were walking along the train tracks. Derry, Pennsylvania, on a warm summer morning. You'd just gotten a Walkman for your birthday. You remember."

Drake trembled, frozen in his grip. "I remember."

"You had the music turned up, distracted, thinking about that girl you had a crush on. You didn't hear the train coming up behind you, around a forested bend."

"My brother," Drake whispered, "my brother ran up and pulled me—"

"*No.*" The Enemy's fingers tightened. "Your brother was too slow. And the train was traveling at ninety-seven miles an hour when it hit you."

Drake exploded.

His body burst into a cloud of gore and bone shrapnel, blasting sideways. Torn, ragged viscera splattered across the pyramid steps. Standing in a mist of blood, the Enemy casually stepped over a puddle of unspooled intestine. Then he turned his attention on me as the mist settled at his back.

"You've lived a life of danger," he told me. "How many close calls and near misses have you survived? Events that could have left you scarred, burned, mutilated?"

He held up his hand, fingers outstretched.

"Let's find a few choice examples along your timeline, shall we? Let's *explore*."

I couldn't win this one.

The idea of getting in a knife fight with the Enemy had been just crazy enough to work. But battling a creature who could do *that* with a single touch…everything I knew about magic, everything I'd ever learned, told me what he'd just done was impossible. And yet.

The door to the vault beckoned at my back. I could run, but if the elevator wasn't waiting for me, or if he was faster than he looked, I'd be cornered. Couldn't let him touch me. I needed a distraction, something to buy me a few more seconds.

My thoughts went to the knife, the rough jade hilt tight in my clammy grip. Whatever he'd been doing to the woman inside the blade, I'd put it on hold by breaking his toys. And if I died here, he and Fleiss would go right back to torturing her. I couldn't let—

The wand pulsed against my forearm.

I flexed my wrist. The sheath clicked softly and the wand dropped into my free hand. The world washed out in black and white, static hissing in my ears and giving way to the jangle of a piano playing under a vintage newsreel. Bodiless, I watched Howard Canton on his stage, pulling an endless stream of scarves from his breast pocket. Tied together at the ends, the scarves became an impossibly long rope that pooled around his polished shoes.

"The Grand Multiplicity," his tinny voice said, "is, it must be stressed, a pure illusion. Matter cannot be created *ex nihilo* by the magician. However, with a base enchanted item and clever tradecraft, a few can take on the appearance of many—"

The Enemy's voice jerked me from the vision,

shattering it. The flames in the great brass braziers roared as he pointed at me.

"Canton's wand. You have Canton's wand."

"Apparently I do."

"That isn't *for* you," he seethed, striding down the pyramid steps. "*Give it to me.*"

"Wow," I said. "With an opening like that..."

My deck of cards flew from my breast pocket in a riffling stream, lancing through the air and swarming around the Enemy like a cloud of gnats. Then I brought up the wand, holding it like an orchestra conductor. I felt an invisible hand, cold and gossamer, close over mine. It guided my motions as I drew runes in the air, tracing lines of power with the bone tip of the wand. The runes, arcane sigils I'd never seen in any of my books, sparked and flared aquamarine in my second sight.

Now the cloud of gnats was a tornado, fifty cards becoming a hundred, then two hundred, then a thousand, a pasteboard whirlwind that filled the vault with dancing, spinning chaos and blotted the Enemy from sight.

I turned and ran. Sheathing the wand as I pounded up the endless corridor, overhead bulbs casting dizzy shadows across the bare drywall. The elevator door loomed ahead. And behind me echoed a guttural roar of frustrated rage.

I hammered the elevator button. It chimed, the door sliding open at a molasses pace. I slipped through the second it was wide enough, then punched the button to take me back to the first floor.

At the far end of the hallway, a lightbulb exploded and went dark. Then another. And a third. The Enemy was coming. The elevator door began to crawl shut. I was trapped, cornered in a cage.

He broke into a run. Bulbs shattered in his wake,

painting the corridor in darkness as he closed the distance like a lion bounding in to slaughter his prey. I pressed my back to the wall, watching him streak toward me while the elevator door continued its slow, mechanical glide.

He was two feet away, his outstretched hand grasping for me, when the door sealed shut. I heard his body slam against the sealed door, jolting the cage. The elevator gave a little shiver. Then it whirred, beginning its ascent.

I took a deep, shuddering breath. I tapped my earpiece a few times, trying to reconnect. As I got closer to the surface, reception came back in a burst of sound.

"—going in there," Caitlin was saying, her voice tight. "He's been out of contact for half an hour. Something's wrong."

"Everybody," I said, "get out *now*. Scrub it. Jennifer, wait thirty seconds and blow the generators, backups too, then *leave*. I'll make my own way out."

"Dan?" Jennifer asked. "What's goin' on?"

"They're here. Fleiss and the Enemy."

"*Damn* that Naavarasi," Caitlin snarled.

"I don't think she knew. We just picked the wrong night to show up." I looked to the dagger in my hand. *Or the right one.* "Anyway, we *can't* fight this guy and we don't want him following us—cover your tracks and get out any way you can. Don't worry about me."

The elevator chimed again, rattling to a stop. I was halfway through Drake's mansion when the power died, lights flickering and going dark. I navigated by memory and raced through the silent halls, back to the service entrance.

Outside was pandemonium. The horses, spirit-maddened by Margaux's ritual, had burst from their corral and were running wild through the compound. Their hooves kicked up dust as they whinnied and foamed at the mouths. Flashlights strobed in all directions while the panicked guards tried to stop them. More guards boiled from the darkened bunkhouses, shouting, racing for the utility sheds and the main house.

Hooves pounded my way. The horse, a majestic golden palomino, drew up short. Caitlin sat astride it. She stroked its ivory mane, soothing the horse, and shook her head at me.

"As if I'd leave you behind. Get on."

I slipped the knife into my belt, snug against the loops, and held Caitlin's hips. The palomino exploded into a gallop, leaning into a turn as we raced through the heart of the compound. A security guard jumped out of our way, throwing himself to the dirt and rolling. Another was too slow and went down under a flurry of hooves. Up ahead the ranch gate loomed tall. And locked up tight.

"Cait," I said, clinging tight, "it's too high. We can't jump that."

"Shouldn't have to. Jennifer?"

"Coming in hot," she said over the earpiece. "That thing we didn't wanna do if we didn't have to? I'm doin' it."

Headlights flared as our SUV careened toward the driftwood gate from outside, Jennifer behind the wheel with her foot heavy on the gas. The gate crashed open and debris flew in a storm of splintered wood. She stomped on the brakes, the SUV screeching to a halt, washing the compound in the light of its high beams. We went wide and rode around the side of the car. While we swung down from the palomino's back, Corman leaned out the passenger-side window with a pistol in his fist. He laid down a stream of fire, forcing guards to dive for cover while Caitlin and I climbed in back.

"Jammed," Corman grunted. "Stupid piece of—we ready? Everybody in?"

I slammed the door shut. "We're in. Let's *go!*"

Jennifer threw the SUV into reverse. Wisps of smoke drifted from the battered hood as she drove backward then spun the wheel into a squealing hundred-and-eighty-degree turn. We shot off along the access road, leaving Eastern Pines in our dust.

"Did we get the knife?" Pixie asked.

We got it, all right. My fingers traced the blade, snug in my belt loop.

I had an enemy—*the* Enemy—who could rewrite history with a touch of his hand. A dagger with a living person trapped inside of it. And a stage magician's wand that could teach me occult secrets, but only when it felt inclined.

What I had was a giant mess on my hands. And it was about to get a lot worse. Because no matter what I'd said, no matter what I owed her, there was no way in hell I was giving the dagger to Naavarasi.

21.

The lights of Austin blazed outside the penthouse windows, with dawn coming fast. A silver slice of crescent moon was sinking on the horizon and I wanted to be gone before it was. We'd buried our masks and gloves in a shallow hole about a quarter mile from the interstate. The bag of guns had gone into a second pit after we scrubbed and stripped each piece. We weren't worried about getting our deposit back from the dealer.

Up in the penthouse, Pixie was breaking down her drone, packing pieces into a foam-lined case. Jennifer paced in front of the windows. Caitlin was on the phone with the airline and trying to get our tickets bumped to an earlier flight. As early as possible. Bentley, Corman, and Margaux were doing a quick cleanup job on the room, checking every nook and cranny to make sure we weren't leaving anything questionable behind. Shopping bags, loose receipts, anything that could tie us in any way to the raid on Eastern Pines—it all had to go.

I set the knife on the table. Now every eye in the room was on me. Caitlin finished her call and hung up the phone.

"This...is a lot to unpack," I told them.

"You saw him," Bentley said. "Didn't you?"

"The Enemy. And he's..." I shook my head, searching for words. "To say he's dangerous is like saying a nuclear bomb is dangerous. True, but it understates the situation by a mile or two. I'll start from the beginning. I made my way into the main house and found Cameron Drake—"

"Who?" Pixie asked.

I furrowed my brow at her. "Cameron Drake? The person we were going to rescue?"

A lot of confused faces. I looked around the room.

"Okay, everybody who remembers Cameron Drake, raise your hand."

Jennifer and Caitlin raised their hands. The others just offered blank stares.

"Everybody who was on the scene," I murmured. Everybody who had been close to the house, inside the fence when the Enemy murdered Drake, knew who I was talking about. For everyone else...

"Try this," I said. "Pixie, look up who *owns* Eastern Pines Ranch."

She hunched over her laptop, typing fast. Jennifer came over and pitched her voice low, leaning close to my ear.

"Dan? Why does half the room have amnesia all of a sudden?"

"You remember how the Enemy tossed me into prison, and everybody 'remembered' a trial and a conviction that never actually happened? I got another look at what he's capable of tonight, up close and personal."

"I noticed Drake ain't with you."

"He's not anywhere," I said. And I was pretty sure if I dug into the microfiche for a newspaper in Derry,

Pennsylvania, about twentysomething years ago, I'd find an article about a young boy being hit by a train.

"These records are...weird," Pixie said. "Fragmented, contradictory. Even in the county registry, it's like nobody *knows* who owns the place."

The Enemy's touch could scorch someone from history, but it didn't burn clean. More like a hack job, a tornado of raw chaos searing the fabric of time and leaving the universe struggling to put itself back together.

I turned my back to the table as I gazed across the room.

"That's because, believe it or not, the guy who owns the place doesn't exist anymore. He was murdered retroactively. The Enemy put his hand on him and rewrote his life's story right in front of me. A few hours ago, he was a thirtysomething lottery winner. Now, he died when he was twelve years old, and half of you don't remember that we stood in this very room and talked about him yesterday."

Pixie slumped in her chair and shut her laptop. "Murder by time travel. That's weirder than usual."

"It gets weirder," I said. "The dagger—the Enemy called it a 'Cutting Knife'—was more than a piece of cutlery. He was doing this ritual, some kind of sacrifice to—"

Everyone was staring. Not at me. Past me. I turned around.

The woman in the ivory tunic perched on the table. Her gown was still spattered with Cameron Drake's blood, but less of it now, as if the linen was slowly mending itself. I blinked at her. She blinked back, wide-eyed and curious.

"Right," I said to the room. "Also, the knife is a person."

"Does the...person," Caitlin said, staring, "have a name?"

"Circe." She spoke haltingly, tapping her chest. "I. Circe."

I looked to her. "So, um, at the risk of being rude, what *are* you?"

She shrugged. "Circe."

"Not helpful," Jennifer muttered.

"Turns out, whatever our new friend *is*, Ms. Fleiss is one, too." I glanced back at Circe. "Do you know her? Fleiss?"

Circe's amber eyes darkened. She crossed her arms over her chest, cradling herself tight.

"Not her real name. He made her..." She shook her head, struggling for words. "Forget. Made a hole, inside her. Filled it with *him*."

"Was that what he was trying to do to you?" I asked. "Make you forget, like her?"

Circe's head bobbed. Margaux stepped forward, her face grave.

"Danny," she said, "you know what's right. You know what you gotta do here."

"I know. When Naavarasi wanted me to steal a relic for her, that was one thing. I'm not giving her a *person*."

Caitlin stroked her chin with her fingertips, pacing. "And now we know. The recourse to a culture and a noble title she despises, the insistence on protocol. It was all done in case we learned the truth before handing the knife over to her."

"Well," I said, "I see we're back to the 'Naavarasi can go pound sand' option. I'll buy her a box of chocolates at the airport and send it to her with a sympathy card."

"Pause a moment and think twice. You agreed to this

specific boon, under the dictates of the Cold Peace. She *will* escalate matters. It's likely to become a diplomatic incident between our courts."

"And I'm sorry, Cait, I really am. I know this is gonna make your job a little harder for a while. I'm nobody to claim the moral high ground—I'll make money selling anything that falls off the back of a truck—but I've got to draw a line somewhere. Circe isn't a thing to be sold; she's a person. We're talking about slavery. And I'm not doing it."

"This is going to be a political nightmare. There may be a prior claim involved as well, if she really was Naavarasi's." Caitlin looked to Circe. "Do you know that name? Naavarasi? Did you belong to her once?"

The woman in white squinted at her, not understanding. "Circe belongs to Circe."

"Absolute political nightmare. This couldn't be more inconvenient."

Margaux glared at her. "Caitlin? Do something for me."

"What's that?"

Margaux stepped toward her, hands on her hips.

"I understand, no matter how you look on the outside, you aren't human. That you come from a place where things are done differently. But do me this little favor. Before you say one more word about how *inconvenient* it is that we aren't gonna turn in a fugitive slave? *Try* to remember that I'm Haitian. And watch your damn mouth."

Caitlin's eyes flared, glitters of angry gold sparkling behind her irises. Then the glitters faded. She bit her bottom lip and nodded.

"I'm sorry," she said. "I deserved that. I will...make an effort to be more thoughtful in the future."

I sensed a *but* coming and waited. She didn't say another word.

"First things first," I said. "Regardless of what Naavarasi wants, the Enemy definitely wants Circe back. And me. And he's, like, here in Texas. So we need to *not* be in Texas. Circe, you wanna come with us? We'll do everything we can to keep you safe, I promise."

She poked my arm. As her finger touched my sleeve, it ignited a stinging snap of static electricity.

"With you," she said.

"Great. I hate to ask this, but I'm gonna need you to change back into a knife for a few hours. You can't get on an airplane without ID, and something tells me you don't have a driver's license."

She tilted her head. "Air...plane?"

"Yeah." I sighed. "This is gonna be fun."

* * *

We made it to the airport without incident—and I hoped without a tail, though we doubled back four or five times on our way there. We turned in the SUV, attendants staring in sheer dismay at the crumpled hood.

"Don't worry about it," Jennifer told them. "I paid for the insurance."

As we walked away, she leaned in close and whispered, "Under a fake name, with a stolen credit card."

"That's my girl."

Circe, back in her knife form, took a ride in our checked baggage. Pixie had carved out a bit of extra foam in her drone case to keep her nice and snug. Then we mustered in the Delta terminal, twenty minutes to boarding. I kept an eye on the concourse, half expecting the Enemy to come at us in public, in broad daylight and in front of a half dozen cameras. A move like that would break every rule of the occult underground, but I wasn't sure if he cared.

Caitlin and Margaux were over by the tall windows, having a private conversation in low voices. From the looks on their faces, it was serious but not painful. Margaux put a gentle hand on Caitlin's arm. Caitlin nodded.

I found a patch of open chairs, sat down, and took out my phone. I was saving my call to Naavarasi for later. Putting off the inevitable argument, but mostly I just wanted to get clear of one problem before inviting another to my doorstep. Instead, I called a new friend. Semi-friend.

"Speak of the devil," Carolyn Saunders said. "I was just writing about you."

"You got my attention with your last book. You don't need to do that again."

Carolyn—the Scribe, another victim damned to endless reincarnations as part of the same cosmic story that spawned the Enemy—had reached out to me the only way she could. Through the pages of a fantasy novel, *The Killing Floor*, with a fictionalized account of my time in Eisenberg Correctional. It had come to my attention courtesy of an anonymous email from "a friend."

Neither of us had any idea who sent it.

"Well, that's the thing. Turns out 'Donatello Faustus' was such a popular character, my readers are pretty much demanding a spin-off series. The first book involves a war between thieves' guilds in the City of Burning Lights. After faking his death, Faustus is being blackmailed by a member of the city watch—"

"Damn it, Carolyn, you're just writing down stuff that

actually happened. To *me*. That's shitty storytelling. Have some self-respect."

"I write pulp fiction for a living, it's eight in the morning, and I've just started my second mug of Irish coffee. After lunch I switch to straight bourbon. If you're looking for self-respect, you're in the wrong place."

"I am in the wrong place. Austin. I know this, because I just met the Enemy face-to-face."

I heard her mug rattle against her desk.

"You *met* him? And you walked away in one piece?"

"Ran away, honestly, and it was a close call. Listen, he revealed part of his game plan. We've gotta find the Paladin, *fast*. Before he does."

I gave her the Cliffs Notes version. I heard her keyboard clicking, typing away as I told her about the vault under Eastern Pines.

"Cutting Knives," she echoed. "I've heard the phrase before, I'm just not certain where. So that's why Fleiss is so devoted to him. He corrupted her somehow. Brainwashed her."

"And he was about to do the same thing to Circe. I've seen Fleiss in action, and I have to assume Circe can do everything Fleiss can. *One* of those things on his side is bad enough."

"What's been done could possibly be undone. I'll be conducting some research. And I agree, finding the Paladin is our top priority."

"You've gotta level with me," I said. "Things are moving fast here, and I'm about to navigate one hell of a minefield. Until we figure out how to get this whammy off me, I've been drafted into the story. I'm the Thief. You need to tell me the original ending. How does the Thief die?"

"As I said, it's not likely to—"

"*Please*. I can't protect myself if I don't know what to watch for."

She sighed. "As you wish. According to the story, the Thief pulls off the most dangerous robbery of his life. As he's celebrating, safe and at home, his lover—the only person in the world he absolutely trusts—stabs him in the back. She murders him for the treasure."

I gazed across the concourse. Caitlin, still talking to Margaux, caught my eye. She gave me a wink and a smile.

"Great," I said, sagging into my chair.

"There are variations, of course. The story never repeats itself in exactly the same way."

"Got it. Thanks. I'll call you if I learn anything else. And please, do me a favor? Stop putting real occult-underground shit in your books. You're gonna get yourself in trouble. Or you're gonna get *me* in trouble."

"Come on," she said. "You didn't like *anything* in my last book?"

I took a deep breath. Had to give her something.

"I liked the bit where Faustus slept with the two leather-clad vampire vixens. That was okay."

"I'll make a fan out of you yet."

"Yeah," I said, "but see? That was one of the parts that didn't happen in real life. *Fiction*. Try writing it sometime."

"It *could* happen."

"Vampires aren't real. Goodbye, Carolyn."

I hung up. Caitlin drifted over to me.

"Good talk?" I asked her.

"Good talk." Her placid smile broke like a cloud, turning stormy. "Are you all right, pet? You seem disturbed."

I shrugged. "It's been a disturbing day."

"Fair enough." She pointed to the line gathering by the boarding-ramp door. "Looks like they're about to let us on the plane. Shall we?"

I pushed myself to my feet and took a long look up the concourse.

"Sure," I said. "Let's go home."

22.

Home was three hours away. I held my breath as we walked through the boarding tunnel. A rush of cool outside air seeped through the rubber seal between the tunnel and the plane, engines thrumming. I took a window seat in first class, and a preflight glass of wine. I wanted something harder than that.

"You sure you're all right?" Caitlin said, giving me a suspicious side-eye.

"I'll be all right when we're in the air."

That wasn't true either, but once we hit our cruising altitude, another couple glasses of merlot mostly got the job done. I did my thinking between sips.

I wasn't afraid Caitlin was going to stab me in the back, literally or metaphorically. I'd trusted her with my life before and I'd do it again, without hesitation. Then again, I supposed that's what the Thief thought each time around too. From what I was gathering, if the pawns in this little game didn't feel like playing, the universe would bend over backward to *make* them follow the story.

No. I couldn't do this. I couldn't let myself get suspicious of a woman who had brought nothing but good into my life. That was a long and bumpy trip down

Paranoia Lane, and it wouldn't take me anywhere I wanted to go.

She put her hand over mine. Warm. Reassuring. From the uncertain tension in her eyes, though, I figured she was the one who needed a little reassurance. Couldn't blame her. I'd been locked down like a submarine hatch since I'd gotten off the phone with Carolyn.

"It's going to be okay," I told her. "Just...figuring out how I'm gonna deal with Naavarasi. I thought about telling her we couldn't get the dagger, but..."

"But she'll keep insisting you go back and try again," she said, "and eventually she'll start spying on you—because it's Naavarasi—and realize you aren't. She'll figure it out."

"Bingo. I figure the truth is the best policy." I shook my head and drank my wine. "Wow, those words do *not* feel right coming out of my mouth. So, once I tell her she's not getting her hands on Circe, in dagger form or otherwise, what are her options?"

Caitlin eased back in her seat. She gazed upward for a moment, mentally running through a checklist, and sighed.

"Your status—as my consort, but not formally attached to my court—is both a hindrance and a help. There are obligations which don't apply to you, as well as protections you don't enjoy. There are gray areas in the law."

"Loopholes? That's good, right?"

She gave me half of a smile and sipped from a glass of chardonnay.

"The laws of hell were not designed to be fair or just, pet. Quite the opposite. Don't expect anything to work in your favor. And don't expect you'll be better at twisting it to your advantage than people who have spent centuries doing nothing but. As far as her options, what will most likely happen is Naavarasi will make a formal petition to Prince Malphas, complaining that you've refused to pay your debt to her."

"And then he'll gripe to Prince Sitri, I assume."

"You assume correctly. At which point, well, it's up to him. You aren't a member of our court, so my father can't compel you to hand Circe over."

She pursed her lips. The jet rumbled, hitting a patch of turbulence, as gray clouds drifted past the porthole windows.

"I'm sensing an unspoken follow-up to that."

"He can't compel you directly. But I am his hound. His left hand and enforcer of his will. He can compel me to take Circe from you, by force if necessary, and *make* you fulfill your obligation."

Another rumble. I stared out the window. Not wanting to ask the question, not wanting to go down this road, but I was the one who had opened this door in the first place.

"Would he do that?"

Caitlin shrugged. "Who can say what my father will do in *any* circumstance? He sparks coup attempts against himself when he gets bored just so he has a challenge to occupy his mind. When you chose to sacrifice the Ring of Solomon, back when we were battling the Redemption Choir, you earned his respect. But respect, in his eyes, generally just means you're a more attractive plaything."

"And if he goes that route? What if he tells you to take Circe from me and hand her over to Naavarasi?"

Caitlin set her glass down.

She didn't answer, not right away. Her gaze fell to her lap.

"A man is holding Bentley and Corman at gunpoint," she said. "You can only save one of them. The other will be shot and killed."

"Wait, what?"

She locked eyes with me. "Which one do you save? Who do you love more?"

"That's...that's kind of a fucked-up question, Cait."

"It's an unfair question, isn't it?"

"Well, yeah," I said.

"If I refuse a direct order from my prince, it means I lose everything. My career, my home. I will be disowned. My houndship—the highest honor a demon can earn save for princehood, and an honor I have spent centuries clawing and fighting for—will be stripped from me. What do I love more, all of that, or you? An impossible and cruel choice. *That* is what you are asking me."

"I'm sorry," I said. "I didn't think of it that way."

She picked up her glass again. Turning it slowly in her fingertips, rolling the golden wine around.

"If it comes to that—*if*—we'll work something out. Together."

* * *

After the Redemption Choir pitched a Molotov into my former apartment, I'd spent a while couch-surfing. Too long. Thanks to some working capital from the New Commission and apartment-hunting help from Caitlin, I'd finally remedied that.

My new place was on the east side, a second-floor walkup over a pool hall called Della's. Lousy neighborhood and Della's was a genuine dive; it looked like a great place to get your throat cut over a five-dollar bar bet, mostly because it was. That said, residency had its privileges. For one thing, Winslow's boys hung out here when they weren't at their clubhouse. The Blood Eagles might snicker when I pulled up to their line of bikes in whatever I was driving—this week, a rented Santa Fe—but they always saved a spot at the end of the lot for me. For another, Della was behind the bar most nights. She poured with a heavy hand and comped half my drinks.

The apartment itself, a one-bedroom, had been freshly renovated. It wasn't much on the outside, crumbling brick and sagging eaves, but just past my front door was a span of polished hardwood flooring and warm walls the color of oatmeal. Stained oak cabinets, granite countertops, lots of light—beyond the muffled noise from the pool hall below, a constant companion from sunset to sunrise, it could have been one of the nicer apartments just off the Strip.

"Yeah, I was gonna move in there myself," Della told me. "Then after I did all the renovations I asked myself, 'Who the hell wants to live where they work?' I spend too much damn time here as it is. Besides, I figure you're good luck to have around."

She also satisfied my main requirements as a landlord: she took rent payments in cash and kept the apartment listing officially vacant. I'd taken pains with the old place to stay off the grid and make sure nobody knew where I rested my head. I slipped up once, bringing a stranger under my roof to try to protect him from trouble, and lost everything.

And here I was, doing it again.

I double dead-bolted the door behind me, left my rolling suitcase next to it, and set the Cutting Knife on the kitchen counter. Then I rummaged through the cabinets, mixed myself a gin and tonic, and trudged over to collapse onto the storm-gray sofa. I was bone tired, and all the exhaustion I'd been staving off suddenly hit me with the force of a boxer's knockout punch. Home, safe and alone, I could let my guard down just far enough to crash in peace.

I turned on the television. Wasn't even sure what I was watching, some kind of cooking show, but I just wanted the background noise. I sipped my gin and sank deeper into the sofa cushions.

"Your picture moves," Circe said, standing wide-eyed behind the sofa. Her gown was almost pure ivory now, the bloodstains shrinking to spatters like spilled wine.

"That's a television," I told her.

She pointed. "It talks."

"I'm guessing you've been a knife for a long time."

"Stuck," she said. "First part of ritual—freed me. Second part would have bound me again. But worse."

"Like Ms. Fleiss."

Circe frowned. "Sister. Who she is now...not who she was once."

She circled the sofa and approached the television set. A Hollywood chef with a bogus southern drawl was cooking up hot wings, the camera swooping in to take a close look as he tossed the raw meat in a spice mix. Circe's fingernails plinked against the screen.

I sat up. "Are you trying to...no, you can't—you can't actually take things from inside the TV. It's just a picture."

She frowned at me again.

"My god," I muttered, "I think I just adopted a cat. Are you hungry?"

She nodded. I set my drink down—after tossing back a swig—and ambled back to the kitchen nook.

"I should have something. Just keep in mind that I live alone and I'm not a healthy person in general, so that 'something' is probably going to be frozen pizza or pizza rolls. Or leftover carryout pizza. On a good day, it's leftover Chinese. What can you eat, anyway? I'm still not entirely sure what you *are*."

"Circe," she said.

"I got that part." I rummaged through the fridge. "It's everything past your name that I'm hazy on."

"Words." She pointed at herself, frustrated. "Like...*pythia*, you know this word? Like, priestess."

I grabbed a frozen pizza from the freezer—pepperoni with extra cheese—and set it on the counter.

"Great, now we're getting somewhere. A priestess of who?"

She squinted at me. "You know."

"Uh, no. I don't. Entire volumes have been written about how much I don't know, trust me."

"But...you use the magic. I see it."

I sliced open the wrapper on the pizza, then leaned over to preheat the oven. "Yeah, but what's that got to do with anything? Sorcery isn't a religion."

"But who do you pray to?"

I shrugged at her. "Nobody in particular. I'm not much of a church-goer."

Circe looked crestfallen. "That's so sad."

"I have adopted a religious cat."

My phone chimed. I hoped it was Jennifer, Cait, anyone but Naavarasi. I checked the screen.

Caller: Blue Karma Restaurant.

"Table this discussion for later," I told Circe. "There's a very unfriendly person on the line, and I'm about to make her really, really mad at me. It's kind of my specialty."

23.

"Daniel." Naavarasi's rich voice slithered over the line. "How fared your hunt? Do you have my property? When will you be returning it to me?"

"Well, little problem there. Do you think there might have been something you forgot to tell me about the knife? Just a tiny detail, maybe?"

She hesitated, cagey. "Did I?"

"Yeah. Like, maybe how the knife is a *she*, not an *it*?"

The line went silent. I was about to check the connection, thinking she might have hung up, when Naavarasi spoke again.

"You woke it up."

"Not deliberately, I was just in the right place at the right time to see it happen. You knew, didn't you? You knew that 'knife' was a living thing. And you were gonna let me hand her over like a piece of property, none the wiser."

"It makes no difference," she said. "It *is* a piece of property. Bring it to me. Now."

"I say again, *her*. Her name is Circe, by the way, and she's—" I shouldered the phone. Circe was hiding behind the couch while a chainsaw-wielding madman rampaged on the television screen. "It's just a picture, Circe. It can't hurt you. And that's all special effects."

"*She* is my property," Naavarasi said.

"Huh, no, I was about to say she just figured out how to change channels—good, Circe, just leave it on the cartoon for now, okay? That's probably safest."

Circe pointed at the screen. "Talking ponies."

"Yeah, good choice. Stick with that." I put the phone back to my ear. "Look, we're back to my first offer. You want me to pull a heist, steal something pretty for you, something expensive, or something pretty expensive? I can do that. But you're not getting Circe."

"And why not?"

"Are...are you for real? Are you seriously asking me that question? Because she's a living, breathing, hu—well, she looks human, jury's out on that, but the point stands."

"I am a baron of hell, Daniel. I have every right to own chattel."

"And if we were *in* hell," I said, "you could take me to court and win. But this is twenty-first-century America and the law's on my side here."

Naavarasi snorted. "Speaking to me of laws? You are a thief and a murderer."

"True. And a decent card player, a fair hand as a cocktail mixologist, and—I like to believe—a considerate lover, but nobody ever brings *those* things up when they're trying to push me into doing something shitty. I have to draw a line somewhere, okay? And this is where it stands."

"You forget," she said, "that your precious twenty-first-century America is nothing but a colony of the infernal courts. *All* are subject to the laws of the Cold Peace. Pay your debt to me."

"I'm trying to. The way I see it, you've got two choices."

"Do tell."

"Option one," I said, "you can take my counteroffer. Pick another score, and accept whatever I steal for you as a fair payment for what I owe. We shake hands and everybody walks away happy. Option two, you complain to Prince Malphas, it turns into a big political mess, I find a way to wriggle out of it—and you know me, you *know* I will find a way to wriggle out of it—and you get nothing. C'mon, Naavarasi, be reasonable. Take the deal."

Her voice was a gust of winter wind in my ear.

"I will take what is rightfully mine, Daniel. And I will *not* be denied."

She hung up on me. The stove beeped, letting me know it was nice and hot. I set the phone down and went looking for my oven mitt.

* * *

I was a little worried that Circe couldn't eat any of my food—I wasn't sure what constituted an edible diet for a being who could transform into an inanimate object—but she laid that to rest right away. She jammed half a pizza slice into her mouth, chewing fast and sliding the rest in as she swallowed.

"Might wanna slow down," I said. "Don't want to get an upset stomach."

She snatched up a second slice. "More singing ponies."

"Huh?" I looked at the TV. "Yeah, sure, watch whatever you want."

I'd barely touched my slice. Naavarasi wanted to do things the hard way, so we were going to do things the hard way. I'd managed to make an enemy of a woman who could look and sound exactly like anyone in the world, at any time, on a whim. My one advantage was that after the first time she got the drop on me, posing as my ex-girlfriend, I'd trained myself to sniff out her magical signature. But that wouldn't stop her from fooling other people. Like, for instance, by changing into *my* shape and going on a public shooting spree. Or something more subtle, like turning my friends against me, or against each other. There weren't many limits to the damage a creative shape-shifter could do.

I supposed I did have one other edge: Naavarasi wasn't a rocket scientist. She wasn't stupid by any means, far from it, but her ego was bigger than her brains. She couldn't *not* show off. She was like a stage magician who performed incredible feats of illusion, then insisted on spoiling the tricks step by step so you could marvel at how clever she was. She starved for praise and the spotlight.

Which more or less meant she could come at me and do some real damage, but at least I knew she'd brag about it afterward and let me know exactly what she'd done.

Another call came in. I braced myself, expecting round two. Instead, it was an entirely different pain in my ass on the line.

"Detective Kemper," I said. "Always a pleasure."

"The hell did you do to that Malone guy? The ink dealer?"

I pushed my plate aside. My appetite was dead and buried.

"Me? Nothing, I just got back into town a few hours ago. What happened to him?"

"He stormed into the Metro substation over on West Sahara and demanded to be locked up. Said he wanted to revoke his own bail."

"That's a new one," I said. "Any idea why?"

"He said he was being followed. He figured the guys he

worked for, back in New Mexico, sent somebody to shut him up for good."

I slapped my palm against my forehead. Jennifer had said she was going to have Malone tailed. Whoever she sent was probably about as subtle as a tuba in a string quartet.

"What'd they tell him?" I asked.

"To take a hike. The desk sarge pegged him for a loony, and she didn't want to deal with it. Lemme guess: those were your guys shadowing him, weren't they?"

"Friends of a friend. Don't worry, I know where Malone is staying. I'll swing around and tell him to stay cool."

"Just make sure he shows up for his court date."

Gary hung up. I had another reason to check on our friendly local ink dealer. By now, Dr. Nedry would have reported back to his bosses in the Network—assuming it actually existed and everything he told us hadn't been a pile of bull—and they knew Vegas was going after their drug pipeline. They also knew we'd gotten a heads-up from a formerly magic-roach-infested flunky. Two plus two equaled "Malone talked." If I were in their shoes, I'd either want to bring Malone in or permanently take him out.

I figured my best call was moving him to a safer location, at least until his trial. Not back here, though. I'd already risked opening my home to Circe, and that was more than enough company. Stashing him in a different hotel room under an assumed name would work. I'd just have to put a scare into him, make sure he was too frightened to poke his head outside or use the phone.

I have a few marketable skills. Scaring people is one of them.

"I have to go out for a few hours," I told Circe. "Stay put, okay? You'll be safe as long as you stay here."

She pointed at the screen. "Television."

"Yeah, just...enjoy the TV. I'll be back as soon as I can."

Normally I wouldn't recommend that much TV to anybody, but at least it would keep her out of trouble. I'd have to figure out what to do with her long-term, but for now I just had to weather Naavarasi's wrath.

I cruised over to the Paradise All-Suites. The source of the problem wasn't hard to spot: a couple of Cinco Calles, their rust-bucket car painted the same shade as their brown-and-yellow bandannas, were parked front and center in the lot with their engine idling. I walked up and politely knocked on the driver-side window.

He fumbled his Big Mac, spilling it across his lap while his buddy yanked a janky revolver from the glove compartment. I stood there and waited patiently while they got their act together.

The window rolled down. "Uh, Mr. Faust. *Hola*."

"*Hola, amigos*," I said. "I'm guessing Jennifer sent you over, to keep an eye on Malone?"

"That's right," the driver told me. "We got it covered, no worries."

"You've been parked right here, directly in front of the stairwell where he'd be coming in and out? So, basically the first thing he'd see?"

His partner nodded. "All day long. He only left twice, once to go to the liquor store up the block, once to the cops. We followed him there and back. We stayed *real* close on his ass."

I bit back a sigh. "And I'm guessing you mad-dogged the guy every time he made eye contact."

"He was eyeballin' us like a little bitch," the driver said.

I patted the hood of the car.

"Excellent covert surveillance, guys. Keep up the great work."

I headed inside, through the stairwell door and up the bare concrete steps, hoping against hope that I wouldn't have to chase Malone out the window again. I wasn't alone in the second-floor hallway. Not a resident, either: the man strolling my way was a prim, tight-lipped gentleman in a pressed gray suit. The suit said *detective*, but the alligator-skin attaché case swinging in his pale hand said *lawyer*.

He nodded as we passed. "Good day, sir."

"Yeah, you too."

Malone's door had been fixed since my last visit, if "fixed" meant applying strips of duct tape to the broken lock and fitting a new hinge with mismatched nails instead of screws. Only the best for the denizens of the Paradise All-Suites. I knocked, and the door yawned open under my knuckles.

"Malone?" I said, poking my head in. "It's me, stay cool—"

I froze, catching an all-too-familiar stench. The rotten-copper smell of spilled blood, lots of it, mingled with gunsmoke.

Bracing for a fight, I eased across the threshold. The filthy room hovered in murky shadow, the lights doused and a sunlight glow pushing against the drawn shades over the window. My eyes adjusted fast. Fast enough to see the torrent of gore—blood and bone and bits of gray matter—spattered across the bedspread.

Malone sprawled on the floor, his back to the bed, with the barrel of a shotgun in his mouth and a hole in the back of his head big enough to put my fist through. His big toe was hooked around the trigger.

24.

I darted out of the room, racing up the hallway toward the staircase. Nothing fit right about this scene, and the biggest wrong piece was the guy in the three-piece suit. I hadn't seen him coming out of Malone's room, but I still wanted a word with him.

Empty stairwell. I took the steps two at a time and burst out into the parking lot. Nobody in sight except for Malone's minders. I ran to the rust bucket and hammered on the window.

"Easy, *ese*," the driver said as it whirred down. "What's wrong?"

"Guy just came through here, looked like a cop or a lawyer? Had a suit and an alligator-skin case?"

They looked at each other and shrugged. "From the stairwell? Nobody's been through that door but you."

"Okay, how about a gunshot? From a shotgun, would have been *loud*. I'm guessing no more than twenty minutes ago, maybe less."

The driver shook his head. "You trippin', man? We woulda heard that. Nobody's been shooting nothing. Besides, even in *this* dump, locals would have called the cops if they heard somebody poppin' off with a shotgun."

I stepped back from the car, deflated.

"Okay. Thanks."

I went back inside.

Back to Malone's room, where I gave the grimy paper shutter a yank. It whipped upward and flooded the room with dusty light. Now that I could see better, I took a second look at the scene of the crime.

My stomach churned at the stench, but I got close, circling the bedspread and the body. Malone had blown his brains all over the sheets, and the damage was definitely fresh. I folded over a clean part of the top sheet, rubbing at the gore, and it smeared like raspberry preserves. Not even close to dry.

Malone's minders would have heard the shotgun go off. The desk clerk would have heard it, too, along with everyone else in the building. While I could see a few of the long-time residents turning a deaf ear—the ones with something to lose if cops came searching the place—*somebody* would have called it in. And the ones with something to lose would be poking around, trying to find out what was going down.

Nobody in the hallway outside. Nobody but me and the bland man in the gray suit.

The shotgun itself, that was another problem. Mainly because Malone didn't own one. The only gun he'd had when I rousted him the first time was the pocket .32 he'd just bought. Could he have picked up the shotgun since? Possibly, but walking around in public with a longarm—I glanced around, couldn't see a gun case or a duffel or anything big enough to hide it in—tended to draw attention.

I crouched down next to the corpse and gave it a closer look. Malone had killed himself with a hunting shotgun, a Perazzi MXS Sporter. Smooth wood stock, not a scratch or scuff on it, and a competition-quality trigger. I took out my phone and called my favorite gunrunner.

"Yeah," Winslow grunted. He must have been at the garage; in the background, I heard the squeal of a buzz saw chopping into metal.

"Need a price check," I told him. "Perazzi MXS Sporter. Those are expensive, right?"

"Hell yeah. Perazzi's for high-end game hunting. Sporter's an entry-level model, and even that'll set you back almost seven grand. You shoppin' for something new? Tell ya right now, you don't need anything that fancy for strong-arm work."

"Thanks, Winslow."

I hung up and studied the body one last time.

It didn't play. No chance Malone had anywhere near seven thousand dollars on him. His bail was only five grand, and his lawyers had gone through a bail bondsman to put the money up.

Lawyers. Like the man in the gray suit, who had managed to vanish into thin air.

Weishaupt and Associates had to be a front for the Network. We already knew they were made of smoke, that they'd been involved in the gladiator fights at Eisenberg Correctional, and now they were representing ink dealers. And cleaning up their tracks. The shotgun blast had been muffled by magic; Malone had either been forced to kill himself, or he was murdered and the scene staged after the fact. His case would go down as a suicide, a man terrified of facing hard prison time and taking the fast way out. What bothered me more were the implications.

They'd killed Malone with a hunter's gun. The symbolism there was obvious. They could have used a cheap one; instead, they'd thrown away a seven-thousand-dollar weapon, meaning money was no object to these people.

And the man in the gray suit had ways of coming and going without being seen. Except by me. He *wanted* me to see him.

I walked downstairs, out into the sunshine, breathing deep. The odor of death clung to the back of my nostrils and I fought it with lungfuls of fresh air. The sunlight seemed paler than when I first went inside. The autumn desert air a little colder. I relieved Malone's minders of their duty and walked over to my rented Santa Fe.

The car doors were locked, no sign of a break-in, but somebody had been inside. A business card was neatly tucked into the air-conditioning vent. I plucked it out. *Weishaupt and Associates. Mr. Smith, Esquire.* I dialed the number on the card.

It rang once. The voice on the other end, crisply enunciating his words, matched the man I'd passed in the hall.

"Mr. Faust," he said, "I trust we have made our point."

He hung up.

I dialed again. This time I got three loud, sharp notes in my ear and a canned recording: "*We're sorry, this number is no longer in service.*"

This wasn't the Chicago Outfit, or some penny-ante gang that happened to get lucky and recruit a hired wand or two. The Network was something...different. *The Network has a philosophy*, Nedry had told us. *It's a holy order.* The more I thought about it, the more I suspected they'd flipped the old paradigms. Us, the Outfit, the Five Families, the Cali Cartel—all of our organizations were basically working from the same underworld playbook, same way it had always been done.

We were criminals who used magic. I was getting the feeling that the Network was a pack of magicians who used crime. What they were using it *for*, what their real goals were, that was the million-dollar question.

A question I'd have to be damn careful asking. They'd sent me a warning. I doubted they would warn me twice.

I was so distracted I almost forgot about the threat from Naavarasi hanging over my head. As it turned out, she didn't keep me waiting.

* * *

Not far off the Strip, a neon arrow marked the doorway to one of the hottest clubs in town. As early as nine o'clock, with the Vegas skyline blooming hot and shining brighter than the moon, the line behind the blue velvet rope stretched all the way down the block. I wasn't a big fan of waiting around. The bouncer didn't have to check his clipboard as I walked to the head of the line; he unhooked the rope for me without saying a word, waving me through while a pack of inhumanly pretty twentysomethings groaned at my back.

"Seriously," a kid griped, "you're letting *grandpa* in?"

Grandpa. God. My fortieth birthday was coming up this year. Might as well top the cake with cyanide frosting.

If I was too old for the first floor of Winter, where dance music played at bone-rattling volume and LED snowflakes rained down electronic wall-panels, I was an infant compared to some of the guests who preferred the basement level. It was an even more exclusive club down an unmarked back corridor, invitation only, and the doorman—a hulk in a black leather apron and a gas mask with opaque lenses—sent most wayward clubgoers stumbling in the opposite direction fast. As I walked up, the bass thudded through the floor and sent a ripple along my spine. The doorman punched a string of numbers into a keypad. The door opened with a metallic *chunk* and a faint hiss.

"Hold that door," said a voice at my back.

Nadine strode up the corridor, imperious, her hair in a perfect blond bob and her lips stained cherry-red. She was dressed for the club, in a breezy top and a pleated snow-white miniskirt that used a handkerchief's worth of fabric, but my eyes weren't on her legs. I was more focused on my sudden need to be anywhere but here.

"I came as soon as I heard," she told me. "Took my private jet directly from Saint Louis. You and I need to talk."

"I'm not sure we do. Have I mentioned I'm meeting Caitlin here?"

She hooked her arm around mine, barely breaking her stride, and tugged me down the steps to the basement. We descended into the dark, the basement a labyrinth of honeycomb rooms with black walls and gold neon piping. As we walked I felt a prickly warmth spreading up my arm where her body touched mine. My anxiety fading, my heartbeat slowing. I remembered how much I liked Nadine, how much I wanted to hear whatever she had to say, hanging on her every word—

I twisted my arm and yanked it away from her, hard.

Nadine looked offended, but she held up her open hands. "I'm just trying to soothe you, that's all. No tricks. I have bad news, and I thought I'd make it easier to take."

"You know what I like about my feelings, Nadine? That they're *my* feelings. Let's keep it that way."

We stood in the antechamber. The music from above

faded into a muffled thumping, echoing in time with strained groans of pleasure from deeper in the labyrinth.

"My jet," she said, "is fueled and ready to go. I've spoken to Royce, and our previous offer still stands: we're ready to induct you into the Court of Night-Blooming Flowers, as one of Prince Malphas's favored human operatives, as soon as we land in Chicago. Royce will be waiting on the tarmac for us. We'll perform the ceremony on the spot and have it duly recorded—"

"Wait. Hold up. Take a breath. What are you *talking* about?"

"You broke your pact with Naavarasi," she said. "Not only that, but you're holding on to her property and refusing to give it back to her."

"Yeah, well, she should have told me the 'property' in question was a sentient being."

Nadine rolled her eyes. "Of all the stupid little petty details to get hung up over...Daniel, this is not the hill you want to die on. Do you even understand what you've done?"

"Sure," I said. "She's gonna complain to Malphas, Malphas will complain to Sitri, then we see who blinks first."

"You adorable child. No. That's how civilized aristocrats like myself handle things. Naavarasi, on the other hand, is a primitive masquerading as one of her betters, and doing a poor job of it. The very fact that Malphas conferred a *barony* on that miscreated creature is a constant insult to the rest of us."

"You don't sound like a fan," I said.

"She's not a demon. She has no business holding a noble title. None. Malphas was just amused by the idea of the last rakshasi being part of his court. Like keeping an exotic and endangered animal in his private zoo. *I* said if he wanted her for a pet, he should have put her on a leash."

"Do you ever think," I said, "maybe people do things just to piss you off sometimes?"

She shook her head, her brow furrowed. "Why would anyone do that?"

"Don't know. I can't imagine why, either. I mean, you're so much fun to be around."

"Get used to it. You'll be working directly under me. Now, there will be a slight cultural shift, but I'm sure you'll acclimate—"

"Nadine," I said. "I don't know how many times I have to say this. I am not working for you. Not now, not ever. I'm with Caitlin. It's kind of a committed relationship."

She stepped closer. Close enough to touch. Close enough to smell her perfume, a blend of sweet wildflowers.

"Caitlin can't save you now," she said. "Only I can. Naavarasi decided she couldn't be bothered with our traditions and our courtesies. She's jumped directly to the nuclear option."

"Which is?"

Nadine carried a slim white leather clutch. She opened it and tugged out a sheet of paper, folded neatly down the center. It looked like it had gone through a vintage manual typewriter with a couple of keys dropped. An imposing scarlet stamp, bearing a jagged glyph ringed by a motto in ancient Latin, sat below the terse block of type.

GRAY LETTER CONTRACT

Target: Daniel Faust (Court of Jade Tears, nonaffiliated associate)

Location: Las Vegas / Nevada / United States

Nature: Human / Mortal / Sorcerer / Contact CHINFO for full dossier

Threat Level: NP

Payment: Accelerated schedule / Contact CHACCT for contract annotations

I folded the page and met Nadine's cool gaze.

"You broke the laws of the Cold Peace," she told me. "Naavarasi appealed to the Order of Chainmen. Hell's bounty hunters. Unless you return her property, by midnight, the contract goes live. They're not just going to take your life, Daniel. They'll take your soul."

25.

The darkness beneath the nightclub floor, lit by streaks of neon gold, felt like it was closing in around me. The muffled thumping louder now, like a drumbeat call to battle.

"Bounty hunters," I echoed. "How can she do that?"

"By exploiting the law," Nadine said. "We're demons, Daniel. The law was *made* to be exploited by the clever and the wise. She—despite *not* being one of us, no matter what unearned honors my prince heaps on her head—is just too damn cunning for her own good. You see, she's alleging that the creature she sent you to retrieve—some sort of animated construct, if I understand correctly—was originally her property."

"Sure," I said. "She went out of her way to make my 'debt' all formal, a thing between the courts, so she could hold a political gun to Caitlin's head if I didn't follow through."

"That's the thing. She's not pursuing the debt angle at all. Instead, she's alleging that by seizing her property and knowingly refusing to return it, you have essentially stolen from her. Matters of debts and boons are almost always resolved by diplomacy, and they can take centuries to clear up. When a mortal *steals* from a member of the courts, however, that's a simple matter of direct action. She has every right to summon the Chainmen without any further discussion. It's a crass and ham-fisted tactic, and makes her look like the barbarian she is, but you aren't an official member of any demonic court. You don't have any rights of appeal, any rights of diplomacy...you're free game."

"So if Caitlin got the thumbs-up from Prince Sitri and drafted me into the Jade Tears, that would—"

"Accomplish nothing," Nadine said. "It's still a matter of a human stealing from hell's aristocracy, and making it an intercourt issue just escalates the severity. On the other hand, Naavarasi is with the Night-Blooming Flowers. My court. Bend your knee to me, join us, and Naavarasi becomes your cousin. A dispute like this, between two servants of the same prince, *must* be resolved by mediation. You'll both stand before Prince Malphas, he'll decide on the appropriate distribution of the disputed property, and that's the end of it."

"Basically like *Judge Judy*."

Nadine blinked. She tilted her head, peering at me for a moment.

"Actually...yes," she said. "Much like *Judge Judy*."

"And what are the odds that he finds in my favor?"

"He doesn't like you, at all, so infinitesimal. The point is, this won't end with your destruction; you'll return Naavarasi's property, honor will be satisfied, and there will be no further repercussions."

"Yeah," I said, "that doesn't work for me. Circe is a person, not a thing, and I'm not handing her over."

Nadine reached for me. Just a finger, curling toward the nape of my neck. I took a step back.

"One man, standing alone against the tides of hell," she murmured. "Romantic and stupid."

"I've been called worse. And I'm not alone."

"Your precious Caitlin can't help you, not with this." Her lips curled into a scowl. "You still believe she loves you, don't you? We are daughters of the Choir of Lust, Daniel. The appearance of love is simply a tool in our arsenal, a means of getting what we want. We aren't so weak as to actually *feel* it for anyone."

"We humans," I said, "have this psychological concept called 'projection.' You should look it up."

"You never opened the envelope I gave you, did you? I only later realized that they probably confiscated your belongings when you landed in prison."

She dipped her fingers into her clutch. They emerged with a small square envelope, crisp and ivory, the flap sealed with a lipstick kiss. She held it out to me.

"So I made you another. Inside, you'll find the name and address of Caitlin's *last* human lover. Go to him. See what she did to him. Don't take my word for it, take his."

I stared at the envelope. It swayed between her fingertips like the head of a rattlesnake.

"Keep it," I told her.

"Why? You think I'm lying? Well, then there's nothing to it, is there? Some sort of trick, a deception you'll no doubt see right through." She gave me a slow, cruel smile. "With the strength of your *love*. Or maybe you know, deep down inside, that I'm telling the truth. And as long as you don't open the envelope, you'll never have to confront reality."

The envelope swayed. Beckoned.

"I never thought you a coward," she told me. "If you

were really so sure, if you really believed in her, you'd take this envelope without hesitation."

I couldn't *not* take it after that. I had something to prove. To her, not to myself. I snatched the envelope from her, careful not to brush against Nadine's fingers, and shoved it into my pocket. Unopened.

"Once you see the truth, I'll be waiting with open arms. I *will* save you. And I will never pretend to love you, but you won't mind." She ran one slow hand down her hip. Her fingers traced the pleated ruffles of her skirt. "Some things are much better than love."

"I'll take my chances."

Nadine stepped back. Her gaze took me in, head to toe and back again.

"Then I'll mourn you, very briefly. Something you should know: hunters are already lining up to take the contract. Including my daughter. Nyx has never failed to capture a bounty."

"Are you sure about that?" I asked. "Because last time I was here, I'm pretty sure I heard something about Harmony Black—"

Nadine's eyes blazed, shifting to orbs of swirling molten brass as she barked at me from a mouth lined with shark's teeth.

"*Shut. Your. Mouth.*"

I pointed at her face. "And this is why we could never have a relationship together. We'd be in couple's therapy *so* fast."

A figure emerged from the shadows at the labyrinth's edge. Emma Loomis, in a prim sweater and faded jeans, looking like the picture of a suburban soccer mom. That is, if you ignored the flecks of fresh blood speckling her hands.

"The other reason is he's already spoken for." Emma put her hands on her hips. "Do we have a problem here, Nadine?"

"*We* don't have anything at all, peasant." Nadine glared at her, then looked my way as her voice dropped. "Open your eyes, then come to me. Do it while you still draw breath."

She stormed off, deeper into the maze of honeycombed chambers, her hands curled into claws at her sides. Emma strolled over, watching her retreat with one raised eyebrow.

"What was that all about?"

"Before I answer," I said, "two questions. One, are you still mad at me? And two, why do you have blood on your hands?"

Emma took a deep breath and puffed her cheeks, letting it out as a tired sigh.

"I told you to take my daughter to a safe house. Instead, you placed her in the dubious care of two elderly con artists. Melanie is doing card tricks now, Daniel. *Card tricks.*"

"I had to do what I thought was right. I'm sorry."

"Caitlin eventually impressed that upon me. And your apology is accepted. Melanie and I are just going through a rough patch." Emma rolled her eyes. "I swear. I fought in *two* civil wars, one here and one back home. I witnessed the burning of Atlanta and survived the Massacre of the Tenebrous Deeps. None of it—*none* of it—prepared me for raising a teenage daughter."

"I never knew you were a soldier," I said.

Emma stared off to the side for a moment. She wore a faint, sad smile, something wistful in her eyes.

"When Lucifer abandoned us, when hell tumbled into

chaos...many of us became soldiers for a little while." She shook it off, her shoulders slumping, and met my gaze. "Nadine, for the record, didn't. She sat in her tower and waited to jump on a winning team once the hard work was done. As she does. So what did she want, anyway?"

I unfolded the bounty contract and handed it to her.

"Apparently I'm in more trouble than usual."

Emma's eyes went wide as her finger trailed down the disjointed type. "Daniel, this is...we have to see Caitlin. *Now*. Come on, I'm pulling her out of her meeting."

"You still haven't told me why you have blood on your hands," I said, walking fast to keep up.

"Because I work hard and I play hard."

"That's really not an answer," I said.

"Sure it is."

She hammered her fist against a smooth mahogany door, then opened it without waiting for an invitation. Inside a long, narrow conference room, at a polished granite table surrounded by high-backed leather chairs, Caitlin sat with a pair of Asian men in somber black suits. Emma swept in and handed her the bounty letter.

Caitlin read it in silence. Then she pushed her chair back and rose sharply to her feet.

"Gentlemen, I deeply apologize, but an emergency has come up. Please, enjoy the pleasures of our humble establishment. I'll come and find you as soon as we're finished."

Then she held out her hand and said something in a smooth, flowing tongue that sounded like Mandarin. One of the men responded as he stood, both of them nodding quickly. They backed out of the room, and Emma shut the door.

"New friends?" I asked.

"Emissaries from the Court of the White Harvest," Caitlin said. "We're strengthening our overseas ties. Daniel, this...this has gone too far. You need to placate Naavarasi. Give her what she wants."

"I was kind of hoping you were going to tell me about some cool corporate judo you could do and make this all go away."

Caitlin sank back into her chair. She pressed her hand to her head, her other hand brushing against the letter.

"Make it go away?" She sighed. "I can't even *defend* you. At the stroke of midnight, you become a fugitive under hell's law. If I intervene in any way, or if any of my people do, it's tantamount to an act of war against Naavarasi's court."

"And the bitch knows it." Emma stood at Caitlin's shoulder, folding her arms. "She's backed us all into a corner. Separate corners."

"So, these 'chainmen,'" I said. "What's their deal? I mean, I get the basics, they're bounty hunters, but what are the ground rules here?"

Caitlin counted them off on her fingertips. "One, any ordained chainman may take on any contract. They're freelancers."

"In other words," Emma said, "even if you somehow defeat one or two of them, more will come. And they will *never* stop. Oh, and in the event of the plaintiff's untimely death, the contract stays active. So as much as we'd all enjoy it right now, killing Naavarasi won't save you."

"Two, they can only hunt their designated target, must limit any unnecessary contact with mortals, must conceal their true natures at all costs—of course—and must depart as soon as the hunt is finished. Chainmen are forbidden to directly fight each other when competing for a bounty, but any field assets or employees may do as they wish."

"These are actually guidelines," Emma said, "not rules, and frequently broken for the sake of convenience."

Caitlin gave Emma the side-eye. "I appear to have sprouted an editorial commentator."

"Do you want him to survive this or not?"

"Fair," Caitlin said. She looked back to me. "Three, the Order of Chainmen recruits from all strata of hell and every court. Their members include incarnates, possessors, occult constructs, occasionally cambion, and even—*very* rarely—humans they find worthy of admission."

"And most of them would kill their own mothers for a bent nickel," Emma said.

"And four, there's no time limit, no finish line. There are only two ways this ends. Naavarasi can retract her contract, at which point the hunt is over..."

"Or?" I asked.

"Or," Caitlin said, "the chainmen will hunt you down, slay your mortal body, and drag your soul to stand trial in Prince Malphas's court. At which point the most likely verdict, going off of centuries of prior jurisprudence, is that you will be given to Naavarasi as a slave. For all of eternity. And there is absolutely nothing I can do about it."

"So you have that to look forward to," Emma said.

26.

We went back and forth for a while, tossing ideas in the air, watching them burn to ash at our feet. I told them everything Nadine had said. Everything but the part about the envelope in my pocket, sealed with a cherry-lipped kiss.

"I hate to say it," Emma sighed. "I really hate to say it—"

Caitlin glared at her. "Then *don't*."

"Nadine has a point. If Daniel became a member of the Flowers, this becomes an internal diplomatic issue. The chainmen would have to back off, it would be tied up in the courts while we work to settle things via the usual backchannels—"

"And Nadine sticks her fingers in my brain and swirls 'em around until I'm not me anymore," I said. "Uh-uh. Why are she and Royce so hot to recruit me, anyway?"

"Because of me," Caitlin said. "Nadine despises me. Hates the idea that a 'commoner' could rise to the rank of a hound, while she was passed over for the honor. She doesn't want you. She just knows that I want you, which is all the reason she needs to try and take you from me."

"I don't see any other way out of this," Emma said.

"You hand Circe over, or you face the consequences. I'm sorry, I'm trying to be supportive, but the law is the law. Naavarasi is in the right."

I didn't buy it. I didn't believe in no-win situations, and I'd spent my entire life breaking laws for a living. This was a new rulebook, but every rulebook had loopholes. Nadine had even admitted the Cold Peace was *made* to be twisted. I just had to find an angle of attack.

In a flash, it hit me.

I tugged the glossy photograph that I'd taken from Naavarasi from my pocket, the picture of the knife with the punch tape stuck to one corner, and laid it flat on the table.

"Her angle is that I'm a thief," I said. "The knife was hers, so even though I didn't steal it directly from her, I'm still hanging on to stolen property."

"Exactly," Caitlin said. "If this was simply a dispute over an unpaid debt, which we *thought* would be her angle of attack, there'd be no grounds to summon the chainmen. Not yet, at least, not until all diplomatic options were exhausted."

"So what if she's lying?" I asked.

Emma leaned in, studying the photograph. "Do you think she is?"

"We asked Circe if Naavarasi was her owner. She didn't even recognize the name."

"To be fair," Caitlin said, "she's borderline incoherent and she used to be a piece of kitchenware. I'm not convinced she's entirely sane. Nor do we know if her memory is intact."

"What if I can prove it? The knife was in Damien Ecko's safe. If I can trace its history, follow it back...what if

I can prove she's lying, and Circe was never hers in the first place?"

"Then she'll have egg all over her face," Emma said. A tiny smile rose to her lips. "Invoking the chainmen under false pretenses? A grave offense. Prince Malphas will have to punish her for that. Might even strip her of her title and lands. She'll be lucky if the order doesn't hunt *her* in retribution."

Caitlin nodded, taking it in. "And even if she survives the humiliation, this goes right back to being a diplomatic matter. One we will win, purely by the weight of righteous outrage. You'll owe her nothing."

"And Circe goes free," I said.

"You realize," Caitlin said, "Naavarasi may be telling the truth. In which case you're squandering the last hours of your life on a wild goose chase."

"I'm confident I have absolute, incontrovertible evidence that she was lying," I said.

"Oh? Which is?"

"Her lips were moving when she said it."

Emma shrugged. "Can't argue that."

"Looks like I'm taking a red-eye to Chicago," I said.

Caitlin put her finger on the photograph and slid it across the granite table.

"I can't go with you," she said. "We can't be seen rendering any aid, in any way—"

"Hey," I said. "No worries. I got this. And meanwhile, Circe's safer hiding out in my new apartment than she is anywhere else. It's totally secure."

"Didn't you say that about your last apartment?" she asked me.

"It was, until I trusted the wrong person. And if it turns out Circe is secretly working for Naavarasi and this is a giant setup and my place gets firebombed *again*..." I pocketed the photograph. "Well, the chainmen won't have to kill me. I will literally die of embarrassment. Literally."

Caitlin rose from her chair, filling the space between us with two graceful steps. She pulled me into a kiss. Her fingertips stroked the back of my neck, and I wished this moment could go on forever.

I wished it didn't feel like a kiss goodbye.

"We can't help directly," she told me, "but stay in contact as much as you can. I'll mobilize operatives to gather information and see what we can learn about the hunters on your trail."

"We know one of them," Emma said. "Nyx."

I looked over at her, past Caitlin's shoulder. "Any chance she's secretly a cream puff who loves kittens and rainbows?"

"Oh, no, she'll rip your spine out, sharpen it into a spear, and impale you on it. Not to kill you, just to hold you in place while she twists your limbs off one at a time. She's basically a seething ball of uncontrollable rage."

"I can't imagine why," I said. "Her mom is so *nice*. Hey, one question. On the bounty notice, my threat level is listed as 'NP.' What does that mean, exactly?"

Caitlin and Emma shared a glance. Neither responded.

"Means I'm a scary, world-class badass, right?" I said. "Like, hey, watch out for this guy."

"It—" Caitlin started to say.

"Well—" Emma added, cringing a little.

"I'll take that as agreement," I said. "Okay, so, I guess...I guess this is it. I gotta run."

Caitlin put her hand on my shoulder. Her fingers curled tight.

"Go," she said. "Run swift, run silent. And come back to me."

* * *

I shouldered my way through my apartment door. My arms were heavy with white plastic bags, overstuffed and threatening to split at the seams. I heard a laugh track rippling from the television.

"I'm home," I called out, hefting the bags onto the kitchen counter. "You okay?"

Circe stood at the edge of the kitchen nook. The last of the blood spatter had faded from her tunic, leaving pristine ivory in its wake. Her eyes seemed sharper, her olive skin richer than before.

"I am well," she said. "But you carry a heaviness. I can sense it."

I was in the middle of tugging a package of Oreos from the bag. Pausing, I stared at her.

"Why are you suddenly speaking in complete sentences?"

"Television," she said.

I could roll with that. I laid out groceries, chucking a few packages into the refrigerator.

"I went shopping," I said. "I've gotta go on a little trip, so I bought about two weeks' worth of food. Two days for you, judging by how you scarfed down that pizza. It's all prepackaged stuff. I wasn't sure if you knew how to cook."

"I spent much of the afternoon watching the Cooking Channel. I can cook now."

"You're either overconfident," I said, "or an incredibly fast learner."

"Not learning so much as remembering. I parse word-symbols to unlock the chambers of my history. My past skills facilitate the acquisition of present knowledge, such as your language. Most of my memories during the time I was imprisoned, unfortunately, remain sealed to me. I was sleeping, without dreams. You asked, before, if I knew this 'Naavarasi'. I cannot say for certain."

"Duly noted," I told her. "Can you at least tell me what you are?"

"I already have. I'm Circe."

I opened an overhead cabinet, stocking it with a row of cereal boxes.

"Feels like I'm doing the 'who's on first' routine with an MIT graduate."

Circe moved closer, standing behind me. Just off to the side, watching. "The heaviness I spoke of earlier was not the heaviness of your provisions. What weighs upon you?"

"Well, when I refused to hand you over to a very bad person, I busted a deal, and now I have to pay for it. There's a lot of folks coming to kill me, and that's just the start of what they've got planned. I've got one chance to find some evidence and squirm my way out of this mess. A real slim chance."

"You don't know me," she said. "Why are you taking this risk?"

I set down the groceries and turned to face her.

"For a very long time, I defined myself by the few things I wouldn't do. Not by my virtues, because I don't have a whole lot of those. So I drew lines in the sand. I wouldn't kill an innocent person. I wouldn't pull the trigger on a cop. These were rules I set for myself, so I could look in the mirror every morning and pretend I'm not a complete bastard. You understand?"

She nodded, her eyes deep as an ocean.

"Well, lately, one by one, I've gotten shoved right

across every one of those invisible lines. Or maybe I jumped across and told myself I was pushed. Either way, I don't have much of a code left. And I am clinging—I am clinging tooth and fucking nail—to whatever moral stand I can still make."

"So you can become a better person," she said.

"No," I said. "If I honestly cared about becoming a 'better person,' whatever that means, I wouldn't be in half the messes I get into. No, it's so I can feel good about myself once in a while. Or at least not hate myself. And I do a lot of shady business, but I do *not* deal in slaves. Period. That's one line I won't be pushed across."

She lifted her chin a little as she studied my face.

"Would you like to pray with me before you go? For victory in battle?"

"I told you, I don't pray. You still haven't told me what god you're supposed to be a priestess of, anyway."

"You have forgotten your mother's name, Daniel Faust."

I turned my back on her. Went back to putting away the groceries. Bit the inside of my cheek until I tasted blood. I felt like a violin string had snapped inside my stomach.

"My mom's name was Holly," I said. "She died when I was a kid. Pretty sure my dad killed her."

Circe didn't reply. I heard her walk away, soft footfalls on the hardwood floor.

"I will pray for you, then."

She sat on the sofa and watched television. I put away the rest of the groceries.

* * *

I'd bought my ticket, packed my overnight bag. Changed into a clean black suit with a bronze silk tie.

Sorted the groceries and made sure Circe knew where everything was, what to do if a stranger knocked on the door. Now I was standing at the window and staring out at the starless dark.

I glanced at my watch: 11:59. The seconds rolled over, bumping the minute hand to land on midnight.

The contract was live. And hell was hunting me.

"I've got a flight to catch," I told Circe on my way out the door. "I'll be back."

27.

I rode into a Chicago dawn in a stiff seat overlooking the grimy wing of a 747. The sky bloomed tangerine and the sun rose like a bloody soft-boiled egg, shimmering and wet. A gunslinger's sunrise. And here I was, without a gun.

Laying my hands on some weapons was a priority. I'd spent my last fistful of cards escaping the man with the Cheshire smile, and while I could enchant a fresh deck, it'd take supplies, privacy, and time. I doubted I was going to get any. My best hope was that I'd slipped out of town under the radar, and my hunters were combing the wrong city for me. Before leaving, my last act had been to warn my family and crew to lie low: just because the chainmen weren't *supposed* to involve outsiders in their hunt didn't mean they wouldn't.

I joined a line of weary commuters trudging off the plane, rolling our carry-ons through a cold and drafty terminal where the off-white tile was perpetually smeared with fresh dirty tracks. There was always something grim about flying from Vegas to the Midwest. Flights *to* Vegas were party boats, full of bright-eyed soon-to-be winners.

Outbound flights were a splash of cold water and a few hundred empty wallets.

I stepped out into the crisp morning air, traffic rumbling under a soot-stained concrete canopy and jets screaming as they took to the sky. I waited in line at the cabstand. My cabbie was an Armenian guy, heavy-lidded eyes, short on words. He tossed my bag into the trunk with an obliging grunt. I got into the back seat.

The opposite passenger door swung open and a stranger joined me. He was twentysomething, with feral eyes and a razor-cut shock of dyed yellow hair.

"Hey, *taken—*" I started to say. Then the barrel of a gun jabbed against my ribs.

"Truer words never spoken. Hooo-ee! You're slippery as a sumbitch, but you ain't gonna outrun *us*." He slapped the Plexiglas partition with his other hand. "Let's roll, driver."

The cab pulled away from the stand, merging into traffic and heading for the freeway.

"Us?" I glanced downward. He had a .45 with inlaid ivory grips, a filigreed ornately engraved barrel, and a hammer plated in gold. A gaudy showpiece, not a professional's tool. "Let me guess: you named your gun."

His eyes flooded gooey yellow, and he leered with a mouth of jagged, razor-sharp teeth. "Au contraire, amigo! I'm Dean, she's Belle, and we are the world-infamous Gruesome Two."

He reached through the open partition and grabbed the cabbie's shoulder. I caught the flicker of a shadow passing between them. Then the driver slammed on the gas, the cab's wheels screeching and horns blaring behind us as he lurched into the fast lane. The cabbie cackled, speaking with a woman's voice.

"Forget the rest, you just got lassoed by the best. Where am I drivin', Dean?"

"Wherever's clever," he said. "Just find someplace nice and backstreet, where I can pluck this walking bouquet of sweet, sweet money."

I glanced between them. "A cambion, teaming up with a hijacker. Never seen that before. So she rides around in the back of your head until you're ready to get to work."

"You never seen it before because we are unequaled and undefeated," Dean told me. "Twelve confirmed kills, including two green-letter contracts. We slice 'em and dice 'em—"

"And bag 'em and tag 'em!" his partner crowed.

They were chatty. That was good. They were sloppy. Even better. Dean kept his showboat of a gun trained on me, but every time he talked to his partner he couldn't help turning his head to look at her. I could use that. Right now, though, the cab was red-lining at eighty-five miles an hour, carving through freeway traffic like a reaper's scythe. Brakes squealed and a semi's air horn boomed behind us as Belle swerved into another last-second lane change. I swayed in my seat, unsteady. So did Dean, the muzzle of the gun slipping a little before he leveled his grip.

"I have to ask," I said, "how'd you find me?"

"Client told us," Belle said.

Dean turned his head again at the sound of her voice, but he was right back on me a second later. "Didn't say why, but she knew you were gonna be here. I said to Belle, partner, you *know* early bird's gonna get that worm."

That was the best news I'd heard all morning. Not the fact that Chicago was about to be flooded with demonic bounty hunters, that part I could do without. But if Naavarasi knew I was coming here, she'd have to know why: that I was chasing down the history of the knife, and looking for proof that she never owned it.

And if she was worried about that, there was a damn good chance I was on the right track.

The cab rocketed down an off-ramp, cornering so hard we almost went up on two wheels. Dean's hand swayed again. If I could get his partner talking, make him turn his head and time my move just right...

"So what are you waiting for?" I asked.

"Just lookin' for a cozy spot to park," Belle said. "The human soul only lingers with the body for about a minute after the moment of brain death, give or take."

Dean leered at me. "Gotta scoop that sucker out and bottle it just right for delivery. It's a complicated process, amigo! Not for amateurs!"

"Did I mention we're the best?" Belle added.

"Really?" I asked. "Then how come I've never heard of you?"

In the rearview mirror, I watched the possessed cabbie frown. We sped up, just a little. Belle's foot got heavy when she wasn't happy.

"'Cause you're plum ignorant," she said. "If you weren't, you wouldn't *be* in this situation, now would ya?"

"You tell him," Dean said, his head on a swivel.

"Sure, sure," I said. "Hey, I know what it's like. You're new to this game, you're up and coming. Sure, the real stars like Nyx keep rubbing their success in your faces, but you've got spirit. You'll be successful someday."

"Oh he did *not*," Belle said, jaw hanging wide. The needle started to climb. Thirty-five, then forty, as we barreled down a suburban side street. Industrial sprawl loomed ahead, rows of parked semis and faceless corporate buildings like dirty white bricks.

"I will slap that name right outta your mouth," Dean told me. "Ain't nobody better than the Gruesome Two, and when you get to hell, you can tell everybody who sent ya."

The road kinked up ahead. A mandatory hard left. I glanced down at the gun and judged the distance, adrenaline kicking in like a hot wire in my veins.

"I don't know about that," I said. "I'd be too embarrassed to say I got taken down by a couple of amateurs. I think I'll just tell everyone that Nyx killed me."

Belle swung the steering wheel. The cab's tires screamed and Dean leaned hard against the passenger door, his gun hand wriggling an inch to the left. "You son of a *bitch*—" Belle shouted, and he looked her way like a dog at the sound of his master's voice.

I shoved his wrist and grabbed his elbow with my other hand, twisting hard. He pulled the trigger a half-second too late. The .45 boomed and the bullet punched through the divider, hot lead scoring the side of the cabbie's scalp and spraying blood across the Plexiglas. Belle shrieked and fell against the wheel, stomping the gas.

The cab lurched, swaying like a drunken rhino on a rampage, as Dean threw himself onto me. Acrid drool leaked from the cambion's broken teeth, spattering my face as we wrestled for the gun. It fired again, the round tearing into the back of a seat, and my ears rang like I was a hundred feet underwater. Then the vinyl seat dropped out from under me and the world went sideways as the cab plowed into the side of a parked semi. I saw flickers of shattered glass and blood droplets flying, heard the screaming of steel and the gunshot *whump* of airbags. I rolled, hit the front seats, fell to the floor on top of Dean. Wedged between the seats and stunned, he didn't have room to aim. I put all my weight on his hand, shoving down, and heard his wrist snap. He let out an ear-piercing shriek and I ripped the .45 from his spasming fingers. Then I flipped it around and put two bullets in his face.

He stopped screaming. Or maybe I just couldn't hear it, my tortured eardrums reducing the entire swimmy world to distant echoes.

I shoved open the taxi door. Got out, took one step, and collapsed to the street.

I had to remember how to stand up again. It took a while. The world kept slipping out from under me, icy-slick, like a bad dream where the laws of physics turn traitor. My head throbbed and my shoulder was a bruised and bloody mess, open cuts oozing and plastering my dress shirt to my back. My tie hung loose around my neck, a designer hangman's noose.

I hauled open the dented wreck of the driver's door. The cabbie was dead, pinioned between the seat and the airbag, looking like a human piñata. Belle must have taken off. A hijacker without a body to possess can't hang around for long—they get sucked back to hell where they belong—but they tend to come back like a bad rash. I shoved the corpse's leg aside and tugged the trunk-release lever.

I got my rolling suitcase out of the trunk, tossed Dean's ivory-gripped .45 inside, and started limping. No direction in particular.

About a quarter mile down the road, I passed a couple of guys unloading a truck. They looked at me like I had two heads. "Morning," I said. "Out of curiosity, where am I?"

"Franklin Park," one said.

"And if I wanted to be in Chicago instead?"

They looked at each other. One shrugged. The other pointed.

"Train station's about a mile that way."

"Much obliged," I told them. I kept walking.

At least I had time to think while I waited for my ears to stop ringing and my left knee to stop threatening to buckle with every step I took. Back before we crossed swords, Damien Ecko had run a pawn service for the Chicago underworld; he'd hold on to hot goods that were difficult to sell, like stolen artwork, in exchange for short-term loans to drug dealers. The dealers would purchase product with his money, sell it on the street for a quick profit, then buy the collateral back from Ecko.

Stolen being the keyword there. I didn't need to figure out which luminary of the Chicago dope scene had held the knife last. Naavarasi's photo showed me that once upon a time, before it became a bargaining chip for gangsters, the knife had been safe and snug in a museum display case. If I could figure out which museum and when, that'd give me a powerful lead on tracing its history.

Fortunately, when it came to antiquities of the ancient world, I knew a local authority.

28.

I knew I should have felt more or less safe as I climbed the towering steps of the Field Museum, suitcase thumping at my side. The chainmen might know I was in Chicago—at least some of them—but catching an expected arrival at the airport was a lot easier than finding one man in a city of almost three million. If the other hunters didn't have magical means of tracking me down, escaping Dean and Belle had bought me a little time. I also didn't think anyone would take a shot at me in the middle of a crowd. All the same, I felt like I had a target on my back.

Mammoth Ionic columns rose up at the top of the museum steps, and fifty-foot banners dangled between them, advertising the latest traveling exhibit. Vikings, this month, and I stared up at the prow of a longboat plowing through an icy sea. A cold wind mussed my unkempt hair, a greeting from November. An early winter was coming. I hoped I'd live long enough to see it.

I wasn't thrilled to find the museum lobby mobbed by pint-size kids. Apparently it was a field-trip day, and half the elementary schools in Chicago were here. I had to keep moving. Like I said, I didn't *think* my hunters would take a shot at me in public, but I'd only met two so far and they had seemed crazy enough to try. I wasn't going to risk these kids' lives on a bad roll of the dice. I waded through the horde on my way to a rendezvous with Sue.

Sue, the reconstructed T. rex fossil, reared up on her pedestal. Forty feet of skeletal dinosaur fury, her tiny arms clawing at the crowd as tourists snapped pictures.

"The Order of Chainmen's members include incarnates, hijackers, cambion, and the occasional human," I muttered under my breath. "No dinosaurs. I'm safe."

"You are most certainly not," Dr. Halima Khoury said, striding up to meet me. Her almond face, ringed by a powder-blue headscarf, fixed me with a dour stare. "Come with me. We have to get you behind closed doors."

"Good to see you too, Doc."

"Don't be flippant." She lowered her voice as she hustled me to a side door. "Hired killers on your heels, and you came *here*? There are innocent people here, Daniel."

She punched a code into a keypad next to a door marked Employees Only. Her fingers fumbled. Halima shot a death glare at the pad as a red light flickered. She got it on the next try, pulled open the door and pushed me inside.

"I wouldn't have come if I didn't have to," I told her. "I'm sorry. I'm in a bind."

She sighed. "I know. And Dances is on her way; she's picking up the items you requested."

"Good. I need to arm up. All I've got is a gun with four bullets, and it's a really embarrassing gun."

Halima led me down a sterile white hall under harsh lights, and into her office. It was a cluttered little bolt-hole barely big enough for a desk and two chairs, the desktop piled with papers, folders, and a leaning tower of musty old hardcover books. The clamshell of a laptop computer sat skewed off to one side. She squeezed behind the desk and motioned to one of the visitor's chairs. Then her eyebrows knitted.

"I shouldn't even care," she said, "but...how embarrassing?"

I unzipped my carry-on and tugged out Dean's pistol, showing off the gold-plated hammer and ivory grips. Now that the gun wasn't being pointed at me, I got a good look at the engravings along the barrel. One side read *Certified* in calligraphic script. The other read *Badass*.

She leaned over the desk, eyebrows raised, then sat down again.

"I think I'd almost rather go unarmed."

"Right?" I put the gun away. "I'm not sure who I blame more here: the person who requested it, or the smith who actually did the job."

I passed her the photograph of the knife. She opened her top desk drawer and fished out a slim pair of reading glasses, slipping them on. Her finger trailed over the tape stuck to the corner of the photo.

"I don't recognize this as any kind of standard filing number," she mused, "probably an in-house thing, unique to that museum. Can't tell the location by the case the knife is in...let me check online."

"I tried Googling 'stolen Aztec dagger' and struck out."

She chuckled and opened the lid of her laptop.

"We can be a bit more precise than that. Interpol and the FBI both maintain a database, viewable by the public, of stolen art and archaeological relics. The FBI's is a bit more robust, but we'll try both. There's also the Art Loss Register, private service, but the museum has a subscription and they've got half a million items in their database."

"Half a million?" I asked. "Art theft is that big a problem?"

"When you say 'art theft,'" she told me, "most people think of grand museum heists from the movies. *The Thomas Crown Affair*, that sort of thing. But there are countless thefts from private collections, antiquities stolen in transit, staged robberies for the purpose of defrauding insurance companies...by and large these crimes go under-investigated by the authorities, because they're considered victimless."

"Sounds like I should get in on this action."

If looks could kill, Halima would have claimed the bounty on my head. I held up my hands.

"Kidding, just kidding!"

"For the sake of peace," she said as she turned to her laptop screen, "I'll pretend you are, even though we both know better."

A knock sounded at the door, half a second before it swung wide. Fredrika Vinter, queen bee of the Chicago occult underground, swept in with a sequined tote over one shoulder and a jet-black plastic bag dangling from one casually curled finger.

"*Dahling*," she swooned, leaning in to throw an arm around my shoulder and peck my cheek. Her lips were cold as ice.

"Hey, Freddie, thanks—I hope it wasn't too much trouble."

She passed me the plastic bag and I opened it on my lap. Everything I needed was inside: a few tiny bottles of oil, a packet of dried herbs, and a brand-new deck of cards. Red Bicycle Dragon Backs, my favorite brand.

"It nearly was. I stopped by the Hermetic Inquiry in Wicker Park—Trevor is a tedious little pill of a man with the fashion sense of a naked mole rat, but he does stock the good stuff. As I was leaving, a rather striking young woman was coming in. More black leather than a fetish club on Friday night."

I winced. "Lemme guess. Tall, seriously Nordic, blond braid down to the base of her spine? Never says the word 'I'?"

"That's her." Freddie snapped her fingers at me. "'This one' wanted to speak with Trevor. 'This one' wanted to know if any out-of-towners or unusual customers came by that morning."

"Did he rat you out?"

Freddie pulled back the chair beside me and snickered as she dropped into it.

"Are you kidding me?" she said. "He knows I'd eat him. I would literally eat him. Only reason I haven't done it by now is because I suspect he's as tasteless as his wardrobe."

Halima was typing away, concentrating on her screen. "Show Dances the gun," she murmured.

I showed her the gun. Freddie gaped at it, slowly shaking her head.

"Someone paid money for that," she said. "You killed them, right? Please tell me you killed them."

"Here we go," Halima said. "Found a hit in the FBI's database."

She turned her laptop around to show us. The dagger on the screen mirrored mine, with a picture taken at a slightly different angle.

"'Incident Type: stolen,'" I read aloud. "Doesn't really tell us much, does it?"

Halima held up a finger and scooped up her desk phone, dialing fast.

"Yes, good morning," she said. "This is Dr. Khoury with the Field Museum in Chicago. Would it be possible to speak to someone regarding an item in the National Stolen Art File? We've been approached by a benefactor about a large estate donation, and I believe one of the objects in the lot *might* be stolen, but I need more information to be sure."

"My BFF," Freddie said, "has *skills*."

Halima put the phone against her shoulder and whispered, "They're having someone call me back. This may take a while."

I held up the black plastic bag. "I need to arm up. Don't suppose there's a broom closet or something around here where I can be guaranteed a few hours of privacy?"

"Given that there are people coming to murder you," Halima said, "I don't think anyone can offer that guarantee at the moment."

Freddie stood up and offered me her hand.

"*I* can. Time to get my favorite thief off the grid."

* * *

Cruising the city streets in a lipstick-red Ferrari wasn't my idea of keeping a low profile. We rolled into the Fulton River District on the edge of downtown, northwest of the Chicago Loop. The neighborhood used to be a warehouse district, but time and new money had sanded down the rough edges. Now the warehouses had become condos, retro-styled towers offering skyline views for as much as a million dollars a pop.

"We're going to your place?" I asked her.

Freddie smiled out at the city with her eyes shrouded

behind black Aviators, her hands resting easy on the Ferrari's wheel.

"Oh, no. I love you, darling, but at the moment you're hot in all the wrong ways. I've got someplace much more private in mind. And less likely to be attacked. I have some very expensive *objets d'art* in my loft, and I'd prefer they not be riddled by gunfire."

Our final destination was one of the few real warehouses left in Fulton, a crumbling brick fortress at the river's edge. The Ferrari eased around back, down a narrow wooden-fenced alley, and Freddie tapped a remote clipped to the sun visor. A steel garage door thrummed as it rolled upward. We drove inside, parking in a small garage. The place was stripped down and anything but stylish. The garage door clanged shut as I got out of the car, and overhead fluorescents flickered to life.

"Consider yourself lucky," Freddie said. A key ring rattled as she unlocked a side door, leading the way deeper into the warehouse. "*Usually* when I take dates here, I'm the only one who leaves."

"Wait, you mean this is your—" I followed her across the threshold and got my answer.

Beyond the garage, the warehouse was a labyrinth. Plywood walls rose up to create a tangled maze, with no clue as to how big it really was or what was waiting deeper inside. Off to my left, a standing light shone in a small open room. The beam was cast across a surgical table, fixed directly beneath a long hanging mirror.

The table had buckles and straps. Restraints.

"The word may be out of fashion," she said, "but I've always been partial to 'haunt.' Has an elegant, gothy ring to it. Now then, you needed a cozy space with privacy and quiet. Let's see what we can do, hmm?"

A second door, locked and set with a tiny barred window, yawned into darkness. The room beyond was about the size of a walk-in closet with bare stone walls.

"Freddie," I said, "this is a holding cell."

"It's a cozy space with privacy and quiet."

I gave her a dubious look. She pouted at me.

"I'm *offering* my help," she said. "Do you really think I'm going to lock you in there and do something nefarious? Caitlin is my BFF, darling. She'd never forgive me. And also I'm fond of you. That too."

"Right." I held up the plastic bag. "I'd better get to work."

29.

Some spells require books, elaborate notes, days of fasting and mental preparation. When it came to my cards, I'd done the rite more times than I could count. The ritual gestures, hooking and unhooking my fingers, tracing patterns in the air, were all second nature now. So was the stream of bastard Latin rippling over my lips as I opened the new deck. I fanned the cards, riffled and cut them, then crossed my legs and balanced them on my left knee.

I shook a vial of essential oils, mixed to exact proportions and smelling faintly of red pepper, and dabbed it against my fingertip. Tracing a glyph on the face of each card, one at a time. The glossy pasteboard tingled against my fingers. Slowly the stack of cards migrated from my left knee to my right, one pile shrinking and the other—consecrated and trembling and awake—growing.

Time slipped away from me. I slipped away from me.

Nothing existed but the cards and the dance of my fingers, tracing patterns in oil that glowed hot scarlet in the dark. Finally, the last one joined the stack. I twirled my hand. The cards lifted, floating in the air, spinning around me in a joyous circle.

I snapped my fingers and opened my palm. The deck

landed home, gliding into my outstretched hand. *Now* I was ready for a fight.

I knocked on the cell door. Freddie peered at me through the barred window.

"No," she said, "changed my mind. I'm keeping you."

"*Freddie*—"

The door whistled open. "Fine, fine. Be that way. You've got places to go and people to see, anyway. Person to see."

"Halima called?"

She checked her phone, bringing up a notepad app.

"Let's see...okay, the dagger was stolen from the Oriental Institute twelve years ago. Never made it there, actually. It was part of a touring exhibition, and the thieves stole it—plus a bunch of other random goodies—from the cargo container at the airport."

Made sense that the crime was local. The knife had probably been circulating the Chicago underworld ever since, serving as rolling collateral. "And before that?"

"My BFF Halima, being brilliant and resourceful, found the archaeologist who led the original dig. You're looking for one Dr. Adrian Gladstone who, joy of joys, is currently a faculty member at the University of Chicago. Nobody in the world can tell you more about that dagger and where it came from."

"Can you give me a lift?"

She jangled her keys in her hand.

"Like you have to ask?"

* * *

Freddie dropped me off at the edge of campus. Halima's research, and my card-work, had taken most of the day. Now the clock was pushing past ten, the sun a warm memory, and last night's thin sliver of moon had gone full dark.

"I'll hang on to your luggage for you," Freddie told me. "Call me when you need a pickup."

"You're not coming with?"

"Darling, when you don't have a moving target on your back, I'll be seen with you anywhere. Until then, I'm afraid our little dalliances must be a *bit* more circumspect."

The campus was an odd mishmash of architectural styles. Grand Gothic arches, looking more like a cathedral than a college, rubbed shoulders with modern office buildings. The Joseph Regenstein Library was almost brutalist: a lumpy beige stone fist where narrow windows squeezed between mismatched and uneven blocks. Behind it, the new library extension was a glass-shrouded geodesic dome. A clash of times and worlds.

Just inside the door, a security guard asked for my pass.

"I'm just looking for Professor Gladstone," I said. "I asked over at Haskell Hall and they said he should be here."

"Still need a pass," he told me.

I slipped him a folded twenty. The guard made it disappear, then jerked his thumb over his shoulder. "Last I saw him, he was in the Grand Reading Room. That's the new extension; head *all* the way back."

I passed from the old world into the new through a glass-walled tunnel. The tunnel opened onto the reading room, and it had earned the word "grand." A vast room lined with silent and warm wooden tables, all beneath the steel spiderweb struts of the geodesic dome. The dome wasn't a perfect half sphere: it twisted and coiled at the far end of the oval chamber, making me think of a mollusk's shell.

A few students were scattered around the tables and burning the midnight oil, maybe ten or eleven in a space built for nearly two hundred. I spotted Gladstone right away, recognizing him from his profile on the university website. Fiftysomething, with a sandy blond comb-over and wire-rimmed glasses. He was engrossed in a fat hardcover, his face hovering a foot from the page. He didn't even notice when I pulled up a chair across from him. Then I knocked lightly on the table and he gave a little start.

"Professor," I whispered, "I need a moment of your time. Might need more than that, actually. We'll see how it goes."

"I'm...sorry?" He squinted at me, keeping his voice soft. "Have we met?"

I unfolded the photograph of the dagger and set it on top of his open book.

"You found this knife on an archaeological expedition, back in '98. Twelve years ago it went missing from a cargo container."

He tilted his head, thinking back. Then he tapped the photo and smiled. "That's right, the Teotihuacan dig! Has the dagger been recovered?"

"You could say that. So, this Teot...this place I can't pronounce. What can you tell me about it?"

He chuckled. "More time than we have, the library is only open until midnight. Are you a student, Mr....?"

"Let's just say the dagger may have been found, and I'm trying to authenticate its provenance."

"You're a museum curator?" He gave me a closer look. "No. I'm guessing a field agent for an antiquities dealer."

"Again, you could say that. Please, Professor, indulge me. Tell me about the dig. Just the broad strokes."

He shrugged, easing back in his chair.

"Well, it's a fascinating site. Not actually Aztec in origin. Teotihuacan is a Nahuatl word that means 'birthplace of the gods.' It was a vast city with a towering step pyramid, but by the time the Aztecs settled in the region, it had been completely abandoned by its creators. We *think* the builders were Toltec or Totonac, but honestly, we don't know for certain."

"So...how old is this city?" I asked.

"Twenty-one hundred years or so. We believe it was founded around one hundred years BC. Now, that said, my dig took place in an untouched and deeper strata of the ruin than most. Much of the area has become a modern tourist attraction, and you have to go far afield to get any work done. *This* spot, I theorized, was occupied by the earliest settlers, even before the city's founding. That's where we found quite the treasure trove: this knife, an exquisitely preserved jade bowl, a set of tall obsidian mirrors...clearly a ceremonial site, but nothing matched up with what we knew about Totonac or Toltec religious practices. A delightful anomaly."

"Okay," I said, "here's the important part. This dagger. You're saying it was buried in that dig site for at *least* two thousand years? Untouched?"

He smiled. "Well, unless someone dug it up, then put it back without disturbing a stray grain of dirt...yes, that's a safe statement."

I took out my phone.

"You can't make calls in here," Gladstone whispered. "This is a *library*."

"I'll be quick."

Caitlin picked up on the second ring. "Daniel? Are you all right?"

"Safe as I can manage. I'm sitting with the guy who found the knife in Mexico. Do we know how old Naavarasi is? Or how long she's been visiting"—I paused, glancing at the professor—"these parts?"

"By 'these parts,' meaning Earth? Not sure on either count. But her rights as a baron of hell began when she received her title. That was...nine hundred years ago, perhaps?"

"Well, the good professor can vouch that the knife was buried in historic dirt for the last two thousand years," I said. "That just leaves a gap of twelve years when it was floating around the Chicago underworld, and if we can buy a little time, I guarantee I can trace every minute of it."

Caitlin's sigh of relief gusted over the line. "We've *got* her. Bring this professor to me. I need him to testify before multiple authorities from my court and from hers. I'll call Royce to bear witness—he's no friend of Naavarasi's. It galls me to say it, but I may even call Nadine."

"I'll be on the next flight out. So, in regards to his safety..."

"He won't be harmed," Caitlin said. "And he'll be suitably rewarded. After all, he's saving my consort's life. Come home, Daniel."

I hung up and turned to Gladstone.

"I'd really like to know what this is about," he whispered.

"It's about an all-expenses-paid vacation to sunny Las Vegas, Nevada," I told him. "You, a penthouse suite, Michelin-starred cuisine—"

"I don't gamble."

"Feh. Gambling? Forget about it. Think of the shows. Do you like magic? Topless dancers? Wanna see magicians do things *with* topless dancers? Thing is, Professor, some friends of mine really, really need to hear about your dig, straight from the horse's mouth. You'll be paid for your time. And paid *well*."

He shifted in his chair, buckling under the pressure of the hard sell.

"I suppose I could clear some time in my schedule next month," he said, "but I really need more information—"

"Ah, see, that won't work for us. It's more like 'you and me on the next flight to Vegas.' Time's a factor here."

"I couldn't possibly," he said.

I sighed. Time for the hard sell to get a little harder. I slid back my chair and stood up.

"This is kind of a carrot-and-stick situation," I said, "and while I *prefer* to use the carrot..."

I caught a glint in the corner of my eye. Something gleaming, far beyond the geodesic dome, out along the campus rooftops.

Then a glass pane shattered, broken shards crashing down onto the polished floorboards. A sniper's bullet plowed into the table between us and kicked a confetti rain of shredded paper into the air.

30.

"*Down!*" I shouted. Students ran, screaming, throwing their hands or their books over their heads as they stampeded for the exit. Professor Gladstone dove under the reading table. I ducked down beside him, eyes sharp, looking for anything I could use. The reading room was a sniper's paradise, one vast open floor under glass. Maybe we could dart from table to table, but that was a hell of a risk. The sniper knew exactly where we were; he'd be watching through his scope, just waiting for us to poke our heads out.

"Why are they trying to kill me?" he squealed, cupping his hands over his head.

"They're not," I told him. "They're trying to kill *me*. So stay close."

"They're trying to kill you, so I should stay close?" He gaped at me. "That's *terrible* advice."

"Shut up so I can think. Please."

At least we weren't dealing with a world-class pro. A pro wouldn't have missed with his first shot. Then again, even a rookie could get lucky, and a bullet was just as deadly no matter who pulled the trigger.

My top priority had to be saving Gladstone's life. If he died, all bets were—

Howard Canton's wand tingled to life. A rippling warmth spread through my veins, pulsing in time with my heartbeat. And in an instant, I saw what I'd been missing. The common links when the wand worked—and when it *didn't.*

When I fought Damien Ecko, then raided the Outfit's fortress in the Chicago burbs, all I could think about was ending the gang war and saving my friends' lives. After that the wand went dormant until I was defending Caitlin in the drug factory in Albuquerque. Didn't help me against David Gosselin, but it sparked like wildfire when I was fighting to save Circe from the Enemy.

Powerful as it was, Canton's legacy wouldn't help me, even if my life was on the line. It only worked when I was risking my life to protect someone *else.*

I was a bad guy with a good guy's wand.

"You have *got,*" I said out loud, "to be fucking kidding me."

"What?"

I shook my head at Gladstone. "Get ready to run for the exit. You're about to see something really weird, okay? Just roll with it and try not to freak out."

"*I'm already freaked out!*" he shouted.

The wand dropped into my hand. I crouched, reaching for my new deck of cards, and scanned the library floor all around us. The students had cleared out. Perfect. Doing magic in public, especially in the age of cell phone cameras, is a good way to meet a bad end: the underground protects its secrets, and "I was about to be shot by a sniper" isn't really an excuse. As it was, I'd be paying Pixie a fortune to erase the university's security-cam footage.

I flung the cards, sending them flying, dancing in a pasteboard tornado. The wand flicked up in my other hand. The tip tracing runes, etching sigils in the air that left burning neon streaks in its wake. Now the cards burst, one becoming two, two becoming four, multiplying as they flooded the room and made a fluttering blanket between us and the glass dome. I grabbed Gladstone's shoulder and yanked, hard.

"Go, *now!*" I snapped. We broke from cover and ran for the exit. A bullet cracked to my left, punching through another pane of glass and tearing a chunk out of the hardwood floor. Three seconds later, another shot landed behind us. The sniper was half-blind and firing at shadows. We burst from the reading room into the glass tunnel connecting it to the old library, and I froze in my tracks.

Our sniper wasn't the only one who'd tracked me here. Nyx was at the end of the walkway, between us and the only way out. Snarling as she strode toward us, black leather glistening, and swinging up the mammoth barrel of a Desert Eagle. One of the biggest handguns in the world, and it looks even bigger when you're on the wrong end of it.

Nyx was an incarnate. A demonic killing machine. I'd lose in a straight-up fight, and I'd just spent my fresh deck of cards. I didn't think the chainmen would come after me in public like this, but as long as it looked like an act of *human* violence, some random shooting—

That was it. Demons were bound by the same code of silence that mortal mages were, and then some. And I already knew what trick to use, the same one I'd used against Damien Ecko.

I flipped the wand in my hand. One bone tip for

illusion, one for truth, and my instincts told me which was which. One quick slash in the air, faster than her trigger finger, and Nyx's human disguise tore away like a gossamer veil. The air boiled as she melted into a desiccated, skeletal horror. A corpse coated in insectoid chitin like plates of black armor. Her tail, segmented like a scorpion, whipped the air in confusion and rage.

"Lots of people around here, and the cops are on their way," I said. "Anyone sees you like this, you're in big trouble. What's it gonna be? Take me out and expose yourself to the world, or run and hide until you figure out how to get your human face back?"

She bellowed, a strangled screeching-cat yowl, and crashed through the wall of the glass tunnel. Fleeing into the dark.

Gladstone squeezed my arm, his knuckles white. "What *was* that?"

"I'll explain on the way to the airport. You got a car?"

"I'm parked on Ellis Avenue."

"Great," I said, "you're driving."

We raced through the Regenstein Library, distant sirens screaming in fast. We couldn't get jammed up here: if they'd take a shot at me in the middle of a university library, the chainmen wouldn't have any problem getting at me in a holding cell. We burst out onto the campus commons, running fast, heading for cold lights along a quiet, shadowy street.

Gladstone pointed at a dented Jeep Cherokee. "This is me."

He fumbled in his pocket while I watched the rooftops, searching for our sniper. Too many vantage points, too many perches, and I kept low by the side of the Jeep. I saw the faintest glimmer of movement, a warning that came too late, then the far-off *crack* of a rifle.

The bullet caught Gladstone in the throat.

He dropped to the street, convulsing, blood spurting from his neck. There were bits of his spine on the asphalt. He clutched my hand, eyes bulging, knowing he was dying and knowing there was nothing he could do about it.

The stupid bastard with the rifle had missed again. He hadn't killed me. He'd just killed my only hope for survival.

Gladstone stopped breathing. I patted him down, grabbed his keys, and jumped behind the wheel. No time for sentiment. I left the professor dead in the street and stomped on the gas pedal, screaming down the road before the sniper could get another shot off. Two blocks away, no flashing lights in my rearview, I dug out my phone, set it on speaker, and tossed it on the passenger seat.

"Cait," I said, "Gladstone's dead."

"*What?* What happened?"

"Two hunters attacked us at once. In public. The professor got in the way of a bullet. I'm gonna...I'm gonna figure out where he lives and check his house. Maybe there's some records—"

"Daniel."

"He's probably near the university and that whole place is gonna be radioactive, but I have to try."

"*Daniel,*" she said. "Listen to me. You have to get out of Chicago. Come home."

I slammed the heel of my hand against the steering wheel. "He was proof. He was proof that Naavarasi is lying. Damn it, I have to keep trying. He had to have left something behind. He had colleagues, other people who did the dig with him. If I can track them down—"

"Naavarasi tripled the bounty." Caitlin said. "You've just become the Order of Chainmen's top-priority target. The *entire* order."

I listened to the sounds of the street. The rumbling of the tires. All of a sudden I didn't have anything to say.

"They know you're in Chicago," she told me. "In another hour, they'll have every airport and railway locked down. Get out. Get out while you still can. Come home, we'll regroup, and we'll come up with a new plan."

For one rosy minute, I was leaving Chicago with the proof I needed to clear my name. For one shining second, I dared to hope. Now I was headed home with nothing but bruises, pulled muscles, and another dead innocent on my conscience.

I bought the first seat on the first flight out, sitting in the concourse with my back to the wall and one eye on every new arrival. Nobody got in my way. I almost felt relieved when the plane lifted off, soaring into a midnight sky, but then I remembered there'd just be another pack of hunters waiting for me on the other end. Up in the sky I had exactly three and a half hours of peace and quiet. The second the plane touched down, it was game on, all over again.

I knew the rules. Killing Naavarasi wouldn't stop the contract. She'd already laid her money down, and the chainmen would just keep coming at me until somebody won the grand prize. For the rest of my life.

All the same, if I had to go out, taking her with me was starting to look like a fine way to do it.

* * *

I landed at McCarran Airport a couple of hours before dawn. My ride, the rented Santa Fe, was in the parking garage. I walked fast and kept my head on a swivel. People were sparse; the tourist crowds didn't migrate at three in the morning. In the parking garage, I only had the sounds of my footfalls for company, shoe leather slapping the oil-stained concrete. I was coming up on my car when I realized I wasn't alone.

At first, it was a prickle at the back of my neck. A psychic stirring, like when you know someone's staring at you but can't spot them. Then I heard it. A giggle from the shadows. High-pitched and clownish. I peered around a parked van, looking for the source.

It was a cartoon hippopotamus.

An honest-to-God, three-dimensional, six-foot-tall cartoon, a man's tubby body with a leering hippo's head and an oversized wooden mallet clutched in its stubby paws. It was a black-and-white sketch given life, flickering as it bounced up and down on absurdly flexible knees. It looked and moved like a piece of vintage cartoon art, like Mickey Mouse in his *Steamboat Willie* days.

"Well," I said. "That's new."

The hippo giggled as it charged, the barrel-sized mallet head swinging high over its head. I threw myself back as the mallet whistled down. It crashed into the spot where I'd just been standing, crushing the stone to dust and leaving a ruptured crater in the garage floor.

31.

I rolled, landing hard on my pulled shoulder, as the hippo took another swing. The mallet pulverized the front end of a pickup truck, crushing the bumper like it was made of cardboard and blasting out a headlight.

Come on, I thought at the wand up my sleeve, *I need an edge here, have to save some really important people. Doing hero stuff.*

Nothing. The wand knew better. And it wasn't going to help.

A car swung around the bend, catching us both in the wash of its headlights. I jumped to one side, taking advantage of the distraction and getting some space, while the hippo staggered back and threw one cartoon paw over its eyes. For just a second, caught by the light, its shape sizzled like an egg in a hot skillet. As the driver streaked by—I caught a glimpse of his face, equal parts confused and terrified by what he'd seen—I got an idea.

I ran for my car. My heart pounded as I threw myself behind the wheel, cranking the ignition, watching the hippo skip merrily toward me. Taking its time now, confident—and whatever it was, it didn't seem to be aware of the "no magic in public" rule. Or it just didn't care.

The living cartoon stood in front of the Santa Fe, raising its mallet high...and the engine rolled over, purring to life. I hit the switch for the high beams.

Bathed in stark fluorescent light, the hippo froze, transfixed and shaking. Then it exploded. Thick, translucent goo, like a bucket of mucus, splashed across the hood and windshield. The goo went everywhere, painting the concrete, spattering nearby cars, leaving no trace of the cartoon monster behind.

I slumped back in my seat, let out the breath I'd been holding, and hit the windshield wipers. They just smeared the goo around. I'd deal with it. I rolled out of the garage, headed for friendlier territory.

* * *

"So, I just got attacked by a cartoon," I told Bentley.

He'd met me at the back door of the Scrivener's Nook, ushering me into the darkened bookstore. As I told him my story, he grabbed a spare piece of Tupperware, ducking back into the alley to scrape off a little of the congealed goo with the edge of a business card and take a sample.

"I'll have to run an alchemical trial," he said, "but this looks like ectoplasm."

"Like, from a ghost?"

He peered into the Tupperware. "Among other things. Ectoplasm is just the residue of a powerful mental projection. Willpower given motion and physical force. It looked like a cartoon, you said?"

"Yeah, but not a modern one. One of those really old black-and-white cartoons, where the animation was super simple and bouncy."

Bentley reached under the front counter. He took out a legal pad and a pen, sliding them over to me.

"Sketch it," he said, "as best you can. Any details you

can remember. I'll do some research and try to figure out where it originated."

I nodded back toward the storeroom door. "Why? It's splattered all over my hood."

"There are two possibilities as I see it. Either the Order of Chainmen has a six-foot-tall cartoon hippopotamus on their payroll—which would make it rather hard to *discreetly* hunt a target—or..."

He let me finish his sentence as my stomach sank. "Or it was conjured up by some world-class psychic. The real hunter. And he's still out there."

"I believe you were dealing with a tulpa. An artificially created thought-form. The practitioner creates every aspect of his emissary, obsessing over it for months, years, *decades* if necessary, in order to bring it to life. It's an extremely difficult technique, highly rare, and requires singular focus. More to the point, you disrupted the tulpa, but he can just recreate it and send it after you again and again until he succeeds."

"That's becoming a theme." I looked to the shop windows. Daylight coming. "I gotta get out of here. It's not safe to be around me right now."

The wrinkles on Bentley's forehead got deeper. He was worried about me, and he couldn't do anything to help. I knew the feeling.

"Where will you go?" he asked.

"I'm dead on my feet," I said. "I'm aching, I'm hungry, I need a shower, and if I don't get at least a couple hours of sleep, I won't be able to think straight. I'm going home."

* * *

I didn't want to go home. I didn't want to face Circe. Didn't want to confess how I'd let us both down.

The television was on. Some morning news broadcast.

Circe sat perched on the sofa's edge, half watching the show, half typing on my laptop. From the clutter of empty boxes and torn wrappers along the kitchen counter, she'd been plowing through the groceries.

"Oh, hey, help yourself to my stuff," I told her. I was too tired to put any snark into my voice. Now that I was back, safe as I could be behind locked doors and a string of magical wards, the last dregs of adrenaline in my system petered out and left me running on fumes.

"I required access to the Internet," she said, typing up a storm. "How fared the hunt?"

I slumped onto the sofa alongside her. My head lolled back. I left it that way.

"I fucked up. Had my hands on a guy who could prove Naavarasi's lying about you and he just...slipped away. Idiot with a rifle took the wrong shot, got him in the neck. Anyway, I made it out of Chicago one step ahead of every bounty hunter in hell. And now they know I'm back."

"What will you do?" she asked.

I didn't have an answer for that. I stared up at the ceiling. The talking head on the news was going on about some kind of scandal in the FBI, but it didn't get all the way through my ears. There was too much in my head to fit more words inside. My mind was a swirling soup of half-baked ideas, impossible plans, sparks of hope that sputtered and died.

"I don't know," I said.

Circe stopped typing. She turned her head, staring at me.

"I'm supposed to be the guy with the plan," I said. "The trickster who always pulls something from his sleeve, some big surprise to save the day at the last minute. Problem is, Naavarasi's a better trickster than me. I underestimated her. For way too damn long, we all underestimated her, and now...now I don't know. I don't see a way to win this."

"I'll go," Circe said.

I lifted my head, meeting her gaze. "Go?"

"To her. I'll surrender myself. She'll have to call off the hunt then."

"Do you understand what you're saying? Whatever the Enemy was trying to do to you, that thing with the blood, Naavarasi's probably got something just as nasty in mind."

"And I will submit," Circe replied.

"No." I sat up straight. "No, you *won't*. This fight isn't over."

She frowned at me. "But...you said you can't win."

I looked for a way to voice the feelings raging in my heart. The words I found didn't belong to me, but I could use them all the same.

"My buddy Paolo, he got hurt, hurt bad, not too long ago. He's alive, but he's gonna be struggling the rest of his life just to get back to anything close to normal. He told me, anything worth having is worth fighting for. His art. My life. Your freedom."

"But you can't win."

"Doesn't matter," I told her. "Anything worth having is worth fighting for. And the more you want it, the more you have to fight. That's what makes us human."

I pushed myself to my feet, one knee screaming in protest. A fresh lance of pain twinged along my shoulder.

"Don't count me out," I said. "I might have one or two surprises left. For now I need a shower and some shut-eye, so I can get my head together. I want you to promise me something. Promise me you'll stay here."

"You don't know what my word is worth, or if it's worth anything at all," she said.

"Nope. Promise me anyway. We fight until the last round. No surrender."

She stared at me, her deep, soft eyes unblinking. Then she nodded.

"No surrender," she said.

I stood under the shower jet and let the hot water pound against my back for a while. Then I crawled into bed, dragged the covers over my head, and set the alarm for sunset. When I made my next move, whatever it was, I'd do it under cover of darkness.

That was the plan, anyway. A trilling echo dragged me out of a dreamless sleep. Groggy, I reached for my phone. It was 3:17 in the afternoon.

"Jen?" I croaked, finding my voice. "What's up?"

"Might be trouble. I was shootin' the breeze with Bentley and Corman on the phone, trying to come up with a solution to your present predicament. Bentley had to go take care of a customer. Suddenly the line went dead, and they ain't picking up."

I threw back the covers, wide awake and on my feet in an instant.

"I'm on my way," I told her. "I'll meet you at the bookstore."

According to the rules, the chainmen weren't supposed to involve outsiders in their hunt. According to Emma, the rules were more like guidelines. And if *I* was hunting me, I knew exactly how I'd bait the line.

32.

I pulled into the alley behind the Scrivener's Nook, tires screeching to a stop, and hit the back door running. They'd left it unlocked. I burst through the stockroom and into the shop, bracing for a battle.

I'd missed the fight. Corman's old shotgun lay out on the store counter, and the haze of dirty gunsmoke lingered in the air. The store—dark and with the Closed sign flipped—crackled faintly with the aftermath of spellwork. Bentley and Corman were with Jennifer, looking ruffled but intact.

"What happened?" I said, rushing across the store to pull Bentley and Corman into a tight hug.

Corman snorted. "Idiot thought she was gonna strong-arm us into giving you up. Bentley hit her with the ol' whammy. Then while she was fighting his hex off, I introduced her to both barrels."

"It's going to take forever to clean this up," Bentley said, wringing his hands.

I followed his gaze. A man lay dead in the far corner of the shop, sprawled out with his insides spattered across a wall of vintage hardcovers. He was stocky, in his thirties, with black and broken fingernails. One eye, open and glassy, was runny-egg yellow. A cambion. The marks of his demon blood were already fading, his eyes turning blue, reverting back to human form as the last sparks of infernal energy in his veins went cold.

I squinted at Corman. "You said 'she.'"

"Talked like a woman. Not a *lady*, mind you. Said her name was Belle, and she had a personal score to settle."

"Ran into her in Chicago," I said with a sigh. "The 'Gruesome Two.' It was a team act: she was a hijacker, riding around in her cambion partner's head. I took her partner out, but she got away when the body she was jacking died in a car crash."

"You sure?" Jennifer frowned. "A hijacker shouldn't be able to come back that fast. Usually, once you knock 'em down to hell it takes at least a month or two to build up the juice for another go."

"Usually. Nothing about the Order of Chainmen is *usual*." I walked over and crouched beside the corpse, wrinkling my nose at the stench of rotten meat. "Anyway, either she found a victim to possess, and he just happened to be demon-blooded, or she was stepping out on her former accomplice. She probably has a string of dopes who think they're her one-and-only partner in crime, when they're just vehicles to carry her from hit to hit."

"She ain't gonna stop," Jennifer said. "We gotta pin this Belle down, exorcise her, and stuff her in a soul-bottle."

I rummaged through the dead man's pockets, looking for ID, a phone, any clues we could use to track Belle down. I opened his wallet, a thick black leather fold, and froze.

"We've got a problem," I said.

Corman gave me a gallows smile. "Stating the obvious, kiddo."

"No, an *immediate* problem."

I showed them what I'd found. A gold shield.

"*Detective* Dorset," I said. "LAPD. Belle's backup partner was a cop."

"We gotta pull a Houdini on this body," Jennifer said.

I nodded and pushed myself to my feet. "As far as human law is concerned, Corman just shot a cop. And they're not gonna take 'he was a bounty hunter with a demon in his brain and working for the powers of hell' as an excuse, not unless you're looking for an insanity plea. Okay, Bentley, run upstairs and grab all the cleaning supplies from your apartment. *All* of them. Corman, I need those extra-large Hefty bags from the stockroom and a roll of duct tape. And one of you, please tell me you've got a box of latex gloves handy."

Jennifer and I wrestled Dorset's body into a pair of fifty-five-gallon contractor bags, the black plastic bulging around his corpse. One down over his head, one up over his legs, and meeting in the middle with spool after spool of duct tape. The end result looked exactly like what it was—a dead body wrapped in trash bags—but if we did our jobs right nobody would see it. She stood watch in the alley while I hauled the body out in a fireman's carry. I tossed him into the back of the Santa Fe.

While we struggled with a hundred and seventy-odd pounds of dead weight, Bentley and Corman worked the floor with a pair of mops and a witches' brew of household cleaners. The sharp tang stung my nose hairs, like an over-chlorinated swimming pool.

There were right ways and wrong ways to make a corpse disappear. A lot of guys were serving twenty to life for doing it the wrong way. This was more on the "quick and dirty" spectrum. Ideally, we'd be cremating the body then taking all the little bits of teeth and bone—everything that survived the fire and could potentially tell tales under a forensic microscope—and scattering them across a dozen miles of open desert.

No time for that. But then again, as long as we cleaned the shop spotless, the human authorities wouldn't have reason to suspect Bentley and Corman of anything. After all, they'd never met the man before. The official story was nice and simple: Dorset came into the shop, said he was on vacation, browsed a little, and left, just like twenty other customers every day. Even if his corpse turned up later, there was zero reason to bring them in for questioning.

I was more worried about Belle coming back with a fresh body and shooting first next time. I knew Bentley and Corman could take care of themselves. They'd taught me everything I knew, about magic *and* the art of the con, but I still had to worry. Any trouble on their doorstep was my fault.

Bentley heard me thinking. He took me aside, his hand gentle on my shoulder, as Jennifer got ready to leave.

"Two facts," he said. "One, this isn't your fault. Don't blame yourself."

"Kinda hard not to. She came here looking for me."

"And she may return, or others might, in which case I direct you to fact number two: Cormie and I were getting ourselves in and *out* of worse trouble than this when you were in diapers. Did I ever tell you about the time we escaped a Bolivian jail?"

"Bolivia?" I tilted my head at him. "No. You did not."

"Oh, toe-curling story. You see, the daughter of the governor thought we were vying for her hand, when we were really enraptured by the lovely senorita's diamond necklace. Things did *not* go according to plan. So there we were, scheduled to face a firing squad at dawn—"

"Hate to break this up," Jennifer said from the stockroom door, "but the sun's goin' down and this guy ain't gonna smell any better than he does right now."

The corners of Bentley's eyes crinkled as he flashed a smile. "The point is, we'll be fine. Go."

We put the neon behind us and drove, winding across the flats under a cold desert sky. Two hours on the highway and then we left the road, bumping and jolting across rough ground, looking for a spot I knew.

"Here's good," I said. I killed the engine and got out, grabbing a pair of shovels from the back of the Santa Fe.

Jennifer dug the heel of her sneaker into the dirt. "Okay for digging?"

"Sucks for digging." I tossed her one of the shovels. "Everywhere out here sucks for digging. That's why you're supposed to bring the guy out alive, make *him* dig the hole before you toss him in it."

"Dyin' in the wrong place, then making us come all the way out here to do hard labor. Some people got no basic courtesy."

We dug. It was slow going, carving out a pit six feet long and half as deep, and my lower back was a knot of white-hot pain an hour in. We talked to pass the time, mostly about nothing, the way old friends do.

We used up all the small talk and banter, until there wasn't anything left but honesty.

"What's your next play?" she asked me.

My shovel struck a rock and twisted in my damp grip. Sweat plastered my shirt to my back, running ice-cold in the desert night.

"Thinking about going on the offense. Taking Naavarasi out."

"I thought that wouldn't stop the contract," Jennifer said.

"It won't," I said.

"Make you feel better, though, huh?"

"It would."

Deep enough. We dragged the bagged-up corpse from the back of the car and dumped him in. At least filling in the hole was easier than digging it.

"I like a good mission of mayhem as much as the next girl," Jennifer said, panting as she heaved shovelfuls of dirt down onto the body, "but it seems to me that what you need is some breathin' room. Offense is the right play, you just got the wrong target in mind."

"What are you thinking?"

"I'm thinking we make you one goddamn expensive bounty," Jennifer said. "We get all the intel we can on these 'chainmen,' and we go after *them*. All of 'em, anyone stupid enough to say yes to that contract. The ones we catch? They die slow. And we send what's left of the bodies to their pals. I say we make these guys so afraid of you that they tell Naavarasi to cram her money someplace the sun don't shine. These bounty hunters are all puffed up because they think they've got hell on their side."

Her shovel slammed down on the displaced earth, packing it tight.

"We can *teach* them a thing or two about hell," she told me.

I leaned on my shovel. Catching my breath.

"I like it," I said. "Caitlin and her court can't directly help us, but no reason they can't slip us some intel under the table. Let's flip the script and start hunting the hunters."

A giggle washed across the desert flats. High-pitched and half-mad.

I hefted my shovel like a baseball bat, backpedaling. "Car. *Now.*"

"The hell is that?" Jennifer scrunched her face up, looking around.

The cartoon hippo-man bounded from the shadows, twenty feet away and twirling his oversized mallet like it was weightless. He wasn't alone. On the opposite side, flanking us, he had a friend: another black-and-white apparition, this one a rat with button-down overalls and a wedge-shaped head. The rat's arms were boneless accordions, rippling in a permanent wave and clutching a butcher knife in each three-fingered hand.

Jennifer's back bumped against mine. I turned. A third animation bounced into view on rubbery legs, an inhumanly tall and thin circus clown with his jack-in-the-box head on a wobbling steel spring instead of a neck. He juggled a trio of grapefruit-sized black iron bombs, their cartoon fuses lit and burning down.

33.

I threw my shovel. It went winging through the open air and hit the animated rat dead center. The cartoon didn't even ripple as the shovel passed on through, clattering to the dirt behind it. Apparently these psychic projections were one-way only: we couldn't touch them, but they could touch us.

We ran for the Santa Fe. I hammered the remote-unlock, the doors squawked, and we piled in. The engine roared and the headlights flared to life just as the animated rat charged. It burst like a water balloon and splattered the sand with hot mucus. I stomped the gas. The hippo ran up from behind, swinging his mallet like a Major League batter. The car jolted sideways as the barrel-sized head swatted the back bumper, crumpling steel.

The juggling clown tossed one of his bombs. It landed square in our path and I jerked the wheel hard, veering right. The bomb exploded. My vision whited out, the car rocked and a torrent of heat washed over us.

"And *this* asshole," I shouted as I red-lined the engine, squinting to clear my eyes, "we are hunting in *particular*. I'm gonna kill him just for being creepy."

Jennifer turned in her seat, staring out the back

window at the flickering apparitions. They ran behind us for a little while, slowly falling back, then fading into shadow.

"What the hell was that?" she said.

"Same thing that jumped me at the airport when I got back. Of course, I knew immediately that it was a tulpa: a sort of psychic projection given life of its own through intense and obsessive concentration. Very rare technique."

Jennifer turned back around in her seat, facing front, and folded her arms. "So what you mean is, you were clueless, but you asked Bentley and he told you what it was."

"Exactly," I said.

"So how do we put 'em down permanently?"

"Good news is, you saw the rat: focused light makes the tulpas go pop. Bad news is, it isn't a permanent fix. The guy sending them can just make more. We've got to track down the source."

After the desert dark, the lights of Vegas felt like a welcome-home embrace. We headed for the safest place we could think of: the Tiger's Garden. I'd been warned that the chainmen had a human magician or two in their ranks, but the outfit was mostly made up of demons, and demons couldn't even find the Garden's front door.

There was also the "no fighting inside" rule. We'd never seen anyone break it, and the quiet air of power that radiated from every shuttered window whispered that it wasn't to be taken lightly. The *door* to the Tiger's Garden was on Fremont Street, but the Garden itself was...elsewhere.

We were two steps inside when Amar swooped over, ushering us to an empty table and passing out the drinks we were about to order. A Jack and Coke for me, a whiskey on the rocks for Jennifer. The restaurant was almost empty. Almost. David Gosselin was drinking alone at a corner table. We locked eyes.

"Daniel," he growled.

"David."

"*Boys*," Jennifer said. Her tone made it clear she wasn't putting up with any nonsense tonight.

I looked away and sipped my drink. "Okay, so a tulpa requires constant, hard-core focus. You have to be obsessive."

"And he's got three of the critters, at least. The hippo with the mallet, the clown with the jack-in-the-box head, and the rat with the butcher knives. They all looked like the same...style, I guess? Like the same guy drew 'em."

"And they're animated like vintage cartoons," I said. "I think that's what we're looking at. This guy found a classic cartoon, watched it a few hundred times—or a few thousand—and used his magic to bring the characters to life. So, why *that* cartoon in particular?"

Jennifer tossed back a swig of whiskey and threw one arm over the back of her chair, slouching.

"Why a cartoon at all?" she asked. "If those critters get seen in public by people who aren't clued-in, the guy sending 'em is in a heap of trouble. If he could turn any character on TV into a psychic projection, why not conjure, I don't know, Bruce Lee, maybe? Chuck Norris? Martha Stewart?"

"I'm thinking it's some kind of personal connection. Maybe it's a connection we can trace—like if the guy is related to the original artist or something. We've got to find out everything we can about the..." I paused, feeling a prickling sensation on the back of my neck, and lowered my voice. "He's staring at me, isn't he?"

"Oh yeah," Jennifer said.

I sighed. I was going to have to deal with this one way or another, and I already had too many targets on my back.

"*Fine*," I said loudly, not looking at him. "David, I will give you your hat back."

Silence. Then he replied, "And?"

I turned in my chair, facing him. "And what?"

He folded his arms, glowering. "*And?*"

I waved my hand, floundering for words. "And...I'm sorry?"

"For?"

I couldn't believe we were actually doing this.

"For...stealing the aforementioned hat," I said.

"And?"

We stared each other down. Jennifer reached over and patted my arm. "Be the better man, sugar."

"He threw *doves* at me, Jen."

I heard a faint cooing from under David's table.

"I am sorry," I said, taking a deep breath, "for stealing the hat, and that your museum got shot up when a different team of thieves came to steal the hat."

"*And?*"

I flung my hands in the air. "What 'and'? There is no 'and'! That's all I did to you!"

"You interrupted my *date*," David said. "I didn't even get those girls' phone numbers."

"Oh. My. God." I struggled not to bury my face in my palm. "You weren't on a date, David. The twins were my diversionary tactic. Their job was to get you to shut off the burglar alarms and keep you busy. Did you not *know* that?"

He shifted in his chair, his righteous glare fading fast.

"Of...of course I knew that."

"They locked you in a steel milk jug," I said.

"I just thought they were kinky."

"Oh," Jennifer said, "take it from me, they are."

We both stared at her.

"What?" She sipped her whiskey. "It was one time. I was *real* drunk."

David coughed into his hand. "I think in the interests of the greater magical community, I can show my generosity and understanding. Return the hat, and all is forgiven."

"Gee," I said, "that's swell. I'll drop it off once I'm not being chased by demonic bounty hunters."

"By the way, you're looking for *Bad Clarence*."

I blinked at him. My glass froze halfway to my lips.

"What's that now?"

"The cartoon you were talking about," David said. "Hippo-man, rat with butcher knives? Was the clown juggling bombs?"

"That's right," Jennifer said.

"*Bad Clarence*. It's not really a vintage cartoon; it was just drawn to look that way. Came out in...'64, '65, maybe? I've got a couple of animation cels on display in my museum."

"Your museum's dedicated to the history of magic," I said. "What's the connection?"

David let out a theatrical sigh and rose from his chair. He cradled his martini glass as he walked over to join us at our table.

"This is your problem, Faust: you don't appreciate the history of our art. A little study would do you good."

"Enlighten me."

"*Bad Clarence* was a nine-minute cartoon, drawn and

filmed by one man, a failed stage magician and occult prodigy named Irving Abromovitz. It took him nearly thirty years to create. It was also an absolute bomb. It screened in a few art-house cinemas to thundering boos. I've never seen the whole thing, but it's allegedly incomprehensible and very, very disturbing. Four students from a film club in Berkeley got their hands on a copy back in '69 and watched it while dropping acid. The next morning, they were all found dead. Suicide."

"This Irving fella," Jennifer said. "He still alive? We might need to have a word with him."

"*Also* suicide," David said, "the week after the first screening. He tried to skin himself with a kitchen knife. He got pretty far before the shock and blood loss killed him. The man did not have a happy life. But if somebody's using a print of the cartoon to create tulpas, they've got the right idea. That's exactly why Irving made it. The whole thing is seeded with occult imagery and symbols to boost a magician's focus. Mandalas, one-frame flickers of summoning seals...it was Irving's life's work. His magnum opus."

"I assume we can't just pull this thing up on YouTube," I said.

"You are correct. Only four copies were ever made. After the student suicides, the Berkeley reel was destroyed, and another was chopped up to sell individual cels as art prints. One intact copy went up for auction about five years ago. I put in a bid, and it was down to me and one other customer, but I tapped out when the price hit a hundred grand."

Jennifer eyed him over her whiskey glass. "You can afford that."

"Sure," he said, "but to be honest, the idea of watching

the thing scares me a little. Some doors don't need to be opened."

"The winning bidder might be our guy," I said. "Do you remember anything about him?"

"I've got a name and address," David told me. He sipped his martini. "And as soon as I get my hat back, I'm *sure* I'll remember where I wrote it down."

* * *

The next morning, I met David on the edge of town. I gave him the top hat. He gave me a slip of paper.

It wasn't a name. Well, not a person's name: the buyer was a representative from Astounding Comics and Collectibles, just off the Maryland Parkway. I hadn't set foot in a comic store since I was a kid. I was half expecting a dimly lit dump, packed with boxes of dog-eared comics and resplendent body odor.

What I got instead was a brightly lit emporium with wide, clean aisles and glass display cases, a shrine to geek culture. Blown-up comic pages lined the walls, signed by the artists and writers, and a small spotlight shone on a display of elaborately built Japanese robot models.

All the same, something didn't quite ring true. It was an upscale store, but those robot models were the most expensive things on display at a few hundred bucks apiece. I didn't see this place dropping six figures on a rare film print. I wandered the aisles, obviously a tourist out of my element, until a skinny guy wearing a store-logo polo shirt gravitated my way. He gave me a welcoming smile, his cheeks bristling with a scruffy proto-beard.

"Hey, thanks for coming in," he said. "Can I help you find anything?"

"Possibly," I told him. "Don't suppose the owner is around?"

He pointed at himself. "That's me. I'm Steve. What can I do for you?"

"I'm looking for a film—" I started to say.

"Oh, we've got you covered. Lemme show you our selection. We've got fantasy, sci-fi, horror, domestic and imports. Anime? No, you don't look like an anime guy. We can also special-order anything we don't stock. If we don't have it, trust me, we can find it—"

"*Bad Clarence*," I said.

His smile vanished.

He wavered on his feet and his gaze flicked to the door. Every sign of a man about to turn rabbit.

"I wouldn't," I told him. "The last guy I had to chase got hit by a car. And then his life *really* started to suck."

"Are...are you with the IRS?"

"No," I said, "but I bet there's an interesting story behind you thinking I might be. Tell me all about it."

34.

Steve put one of his worker bees in charge and we stepped into his office. A pair of cartoon gun bunnies in bathing suits flashed peace signs from a glossy poster over his computer. I grabbed a folding chair, sitting almost knee-to-knee with him in the cramped room.

"Are you a cop?" he asked. "God, I knew something like this would happen eventually."

"Steve, Steve, relax. I'm not a cop. What I am is an interested party seeking information. If you tell me everything I want to know, and if you tell me the truth, I'll be a happy man. I'm very generous when I'm happy."

"What...happens when you're not happy?"

I leaned in, fixing him with a graveyard stare.

"Better that you don't find out," I said. "You won a copy of *Bad Clarence* at an auction five years ago. Tell me all about it."

"Man, I had never even heard of the thing before that, and I know my animation, all right? *Super* obscure."

"You were curious enough to drop six figures on it?"

Steve shook his head. "It was a commissioned job. See, I meant what I said: if we don't have something in stock, we can find it for you. I've got a reputation in the collectibles industry for being a bloodhound. So this guy contacts me, says he's heard I'm good, and wants me to find a copy of *Bad Clarence*. I got the impression I wasn't the only person he'd hired, too. Threw down a cash retainer, five grand, no questions asked."

"This guy," I said, "what'd he look like?"

"All communication was from a throwaway email address. The cash? Sealed in an envelope and tossed through our mail slot overnight."

"You didn't think that was a little weird?" I asked.

"It was a *lot* weird," he said. "It was also a lot of cash. And at that point I was too curious not to go looking for the film. I spotted it coming up for auction and, well..."

His voice trailed off. He wore his guilt like a hair shirt.

"This is the part," I said, "that made you worried about the IRS."

"He said money was no object. I mean, he literally said that. We agreed that I'd get a five percent commission on whatever the final price came out to, on top of my retainer. So I won the auction for a hundred grand and paid it out of pocket. Normally, a buyer would cut me a check at that point—in this case, for a hundred and five thousand."

"But," I said.

"No checks. He'd only pay cash. Didn't want a paper trail. So I get another envelope through the mail slot. A hundred and five g's in hundred-dollar bills. Unmarked, untraceable. And I realized, well, nobody could prove the copy ever changed hands. As far as anybody knew, I'd bought the reel as an investment piece and I still had it."

I edged a little closer. The folding chair squeaked on the linoleum floor. My knees bumped against his.

"What'd you do, Steve?"

He cringed. "The store had a, um...small and unfortunate fire."

I couldn't help but smile. "So you collected an insurance payout on the film reel that 'burned up.' You're a clever little criminal, aren't you?"

"I'm...I'm *not* a criminal," he said. "It was just the one time—"

"I'm not here to judge. So how'd you deliver the goods?"

"He sent me an address. A coffee shop in Boulder City. This woman shows up, dressed sort of like a nurse on her lunch break. Like, wearing those—" He gestured at his chest, wriggling his hands up and down.

"Scrubs?"

"Yeah. She sat next to me, I asked if she was the buyer, and she just gave me this *look*. Like I'd stepped in dog crap on my way into the shop and was too dumb to notice. She held out her hand, I gave her the reel, and she left. Never spoke a word."

"So that was the end of it?"

He smiled, pleased with himself. "Not entirely. I followed her. I was just...too damn curious, you know? So I tailed her car to a warehouse about three miles outside town. Place was packed with moving trucks. Moving *in*. I saw guys bringing in film equipment, photo-processing stuff, projectors...and a hospital bed."

"What happened next?" I asked.

"I got out of there." His smile faltered. "The guys doing the moving? They had guns. And it occurred to me, you know—if there's no trail of the deal, there wouldn't be any trail if I suddenly went missing, either."

"Smart move." I pulled out my wallet. I took a pair of twenties, folded them around my fingertips, and held them up. "Now, to win the grand prize, you only have to answer one more question correctly. Where exactly can I find that warehouse?"

* * *

Boulder City was half an hour southeast of Vegas, a stone's throw from the Hoover Dam. A lot of small-town charm with a big retiree population, not a lot of trouble to be found.

We decided to bring our own trouble with us.

Two unmarked panel vans set out on Interstate 515. I was behind one wheel, Jennifer behind the other. Each ride had a full load; eight hard-eyed hitters from the Cinco Calles who had volunteered to earn a little combat pay. One sat beside me in the passenger seat, playing with one of the industrial-strength Maglites we'd passed out to the entire crew.

"What are we supposed to do with these things? Whack 'em over the head?"

"You see any weird shit, train your beams on it until it pops." I glanced at the GPS. Almost there. "Save your bullets for anything flesh and blood."

"Whatever you say, ese. You're *the guy*, after all."

I narrowed my eyes at him. I'd asked people to stop calling me that. I had not been successful.

Outside town, the target loomed in a cloud of rolling dust. It was a plain beige brick of a warehouse, no windows, no sign out front, and the loading bay doors sealed up tight.

"Thirty seconds," I said, glancing in the rearview. "We're gonna hit that side service entrance. You got the key to the city?"

One of the Calles held the police-issue battering ram, three feet of black steel with a pair of handle grips, between his knees. He gave it a solid whack with his open palm.

The vans screamed up to the warehouse, pulling in tight, side doors rattling open before we'd even come to a stop. The two hitters with the battering ram led the charge. They swung the steel back, then slammed it against the service-entrance door. The door buckled open under the second hit, lock snapping, and they jumped out of the way while the rest of us streamed inside.

Pitch darkness warred with flickering light, my vision blurring as I struggled to come to grips with what I saw. The warehouse was a maze of film screens of all different sizes, standing on tripods, forming cloth walls, while projectors played copy after copy of *Bad Clarence* on an infinite loop. Insane giggling boomed over ceiling-mounted speakers, rock-concert loud, accompanying disjointed piano music. On my left, the hippo-man was sawing his own skull open, giving the camera a dopey grin, while behind him, a shining sun with an agonized face wept fountains of tears. Ahead of me, at a skewed angle, the clown's head bounced on its jack-in-the-box spring. On my right, the rat with the knives was coming in fast and—

That wasn't a screen. I turned and brought up my Maglite.

"To the right!" I shouted. "Get lights on it!"

A half dozen beams fixed on the rat's face. It shuddered, wavered, and burst, splashing goo across a rippling movie screen.

We spread out, two columns winding through the maze. I heard a scream behind me, and a screen ripped in half as the hippo charged through, mallet swinging. The hitter in his sights went with his instincts and pulled his gun instead of his flashlight. The bullets billowed through the hippo's gut as the mallet whistled down.

The kid's head exploded in a spray of blood and splintered bone. His corpse fell at the animated monster's feet. The hippo was next to go, blasting apart under our flashlight beams. More gunshots, off to my left. More screams, and the sound of a projector clattering to the concrete floor. There were too many angles, too many corners, not enough light. Ahead of me, an image of the hippo opened his mouth wide. His front teeth sprouted anguished faces, crying and trying to force themselves out of his gums with tiny arms.

I had to get to the center. I shouldered a screen aside, forcing my way through the maze, and stopped dead in my tracks.

A hospital bed stood at the heart of the labyrinth, flanked by softly beeping life-support equipment. The withered figure in the bed, hooked to IV drips and tubes and a catheter, made my stomach clench with revulsion.

He had been a man, once.

His legs had been amputated at the knees, leaving cauliflower stumps. One of his arms had no bones in it. The skin hung limp at his side, his hand and fingers like an empty, fleshy glove. On the other hand, the flesh of his fingers had melted together. His face was wrapped in gauze, all but his lipless mouth and one staring, lidless eye, but from the mass of third-degree burn tissue along his neck and chest I could only imagine what he looked like underneath. The gauze was wound flat. No nose to get in the way, just the lump of an oxygen tube.

"Daniel Faust," he rasped from under his bandage mask, his accent faintly refined, English. I stepped closer to the bed to hear him over the booming piano and mad laughter from the speakers overhead.

"You've been trying to kill me," I said. "So you know why I'm here."

"Wasn't trying that hard." His attempt at a chuckle became a hacking cough. "Part of me hoped we'd meet. My name is Dustin Hall. I used to be quite the professional life-taker. Then...this happened, and I had to find another means of returning to my old practice. The world's first quadriplegic assassin."

"The tulpas," I said.

He nodded, just a little, wincing at the movement. "It's important, the doctors told me, to stay mentally active. I took them at their word. Five years, it took me, and almost all of my money. Five years of lying in this bed, drinking in every detail of that damned creation twenty-four hours a day without cease, *living* it until it became part of my soul. My will. You were my very first post-retirement bounty."

I looked him up and down, still not sure how he managed to go on breathing with his body mangled and broken.

"What happened to you?" I asked.

"You really don't know, do you?"

That coughing chuckle again.

"Caitlin," he said. "Caitlin happened to me."

35.

More gunshots echoed off to my left. Caught the sight of Maglite beams straying dizzily across the warehouse roof. "Go back to back," Jennifer was shouting. "Don't let 'em box you in!"

"They keep coming!" one of the Calles screamed. "That fucking rat, I killed it three times alre—"

His shout ended in a high-pitched shriek of pain. I looked to Hall.

"Call them off. *Now.*"

Hall's head lolled on his pillow. "Can't. Literally can't. They're a part of me, Mr. Faust. They're my friends, and you've invaded my home. They want to protect me."

I needed to end it. Needed to end *him*. The tulpas were fueled by Hall's brain. All the same, I wavered on my feet.

"What do you mean, Caitlin happened?" I demanded. "How do you know her?"

"The same way you do. We were lovers. Did you think you were her *first* human plaything? You're just the latest member of a very sad and exclusive club. And soon she'll use you up, break you, and toss you away just like the rest of us. She's...hard on her toys."

"No." I paced beside the bed and pointed at him. "You're lying."

"Oh, it was grand at first. I'd never been so deeply in love, so fast. It wasn't until later that I realized she was controlling my thoughts. Playing with my emotions, with every touch of her fingertips. I resolved to break it off. Drove to her penthouse with every intention of dumping her. Two hours later I was down on one knee, proposing marriage."

Hall's laugh was a bitter, choking rasp.

"She said no. She wasn't ready. Can you imagine that, Mr. Faust? The sick, sadistic bitch actually made me *propose* to her, just so she could turn me down. Then, just to make sure I wouldn't stray again, she kissed me. The *real* kiss, the heroin kiss, the one that turns your insides out and makes you willing to knife your own mother just for one more hit."

"Danny!" Jennifer shouted. "Where are you? We're cornered back here and we need help *now!*"

"Oh, the things I could tell you about your dear, beloved Caitlin," Hall hissed. "The filthy secrets I could share—"

"Danny, *please!*" Jennifer screamed.

I yanked the pillow from under Hall's head and shoved it into his face. I leaned in with all my weight, smothering him, as his body bucked and shook. It wasn't hard. He couldn't fight back, not with his tortured flesh, not anymore. He gave one last twitch and fell still.

The gunshots and the screams went silent.

* * *

It was quiet on the ride back to Vegas.

We'd raided Hall's hideout with sixteen men. We were coming back with twelve. Three of them were in the other van, critical, being rushed to Doc Savoy's for a patch-up job. After the things we'd seen in that warehouse, nobody was in the mood to talk.

That suited me just fine.

I dropped everyone off, ditched the van, and headed home. There was something I had to do, and I didn't want to do it.

Circe was watching television. She looked over as I came through the front door. "Victory?" she asked.

"Pyrrhic victory," I said.

I walked into the bedroom and opened my top dresser drawer. Found what I was looking for, right where I'd tossed it.

Nadine's little white envelope, sealed with a cherry-lipstick kiss.

I tore the flap open and slid out the card inside. Nadine's "gift" to me, the identity of a man who could supposedly prove that Caitlin had been manipulating me since the moment we met.

Dustin Hall, read Nadine's delicate handwriting. *Boulder City, Nevada.*

"I have to go out," I told Circe on my way to the door. "Don't wait up."

* * *

Caitlin met me at her penthouse door. She cradled a fresh glass of Chianti. Expressions flickered across her face, relief and pleasure and worry, like she was deciding which mask to wear for me.

"Daniel," she said. "I'm pleased to see you alive and intact, but you really shouldn't *be* here. We can't give Naavarasi any grounds to claim our court is aiding you—"

"It's important," I said. "We need to talk."

She welcomed me in. Her living room was an expanse

of polished hardwood and black leather under sleek track lighting. An original Nagel painting hung over her sofa. She had her stereo on, a Duran Duran album playing low and soft.

"We just took down another one of the chainmen," I told her.

"That's appealing news," she said. Her back to me, walking toward the kitchen. "I'll get another glass. We can celebrate—"

"His name was Dustin Hall."

The glass slipped from her fingers.

It shattered on the floor, crystal rupturing, irreparable, dark red wine splashing across the wood like heart blood.

She turned to face me.

"I smothered him with a pillow," I said. "He's dead now. But we talked a little first."

Caitlin wore a poker face now. Nothing slipping out past the icy prisons of her eyes.

"Did you?" she said.

"Funny you never mentioned him before."

"I haven't mentioned most of my lovers. I've been alive for centuries and I'm a daughter of Lust; I've had quite a few. You *know* that. It's never been an issue before."

"Generally it isn't," I said. "Except when I find out one of your former lovers was tortured and mutilated to the point he barely looked like a human being anymore, and he says you did it to him, I get a little concerned."

I didn't want to say the other thing. It took me a minute.

"When he says you used your powers on him to control his mind, and he didn't even know you were doing it at first...I get a little concerned."

Caitlin took a step toward me. Just one step.

"I broke him," she said. "I took great pleasure in it. I'm assuming he didn't tell you why, though. Funny thing about stories. They tend to have two sides."

"I'm all ears."

"Dustin was obsessive. Jealous. You—at least, before now—never cared about my past or where I'd been before I was with you. He was the exact opposite. And every moment I wasn't at his side, in his sight, he was convinced I was visiting a retinue of lovers behind his back. He actually proposed marriage to me, without understanding or even asking what that means to my people, to my culture."

"He said you made him do it."

Caitlin's eyes narrowed. "The moon is purple. Look out the window. Is it true? I just said it, so it must be. Or do you only believe in deathbed confessions from homicidal maniacs?"

"How did he end up...like he did, Cait?"

"His jealousy," she said, "reached a boiling point. He decided that the only way he could guarantee my faithfulness was to bind me with magic. To strip me of my free will and turn me into a slave. I've told you before, my people become very, very frightened when our freedom is threatened. We lash out."

The crystal stem of her fallen glass cracked under her heel. She paced the living-room floor, slow, a lioness in her den.

"I didn't want to believe it when I caught him making the preparations. Researching my true name, the seals of my lineage, tokens to bind and compel me. I spent a month in abject denial. And then...then he lured me into a trap. An imperfect one. I wept when he told me why he'd done it. I wept for him, for us, for the consequences of his madness."

"And then?" I asked.

She stopped pacing. She turned to meet my gaze.

"And then I punished him. I ravaged his flesh and his mind with every means at my disposal, every new agony carefully layered atop the last, but leaving him alive. Leaving him alive to spend the rest of his mortal years contemplating what he'd done. Now that you've sent him to hell...well, I imagine one of my sisters is greeting him at this very moment. Preparing him for a refresher course in pain. His screams will begin anew, and they will never cease. They will never cease until I grow bored of hearing them. And that won't be anytime soon."

She closed the gap between us. She studied me, faint glitters of molten copper swirling in her eyes.

"Daniel," she whispered. "Did you forget what I am?"

"Never," I whispered back. My throat suddenly bone-dry.

"You have a question. Ask it. Let there be nothing but honesty between us."

I'd never been so deeply in love, so fast, Hall had told me.

I remembered standing at the mouth of the storm tunnel, after sending Stacy Pankow's wraith to hell. Caitlin's hand curled in mine.

I'm not sure what there is to celebrate, I'd said.

Us, she'd replied. *Us, and today, and tonight, and tomorrow.*

I remembered the Ring of Solomon. The most powerful relic on Earth, a tool that could bind and enslave demons with nothing but its bearer's will. I remembered holding it in my clenched fist, contemplating my future. For one moment, I saw something I thought had been lost to me forever: the possibility of redemption. I could have become the champion of humanity, a warrior against darkness, an unstoppable threat to the powers of hell. I remembered looking at the ring, deciding what mattered most to me.

I remembered throwing it away. Watching it tumble into a starless void.

"Caitlin," I said softly, "I need to know something. And whatever you tell me...whatever you tell me, I'll believe you. I promise I'll believe you, and that'll be the end of it. I'm sorry. I shouldn't have to ask, but I need...I need to hear you say it."

"Ask me," she said.

"Have you ever used your powers on me?"

She thought about it. Then she nodded.

"Yes," she said.

36.

I had expected a denial. I had expected a rebuttal. I had expected anything in the world but *yes*. I felt the ground sliding out from under my feet, pitching me toward a yawning abyss. Nothing to hold on to. No safe harbor. Not even in Caitlin's arms.

"Yes?" I echoed. Part of me hoping I'd somehow misheard her, that she'd correct me.

"Yes," she said. "And I'm sorry. I never wanted to have this conversation. I hoped—vainly, foolishly—that it might never happen. But it was always going to, eventually, and we might as well have it now. Yes, Daniel. I have influenced your mind."

"When?" The word came out as an uneven croak. I was having trouble finding my breath.

"The night you freed me," she said.

For a heartbeat I was back in Artie Kaufman's kitchen. Artie was dead. The parts of him that Caitlin hadn't eaten, spending slow hours torturing him to death while I watched, trapped in my circle of salt, were splattered across the cabinets and the floor. Artie's cop buddy was slug-belly pale, down on the linoleum with his hand cut off and his neck snapped.

The circle was a ruse. Powerless. Caitlin had slid her foot across it, stepping inside with me. Her fingers curled in my hair. She kissed my cheek.

"I couldn't get you out of my head after that," I whispered.

"No," she said, "you couldn't. You'd just saved me from a horrible fate, given me a wonderful gift. I wanted to reward you. I wanted to make you love me."

"How is that a reward?"

She tilted her head. The molten-copper sparks in her eyes swirled like tiny whirlwinds.

"Daniel," she said. "Did you forget what I am?"

"That's not an answer."

"You were alone. You were lonely. You thought you were heading for wedding bells with that girl, Roxy—what you got was one less suitcase and an empty apartment. You were going to bed with a bottle of Jack Daniels every night of the week, drinking until the aching stopped. You were blaming yourself—"

"I was blaming myself," I said, "because Roxy walking out was my fault. I was a shitty boyfriend."

"You say that as if I care. I wanted you to stop *destroying* yourself. So I gave you the best gift I had to offer. I brought the bloom of new love into your life."

Her words were so well rehearsed I almost believed them. Then I thought about the ring.

"And it was just a coincidence that the Ring of Solomon was in play, and you needed a human agent—who couldn't be touched by its magic—to do the job you couldn't."

"Speak directly," she told me. "Ask what you want to ask."

I held out my open palm, cradling a memory.

"I had the ring. I had it in my hand. And I *threw it away*." I looked from my palm to her eyes. "Did you make me do it?"

"No. And you know why you threw it away. It would have put everyone you've ever known, everyone you've ever loved, in mortal danger for the rest of their lives. Every sorcerer on Earth would be flocking to Vegas looking to claim the ring for their own, and all of hell would be plotting your doom. *That* is why you threw it away. The choice was made of your own free will."

I started to reply. My voice cracked, the words choking in my throat.

"How can I believe you?"

Caitlin lowered her head. She stepped back, drifting to the black leather sofa. Her hand clutched at the air. Grasping for something ethereal.

"I could have used you as an agent. Thrown you away when I was done. I've done it to mortals before, so many times. But something happened." She looked over at me. "I fell in love with you, for real. Wasn't supposed to. But it happened. And that was the end of it. The moment I realized that I wanted you—that I wanted *you*, the real you, not some puppet on a string—was the last time I *ever* used my magic on you. Because I wanted you to choose to love me back. For real, with your real feelings and your real heart. And that moment was long before you seized the Ring of Solomon."

I squeezed my eyes shut. Felt tears gathering, and I fought them back with everything I had.

"How can I know that?" I asked her. "If your power is so subtle that you can influence me without me knowing about it, how can I possibly know you're telling the truth?

You could still be doing it, right this minute. How can I know?"

Caitlin walked up to me. Her fingernails pressed gently over my heart.

"What you're feeling right now," she said. "Does it hurt?"

I opened my eyes. A tear trickled down my cheek. I couldn't stop it. Wasn't strong enough.

"Yes. It fucking *hurts*."

"That's how you know," she said. "Because if I was using my powers on you, you would never, ever hurt. And I can't tell you how badly I want to. I want to wipe your pain away, make you smile, make you forget all of this. But I won't. I can, but I won't. Because I've learned that people in love—*real* love—hurt each other sometimes. And you have to deal with it, and work through it, and find a way back somehow."

"I don't know if there is a way back," I whispered.

"I hurt you," she said. "And I'm sorry. Will you forgive me?"

I stood there, torn between *I can't* and *I already have*, and I wasn't sure which was true.

"It's not about forgiveness, Cait." I rubbed at my cheek with the back of my hand, smearing the fallen tear away. "It's about trust. How do I know I can trust you?"

She shook her head. "I can't give you some magical proof. It doesn't exist. All I can ask is that you give me a chance."

"I have to go," I said.

Her jaw tightened. "Please don't."

"I'm not...I'm not *leaving* leaving. I just can't—" I sighed, frustrated, looking for words I didn't have to express a tangle of emotions I couldn't unsnarl. "You want forgiveness. And I can't give it to you right now. I can't say the words. I have to go and feel hurt for a little bit, while I work this all out in my head. I just...I need some space."

I walked to the door. She could have stopped me. By force, by magic. She did neither. She just stood there, with her bottom lip trembling, as I walked out the door.

* * *

I didn't care about the bounty on my head, the demons combing the city for me. I didn't care about much of anything beyond the bitter taste in my throat, and how badly I needed a drink to wash it away. I headed for the heart of the Strip. I needed neon and crowds and glitter. I'd overdosed on the truth, and the lying facades and false promises of Las Vegas felt like the only antidote.

I wound up at the Monaco, at the little bar on the edge of the casino floor. Halfway through nursing my second Jack and Coke, the guy sitting on the stool to my left nodded to get my attention.

"Girl problems, right?"

He was in his seventies, maybe, with bright eyes and a tailored gray suit, and what remained of his hair was perfectly groomed. A silver fox. I lifted my glass.

"Is it that obvious?"

"When you've been around the block as many times as I have, you recognize the look. Did you break up?"

I had to think about that one.

"I don't know. Guess I'm trying to decide." I shrugged. "We had our first real fight as a couple."

He chuckled. "Show me a couple that never fights and I'll show you a couple that lies about *everything* to each other. Stress and occasional heartache are the price of honesty."

"Well, it wasn't a *little* fight."

"What'd you do?" He squinted at me. "No. It's what she did. Did she step out on you with some other beau?"

I contemplated my glass. One last swallow of Jack, rolling around in the bottom of the cup. I tossed it back and drank it down.

"No. Nothing like that, it was..." I tried to find a way to word it. "When we first met, before we got serious, she betrayed my trust. I mean, really, *really* betrayed it. She came clean about it, says she's sorry, but..."

"Has she done it again since?"

I had to think about that one, too. The silver fox waved for the bartender.

"Another martini, my good man. And another drink for my new friend here. It's on me."

The drinks slid over on fresh napkins. I lifted mine with a nod of thanks.

"I don't think so," I said. "I really do believe her. And I believe she's sorry for it."

The crow's-feet at the edges of his eyes crinkled as he gave me a rakish smile. "So this isn't really about *her* at all, is it? Like many a man before you, your pride's been bruised. A dire wound to the ego."

"It's not that simple."

"Isn't it?" He sipped his martini and closed his eyes for a moment. "Mm. Perfectly made. Would you indulge an old man in a memory?"

"I've got nowhere else to go," I said.

"Before I retired," he said, "I was an architect. A damned good one, too. My best friend and I went in on a new undertaking together. It was a housing project. Enormous, you wouldn't believe how big. Ecological, entirely self-sustaining, a landmark to end all landmarks."

"How'd that work out for you?" I asked.

"Great. At first." He gave a tiny shrug. "Soon enough, the arguments started. We disagreed on *everything*, from the aesthetics to the heating system. Finally, we had a mother of a fight and I stomped out. Said fine, hell with it, I'll do my own thing and show him just how wrong he is."

The old man's eyes went distant. He stared at his martini glass, but he was a million miles away.

"I'll cut to the punch line," he told me. "Turned out he was right about almost everything. I was a damned fool. And not only did it cost me the contract of a lifetime, it cost me something even more dear: my best friend. And I know, to this very day, that we could be friends again. All I'd have to do is go to him and tell him I'm sorry."

"So why don't you?"

He paused, just a heartbeat. The distant look snapped away. Fully in the present, eyes twinkling, he clinked his glass against mine.

"Because pride, my young friend, is a *bitch*. I let my pride ruin the best thing I ever had, and I see you walking that same lonely road. Let me ask you something. Dig deep. Really think about it. Do you love this girl?"

That was the first question I didn't have to deliberate over. It was the only thing I knew for certain.

"Yeah," I said. "I love her. I really do."

"Relationships are hard work. But anything worth having in this life is worth fighting for. And the more you want it, the more you have to be willing to fight."

I smiled. "Funny. Friend of mine said the same thing, a few days ago."

"That's a friend worth listening to, then. And right this minute, while you're drinking booze with a washed-up old nobody, that lady of yours is at home. Pacing the floors, fretting, fearing." He put his hand on my shoulder and gave it a squeeze. "Go to her. Quiet her fears, and tell her you're on her side. If you've decided she's worth fighting for, *tell* her that. She needs to hear it from you. If I judge that look in your eye right, what you've got is a one-in-a-million girl. That means *you've* got to be a one-in-a-million man."

He was right. I believed Caitlin. And yeah, she'd hurt me, but I wasn't some perfect prize either. We could get past this. We could move on, together. The only thing stopping me from forgiving her was the thorn of pride sticking in my heel. Time to yank it out.

"You're right," I told him. I set my unfinished drink on the bar. "I'm going. Right now."

"Attaboy." He patted my shoulder as he hopped off his stool. "If love was simple, poets and playwrights wouldn't have spent centuries obsessing over it. Just keep working at it. You'll figure it out, Daniel."

He disappeared into the churning crowds, swallowed by the city. I tilted my head, feeling suddenly off-kilter, and then I realized why.

I had never told him my name.

37.

I didn't call ahead. This was a conversation to have face-to-face, eye-to-eye. I speed-walked through the Taipei Tower lobby, across the scarlet-and-black chrysanthemum-patterned carpet. You needed a keycard to ride all the way up to the penthouse floor, but the desk clerk knew me; he gave me a wave and called the elevator remotely.

I wasn't the only one waiting. A couple of tourists, a prim woman cradling a plastic margarita cup and a stringy-haired, over-tanned man in an *I Heart Las Vegas* T-shirt, were ahead of me. We got onto the elevator together.

The woman got off on the fourth floor. The car stopped again on seven. A little girl got into the elevator alone. She was maybe eight or nine, dressed in pigtails and a frilly smock. I had a brief moment of nostalgia, thinking of the days *before* Vegas became a family destination. She hit the button for twelve and the elevator started moving again.

The little girl looked up at me. She had disconcertingly flat eyes, like a dead fish.

"Hey, fucko," she said.

I blinked. "*Excuse* me?"

"Got a riddle for ya. What's black and yellow and delivers two-point-one milliamps of electricity?"

My gaze shot to her hands. Empty. Then the man standing behind me put his stun gun to the base of my neck and pulled the trigger. The floor of the elevator rushed up to greet my face, and everything went dark.

* * *

The world swam around me. It felt like I was underwater, voices echoing and faint. My hands were puffy and numb, wrists and ankles bound tight with zip ties. I was lying on my back in a dry bathtub. My vision came back into focus, and I realized they hadn't taken me out of the building: we were in a tower guest suite, somewhere below Caitlin's penthouse. I wriggled myself into a sitting position, as best I could with the hard porcelain pressing against my bound and aching wrists.

The over-tanned man and the little girl were in the suite's parlor. I watched through the open doorway as they labored over a small metal bowl. The face of the bowl was engraved with swirling runes, and black wisps of smoke drifted from its lip, curling in the dim light of an end-table lamp.

I shook my head, trying to clear it. I was wide-awake, but their voices seemed oddly muffled and distant. The man looked over at me.

"Aw, good, he's up." He spoke in a slow and easy Louisiana drawl, the voice of a riverboat gambler. "Would you do us a kindness, friend? Just scream real loud. Call for help. Go crazy with it."

I was going to do that anyway. I took a deep breath and shouted at the top of my lungs, kicking my bound feet against the bathtub, trying to get someone's—anyone's—attention.

Nobody came running.

"Now y'see?" the man said to the girl. "That's why you always bring a sonitus baffle on a job where you might have to deal with the target in a public place. He can scream all day long, won't cause a bit of trouble. Worth every penny. C'mon, let's go introduce ourselves."

As they stepped across the bathroom threshold, their footsteps snapped into sharp clarity. The distant, swimmy sound of their voices became crystal clear.

"Evenin', friend," he said. "The name's Fontaine, proud to represent the hallowed and distinguished Order of Chainmen, and this here's my new apprentice Rache. I'm kinda showing her the ropes, so I hope you'll grant us a little extra patience."

"You're gonna fuckin' *die*," the little girl told me. She brandished a stun gun in her tiny fist and looked like she was itching to use it.

Fontaine winced. "Sorry. She's very new at this. Rache has a pair of problems, in that she's inexperienced and also she hates everyone. Only one of those problems, I fear, will be cured by the passage of time. Rache, why don't you go get my kit bag?"

As she scurried from the room, her footsteps swallowed by the sound enchantment, Fontaine gave me an apologetic look.

"Between you and me," he murmured, "I got saddled with the girl *very* much against my will. I think I can make a decent hunter out of her, but it's an uphill fight. Choir of Wrath. They're difficult to work with."

Rache came back, lugging a bowling-ball satchel in white calfskin leather. It clanked as she plopped it down on the tile floor.

"Okay," Fontaine said to her, "now then. We've pulled

off the capture. The mission's gone picture perfect, the target's been corralled, so what now?"

Rache rummaged in the bag. She came up with a scalpel in one hand and an implement in the other that resembled an ice-cream scoop with jagged, razor-sharp edges.

"We employ our surroundings," she dutifully recited, looking ten shades of bloodthirsty. "Using a bathtub means minimum mess. We flip him onto his stomach, cut his throat, and monitor his pulse. The second he goes cold, we melon-ball him."

"Correct. And how long do we have for soul extraction?"

"Sixty-six seconds," Rache said. She rolled her eyes. "Are you really gonna keep schooling me on the basics?"

"Until you get 'em right. Now what'd you forget?"

She scrunched up her face. "I don't know. Tase him in the balls before we kill him?"

Fontaine frowned. "That ain't how we do things, Rache."

"It *could* be, though."

I felt obligated to toss my two cents in. Mostly because my only option, at the moment, was to keep them talking while I figured out an escape plan.

"You might be surprised," I said, "but she's not the first person to threaten me with that."

They both ignored me. Fontaine held up three fingers.

"Research, research, and research. It's not just about knowing your target's threat assessment—"

"I read the bounty notice," Rache snorted. "He's an NP, and it's only a gray-letter contract."

"Will someone please tell me what 'NP' stands for?" I asked. They kept ignoring me.

"If you'd done the homework I assigned you," Fontaine told her, "you'd know that Mr. Faust here is the consort of *Caitlleanabruaudi*. You know? Hound of the Court of Jade Tears? So we're holding a bit of a political football."

Rache glanced askew at him. "Our order isn't political."

"Aw, sweet child, you gotta learn. Everything is political. So before we do anything we can't *un*do, I'm gonna make a quick phone call. Keep an eye on our friend here."

My hands flexed behind my back. The zip ties were brutally tight, not an inch of give as they bit into my skin. It made sense: I was supposed to die wearing them. Fontaine walked out and Rache watched him go, her fish-eyed face equal parts bored and annoyed. If I could go to work on her, get her on my side before her partner came back...

"Rough boss, huh?" I asked. "Doesn't sound like he respects you very much."

Rache sighed at me. "Oh wow, you're actually trying it. You know, the thing where you masterfully turn us against each other with genius mind games, get us fighting, and you make a miraculous escape in the confusion. How stupid do you think I am?"

"Do you really want an answer to that?"

She picked up the stun gun and glared at me.

Fontaine paced by the bathroom door, shaking his head, as his muffled words drifted across the threshold. "Yeah, sorry, darlin', it's *that* phone call. No, ain't done it yet. I wanted to pay my respects and call you first."

"*Caitlin!*" I shouted. "We're in a room in the tower. We're right under—"

Rache hit me in the shoulder with the stun gun and

the world became a burning wire of pain. As I flopped around in the tub, banging the back of my head against the porcelain, she loomed over me.

"She can't hear you, dumbass. Sound enchantment, remember?"

"Then why," I managed to gasp, "did you tase me?"

She shrugged. "Because it's fun."

"Now, now." Fontaine was gently chiding Caitlin on the phone. "You know I can't let you see him. You show up, you're gonna feel compelled to stage a dramatic rescue, it's gonna cause a massive rift between your court and my order, and next thing you know it's a hot mess or a hot war. I'm protecting you from your own worst instincts. I hope you appreciate that."

"I can pay you," I told Rache.

She held up the stun gun. "To tase you? Damn, go hire a dominatrix, ya sicko."

"To let me *go*," I said.

"Lemme think about that." She glanced up at the bathroom ceiling. "Thought about it. No."

"—always had a good working relationship," Fontaine said, walking by the doorway again. "So I really hope this won't—no, of course not. He won't suffer. My word on it. Look, I know there's no upside here; I'm basically the vet callin' to let you know we gotta put your dog to sleep. But I hope you can take some comfort knowing it was me who caught him. This town's infested with hunters right now, and most of 'em would take their sweet time making the kill. Nyx is here along with half the House of Dead Roses—hell, I saw Henry Holmes at the airport. You knew this was only a matter of time."

Fontaine stopped pacing. He stood still, listening, his eyes grave.

"You sure you don't wanna just say goodbye? I'll give him the phone." He fell silent again. "One hour. For you, I can do that."

He hung up the phone and stepped across the threshold. The sound barrier rippled around him like the skin of a soap bubble. Then he cracked his knuckles behind his back.

"Well, we got a little time to kill." He looked my way. "Your lady asked for a brief stay of execution before we do the deed. You got one hour to live."

"One hour?" I shook my head. "Why?"

"My best guess? She's gonna pull out all the stops to try and find us, and...well, she bursts in, dramatic rescue, massive political fallout, yadda yadda. Except she won't find us."

"So let's just kill him now," Rache said. "I got shit to do today."

Fontaine wagged his finger at her. "Now, now. You do not break your word to a hound. We don't *answer* to them, as agents of an independent and sacred order, but you never know when you're gonna need their cooperation. Caitlin's a good ally to have. We can give her an hour of our precious time."

"Can we torture him?"

He slapped his forehead. "Did you not hear the part about 'no suffering'? No. Go play your stupid phone game or something. *I* will watch Mr. Faust."

She skipped off. Fontaine watched her go, shaking his head.

"Don't even worry," he told me. "When the time comes, she ain't gonna lay a hand on you. I'll be doing the deed. Can I offer you a goodbye shot? Got half a fifth of good scotch in my kit bag."

"Will you untie my hands so I can drink it?" I asked.

He flashed a grin. "Nice try."

After that, there wasn't much to do but wait. I knew Caitlin was on her way. She would find me somehow. I waited for the sound of the door bursting open, the window crashing, a rescue team coming in loud and hard. Any minute now, she'd be here.

Any minute now.

The alarm went off on Fontaine's phone, a merry chime. He clicked it off, and gave me a little sigh.

"Sorry, friend," he said. "Looks like your time's up."

Then he picked up the scalpel.

38.

Fontaine rolled me onto my stomach in the bathtub. I thrashed like a fish out of water, kicking with my bound feet, but he held me down with an iron grip.

"Gonna have to ask you to go out with some dignity here," he grunted. "I can make this quick and easy, but it takes a little cooperation on your part."

Hell with that. I was going out fighting. He tightened his fingers in my hair, pulling my head back. I bared my teeth, yanking my neck, my bound hands scrambling at nothing. I saw the flash of the scalpel, felt cold sharp steel against my jugular vein—then tinny music flooded the bathroom. A recording of Marvin Gaye singing "Heard It Through the Grapevine."

Fontaine paused. He let go of me, pulling the scalpel away, and picked up his phone.

"'Scuse me a second. That's my agent, I gotta get that." He answered it. "Fontaine. Yup. Mm-hmm. You're kiddin' me. Well that's a lotta—you know I invested some money in this hunt. I know, I know, that's the life. Okay, well, thanks kindly."

He hung up.

"Huh," he said. "That was almost a big ol' mess."

I craned my neck to look up at him. "What was?"

"Hunt's over." He crouched over me. "Hold your wrists real still, okay? Gotta cut these zip ties off, don't wanna nick you."

"Wait. Over? What do you mean, *over?*"

"I mean over. Called off. Canceled. Finito. Word from the head office: the bounty on your head's been officially rescinded. My good day just went sour, and your sour one just became a ray of ever-lovin' sunshine." The scalpel snicked through the wrist ties and my blood-starved hands tingled as circulation flooded back in. "Watch yourself, though. Gonna be a lot of real pissed-off hunters in town feeling like they got cheated out of a paycheck, and they don't all follow the rules like I do. Hold on, gonna get your ankles now."

I rubbed my wrists and ankles, willing the life back into them. Fontaine held out his hand and helped me up. I stepped out of the tub, still feeling like I'd been blindsided. It should have been good news. I should have been overjoyed.

I wasn't. This was all wrong.

"No hard feelings, I hope," Fontaine told me.

I didn't know what I could even say to that.

On the elevator up, I worked the angles. What could make Naavarasi pull the contract? Killing her wouldn't do it, and the rakshasi queen lived more than an hour away. She wasn't going to do it out of the goodness of her heart. She didn't have any. Obviously Caitlin had requested my stay of execution for a reason. What could she possibly accomplish in one hour that would—

Circe.

One hour was plenty of time to get to my apartment, take Circe by force, and promise her to Naavarasi. Paying my debt for me. Naavarasi still wouldn't *have* to pull the contract, but she'd have to choose which prize she wanted more: my soul or Circe.

I ran up the ivory hallway and hammered my fist on Caitlin's penthouse door. No answer.

Ten minutes later I was leaning on the horn, weaving through sluggish traffic, fighting my way across town. My heart pounded against my ribs as I charged up the steps to my apartment, fumbled with my keys, burst through the door.

Circe was sitting on the sofa, watching television. She gave me a curious look.

"Is something wrong?" she asked.

"You're okay." I shut the door and double-locked it, pressing my back to the wood. "Was Caitlin here? Was anyone here?"

She shook her head, rising to her feet. "No. No one. What's wrong?"

"That's what I'm trying to find out."

I dialed Caitlin's cell; it went straight to her voicemail. Next I called the Southern Tropics head office and braced for my usual fight with the receptionist. The second I gave my name, she patched me through to Emma's desk.

"Daniel," she said, breathless, "is Caitlin with you?"

"No, I was gonna ask if she's with *you*. What's going on, Emma? Naavarasi yanked the bounty and—"

"I got a call from Legal," she said. "Caitlin filled a Writ of Claimance on you about an hour ago. This is bad. This is really, *really* bad."

"Wait, hold on. What's a Writ of Claimance?"

"It's a document officially registering you, via our court, as her thrall. Her legal property."

I leaned my head back against the door and shut my eyes.

"We had a fight," I said, sighing. "I don't know what she's doing, but if she thinks this is how to make up—"

"No," Emma snapped. "Shut up. Listen. Thralls are like...minors in human law. Not competent, you understand? Can't sign contracts. A demon who owns a human thrall is fully responsible for that thrall's actions. Their *debts*."

"The bounty wasn't called off," I breathed. "It was moved. Caitlin's taking the hit for me."

"She'll be treated the exact same way you would have been. Prince Sitri will have no choice not only to rescind her status as his hound, but to come to terms with Naavarasi. Caitlin will be handed over to her. As her slave. For eternity. She's *sacrificing* herself for you, Daniel."

I was standing in a pit of misery a thousand miles deep, and still, buried in that bleakness, I almost had to laugh.

I'd asked Caitlin how I knew I could trust her. How I knew she really loved me. She said she couldn't prove it.

And then she found a way.

"Is there any way around this? Could she have something up her sleeve?"

"No," Emma said. "She can request a trial by combat, but Naavarasi doesn't have to accept. And there's nothing for Naavarasi to gain by dueling her, compared to what she's already going to win. Our court loses face, we're destabilized until a new hound is chosen—and that's a long and bloody process—and she *owns* Caitlin."

I fell silent. The pieces of the puzzle turned, clicked, showing me a new picture. I'd been wrong this entire time. Chasing the wrong clues to the wrong plot.

"Daniel?" Emma said. Standing by the sofa, Circe peered curiously at me.

"She played us," I said. "All this time, we thought Naavarasi wasn't a real threat. That she was too egotistical for her own good. That she couldn't put together a plan if her life depended on it, because she just *had* to show off. It was a fucking act, Emma. It was all a fucking act and we bought it. While we were treating her with kid gloves, she was working the long con. *Studying* us. Laying the pieces for her masterstroke."

"Explain," she said.

"It was never about Circe. She never wanted Circe in the first place." I pushed away from the door, pacing the apartment. "First Naavarasi got me firmly in her debt, and even made me think I was getting a bargain when she did it. Then she sent me on the heist, backing everything up through Caitlin and the laws of the courts. We thought she did that for leverage, just in case I found out Circe was a real, living person and balked at handing her over."

Emma's voice went soft as she followed the trail. "It wasn't a contingency. You were *supposed* to figure it out. She wanted you to refuse."

"Exactly. She sent me on a job that she knew I wouldn't finish. Suddenly, I'm a thief, and thanks to all that groundwork she's got the green light to send the chainmen after me. I tried to find proof that she was lying. When I was in Chicago, a sniper took a shot at me. Their first shot *missed.* A professional killer wouldn't have missed. The second shot took out the guy I was trying to save. Emma, do you know how long the human soul stays with the body after death?"

"Sixty seconds, give or take."

"Right," I said. "So why would a chainman use a sniper

rifle? They *have* to get up close and personal so they can harvest their victims. That wasn't a bounty hunter up on the roof. It was Naavarasi or somebody working for her. She wasn't trying to kill me, she was trying to destroy the evidence. Which she did, and I had to flee the city just ahead of a demonic posse. Step by step, she cut our options down. Maneuvered us into a corner with no way out. And her whole plan hinged on one thing. One thing she knew for an absolute fact."

"Which is?"

"That Caitlin loves me," I said. "And that when we finally ran out of moves, Cait had one last play up her sleeve: taking the fall in my place, just like I would do for her. This was her plan all along, Emma. It wasn't about Circe. It wasn't about me. She wanted *Caitlin*."

"We can't let this happen—"

"We won't. *I* won't. I promise. This ends tonight."

I hung up the phone. Circe stared at me. Her head tilted slightly, contemplating.

"What will you do?" she asked.

"I'm going to do whatever I can to save her," I said. "Whatever it takes."

"Bring me with you."

I shook my head. "You don't owe us anything."

"Will you go where Caitlin goes? Even into hell itself?"

"If I have to," I said.

"Then you may need a guide. Catch me."

Circe ran toward me, jumping and twisting in the air as her body jackknifed. Collapsing upon herself, shrinking, flesh turning to hard, cold obsidian.

The jade-hilted dagger landed in my outstretched hand.

* * *

The line outside Winter stretched around the block. A bouncer in a muscle shirt unhooked the velvet rope for me, but he gestured me aside.

"Hey, Mr. Faust. Uh...tonight might not be so good."

"Lousy DJ?"

He forced a chuckle. "You kidding? We never have a lousy DJ. No, uh, it's...kind of a rough crowd downstairs, if you know what I mean."

"Suits my mood just fine," I said.

Down the back corridor, along a winding path of blue neon, the gas-masked sentry stood beside the door to level two. He keyed in the code and ushered me through. I descended into the honeycombed labyrinth below, the driving dance music reduced to muffled thumping, and navigated the gold-and-black halls by memory.

I emerged into a shadowed gallery, with my target in sight at the other end: a windowless steel door with a second keypad alongside it. The door to the third level.

I wasn't alone. Figures emerged from the alcoves and archways around me. Most I didn't recognize. A few I did. Nyx, in her Nordic-goddess disguise, planted herself square in my path. The others, gathered around me in a loose circle. Eight in all. No way out.

"Wow," I said. "You assholes *really* picked the wrong night to start something."

39.

A yellow-eyed cambion to my right raised a broken fingernail, pointing at me.

"You cost us *money*, Faust. I chased your ass from here to Chicago and back again, and got *nothing* for it."

"What do you want me to say?" I asked. "Sorry you're a loser?"

Nyx swept out her hand. "This club is neutral ground for our kind. *You* are nothing but easy prey, especially with your whore of a lover about to be kneeling at Naavarasi's feet."

"We won't get paid for tearing you apart," said one of the hunters at my back, "but that doesn't mean we can't get some satisfaction out of it."

I turned, slow, taking them all in. Marking every face in the room in my memory.

"You all know who I am," I said.

"This one knows exactly what you are," Nyx said. "A human gutter-mage."

"That's what Lauren Carmichael and her cult thought," I said. "I'd tell you to go ask them, but they're all dead. The Redemption Choir wasn't too impressed at first, either. If you want Sullivan's opinion on the matter, you can find him buried under a parking lot. Oh, hey, here's a name you'll all know: Damien Ecko. He was the hottest bounty around, wasn't he? Every hunter in America was gunning for his head."

I locked eyes with Nyx.

"Except you're too late, because I killed him. And when I got finished with Ecko, there wasn't enough left to bury. Here's a friendly tip for you: when my back's against the wall, sometimes—just sometimes—I manage to punch above my weight class."

"You can't take all of us at once," the cambion hunter snapped.

"And I won't have to."

I counted heads.

"Let's see, we've got one, two, three...eight of you. Impressive little pack. Only problem is, you're not friends, are you? You're not allies. You're competitors. Not one of you would shed a tear if the other seven got hit by a bus, am I right?"

Narrow-eyed glances and muffled grumbles, but not one word of disagreement.

"None of you want to make the first move. That's a sucker bet. You don't know what I'm hiding, what tricks I've got up my sleeve. Nah. Better to let somebody else take that chance. Now here's another tip, something I really hope you'll take to heart: for most of my life, I felt like I didn't have anything to lose."

I flexed my wrist. The wand dropped into my fingers, thrumming with power as I pictured Caitlin's face. I drew the Cutting Knife in my other hand, feeling Circe's dormant energy tingling hot against my grip.

"Tonight," I said, "I've got *everything* to lose, and it's not just my life that I'm fighting for. So I'll promise you something. The first one of you who lays hands on me is going to die. The second one who lays hands on me is going to die. Eventually, yeah, you'll wear me down. I can't beat all eight of you."

I took a good long look around the circle.

"And if you really want me that bad, all you have to do is decide who goes first."

"He's bluffing," Nyx seethed. "Destroy him."

One of the other hunters glared at her. "Then why don't *you* do it, big shot?"

"I don't have a lot of time," I said. "So are we gonna do this or not? Either throw the fuck down or get out of my way."

All eyes fell on Nyx.

"This one..." she said, hesitant, "will not diminish herself by wasting effort on such insignificant prey."

She stepped aside.

I walked past her without a word and keyed in the access code for the steel door. It yawned open, revealing the rough stone staircase beyond.

The stairs wound down into a musty chamber lit by a single white pillar candle. The candle stood at the heart of the room, erected upon a stand of serpent-scaled brass. Its flame fluttered, struggling to reach the shadow-drenched corners. The air smelled of spices and dried oranges.

Chains rattled in the darkness.

A stench wafted from the far corner of the chamber, like roadkill festering in the desert sun. Then a figure, skeletally emaciated, shambled into sight. His face was a mass of burn tissue, eyes and nose obliterated, buried under twisted scars. Only his mouth was untouched. He wore long, once-regal emerald robes, now caked with dried excrement and filth. His wrists and ankles were bound in golden chains that snaked into the shadows. He wasn't tethered with manacles; the final links of the chains had been hammered through his flesh and bones.

"Fear me," rasped the Conduit in a reedy voice, "for I only speak the truth."

I'd been down here twice. I had never wanted to come back again. But the Conduit—a torn-souled creation that existed in both our world and hell, with a foot and a voice in both realms—was my one and only pipeline to the top.

"Prince Sitri," I said. "I need to talk to him."

"The prince is unavailable. He's attending a court affair at the moment. A dispute to be resolved."

My stomach clenched. I might already be too late.

"I need to get there. I need to get to Caitlin. Tell me how."

The Conduit pulled back his lips in a mad rictus.

"Die," he said.

My hopes shattered. "Caitlin is already back in hell."

"Actually...no. Prince Sitri requested a break with tradition, for reasons he did not care to divulge. The trial regarding the matter of his hound is taking place in the Low Liminal."

I shook my head. "I've never heard of it."

"It goes by many names. Limbo. The Big Empty. The place where worlds touch, where spirit and flesh may mingle. Where the lost and the damned float adrift and dogs bray in the endless mists. No place for an untrained wanderer. I could send you there, but you likely won't return."

"I don't care," I said. "If you've got a way to get me to that trial, *do it*."

He parted his robes. His chest was a fleshless mass of

interlocking bones, like the lid of a scrimshaw trunk. And at the heart of the puzzle of bone, a keyhole.

"Open me," the Conduit said. "*Enter* me."

"I don't have a key."

His eyeless head nodded at my hand. At Circe. "Of course you do."

I raised the knife and it began to change. Folding, twisting, sprouting a wave of black glassy spikes like a hedgehog's rippling quills. Finally it sat dormant, its transformation complete.

In my hand I held a key of obsidian and jade.

I unlocked the door. The Conduit hooked clawed fingers in his chest, bones crackling as he wrenched his ribs open. Beyond the bones a tunnel of flesh, like a red and inflamed throat, snaked into darkness.

"Careful," the Conduit said. "It's a tight fit. And a long way down."

He stood still, almost serene, as I crawled into his chest. The throat-tunnel squeezed tight around me, the wet flesh slick and quivering, and I had to pull myself forward on my forearms. I squirmed in, deeper, a few more feet...and I heard the door of bone slam behind me. Sealing me in.

I couldn't see a thing. The tunnel of flesh, stinking of rotten meat, clung to me. Fighting me every inch of the way. All I could hear was my heart pounding in my ears. All I could do was keep moving. For a nightmare moment I thought the flesh tunnel would never end, that this was my hell, this claustrophobic and endless squeezing dark.

I noticed a shift. The tunnel was beginning to slant. Downward, just a little.

Then a little more. I wriggled faster, able to use my weight. The tunnel grew slicker, like the lining of the throat was coated with grease. The next thing I knew, I was sliding. The tunnel dropping hard, almost vertical.

Then it spat me out, and I fell.

Wind whistled in my ears. The world became a blur of color and light, spinning too fast to see as I plummeted through the air. Then a sudden jolt of pain as I landed on my shoulder, tumbling, rolling down a hill that clattered and clanked. Bones. I'd crashed onto a mound of bones, stripped clean and tossed together in a chaotic jumble. I bounced all the way down, landing flat on dead, dusty earth.

The hit knocked the wind out of me. I lay flat on my belly, stunned, staring bleary-eyed at the scattering of bones at the edge of the dead pile. A cracked bottom jaw, a leg bone...and bits and pieces that didn't seem to belong to any earthly animal. Bones with strange curves and sharp edges.

A pair of sandals stepped into my field of vision. Circe, back in her human form, stood over me.

"We can't stay here," she said. "It's not safe."

I groaned and pushed myself to my feet. What I saw almost stole my breath a second time.

A parched plain stretched off in all directions, the cold earth cracked and barren. The dirt had an aroma to it, a faint, dry and spicy smell that made me think of church incense. Banks of white mist roiled in the distance, drifting by like clouds. The sky hung in perpetual twilight, somehow bright and dark at the same time, so perfectly azure it made my eyes ache.

There were three moons in the sky. A trio of crescents, so big and close I felt like I could reach up and touch them. I stared up at the craggy, ancient rock, the moons lit from behind by a soft scarlet glow. I could make out words there.

Runes—they must have been unspeakably massive to be seen with the naked eye—were carved into the faces of the moons. Something tickled my left ear. A puff of breath. A whispered promise. I couldn't move, couldn't do anything but gaze up in rapt wonder. If I could study the runes, learn the secrets they could teach...

Circe grabbed my chin and yanked my face toward her. I reeled, the spell broken.

"*Not. Safe.*" She shook her head, frowning. "Nothing here is safe. And those are not for you."

She licked her index finger and held it in the air, a ship's navigator reckoning the flow of the wind. But there wasn't any wind. All the same, she nodded to herself and picked a direction. I walked alongside her, carefully keeping my eyes at ground level.

I lost track of time. My feet ached like we'd hiked for hours, but it was still twilight. At one point Circe stopped short, throwing her arm across my chest.

"Wrong way," she whispered and pointed.

In the distance, beyond a rolling bank of fog, a shadow swayed. The outline of a towering tree, a weeping willow at least a hundred feet high, its dangling boughs rippling in a breeze I couldn't feel. Birds with vast wings and hard outlines, like living pterodactyls, wheeled in the air around it.

"What is that?" I squinted. "Looks like a—"

The boughs rose, snapping, and lashed around one of the birds' wings to pluck it from the air. I heard the beast's shrill screams as the tree bent back, its trunk splitting to open a gaping and toothy mouth.

"A faded god," Circe said. "Give them no prayers, make them no offerings, pay them no mind. No gain in it. Faded gods are greedy, and they lie."

We changed direction. I didn't look back.

40.

We walked. Circe hadn't looked happy since we got here, and the longer we hiked across the desolate, cold plain, the deeper her frown grew.

"You'd tell me if we were lost, right?" I asked.

"It has been a very long time since I've been free to walk these roads," she said. "The Low Liminal has become...more troubled in my absence. Many faded gods prowling for food and worship, more than there used to be. My queen's way-markers are in disrepair."

"Your queen?"

"And yours, though you've forgotten her name. She still rules this place. I think."

I glanced sidelong at her. "This queen of yours, is she one of these 'faded gods'?"

Circe lifted her chin. Her worry vanished, replaced by an air of strength and a prideful smile.

"She is no *faded* god, Daniel Faust." She paused, pointing, and we changed direction again. "This way. Have to be careful. This road shows signs of recent passage, and the tracks are...unclean."

I looked around. "You keep saying 'road.' There's no road."

She stopped, turning to face me. She moved close and murmured an incantation under her breath. Twisty words with hard edges and sharp loops.

"See as I see," she whispered. Then she stood up on her tiptoes, leaning close, and spat in my eyes.

I flinched, pulling away, wiping at my face. "What the hell, Circe? What was—"

I froze. The endless cracked-earth plain was gone. Now we stood on a dirt road in the heart of a forest, the wilderness still cloaked in eternal twilight. A gray stone, maybe three feet tall, stood off to the roadside. Ancient Greek letters were engraved across its rough face, faded instructions I couldn't quite make out.

"Where did we just go?"

"Nowhere," Circe said. "I took away your illusion and gave you my illusion instead. Now we see the same way."

"So what does this place *really* look like, then?"

Circe frowned, as if she couldn't quite grasp the question.

"It doesn't," she said.

"The word 'illusion' implies an underlying truth."

She shook her head at me. Her smile was almost pitying.

"You have much to learn. Come. This way."

We followed the path. Lights shone up ahead. They were torches, spaced along the forest road about fifty feet apart, one after another. Their flames guttered, the pitch-dipped wood spitting curls of black smoke. I glanced at Circe. She was biting her bottom lip almost hard enough to draw blood.

"What is it?" I asked.

"She found us. I was hoping to take you to your lover and part ways before this happened."

That didn't sound good. "Can we take another road? Change direction? Look, I'm running out of time. I've got to get to Caitlin before—"

I heard the distant braying of hounds. A high-pitched howl that faded into echoes.

"She found us," Circe repeated. "*All* roads lead to her now."

The forest path ended at a crossroads.

Torches burned at the intersection where three roads met. Ours ending dead ahead, and two more stretching out to the east and west.

A woman stood at the crossroads. A spectral blur at first, her motions delayed, trailing, so that as she turned her head she seemed to have three faces. Then the three united and she took on color, form, and life.

The Lady in Red. That's what I instantly dubbed her in my mind, seizing on her dress—an elegant gown, cut high along one leg, like something a torch singer from the twenties might have worn. She had pale skin and piercing dark eyes, her hair a sculpted wave of midnight black. A key of antique brass dangled around her neck on a slender chain.

Circe dropped to her knees. Her fingertips brushed the dirt, her head bowed. Then the Lady in Red turned her gaze upon me, and every muscle in my body wanted to do the same. I only stayed on my feet by sheer force of will as my knees threatened to buckle. Her lips curled in a playful smile, and I realized she was toying with me.

"Circe," she said, her voice rich and cold, "come to me."

Circe rose and walked toward her on wobbly feet. She leaned close and whispered in the Lady's ear. They both glanced my way, and the Lady murmured a question in response. Circe nodded, blushing.

"I understand," said the Lady in Red, "that you did me a service. You've returned one of my wayward daughters."

I shrugged. "Circe? She was in a jam. To be honest, I didn't know what she was at first. Still not entirely sure."

"Once upon a time, nine beasts emerged from the Shadow In-Between. Nine of my daughters, war-witches all, pledged to slay them. But they were tricked and led into an ambush." Her hand played in Circe's hair, affectionately coiling one lock around her fingertip. Then she yanked it tight. "*Weren't* they?"

Circe winced. "Yes, my queen."

The Lady chuckled softly as she loosened her grip.

"They were bound, trapped in the form of *tools*, their powers to be commanded by any man who wielded them. A calculated insult. But men die, and ages pass, and they slowly slipped across the wheel of worlds. Scattered and sleeping, their legend forgotten. I've been making efforts to recover them ever since."

I thought about Ms. Fleiss. "I know where you can find another one."

"So do I." Her eyes twinkled, her smile sly. "But there is little time for talk. I know why you've come, and I can feel the blight of hell intruding upon my realm. They've chosen their battleground, and even as we speak, your lover is facing judgment."

Terror surged up inside me, my throat going tight. "Is it close? Can I get there in time?"

The Lady in Red lifted one idle hand, the other still stroking Circe's hair, and twirled her fingertips. I felt the world lurch under my feet—a sudden, dizzying shift—then it fell still.

"*Now* it is close. My gift to you, for saving my daughter. You'll arrive in time if you follow the path. I wonder, though: what will you do when you get there?"

"I...I don't know," I said. "Naavarasi's been in total control from the start of this mess. She hasn't made a single mistake. She worked us all like puppets...there's got to be a way to win, I just can't *find* it."

The Lady strode toward me. Imperious, the tail of her gown rippling behind her like gossamer on an autumn wind. My knees went rubbery again, and I fought to hold her gaze as her eyes met mine.

"Poison, as all of my daughters learn, is a witch's most potent tool. There are many kinds of poison. Some ingredients can be found growing in the wild, some harvested from beasts, and some—the most potent—arise from cauldrons of carefully harvested words, mixed and heated to dark perfection. Words to blacken the heart with greed, with rage, with lust. So what sort of poison did your enemy use on you?"

I thought it over, walking my way back through Naavarasi's game.

"She suckered me into a bad deal. I thought I had the upper hand, getting something I needed for a favor later down the line, but I was being conned from the jump. Then she played on my connection with Caitlin, using infernal law against us. I realized too late that what I thought she wanted was never the real goal."

"I find it the sweetest irony, and highly amusing, to use an enemy's own weapons against them. You should reflect on that." The Lady raised her hand and pointed up the eastern branch of the crossroads. "Now go. That way, and stay to the path. Your battle awaits. I do hope you survive it."

"Will you tell me your name?" I asked.

She loomed over me, taller now, and her eyes faded to orbs of inky black. Doorways into the depths of space where ancient stars shone, pinpricks of cosmic light.

"You know my name," the Lady in Red replied. "You've only forgotten. When you remember it, and if you are brave, light a candle under the dark of the moon and whisper it to the wind. If you're lucky, I just might answer. If you're unlucky...I just might answer."

I backed away slowly, edging down the crossroads path. Turning my back on her felt like an unwise thing to do. Circe moved to stand at her lady's side, offering me a tiny smile and a farewell wave.

Then a fog blew in, white and blinding, and washed the world away.

I walked through the mist, stumbling and lost, but my feet seemed to know the way. The fog grew sparse, dark shapes looming up ahead, and finally it cleared.

I stood at the edge of a vast marble chessboard. Stone pieces as tall as me lined each side, ready for battle. And behind the pieces, the players, sitting on thrones of ivory and black basalt. I was on the side of the white pieces and closest to the ivory throne. The player turned my way with an curious look, and I knew him in a heartbeat.

Prince Sitri.

He was tall and lean and perfect, every angle of his face and every cut of his vanilla three-piece suit delicate and precise. Sleek, androgynous, with a cool and feminine smile. His eyes were never the same color twice and never matched, shifting along a rainbow spectrum as he tilted his head and looked me up and down.

"Well, well," he purred. "Look what the cat dragged in. This might be entertaining after all."

On the far side of the board, squatting upon a basalt throne, sat Prince Malphas. He was the size of an elephant, his bulk cloaked in dirty ashen rags. A trio of heads poked out from under shaggy hoods: a crow, a ram, and a buzzard. All three sets of eyes flared scarlet as they fell upon me.

Royce, Prince Malphas's hound, stood on one side of the throne. He wore his usual Armani best, the edge of a black thorny vine tattoo poking up from the collar of his tailored shirt. Nadine stood beside him, dressed like a fashion plate, her arm hooked around his. On the other side of the throne, Naavarasi fixed me with a glare of irritation and folded her arms across her chest.

My eyes were on the center of the chessboard. A pillar stood there, engraved with coiling white and black serpents, each devouring another's tail in an endless wheel of destruction. And there was Caitlin. Standing hoisted to her tip-toes, her wrists shackled above her head and chained to a ring at the pillar's summit. Her jaw dropped when she saw me.

"Daniel! You shouldn't *be* here."

I set foot upon the chessboard. It thrummed softly under my shoe, some dormant power buried in the stone.

"I know what you did, Cait. I know you're trying to sacrifice yourself to save me."

I shook my head.

"Can't let you do that."

"Too late," Naavarasi snapped. "You've served your purpose, Daniel. *Leave.*"

I turned, staring her down. "Oh, yeah. I figured out your con. Have to give credit where credit's due, you got us good. Everything fell out just the way you wanted it. But the game's not over yet."

She pointed at me. "I want him removed from this

trial. He's an outsider. He has no place interfering in court proceedings."

I remembered what Nadine had told me. "*The law was made to be exploited by the clever and the wise.*"

"Actually," I said, "I do. The only reason Caitlin's here is because she filed a Writ of Claimance on me. Making me her thrall, ergo, making me a member of the Court of Jade Tears. Hey, guess what: I'm not an outsider anymore. Looks like I'm staying."

Naavarasi's lips curled in a predatory grin. Her eyes flooded with blossoms of tiger orange, like droplets of ink billowing in a glass of water, as she took a step toward me.

"Oh, are we *educated* now, Daniel? Are we a *lawyer?*" She snickered. "Fine. In that case, you're a thrall who's speaking out of turn to a noblewoman. In accordance with my rights, I demand that this insolent mortal be taken from my sight. I also want him whipped. One hundred lashes, I think, would suffice to satisfy my wounded honor."

I needed a friend here, fast. And as I looked around for help, my eyes fell on the unlikeliest one in sight. Nadine. She hated Caitlin with a passion, but I was gambling, based on our talk at the nightclub, that she hated Naavarasi even more. *She* wanted to destroy Caitlin; the idea of her archrival doing it had to be eating at her.

Nadine caught my gaze and replied with a mischievous smile and a wink.

"Point of order," she said, "Daniel is Caitlin's property."

"So?" Naavarasi demanded.

"So, the only person who can punish him is *her*." Nadine smirked. "Would you like to release her from those chains and hand over her whip now, or wait until after the trial?"

Naavarasi's eyes narrowed to burning slits. "When the trial is done, Caitlin will be *my* property."

"Well in that case," I said, "I guess my entire legal status is in question. I mean, property can't own property. That's just illogical."

Royce shrugged. "The good chap's right, you know. Speaking as a *completely* impartial observer—"

Malphas's crow head let out an ear-piercing squawk. The buzzard head shrieked, "*Silence!*"

The chessboard fell into a deathly hush.

"No more delays," the buzzard head croaked. "No more distractions. Let the trial begin."

41.

Naavarasi paced the chessboard, circling the pillar, her hands clasped behind her back as she delivered her opening argument.

"Good princes, I—an esteemed noble, a loyal and faithful servant of the Court of Night-Blooming Flowers—have been wronged. I was formally owed a boon by this human, Daniel Faust. The boon was confirmed by Prince Sitri's very own hound. To prove my case, I hereby call upon the sphere of memory. Witness, I beg you."

From the mists surrounding the chessboard, a soap bubble—massive, fifteen feet across and rippling as if it might pop at any moment—floated into sight. It hovered over our heads. Sparks danced beneath its surface, shimmering and bouncing, slowly resolving into a three-dimensional picture. I looked up at a replay of our meeting at Blue Karma, when I'd gone with Caitlin, but seen from behind Naavarasi's eyes.

"And yet," I watched Caitlin tell her, "here I am. You should have known I'd be here, Baron. You chose to make this a formal matter between the courts. If my prince's name is invoked as part of Daniel's debt to you, then I *will* be present to oversee the discussion."

The image froze.

"The debt was acknowledged," Naavarasi said. "As you can clearly see, there was no question that it was a formal boon, subject to the laws of the Cold Peace."

Malphas's three heads bobbed as one. Sitri sighed, slouching in his throne with his chin resting upon his slender fist.

The image fast-forwarded. I watched myself picking up the photograph of the dagger, stepping away from the table with Caitlin, coming back again, all at high speed. Then the memory lurched back into focus.

"Maybe we can talk about that," my image said. "After the job."

"After the job," Naavarasi's voice echoed across the chessboard. "That's a yes, then?"

"That's a yes."

The image froze again.

"And yet," Naavarasi said, "after obtaining my property, Daniel refused to render it unto me. Making him just as guilty as the original thief."

"Circe was never your property and you know it," I snapped.

"Oh?" She looked my way, sneering. "Can you prove that?"

"I can't prove it, because you shot my witness before he could testify!"

"A convenient story." She turned her back on me, looking to the princes. "There is no ambiguity. The law is crystal clear. I have been wounded and I am entitled to redress. I ask for nothing more than the standard punishment. That the offender—or, in this case, Caitlin, as she is responsible for his deeds—be granted to me as my property, to do with as I see fit."

"*We must deliberate!*" shrieked Malphas's three heads in unison. They darted close, the hoods of their ragged cloaks brushing as they whispered. On the opposite side of the board, Sitri slouched further into his throne. His eyes had gone dark, like burned-out coals. The arch-manipulator, the chess master who thrived on plots and intrigue—and even he couldn't find a way to save her.

It was all on me.

"You're going to regret this," Caitlin said to Naavarasi, her teeth gritted. "I promise you. If it takes a hundred years or a million, you *will* regret this."

Naavarasi sauntered over to her, pitching her voice low.

"The first thing I'm going to do," she murmured, "is take you to that delightful little nightclub in Vegas. And I'm going to parade you through it, on your hands and knees, wearing a leash. So all of your former friends and all of your court can witness my victory."

My hands curled into fists. Nails biting into my palms hard enough to leave welts. I was running out of time. Seconds left on the clock, and I still didn't have a plan. Naavarasi looked my way.

"I'll make you an offer, Daniel. Join her. Give yourself over to me willingly, and I promise Caitlin's treatment will be...merciful. You can make things so much easier on her. And you can still be with her. Don't you want that?"

It wasn't just a cruel taunt. Naavarasi was more cunning than any of us thought, pulling this off, but she couldn't help reaching a little too far. There was real greed in her eyes as she made her pitch. A crushing victory wasn't enough for her: she still wanted more.

And then I knew exactly what to do.

It all came to me at once. Nadine's admonition that

hell's law was made to be twisted. The way Naavarasi had used our own natures against Caitlin and me, finding the perfect openings in our armor to manipulate us into her trap. And the Lady in Red's parting words, her lesson on the uses of poison.

"*We are prepared,*" Malphas's heads screeched, "*to render our verdict.*"

"As am I," Sitri sighed. "We are, I'm sorry to say, in agreement. The law is clear. We must—"

"*Wait!*" I shouted.

The demon princes fell silent, both of them staring incredulously at me. I gathered they weren't used to being interrupted.

"Caitlin," I said, "challenge Naavarasi to a duel."

She blinked. "What?"

"Emma told me you can challenge her to a trial by combat. Do it."

"She doesn't have to agree," Caitlin said.

"Please," I said. "Just do it."

"Very well." She gave me a curious look. "Naavarasi, by my authority as the hound of Prince Sitri—"

"Save your breath," Naavarasi said. "Denied. Why would I possibly grant you the slightest sliver of hope when I've already won? Besides, how are you going to fight me with those manacles on? Kick me to death?"

"Can I fight in her place?" I asked.

No one spoke.

I looked to both sides of the board. "Can I fight in her place?"

"You may," Nadine said, her eyes bright and curious. "If unable to fight, the challenger can appoint a champion of their choosing."

I held up my hand. "I volunteer. I'll be Caitlin's champion."

"Preposterous," Naavarasi said. "You forget, Nadine, he is a thrall. Or an outsider. Whatever we've decided. In either case, he's utterly beneath me. I'd lose face by fighting him."

Prince Sitri rose from his throne. Faint sparks of color had returned to his shimmering eyes, like the rainbow flecks of a polished opal.

"What if he wasn't?" he asked.

Everyone turned his way.

"I find it unseemly," Sitri observed, "that my hound is sharing her bed with a mere thrall. It reflects badly on both of us. He should be a knight of my court, at least."

Naavarasi took a step back, halfway between confusion and outrage. "But...but he—"

"You could duel him then," Sitri said. "A perfectly honorable battle."

"A battle I have *declined*," Naavarasi said.

"What if I sweeten the pot?" I asked her.

She pursed her lips, studying me. "I'm listening."

I took a deep breath. Time to make the biggest gamble of my life.

"Double or nothing," I said. "You pick the battleground, I pick the weapons, and we go at it until one of us taps out. If I win, Caitlin goes free, my debt is canceled, and we're square. If you win, you get Caitlin *and* me."

"Daniel," Caitlin said, "she'll kill you. You've seen Naavarasi fight. You *can't* win."

Naavarasi trailed her index finger along her lip. Thinking. Sorting through my proposal, looking for a trap.

"She's right," Naavarasi said. "I'm faster than you. Stronger than you. Superior in every way. Why would you make such a reckless bet?"

"Because of what you said. Your offer." I swallowed hard, looking to Caitlin, selling the bluff with everything I had. "You're right. More than anything in the world, I want to be with Caitlin. Doesn't matter where. Doesn't matter how. So it's not really a gamble, not for me. Even if I lose, I still win."

"That's *adorable*," Naavarasi said, putting her hands to her heart as she dramatically swooned. "Except you're a neophyte trickster still trying to beat the mistress of the game. Did you think I wouldn't catch what you oh-so-casually inserted into your terms? *You* pick the weapons, for both of us? I think not. You'd pick a broadsword and give me a Wiffle-ball bat. How about this: you choose your weapon, and I choose mine. Still game for a duel?"

I slouched, sagging like a tire with a bad leak. Acting like she'd caught me in a desperate ruse.

Hell, I was counting on that.

"And the battleground?" I asked.

"Why delay? Here and now."

I nodded. "You're on. Deal."

"Let's make this official," Prince Sitri said. "Daniel, if you would, please?"

I stood before him. He gestured to the marble board, and I sank to one knee.

"You understand," he said in a low voice, "that this will bind your fate to mine, and my court, forever. If you had any hope of salvation—"

"She's worth it," I told him. No hesitation.

His mismatched eyes glimmered emerald and amethyst as he looked up, staring over at Caitlin.

"She certainly is. And you continue to make my life entertaining, which is more than I can say for ninety-nine percent of my subjects. Raise your left hand. Do you, Daniel Faust, solemnly pledge to stand for the Court of Jade Tears? To be faithful to me, as your sworn prince, and to fight in the defense of my people and my territories?"

"I do," I said.

He placed his hand upon my shoulder.

"So mote it be. You knelt before me as a thrall. Rise as a knight of hell. Rise, and see to it that my enemies are laid low. This I command as your liege and prince."

As I rose, Sitri leaned in close. He dropped his voice to an amused whisper, his words like honey in my ear.

"Pomp and circumstance aside, I hope I didn't just do that for nothing. Please tell me you're not as pathetically desperate as you look right now. You've got one last ace up your sleeve, yes?"

"Only a little desperate," I whispered back. "I'm going to—"

He held up a finger, cutting me off, then fluttered his hand at me. "Uh-uh. No spoilers. Don't ruin the show. Go on, shoo."

While we conferred, Naavarasi was preening, already celebrating her victory.

"A hound *and* a knight," she said, "soon to be subjugated for the glory of Prince Malphas. And my glory too, of course. Such an embarrassment, Prince Sitri. How will you ever live it down?"

His opal eyes glittered, cold and hard. He looked from me to her and back again.

"I need to be perfectly clear," he said. "Daniel, when I charged you to lay my enemies low?"

"Yeah?"

"By 'enemies,' I meant her specifically. And by 'laid low,' I meant—"

"Ass kicked," I said. "Yeah. Loud and clear, big guy."

The prince gave a solemn nod. And a thumbs-up. I turned back to face Naavarasi.

"Ladies first," I told her. "Choice of weapons?"

She raised a hand. It rippled, sprouting orange and black striped fur, fingers melting into an oversized tiger's paw. Five claws curled out, each one harder than steel and ending in a razor-sharp point.

"I am my weapon," she replied. "I am a mistress of magic. Illusions are my playground, and my flesh becomes whatever I will it to be. No mortal can stand against me. No mortal ever has. Daniel...I understand why you're doing this. The real reason."

"Do tell," I said.

"You're so pathetically easy to read. The look on your face, after I made my offer to allow you to stay with Caitlin, told me everything I needed to know. You want to say yes, but you can't. Your pride's in the way. You know perfectly well that I'm going to defeat you in this duel, but being beaten down and *forced* to submit is so much easier on your ego than kneeling of your own free will." She turned her paw, studying it. Her claws glinted. "Don't worry. I'll be happy to deliver the defeat you're secretly craving. I'll try not to maim you too badly."

"Wow," I said, "you've got me all figured out. Huh. Well, I hope you understand that I'm still going to fight as hard as I can."

She gave me an indulgent smile. "I would expect nothing less. If it makes you feel better, I'll even lie and tell people I was worried."

"Mighty kind of you."

“I can be a gracious mistress,” Naavarasi said. “You’ll see. Now then, choose your weapon.”

“I really have to say it? C’mon, Naavarasi, you’re slipping. All the studying you had to do to pull this off. All the mind games you had to play, all that effort planning and plotting, and you honestly don’t know which weapon I’m going to pick?”

“Your deck of cards?” She tilted her head. “A *gun?* No, you wouldn’t possibly be that foolish.”

“Nope.”

I couldn’t help but smile as I raised my empty hand and pointed.

“I choose Caitlin.”

42.

Naavarasi stared at me, uncertain. "That's...no, that's ridiculous. *She* is not a weapon."

"If it pleases the court," I announced, "I can prove that Naavarasi agrees with me."

"But I *don't* agree." She looked to Prince Malphas. "This is absurd."

I pointed to the soap bubble, still floating over the chessboard, frozen at the end of Naavarasi's memory.

"Please rewind that back to the beginning. And this time, don't skip the next part."

"No," Naavarasi snapped. "I refuse!"

Prince Sitri leaned forward on his throne, grinning from ear to ear.

"You've already submitted it into evidence," he told her. "You *can't* refuse, unless you want to withdraw the entire memory, in which case you have no proof of anything owed to you and there's no case to be argued in the first place. What will it be, Baron? Drop your claim, or show us the rest of the memory?"

Glowering, she gazed up at the shimmering bubble. The memory replayed from the beginning—the clip seen from her eyes—as Caitlin confirmed she was there as a representative of the prince.

"Indeed." Naavarasi's voice echoed across the misty chessboard as everyone listened in silence. "'A hound is a prince's weapon. His sword and his shield, his whip and his crook.' I understand perfectly."

Caitlin's image replied, "Verse thirty-nine, chapter eight of the Dictates of the Cold Peace. You've been studying the law."

"So I have," her voice answered.

The bubble quivered, agitated—then burst. Wet cinders rained down upon the polished board and the air filled with the smell of brimstone.

"'A hound is a prince's weapon,'" I repeated. "Straight from your lips, quoting your own book of laws."

Naavarasi went red in the face. "But that's—that's not, I mean—that's a metaphor!"

"Unless it isn't. I've been told by an expert that the law is highly open to interpretation."

I shot a look of thanks at Nadine. She flashed a wicked smile, utterly smug.

"*It's a technicality!*" Naavarasi shouted.

"Gosh," I said, "tricked into a bad deal then screwed on a technicality. I can't *imagine* what that feels like. That must really suck for you."

Standing next to Nadine, Royce put his hand to his mouth and delicately cleared his throat.

"Actually, my good baron, I'm inclined to support Daniel's reading. As Prince Malphas's hound, I find it sets some interesting precedents vis-à-vis my own enforcement of the law."

"As do I," Nadine said. "Caitlin may be a cheap, shabby, poorly made weapon—an unworthy and laughable one at that, more suited for the hand of a manure farmer than a true knight—but I essentially agree with my colleague."

Naavarasi wheeled around, bellowing across the chessboard. "Who even *invited* you?"

Nadine shrugged. "I go where I like."

Sitri stared across the board, looking to Malphas. "What say you, old friend?"

The three heads conferred in whispers, bending low beneath their ragged hoods. I held my breath.

The crow head emerged. Raising its beak to the mist-shrouded sky, it let out a strangled and frustrated *caw*. Sitri clapped his hands.

"Then we are in near-unanimous agreement."

"Prince Sitri," I said. "May I borrow your weapon, please?"

"You certainly may."

He clapped his hands again. The manacles burst open. Caitlin fell. She dropped to one knee on the ivory marble square beneath her and rubbed her chafed wrists.

She rose slowly, her eyes molten orbs of copper and seething rage. Naavarasi cringed, inching back a step, as Caitlin's gaze fell upon her.

"I understand that we're fighting until one party yields," Caitlin growled. "So I'm going to give you a choice. Yield. Get down on your knees and beg me for mercy, and this can all be over."

Naavarasi pursed her lips. Her jaw was clenched so tight I could see it tremble.

"And if I don't?"

"If you don't," Caitlin said, "then I'm going to hurt you. I'm going to hurt you a great deal, in a variety of exceptionally cruel and potentially permanent ways. And then you'll yield anyway."

"I can still win this fight," Naavarasi said. Fur rippled down her arms and her back, orange streaked with black, as her other hand sprouted killing claws.

"I am so glad you said that," Caitlin replied.

She smiled, opening a mouth lined with the teeth of a great white shark.

"I must confess, I lied a little, Naavarasi. I don't *have* any mercy tonight."

Caitlin charged, barreling across the chessboard like a runaway train, her fist cocked back. She threw all of her force into hurling one lethal punch—and went staggering, off-balance, as Naavarasi vanished. The rakshasi queen burst into a woman-shaped cloud of dust, spinning away like a miniature tornado.

"I didn't know she could do that," I said. Eyes sharp, putting my back to Caitlin's as we watched in all directions.

"Oh, Daniel." Naavarasi's voice seemed to echo from all around us. "I am the mistress of illusion. Your eyes see what I *tell* them to see."

The towering chess pieces, flanking us from both sides, erupted. The stone burst into clouds of debris, and from within, marble tigers carved from ebony and ivory leaped forth to do battle. The mammoth beasts charged. Circling, emitting roars that sounded like gravel in a blender. Each one had Naavarasi's baleful orange eyes.

I flexed my wrist and Canton's wand dropped into my hand. It twirled in my grip, truth-bone outward, as one of the tigers broke from the pack and streaked toward me. I slashed the wand like it was a knife and the air between us shimmered. The tiger exploded into a cascade of ebony shards, broken pieces that skittered and spun across the polished chessboard. Behind me, Caitlin went on the offensive. She charged into the circling pack, threw herself onto a tiger's back, and wrenched its ivory head until it snapped. The apparition went down on its forepaws, sliding, and detonated into rubble beneath her. She rolled onto her back as another tiger pounced. She thrust upward with both feet, kicked it in the belly, and watched it buckle and burst.

There were more tigers. The illusions were multiplying out of nowhere now, replenishing their numbers as fast as we could destroy them, and Naavarasi was still here somewhere. Invisible and—

A tiger plowed into me from the left, slamming me to the marble ground. The ivory beast stood atop me, paws on my chest and squeezing the breath from my lungs.

"Sorry," it said in Naavarasi's voice, chuckling darkly as it raised a killing paw above my face. "*This* one was real."

Caitlin ran in, blindingly fast, baring her teeth as she launched herself into a spin. Her foot lashed out and delivered a brutal kick to the side of Naavarasi's head. She yowled, tumbling off me, juking to one side on four unsteady legs. Then the rakshasi queen thundered into the circling pack of illusions, getting lost in the herd.

"Which one is she?" Caitlin said.

"I don't know!"

I slashed Canton's wand in all directions. Tigers burst right and left, showering the board with ivory and ebony rubble, and more shimmered into being in the corner of my eye. Then one lunged at Caitlin. Naavarasi bounded up and chomped her marble teeth into Caitlin's shoulder. Caitlin howled as the teeth dug deep, tearing muscle and bone, leaving her arm a slick curtain of glistening plum.

Dark blood guttered to the chessboard. She threw a punch with her opposite hand, slamming her knuckles into Naavarasi's snout. The tiger fell back, shaking her head, stunned, then galloped back into the herd.

"Are you okay?" I shouted.

Caitlin winced. She gripped her shoulder and wavered on unsteady feet, her eyes fixed in a dazed squint.

"No," she said.

Naavarasi had the battlefield locked down. She could keep this up all night, hit-and-run attacks until she'd worn us down to nothing, and she could sprout new illusions faster than I could banish them.

We were going to lose.

My mind raced, hunting for a new tactic. Matching her blow for blow wasn't working. I had to fight smarter, not harder. She was an illusionist. So was I. What did I know?

I knew she wouldn't attack me again. That'd just invite another kick in the head from Caitlin. I wasn't the threat here, Cait was, and once Naavarasi had taken her out I wouldn't stand a chance. I also knew these weren't simple illusions. As good as Naavarasi was, she had to be spending some mental effort on keeping them up and moving. She'd have some kind of a tell, something that made her stand out from the pack. I just couldn't *see* it.

I turned my back on the circling horde, looking directly at Caitlin. Watching the herd of tigers, eyes open for another charge. The thrum of stone paws was a thudding, pounding rhythm that kept time with the race of my heartbeat.

Rhythm. *Your eyes see what I tell them to see*, Naavarasi had said.

I closed my eyes.

Listening to the cadence, the steady galloping echoes

around me. All the illusory tigers had the same gait, the same identical stride.

Except for one. One was just a beat off from the rest.

My eyes snapped open, staring dead ahead. There she was. Ebony now, on the move, and her sly gaze flicked to one side. Lining up her attack. I didn't say anything, didn't play my hand. I braced myself, waiting for the tell—then she peeled off from the pack and lunged.

"Caitlin! Six o'clock!"

I slashed my wand through the air, a wave of raw power crackling toward Naavarasi. It hit her in mid-leap. The illusion melted away, ebony turning to orange fur and bare flesh. The wand's power wrenched her into her natural form, a human woman with the head of a Bengal tiger—and Caitlin turned just in time.

She grabbed Naavarasi by the throat and threw her down onto the marble chessboard.

The illusions erupted around us. The entire pack detonated as the rakshasi's concentration shattered, billowing upward like volcanoes of ebony and ivory shards, then raining down in a storm of choking dust.

Caitlin dragged Naavarasi up by the throat, hauling her across the battlefield, then slammed her against the marble pillar. Then she did it again. And again, the stone buckling as Naavarasi struggled to push back against her. Caitlin spun her around, trapped Naavarasi's scruff in her fist, and smashed her face against the bloody stone.

The rakshasi flailed at her. Caitlin seized one of her wrists, hauled it behind her back, and snapped Naavarasi's arm in two places. "*I yield!*" she shrieked.

"No," Caitlin grunted, "not yet."

Caitlin threw Naavarasi back to the floor, standing over her, and brought her foot down on Naavarasi's throat. She slowly leaned forward, putting her weight into it as Naavarasi struggled to shove back with her one good hand.

"Yield," the rakshasi croaked. "*I yield.*"

"Cait," I said, moving up behind her. "C'mon. She tapped out."

Wisps of black smoke drifted from Caitlin's molten eyes. "Not. Yet."

"Caitlin," Royce shouted from the sidelines. "Stop it, you're going to kill her!"

Nadine leaned against the side of Malphas's throne, wearing a lopsided smile. "Works for me."

Prince Malphas shot to his feet, his elephantine bulk jiggling as his three heads squawked in shrill outrage. Sitri waved a tired hand, nodding at his counterpart from across the board.

"Caitlin," Sitri sighed. "Stand down. That's an order."

She took a deep breath, nodded, and pulled her foot away.

Then she drove her heel down like a sledgehammer, square into Naavarasi's stomach. Naavarasi curled into a fetal ball, gasping for breath and writhing at Caitlin's feet.

"*Now* you are allowed to yield," Caitlin told her. She looked to Royce. "You should remove her from the battlefield before I change my mind."

Royce hustled over, getting his hands under the fallen rakshasi's arms, trying to ease her up.

"Aren't you going to help?" he asked Nadine.

"Just got a manicure," she replied, "so...no."

Caitlin drifted to the far edge of the board, silent, fingers massaging her bleeding shoulder. I followed her.

43.

The mists of the Low Liminal drifted around us. They closed in, erasing the edges of the chessboard, the towering thrones. Narrowing down the world to just the two of us.

"Hey," I said. "You okay?"

She kept her back turned.

"My wounds will heal," she said.

"Not what I meant."

"I was...frightened." She turned to face me. Her eyes had changed back to human. Deep, soft, holding some distant sorrow. "When I'm not in control, it reminds me of when you first met me. Enslaved by that...*human*. To think I might have spent eternity trapped. My worst fear. If you hadn't come along."

"But I did," I said.

"But you did."

"Your worst fear," I said, "and still. You were going to give yourself up for me tonight."

She gave me a tiny, almost embarrassed smile.

"I told you," she said. "I love you."

"I love you, too," I said.

"Daniel, I can't...I can't undo what I did to you when

we first met. I can't go back in time and change things. That will always be a wedge between us—"

"No."

I reached out. My fingertips caressed her good shoulder. Gently pulled her a little closer.

"Because it's forgiven," I said, "and it's in the past."

"Can we start over?" she asked.

I thought about it. It wasn't hard to decide. "Yeah. Yeah, I'd like that."

She leaned against me, and I cradled her in my arms.

"You know we've gotta kill the fuck out of Naavarasi now, right?" I added. "I mean, glass-parking-lot levels of carnage."

"Unquestionably."

"*Super* dead."

"Painfully," Caitlin said. "Very painfully."

"So painful the Marquis de Sade will go 'damn, why you gotta be like that?'"

Caitlin nodded to me, utterly deadpan.

"We have to nuke her from orbit, Daniel. It's the only way to be sure."

"And that," I said, "is why I love you."

"I know."

A figure sauntered from the swirling mists. Prince Sitri. Caitlin lowered her head, good shoulder slumping in an exhausted half bow.

"Well fought, my hound." He turned his mismatched eyes my way. "And while I applaud your bloodthirstiness, you *do* realize you can't just drive to Denver and go on a killing spree, yes?"

"It's not a spree if you only kill one person."

Sitri laughed. "Caitlin, please enlighten your consort."

She leaned against me again. Smiling, her head on my shoulder.

"You're one of us now," she said. "My knight in tarnished armor becoming a real knight, who would have thought?"

"Meaning you are bound by our laws," Sitri said. "A direct attack against a member of another court is an act of war. So don't do it. Ever."

"What about indirect attacks?" I asked. "Seems to me like most of these 'rules' boil down to not getting caught."

Sitri looked to Caitlin. "My dear, are you *certain* he doesn't have any of our blood in his veins?"

"One hundred percent human," she said. "I've checked. My cherished pet is simply a quick study."

"He'll need to be. There will no doubt be those looking to test his strength. Humans rising to any level of stature within the courts are...not well loved by most. On the plus side, Daniel, knighthood does confer some minor privileges to accompany the burden of duty. It's customary to grant a one-acre plot of land within my infernal domain. My aide has already drawn up the deed for yours."

"Yeah?" I said. "Is it nice?"

"It's lovely. Absolutely beautiful."

Something in his gaze, some hint of playful malice, gave me pause.

"You're lying, aren't you?"

"It's in the middle of a septic wasteland," Sitri said. "Utterly horrific, never go there."

"Gee, thanks."

"I am a gracious and benevolent prince," he said. "And...thank you. I almost lost my favorite servant today. I would have been very displeased if I had to replace her."

Sitri gazed at Caitlin, quietly admiring her. Not as a

servant. His face said what his words wouldn't. He looked at her like a father looks at his daughter.

"My pleasure," I said. "Though you know, we caught a lucky break."

"Mm? How's that?"

"Well, when I talked to the Conduit...I understand trials like this would normally take place in hell, where I can't go without, y'know, dying first. Pretty fortunate that it was held here instead, and that the Conduit had a way to bring me here. If I didn't know better, I'd say it felt like *somebody* wanted to give me a shot at crashing the party and sabotaging Naavarasi's plan. You know, in a totally deniable way, so nobody from Malphas's court could point a finger at him."

Prince Sitri rubbed his chin. He nodded thoughtfully.

"Now that you mention it, goodness, that *is* an amazingly lucky coincidence." The ground rumbled under our feet, like the warning signs of an earthquake. "And on that note, it isn't wise to stay in the Low Liminal for long. We'd best be going. Daniel, I'm afraid that while we have our own means of egress, for one of mortal flesh and blood..."

He gestured with his left hand, fingertips curling in a ritual sign. The ground between us cracked and a sinkhole yawned open in the marble chessboard. Chunks of stone fell, tumbling into a tunnel of inflamed throat flesh. The living abyss shivered, its skin glistening wet.

"...you have to leave the way you came in," he told me.

I gave Caitlin one last careful squeeze.

"See you on the other side?"

"See you on the other side." She leaned in. Her lips brushed against mine.

Then the fog rolled in, washing the world in winter mist, and she was gone.

* * *

I went home. Aching, disheveled, and dirty, I needed a shower and a new suit before I did anything else. The television was off. Circe had only been in my life for a couple of days, but I felt her sudden absence. Usually I didn't mind living alone. *Alone* didn't mean *lonely*.

Tonight it did. I turned on the TV and let it play in the background, just to hear human voices while I cleaned myself up. I liked imagining Circe sitting on the couch, obsessing over the moving pictures. I almost thought she might be there when I stepped out of the bedroom.

She wasn't. Of course she wasn't. Neither was her queen, her goddess, the Lady in Red. I couldn't get her out of my mind. Her image, her voice—I felt like I should *know* her. Her memory was a spur in my side, commanding me to speak her name.

I pushed the thought aside. I grabbed my keys, heading for the door. Then I paused.

A trace of perfume hung in the air.

Roses.

* * *

I knew exactly where I'd find Caitlin. Gordon Ramsay's, right where we'd had our first dinner together. She even had the same two-seater table with a kitchen view, sitting alone, sipping a ginger liqueur with lemon and bitters. My drink, a Vesper martini, was waiting for me.

"Come here often?" I asked.

"Every now and then." She nodded to the open chair. "Join me, if you like."

"Thanks, this place is packed." I sat across from her and offered her my hand. "I'm Daniel."

Her fingers, warm and soft, curled around mine.

"Caitlin. A pleasure to meet you."

"Likewise."

Then our eyes met, and we had to laugh. Then we couldn't stop laughing, until the diners around us started looking anxious.

"Starting over" was a fine daydream, but it just didn't work in real life. We were who we were, and our relationship was built on the bricks of the choices we'd made. Some good, some bad. Some memories we'd cherish together, and others we'd never talk about again. All we could do was keep moving forward.

All we could do was forgive.

"I've already ordered for both of us," she said.

"I fully expect you have. Beef Wellington?"

"As if there was any other choice." She frowned, glancing down, and pulled her phone out. "Sorry. Office. Have to take this."

My phone buzzed in my pocket. Jennifer calling.

"Yeah, I—same, sorry." I answered it. "Hey Jen."

"You still breathin' over there? I haven't heard from you since the raid went down, thought one of those hunters mighta gotten lucky."

"Sorry, I've been...well, first I was tied up in a bathtub, then I was in another dimension. Long story. But we're all good, crisis over for the moment. Also, I'm a knight now."

"That so?"

"Yep. You have to call me Sir Daniel from now on. It's the law."

"Yeah," Jennifer said. "I ain't gonna do that. As your best friend, it's my job to keep you humble."

"You do excel at that."

Across the table Caitlin was leaning into her phone with her hand over her other ear. "Emma, we can't—no, damn it, we can't just expel them *all* from the city. You need a legal pretext. All right, no, I understand—"

"Anyway," I said, "can I catch you up later? We just sat down to dinner."

"No can do, Dan. Mayor Seabrook just called and we got a problem on our hands. Malone wasn't the only ink dealer in town."

"They arrested another one?"

"Worse." Jen sighed. "Cops answered a noise complaint. Teenagers throwin' a house party. Looks like they got a bad batch of the stuff. They...*did* things to each other. Twelve of 'em are dead. Three are sitting in a rubber room. Total psychotic break."

"Damn," I breathed. "Okay, this isn't just about getting the mayor's goodwill anymore. We are *moving* on these Network assholes."

"One more thing," she said. "One of those kids, he's asking for you by name."

I tilted my head, not sure I'd heard her right. "Me? Do I know him?"

"I don't think it's *him* asking. He's sayin' he's the King of Worms. And he wants to talk to you."

The music, the light, the heat all drained from the room as my vision turned pale, sickly gray. I glanced to my left, where a diner lifted a forkful of steak to his mouth in slow motion.

Maggots squirmed from the putrid meat, plopping onto his lap.

I blinked. The illusion tore away, the world lurching back to vibrant life.

"I'll meet you in twenty minutes," I told her.

Caitlin hung up three seconds after I did. She sighed and folded her cloth napkin.

"I'm sorry, pet, but dinner has to wait. Apparently a number of errant chainmen, instead of leaving town as they were instructed to, threw a bit of a wild party at Winter. A party involving property damage and multiple injuries. I have to go and sort out who did what to who, and dispense punishment as appropriate."

I held up my phone. "Same here, I've got a thing I've gotta deal with right away. New Commission business."

She took a long, quiet look at me, shaking her head, and smiled.

"Power couple," she said.

I laughed. "Power couple. Call me. We'll do lunch."

At least we had time to leave arm in arm. At least we had time for one long, lingering kiss in the doorway.

Some nights, you take what you can get. It was enough for now.

Epilogue

Naavarasi sat at her feast table in sullen silence.

Her arm still burned every time she moved it, and her head hadn't stopped aching since Royce dragged her from the battlefield. She didn't have a demon's resilience: healing, for her, meant slow, agonizing shifts and re-shifts, altering her form again and again until everything knitted together just right. Recovering had hurt worse than the beating she'd suffered at Caitlin's hands.

Still, she couldn't help but smile.

A man stood in the restaurant doorway, just inside the beaded curtain. His features were inked in shadow. He hovered like a nervous animal at the edge of the bloodstained carpet.

"I told you," Naavarasi said. "No face-to-face contact until your part of the plan is complete. It's too dangerous."

"I had to come." His voice was uneven, anxious. "I heard...I heard you'd been hurt, Mistress."

"That was unfortunate, yes. I'll be honest: I *wanted* Caitlin. It would have been a sweet victory, and she would have made an extremely useful servant." She beckoned to him. "Come. Dine with me. You've earned this."

As he sat beside her at the feast table, she lifted one

of the silver serving-tray lids. Steam gusted up, carrying the rich scents of saffron and curry. Strips of meat, pink and tender, nestled in a yellow sauce flecked with herb shavings. Her jade fingernails plucked one of them from the tray.

"Open wide," she said. "Just like I taught you."

The human tilted his head back, lips parted. She dropped the slice of meat into his mouth and chuckled.

"There you go," she murmured. "Nothing makes you stronger than the flesh of your own kind. And your mission status?"

"Successful," he said, chewing contentedly. "I've ingratiated myself with Ms. Fleiss and won her trust. Your psychological profile was invaluable."

"Of course it was. She thought I was mooning over her master, when I was spending my time studying *her*. Stay valuable to her and keep a low profile. It's almost time for your turn in the spotlight."

"But...isn't it all over? Didn't we lose?"

"Lose?" Naavarasi arched an eyebrow, irritated. "Why would you think that? I told you, Caitlin was only a bonus prize. She was never the real goal. If anything, this helps us. She and Daniel are convinced they uncovered my master plan."

She picked another strip of meat from the tray. She threw her head back, held it high, and dropped it down her gullet. Swallowing it whole.

"More importantly, they think it's over."

"But what about the Cutting Knife? It's gone now. Didn't you need it?"

Naavarasi burst into laughter. She closed her eyes, beaming, and patted the man's knee.

"That old thing? Oh, no. What I needed was for Daniel

to have access to one. More importantly, I needed Sitri and Malphas to *know* he had access to one. It's true, I will need a Cutting Knife for my plans to manifest..."

She reached for another serving tray and lifted the lid.

Underneath, on a velvet pillow, rested a dagger. A Tibetan phurba, brass with a three-bladed tip. The brass had oxidized from time and neglect; the once-grand designs carved into its ornate hilt were encrusted with a sickly green patina.

"So it's very fortunate," Naavarasi said, "that I already have one."

* * *

The glass elevator slowly climbed Northlight Tower. One man stood inside. Mr. Smith, Esquire, was prim, pressed, and precise. Gray suit, gray tie, and a white pocket square folded with laser-sharp edges.

He reached into his breast pocket and took out a plastic makeup compact, flicking it open with his thumb. Instead of reflecting his face, the mirror inside was a pit of inky darkness. A man huddled in the depths of the image, head bowed, clutching himself in mortal terror.

"Dr. Nedry," Smith said. "Just thought you'd like to know that I'm working on remedying your lamentable error of judgment."

"Please," Nedry's voice whimpered from the glass. "Let me out."

"You'll stay where you are until I'm certain you've learned the importance of discretion. You betrayed our trust when you revealed our existence, Doctor. Your knowledge and experience are the only reasons we haven't simply eliminated you. So be thankful."

Nedry's shadow slapped at something on his arm. He squirmed to one side, flinching.

"There are...*things* in here with me."

"I know," Smith said. "I put them there. If I was truly being cruel, I'd turn the lights on so you could see them."

He snapped the compact shut and slipped it back into his breast pocket.

The elevator chimed. Smith strode through the coldly lit halls, past mahogany walls and plate-glass windows overlooking a city skyline. He moved, as he always did, unseen and unimpeded.

As the penthouse office doors swung open, light from the waiting room flooding the near-pitch darkness, the Enemy flowed up from his chair with an electric crackle. Smith held up an open hand.

"Please don't be alarmed," he said. "My name is Mr. Smith, legal counsel for an organization of forward-thinking entrepreneurs. We've been watching you for quite a while, sir."

"You've *what*? How are you even here? How did you get past—"

"I have a talent for opening doors. As I was saying, we've seen your work—and we *like* what we see."

The Enemy swirled around him, circling like a school of piranha in the crude shape of a man. "Do you now?"

"We do. And we couldn't help but notice you've been having some trouble in Nevada. There's no shame in it. We've had some difficulties there ourselves lately."

"I'm not having any *difficulties*. Everything is under control."

"I wouldn't imply otherwise," Smith said, standing still as a statue. "But there comes a time in every corporate life cycle when expansion proves problematic. When such occasions arise, a merger between like-minded parties is only prudent."

The Enemy stopped circling. His etched-negative form hovered in front of the lawyer. He leaned close, pearly teeth clenched.

"Why..." he breathed.

"Is there a problem, sir?"

The Enemy loomed closer.

"Why don't you have a *history*? Your timeline is completely empty."

"We'd like to help you, sir. We'd like to collaborate on this Nevada situation by lending you some valuable resources and aiding in logistics. We feel that by doing so, it would create a win-win situation. Positive synergy. You're aiming to accomplish big things. So are we."

"Why don't you have a history?"

Mr. Smith smiled thinly.

"I'm just not very memorable, sir. Afraid I'm quite boring, really. No life outside the office." He held up a business card. "Will you consider our offer? Call me, day or night. No strings attached."

Crackling, flickering fingertips plucked the card from Smith's hand.

"I'll consider it."

Mr. Smith stepped back, bowing with a quick nod of his head. "Very good, sir."

He walked to the door, pausing to glance back over his shoulder.

"And welcome. Welcome to the Network."

Afterword

Daniel's a knight now. So he has that going for him (which is nice). Of course, Prince Sitri never does anything without a reason, and we shouldn't forget the timeless words of the Notorious B.I.G.: "mo' connections to the courts of hell, mo' problems."

(I may not be remembering those lyrics right. Oh, well, close enough.)

At least he and Caitlin weathered this latest storm — which is good, because with all the trouble headed their way, they're going to need each other more than ever. Almost as much, I daresay, as I need my support team: thanks as always to Kira Rubenthaler for her editorial prowess, James T. Egan's cover design artistry, Adam Verner for his audiobook narration, and my priceless assistant, Maggie Faid. And thank you for reading! My readers have stuck with me through thick and thin, and I can't tell you how much it means to me. As for Daniel, he'll be back in 2018 — though the actual story will begin, oh, about twenty minutes after this one ended. No rest for the wicked.

Want to get the advance scoop on new books and projects? Head over to http://www.craigschaeferbooks.com/mailing-list/ and hop onto my mailing list. Once-a-month newsletters, zero spam. Want to reach out? You can find me on Facebook at http://www.facebook.com/CraigSchaeferBooks, on Twitter as @craig_schaefer, or just drop me an email at craig@craigschaeferbooks.com.